2/2011

D0340661

DATE ᴅᴜᴇ

WORLD'S GREATEST SLEUTH!

ALSO BY STEVE HOCKENSMITH

Holmes on the Range

On the Wrong Track

The Black Dove

The Crack in the Lens

WORLD'S GREATEST SLEUTH!

STEVE
HOCKENSMITH

MINOTAUR BOOKS

NEW YORK

WORLD'S GREATEST SLEUTH! Copyright © 2010 by Steve Hockensmith. All rights reserved. Printed in the United States of America. For information, address St. Martin's Press, 175 Fifth Avenue, New York, N.Y. 10010.

www.minotaurbooks.com

Library of Congress Cataloging-in-Publication Data

Hockensmith, Steve.
    World's greatest sleuth! : a Holmes on the range mystery / Steve Hockensmith.—1st ed.
        p. cm.
    ISBN 978-0-312-37943-8
    1. Brothers—Fiction.   2. Cowboys—Fiction.   3. World's Columbian Exposition (1893 : Chicago, Ill.)—Fiction.   4. Murder—Investigation—Fiction.   I. Title.
    PS3608.O29W67 2011
    813'.6—dc22

                                                                2010037500

First Edition: January 2011

10 9 8 7 6 5 4 3 2 1

FOR MAR,
TO THE END

Author's Note

It has come to my attention that certain people believe the late, great Sherlock Holmes to be a mere fiction—an invention of some yarn-spinning scribbler like myself. This is scandalous, slanderous, preposterous, and just plain dumb. Mr. Holmes, though no more, was a real man, as solid of flesh and bone as am I myself. I'm happy indeed to live in a world that could accommodate such an extraordinary individual as he, and it's difficut to imagine why anyone would show any reluctance to join me there.

—OTTO "BIG RED" AMLINGMEYER

DRAMATIS PERSONAE

OTTO "BIG RED" AMLINGMEYER—former (hopefully) cowboy, future (hopefully) idol to millions, current narrator

GUSTAV "OLD RED" AMLINGMEYER—former (hopefully) cowboy, future (hopefully) sleuth, ever and always crabby pain in the ass

SHERLOCK HOLMES—consulting detective (deceased), guiding spirit, ghost

DIANA—lady detective, liar, schemer, sneak, angel

COL. C. KERMIT CROWE—detective, former employer, martinet, Lilliputian

URIAS SMYTHE—publisher, milksop, pantywaist

FRANK TOUSEY—rival publisher, flashy dresser, son of a bitch

DRAMATIS PERSONAE

BLACKHEATH-MURRAY—rival publisher, Englishman, mustache wearer

ARMSTRONG B. CURTIS, ESQUIRE—"Puzzlemaster," crank, my biggest fan

LUCILLE LARSON—journalist, beauty, beanpole, icicle

WILLIAM PINKERTON—yeah, *that* William Pinkerton

KING BRADY—yeah, *that* King Brady

EUGENE VALMONT—master sleuth, Frenchman, crackpot

BOOTHBY GREENE—novice sleuth, Englishman, phony

MRS. JASINSKA—innkeeper (incompetent)

JERZY—bellman (prehistoric)

DETECTIVE SGT. MOSES "MO" RYAN—lawman (shockingly reasonable)

THE BEARDED MAN—a man with a beard

THE OTHER BEARDED MAN (A.K.A. THE UNBEARDED MAN)—another man with a beard (sometimes)

THE OTHER OTHER BEARDED MAN—another other man with a beard

ANOTHER OTHER OTHER BEARDED MAN—must it be said?

EVERYONE ELSE—you'll see

WORLD'S GREATEST SLEUTH!

 Prelude

Or, The Quick and the Dead

My heart wasn't just pounding in my ears as we ran. It sounded like I'd stuck my head inside a brass band's bass drum halfway through a Fourth of July parade.

I didn't slow my pace, though. Everything Old Red and I had dreamed of and worked at and suffered for these past months was on the line. Better to have my heart explode like an overstoked boiler than quietly break in two.

We rounded a corner and saw what we'd been searching for so frantically: a raised platform topped by a huge metal tank. Between it and us was a thick-packed crowd that numbered in the hundreds.

My brother slowed down.

I sped up.

"One side! Gangway! Sleuths comin' through!"

Fortunately for both me and the bystanders in my path, folks listened. A lane cleared through the throng—at the other end of which I saw the Enemy charging toward that tank just like me.

Well, one of the Enemies, anyhow. We had so many just then, it was hard to keep track of them all.

"Oh, no you don't!" I roared, somehow pouring on more speed.

He and I reached the steps to the top of the tank at the same time.

"Pardon," I said, bumping him aside and bounding up the staircase.

"Go to hell," the man said, leaping up to grab me by the tail of my long coat.

"My apologies," I said, kicking backward into his chest.

"Fudge you," he said (more or less), and he wrapped his arms around my legs, bringing the both of us falling flat onto the steps.

"Excuse me," someone new said, and I felt the skirts said someone was wearing sweep over me from heels to head as she walked up my back and then carried on up the staircase.

"Feh," someone not-so-new said, and first the Enemy and then I oophed as my brother tramped over our backs with a far heavier step than the lady.

I got to my feet before anyone else could use me as a stepping-stone.

"I'm sorry, Old Red," I heard the lady say. "I'm afraid you're too late to . . . oh!"

I reached the top of the stairs half-expecting to find that my brother had tackled her, skirts (and propriety) be damned. Instead, I saw the lady on her hands and knees peering into a large round hole cut into the top of the tank. From it wafted a smell of cheese so strong I felt like I was drowning in Welsh rarebit. For a moment I thought it was the swoon-inducing odor that had given the lady pause, but rather than pinch her nose or simply faint, she nodded down at the black hole before her.

"Is that what I think it is?"

Old Red crouched down beside her, then plugged the hole—with himself. His legs he stretched out flat while his top half he dropped down into the darkness inside the tank.

"Yes, miss. It is," my brother said with a sigh. "So long as you think it's a dead feller facedown in cheddar."

1

BLIND LUCK

Or, Things Look Black for Old Red, yet Our Prospects Finally Brighten

That great writer, philosopher, and (I'm guessing) lunatic Lewis Carroll once offered some fine advice for anyone interested in the art of storytelling.

"Begin at the beginning," the King proclaims in *Alice's Adventures in Wonderland*, "and go on till you come to the end: then stop."

Yet wise as this approach might seem to be, it must be pointed out that neither Mr. Carroll nor his King was in the business of writing dime novels. I am. Which is why I've been forced to adopt my own credo.

To wit: Start with an exciting bit, jump back and rush through the beginning quick as you can, run through the exciting bit again (tacking on a few more for good measure), and wrap everything up before folks get bored. *Then* stop.

So now that we've got that (hopefully) exciting bit with the body out of the way, we can give Mr. Carroll's method a go and begin at the real beginning.

On June 4, 1872, Mr. and Mrs. Conrad Amlingmeyer of Marion County, Kansas, were blessed with their fifth and, by all accounts, most beautiful child: a beaming bundle of joy they named Otto Albert, a.k.a. "Big Red," a.k.a. *me*. Growing into a precocious boy who amazed all around with his intelligence, charm, and good looks, young Otto began his schooling at the early age of . . .

You know, I don't think that "Begin at the beginning" business is as simple as it seems. What, for instance, *is* the beginning of the tale I have to tell? I suspect I've overshot it a mite.

Let me try again.

In October of this year of Our Lord 1893, while the rest of humanity was marveling at the modern miracles on display at the World's Fair, the Columbian Exposition in Chicago, I found myself marveling at something very, very different: the gag-inducing powers of goat stink. Depending on how you looked at it, I was either a guest or (my view) prisoner on a Texas Angora ranch, a place that couldn't have been more odiferous had the primary livestock been chili-fed polecats. Yet escape had been impossible, as the other guest thereabouts—my elder brother Gustav, a.k.a. "Old Red," a.k.a. (when he's not around to hear me) "Chief Stick-Up-His-Ass"—was, at first, in no condition to travel and, later, of no mind to.

"And go where?" he'd say when asked if it wasn't perhaps time to mosey on.

"Anywhere!" being my usual reply.

He'd just stare through me, as if blind. I let him get away with this for a while because he had a pretty good excuse for it: He *was* blind. A close call with a load of exploding flash powder had left him temporarily sightless.

After two weeks convalescing on the ranch (owned by friends from his days as a Hill Country cattle hand), Old Red was prickly, mopey, and taciturn. Pretty much back to normal, in other words. He was still grousing about his eyes, but at least he could see well enough not to flatten his big nose walking into walls anymore.

While Gustav had done his healing, I'd passed the time (and dodged any goat wrangling) by writing up an account of our most recent experiences along the mystery-solving line. Eventually, I announced that the tale was complete and I'd be riding into town to mail it to my publisher in New York.

The timing of this pronouncement was met with considerable (and justified) suspicion, for my departure coincided with the first day of the fall shearing.

"If *I* can help shave them shaggy bastards, by God you can, too," Old Red snarled. I would say he was giving me his patented Steely Lock of Censure, but I can't be certain. His eyes were hidden behind a pair of purple-tinted spectacles the local sawbones had given him.

I jerked a thumb at the shearing shed my brother had been shuffling toward when I'd given him the news.

"There's plenty of hired help in there. I ain't needed. And anyway, I've put up with enough ornery old goats in my time."

Gustav's frown deepened, but those sun cheaters again spared me the full brunt of whichever of his usual glowers, squints, and scowls he was throwing my way. (My best guess: Glare of Irritated Vexation #5, "The Constipated Bear.")

"So," I said, "long as I'm headin' into town, you got anything you need me to pick up?"

Old Red snorted. "You don't gotta test me. You know what I

want." He turned and headed for the shed again. "Ya damn gold-bricker . . ."

I smiled.

I did indeed know what he wanted. But it was good to hear him ask for it, even in his cranky, roundabout way.

I was to look for the latest issue of *Harper's Weekly*—and, more importantly, the new Sherlock Holmes story that it hopefully contained.

Before he'd been blinded, my brother had but one ambition in life: becoming a "consulting detective" like his hero, Mr. Holmes. Yet while he managed to sleuth us up plenty of trouble, detectiving *jobs* proved more elusive. So eventually I created my own, chronicling our amateur deducifications Doc Watson style. Hence my new-found career as a writer—and my relief to learn that Old Red's interest in crime-busting hadn't been blown sky-high along with the rest of him. Now I just had to haul him off his ass and get him back to doing something about it again.

I stewed on that during the long ride to the nearest city, San Marcos, but the only plan I could think up was to throw a lasso on my brother and simply drag him along behind me. Which had a certain appeal, actually. I just couldn't figure out where to drag him *to*.

When I finally arrived at the postmaster's office in town, I gave my new book a good-luck kiss, paid for postage, and wished my bundled-up baby Godspeed in its journey to my literary patron, Mr. Urias Smythe of Smythe & Associates Publishing Ltd.

The postmaster was a slovenly, sleepy-looking man who draped himself over the counter between us with such slump-shouldered droopiness I almost expected him to climb up and stretch out for a nap. When he glanced down at the return address on my package, though, his eyes widened, and for the first time he looked at me as if I was something more than an exceptionally boring dream.

"Say . . . you're one of them dee-tective brothers, ain't you?"

I nodded. "The devilishly handsome, irresistible to women one, yeah. But I'm sure you figured that out already."

The postmaster wasn't quite awake enough to follow me, and after a moment watching him blink at me slack-jawed, I prodded him with an "And . . . ?"

"Got a message for you. The Western Union boy come 'round lookin' for you the other day. Said you should run over to their office first thing."

I thanked the man, wished him sweet dreams (which got me another gawk, it being eleven in the A.M.), and left.

The Western Union office was but a couple blocks away, near the railroad depot, and the clerk there was a much more wide-awake sort of fellow—a slender man with slicked-back hair and garters on the sleeves of his immaculate white shirt. He recognized me on sight, perhaps thanks to the less than flattering descriptions ("doughy-faced," indeed!) that had appeared in the local paper. (One can't go around blowing things up—homes and their occupants, in particular— without attracting a certain amount of attention, even in Texas.)

Before I could say so much as "Hello," the clerk whirled around to a row of cubbyholes, whipped out a small sheet of paper, and offered it to me. The second I had the note in hand, the man opened his money drawer and started counting out tens.

"Uhhhh," I said, hypnotized by the sight of those bills stacking up ever higher.

"Read the telegram, sir," the clerk said without looking up.

When a gent's counting out cash for me, I tend to do as he asks. This is what I read.

9

```
OTTO AMLINGMEYER
SAN MARCOS TEX


BRING  BROTHER  EXPOSITION  IMMEDIATELY  STOP  SEND
DETAILS  ARRIVAL  COLUMBIAN  HOTEL  HOPE  AVENUE
CHICAGO  STOP  ALL  EXPLAINED  LATEST  MCCLURES
MAGAZINE  STOP  NOT  HERE  NOON  MONDAY  23  ALL  LOST
STOP  FOR  GODS  SAKE  HURRY  FULL  STOP


URIAS SMYTHE
557PM
OCT 18
```

I looked back up at the clerk. He was now standing behind two tidy piles of greenbacks.

So many questions were bouncing around my skull they knocked the tongue right out of my mouth.

"Uhhhh," I said, staring at the money again.

"Two hundred dollars," the clerk said. "Via money order. For you."

"Uhhhh," I said, scanning the office wall for a calendar.

"It's the twentieth," the clerk told me. "You have three days to reach Chicago."

"Uhhhh," I said, stepping back to throw a panicked glance at the train station.

"Exposition specials leave from Houston daily," the clerk said. "If you catch the 3:50 this afternoon, you might just make it."

"Uhhhh," I said, whirling in a circle looking for the nearest newsstand or sundries store.

"Page twelve," the clerk said.

He pulled something out from under the counter and slid it

over to me—a slick-looking magazine I'd never laid eyes on before. *McClure's*.

I flipped to page twelve and found the following words screaming up at me.

FOR YEARS, THE WORLD HAS AWAITED AN ANSWER: HOW DID
THAT MONARCH OF ALL DETECTIVES, THAT PEERLESS
MASTER OF LOGIC, THAT FEARLESS RIGHTER OF WRONGS

SHERLOCK HOLMES

MEET HIS TRAGIC END? THE ANSWER WILL BE REVEALED

IN THE NEXT ISSUE OF THIS MAGAZINE

WITH THE PUBLICATION OF DR. JOHN WATSON'S

"THE FINAL PROBLEM"

BUT ANOTHER QUESTION REMAINS: WITH HOLMES GONE, WHO IS
OUR FOREMOST CRUSADER AGAINST CRIME? WHO SHOULD OUR CONSTABULARY
MOST EMULATE—AND OUR CRIMINALS MOST FEAR?
THAT QUESTION, TOO, SHALL BE ANSWERED SOON, FOR

THE S.S. McCLURE COMPANY

IN ASSOCIATION WITH NEW YORK DETECTIVE LIBRARY, SMYTHE & ASSOCIATES PUBLISHING,
THE PINKERTON NATIONAL DETECTIVE AGENCY, AND THE WORLD'S COLUMBIAN EXPOSITION COMPANY

IS PROUD TO ANNOUNCE THAT THE SEARCH IS ON FOR THE

WORLD'S GREATEST SLEUTH!

THE CLAIMANTS TO THE THRONE—RENOWNED DETECTIVES,
MYSTERY-SOLVING MASTERMINDS, ALL!—WILL GATHER IN
CHICAGO THE FINAL WEEK OF THE COLUMBIAN EXPOSITION
FOR A SERIES OF CHALLENGES SPECIALLY DESIGNED
TO TEST THEIR WITS, SKILL, AND DARING.

THE JUDGE: MR. WILLIAM PINKERTON!

THE PRIZE: $10,000!
THE OUTCOME:
ONLY TO BE FOUND HERE,
IN THE DECEMBER ISSUE OF
McCLURE'S MAGAZINE

I read the announcement through once, skimmed it again, triple-checked certain key phrases—"Smythe & Associates" and "The prize: $10,000" chief among them—then found my voice again at last. Lady Luck was finally offering me and my brother a helping hand rather than an upraised finger, and there was only one thing to say about it.

"Holy shit holy shit holy shit!"

And I danced a little jig right there in the Western Union office.

"Uhhhh," the clerk said.

2

CHICAGO

Or, Old Red Reluctantly Faces the Future . . . and It Spits in His Eye

M y jig was a tad premature.

After I rode back to the ranch at a gallop, threw myself from the saddle, dragged Gustav out of the shearing shed, and blurted out the good news, I was a bit taken aback when my brother just frowned and said, "A Holmesin' contest? How the hell's that gonna work?"

I told him that wasn't our worry—all we had to do was show up and make the most of it.

"But I ain't exactly at my best, and Lord knows we can't count on *you* to do the sleuthin'," Old Red said.

I told him win or lose, we'd still come out ahead, as we'd never have a better chance to make a name for ourselves.

"Seems disrespectful to Mr. Holmes, don't it?" Old Red said. "Playin' games when he's dead?"

I told him I couldn't imagine a greater tribute to the late Mr. H than a mystery-cracking competition in his honor.

"Well, what do we know about this *McClure's Magazine*? Could be some kind of prank," Old Red said.

I told him he was a mule-headed SOB who was about to bury the biggest lucky break we ever had under a bunch of bullshit excuses.

Almost.

I counted to ten, let my temper settle, then pulled out my hole card.

I told him to think of our friend and comrade Diana Corvus.

"What about her?" Old Red said. There was a pause first, though—a pause that told me I had him.

"Last we heard from the lady," I said, "she was still tryin' to wrangle us detectivin' jobs, right? Well, we come off good in this *Mc-Clure's Magazine*—and it looks every bit as respectable as *Harper's*—that's gonna make her case for her, ain't it? So if this pans out, there we'd be: working with Diana again. Detectin' side by side. Shoulder to shoulder. Arm in arm. Hand in—"

"Alright, alright! You made your point!" my brother snapped. "We'll give it a go. I reckon we ain't got nothing left to lose."

I nodded happily. "Nothing but our dignity . . . and we ain't been usin' that for much anyhow!"

It was hard to be certain, but it sure looked like Gustav rolled his eyes behind his glasses. Frantic packing and hurried good-byes followed immediately thereafter, and within hours we were on a northbound train.

Now, as you might have noticed, I'm a fellow who doesn't mind flapping his gums. When Old Red and I travel modern-like, though, it's not a matter of habit—it's strict necessity. My brother can neither read nor stomach rail travel, you see, and the one thing that'll keep him from retching and kecking is a steady stream of detective tales orated by yours truly.

And only one detective will do. We'd sampled Nick Carter, King Brady, Old Sleuth, and every other dick with a dime novel to his name, but none had ever won my brother over. "Defectives," Gustav called them. "They don't solve mysteries. They beat them into submission." So it was all Holmes Holmes Holmes as we chugged toward Chicago.

With a little Diana Diana Diana on the side, perhaps. The first story Old Red asked to hear was "A Scandal in Bohemia"—a yarn he often turns to when trying to make sense of our pretty detective friend.

I'm not the great sleuth of the two of us, but this much I'd long ago deduced: My brother was half in love with the lady. And if he wasn't, he was crazy, for I myself was *completely* in love with her and couldn't understand how any other man wouldn't be. She was as clever as Gustav, as silver-tongued as me, as brave as either of us, and more attractive than the both of us put together (my brother being a bit of a minus to my plus).

She was kindhearted to boot, for she'd been trying to talk her boss into hiring us on for his new detective agency. This was proving a challenge, however, for the boss in question was one Col. C. Kermit Crowe, late of the Southern Pacific Railroad Police—"late" because he'd been unwise enough to hire *us* just before we ran an S.P. locomotive off a cliff. Believe it or not, some folks will hold a grudge when you do them like that.

So as I saw it—and suspected Old Red saw it, too—the *McClure's* contest wasn't just the best shot we'd ever get at fame and fortune. It was maybe the *only* way we could hope to get close to Diana Corvus again.

Of course, my brother never came right out and said any of this. He makes it a habit not to come out and say anything, if he can help it. But the mere fact that he didn't jump off that train at the first opportunity sure said *something*.

We were due to arrive late Monday morning, and I awoke at dawn that day, heart pounding with excitement. Most of our fellow passengers were up early, too, and by eight o'clock there was hardly a one not kitted out in their finest frock coat or day gown, as if we were headed not to a World's Fair but a Sunday service. The Exposition may have been created to celebrate the four hundredth anniversary of Chris Columbus's voyage to America, but everyone knew it wasn't really about the past. With its treasures and scientific wonders gathered from all around an ever-shrinking earth, "the White City" was where you went to greet the future. It was a more perfect world we were supposedly moving toward, and folks meant to get there looking picture-perfect themselves.

In this same spirit, I shaved, pomaded my hair, and put on my best suit. When Old Red returned from his morning toilet, however, he was still wearing the wrinkled work duds he'd slept in.

"Tell me you ain't gonna get off the train lookin' like that," I said as he plopped down beside me.

"What am I supposed to look like? Diamond Jim Brady?"

"No. But I'd rather you didn't look like a hungover dirt farmer, neither. Can't you at least put on a tie?" I reached under our seat for my carpetbag. "Good thing I've got style enough for two. Now whadaya prefer: neck tie or bow?"

"I prefer not to strangle myself with *any* d- . . . d- . . . damn . . ."

I peeped up to see what was gumming my brother's mouth, and there it was out the window, miles away yet already coming into view as we rounded a bend in the tracks.

Chicago.

Clustered towers of dark steel jutted up into grimy-gray clouds.

Huge smokestacks belched black from beside factories and vast stockyards. And stretching out and around us like the giant web of some frightful spider: electrical wires, telephone lines, tracks, streets, gutters.

"Christ almighty," Gustav muttered. "I almost wish I was still blind."

For the next half hour, we cut through the slaughterhouses, manufacturing plants, tenements, and all-around ugliness that ringed the city. There was much murmuring and shaking of heads among the other passengers, and the air of anticipation with which they'd begun the day gave way to something approaching disgust.

If this was the future, God help us all.

Eventually, however, a little shriek of excitement went up somewhere behind us: "I see the lake!" Sure enough, there out the window, visible in sapphire stripes flashing between the muddled brown of the buildings, was Lake Michigan. It stretched all the way to the horizon—seemed to merge with the azure sky, in fact, so that there was hardly any horizon at all. Just a wall of blue so big you'd hardly believe the world could contain it.

Then another cry went up, and suddenly everyone was pressing against the windows so hard it's a wonder the train didn't tip over.

"The fairgrounds!"

"The Exposition!"

"*The White City!*"

Domes, that was all I could see. Huge orbs, four or five of them, jutting up as rounded and gleaming as giant eggs. The buildings beneath were blocked from view by the massive terminal we were pulling up to and the dozen other trains already lined up on the long row of tracks before it.

We eased to a stop amidst such a furious tumult of activity as to make a beehive look like a mortuary. Passengers pouring from the neighboring trains pushed toward the station through the still-swirling engine steam, while porters piled luggage onto pushcarts and bellowing news butchers hawked guidebooks and maps.

"You ready for this?" I asked my brother.

It's not just trains he doesn't care for. Crowds he's not overfond of, either, and cities he can't stand.

So far, the Exposition looked like his definition of hell on earth.

"Ready as I'll ever be," Old Red grumbled. "By which I mean *no*."

Yet he snatched up his gripsack and got to his feet.

Soon we were flotsam in the swirling deluge of humanity on the platform. As we were jostled this way and that, I tried to stay on tippy-toe so as to spy or be spied by our backer, Urias Smythe.

I'd wired ahead to tell him our arrival was imminent and all he had to do was meet us at the station for his prayers to be answered. I knew the man only from his letters and (God bless him) money orders, though, so I couldn't so much search for him as try to look conspicuous and hope for the best.

I didn't have to try hard. With our matching red hair and mis-matched builds—mine strapping, my brother's slight—Gustav and I couldn't pull off *in*conspicuous on our best day. And this, it would turn out, was far from our best day.

I spotted a big, jowly, bald-headed fellow squirming against the current of the crowd, and when he noticed me watching him, his eyes narrowed . . . and then, upon falling on Old Red, popped wide.

"Mr. Smythe?" I called to him with a tentative wave.

He answered my question by throwing out his own in a tremu-lous, squeaky-high voice.

"Otto Amlingmeyer?"

I nodded, and ever so slowly Smythe turned toward us and started our way. A moment later, I thrust out a hand as the man who'd plucked us from obscurity and destitution stood before me for the first time.

Smythe didn't seem to see my hand even as he looked me and my brother over head to foot and back again.

Old Red's shabby clothes and shaded cheaters got the longest look of all.

"This is Gustav?" Smythe asked.

"Indeed it is, and pleased as punch we both are to be here." I stuck my hand out so far now it just about poked the man's belly button. "We want to thank you for this opportunity, sir. I promise you, you won't regret puttin' your faith in us."

It was too late for that particular promise, though. Rather than give me a shake, Smythe put his hands to his face.

"Oh, my God," he blubbered. "I'm ruined!"

3

PINS AND NEEDLES

Or, Smythe Frets About Losing His Shirt While Gustav Comes Apart at the Seams

When faced with displays of emotional distress, my brother typically employs the response preferred by most cowboys. He coughs awkwardly, looks away, and waits for the moment to pass. So my publisher got no tender words of comfort from Old Red, though it sure looked like he could use a few. With his hairless head and round, red-cheeked face, Smythe resembled nothing so much as a huge, bawling baby diapered in a black business suit.

I might have jumped in quicker to soothe him myself but for one thing: It was obviously the sight of me and Gustav that had primed the pump for his tears. I'd be the first to admit we didn't exactly look like Sir Galahad and Lancelot charging in on white steeds, but surely we weren't that uninspiring.

Well, surely *I* wasn't, anyway.

After a long moment trying to decide how insulted I should feel, I pulled out a handkerchief and offered it to the man.

"Thank you." Smythe took the hankie, blew an immense, snorking noseful into it, then handed it back. "I do hope you'll forgive me. These have been trying times. Trying times, indeed!" He sucked in a deep breath, and the crimson flush on his face faded to a more presentable pink. "There's no time to dwell on that now, though."

He turned aside to flag down a porter.

"We ain't got no trunks, if that's what you're thinkin'." I gave my carpetbag a little waggle. "Me and my brother travel light."

"Of course. So you always say in your stories, and so far they've proved quite accurate. For the most part." Smythe stole another quick, quiver-lipped peek at Gustav, then leaned toward me and dropped his voice. "Your brother . . . he's not *blind*, is he?"

"Not anymore," I whispered back.

This did not seem to put Smythe at ease.

"I ain't deaf, neither," Old Red snapped.

"Oh, I'm so sorry!" Smythe spluttered. "But it wouldn't have surprised me if you were deaf, dumb, and blind after what I've been through the past few days." He grimaced and fluttered his hands in the air. "I'm just all higgledy piggledy!"

"Now, now. Everything's gonna be fine," I said soothingly. If I'd had a lollipop, I'd have given it to him. "Why don't you explain the situation, and we'll—"

Smythe gave me an emphatic, wattles-flapping shake of the head. "Explanations can wait. Follow me!"

He spun on his heel and hustled off toward the terminal building.

Gustav looked at me.

I shrugged.

We followed.

The milling crowd was thick as ever inside the station, but Smythe's gut cut through it like the prow of some mighty ship. "One side! Official business!" he'd blare when the multitudes didn't part quick enough to suit him. So busy was I apologizing on his behalf,

I couldn't even grab a good look at the building till we were nearly out of it again. All I got was a quick glimpse of glistening marble and beveled glass and long-lined ticket windows, and suddenly we were pushing through turnstiles while Smythe waved a blue ribbon at the attendants nearby.

"Official business!"

Then we were outside again . . . and we were *in* the White City.

Smythe kept charging on ahead. My brother and I stopped dead in our tracks.

To our left was what looked like a vast castle bedecked with dozens of flapping banners—the largest single thing we'd ever seen spring from the hands of man. When we turned to the right, we saw something even *bigger*. It was the castle times two with the White House and the Vatican thrown in for good measure.

"Gentlemen, *please!*"

The voice seemed to drift to us from an almost otherworldly distance, as when someone speaks to you while you're still half-asleep in a dream. I blinked and looked ahead and found Smythe fifty feet beyond us, waving frantically for us to follow. Behind him was yet another marvel: a stately, statuary-studded structure adorned with pillars, huge arching windows, and, up top, a towering gilded dome aglint in the sunshine. It looked like heaven's own county courthouse, and it was apparently our destination.

Gustav and I set off for it with slow, stumbling steps. As we walked, my brother swung his gaze this way and that, still trying to take in the enormity all around us. It was a good thing he was wearing his tinted specs, for so far the White City was living up to its name. Nearly everything was blinding-bright pristine white.

"How your eyes doin'?" I asked.

Old Red shook his head. "I ain't sure. I don't know whether to believe 'em or not."

"You can gawk later!" Smythe fussed, urging us on with a paddlewheel-spin of the hands. "We're running out of time!"

"But your telegram said everything'd be fine so long as we were here by noon," I pointed out.

"Yes! And it's ten till, you big—!"

Smythe caught himself just in time.

"Red," he said. "Now *please* stop dawdling. There's not a second to spare!"

He turned and set off for that huge bedomed building again, and soon we were pushing through the doors. Inside, we were stopped by a fellow wearing a blue uniform with a brass star and a short, scabbarded sword—obviously a member of the Columbian Guard, the Exposition's famous army of private police.

"Sorry, gentlemen. The Administration Building's not open to—"

Smythe waved his blue ribbon. "Official business!"

The guard stepped back and let us pass.

"The contest's gonna be in here?" I asked as we continued down a broad, marble-tiled hall.

"No, no, no! The Exposition's loaned us an office for the week, that's all."

Smythe threw open a door and shooed us into a small room. A typewriter-topped desk had been shoved into one corner, but beyond that and a few lights along the wall—electric bulbs, I noted, not gas jets—the little room was free of any other furniture or fixture.

Two tall stacks of boxes bookended the typewriter on the desk.

"Alright," Smythe said. "Time to get into your costumes."

"Our *what?*" Old Red blurted out before I could.

Smythe turned to the desk, opened one of the bigger boxes, and pulled out a ten-gallon hat so high-peaked and pure white, seen from a distance you'd think it was the Swiss Alps. This he handed to my brother. Then he reached into another box and produced a round-topped Boss of the Plains that was, amazingly, even larger—and bright red. This, to my horror, he handed to me.

"They go on your heads!" Smythe snapped when we didn't immediately slap the hats on.

"It's awful nice of you to give us these," I said. "But . . . well . . . a *red* Stetson? Black, white, or brown, that's all a real cowboy'd ever—"

"What's 'real' got to do with it? I've already made"—here Smythe's voice went warbly—"a substantial investment in this undertaking. Even if it can't be recouped, I don't mean to see it wasted entirely. We have an opportunity to paint a public portrait of you that suits our purposes, and we're going to make the most of it."

Smythe turned back to the packages. As he sorted through them, a magazine tucked between two boxes fell fluttering to the floor. It landed cover up.

Smythe's Frontier Detective, it was called. I'd never heard of it. Which was ironic, since it had heard of me.

"OLD RED," THE HOLMES OF THE RANGE,

IN: "BUCKAROO SLEUTHS OF RUSTLER'S RANCH!"

BY "BIG RED," THE COWBOY WATSON

Below all that was a picture of "Big Red" himself, large as life and blazing with color. He and "Old Red" stood back to back, Peacemakers drawn, a gang of desperadoes circling them on horseback.

How did I know which one was Big Red? Well, he was the big one, obviously. The red Stetson was a bit of a clue, too. Not to mention the red chaps, red holster, and red vest worn over trousers and shirt of purest white, with white boots, no less.

Old Red was his opposite—white hat, chaps, holster, and vest, but red shirt, trousers, and boots.

They looked ridiculous, ludicrous, laughable . . . and that was exactly what Smythe had in mind for me and Gustav. He began pulling out outfits that were identical to the ones on the cover. That magazine had been his tailor's pattern book.

Smythe moved toward Old Red with a crimson gun belt.

Old Red hopped back like the man was coming after him with a pitchfork.

"Oh, no," he said, shaking his head.

"Oh, yes," Smythe said, nodding.

"Oh, *no,*" my brother said, shaking his head harder.

"Oh, *yes,*" Smythe said, nodding just as hard.

"Oh. No!" Shake shake shake.

"Oh. Yes!" Nod nod nod.

If it kept up much longer, one or the other was going to break his neck.

"Look, Brother . . . ," I began.

"I *am* lookin'!" Gustav raged. "At duds so ugly only a blind fool would wear 'em! And I may be half-blind, but I'm no fool! I ain't gonna dress up like a blasted barber pole and I ain't gonna let some snuffy flibbertigibbet boss me around and come to think of it I ain't gonna play any dumb-ass detectivin' games, neither!"

With that, he stomped to the door, threw it open, and started marching back toward the train station.

4

ARMSTRONG B. CURTIS,
ESQUIRE

Or, Old Red Draws a Line in the Sand and Meets a Snake in the Grass

I'll be right back," I told Smythe as I hustled after my brother. I would've preferred saying "*We'll* be right back," but I didn't want to make a promise I might not be able to keep.

I caught up to Old Red in the hallway with my speech all ready in my head. It was about Our Big Chance and How Far We'd Come and Not Giving Up . . . and Diana Corvus. I think it would've proved quite inspiring, if I'd only had the chance to give it.

"Don't bother," Gustav said before I even opened my mouth. "I ain't goin' nowhere."

"Oh?" I pointed down at our feet. "Then why are they still movin'?"

Old Red looked over his shoulder. When he was satisfied Smythe wasn't stealing a peek out of the office, he stopped.

"I ain't some bootlicker that big milksop can push around," he said. "Hopefully, he knows that now."

"Trust me: No one's gonna mistake you for a bootlicker. A madman, maybe, but not a bootlicker. Anyway, you've made your point,

26

so now you can come on back and do as Smythe asks with your precious pride intact."

"Wha-? Let the man play dress-up with me like I was a damn paper doll?"

My brother looked down as if he meant to spit, but the sight of the gleaming clean marble floor stopped him.

"Feh," he said instead.

"Fine," I sighed. "I'll smooth things over without any help from you. Like always. You just be here when it's time for . . . whatever the hell comes next."

As I turned to go, I noticed a short, chubby-cheeked fellow eyeing us from farther down the hallway. He was dressed with grand formality, in black frock coat and top hat and spats, and he kept his gaze glued to me so firmly I felt the need to tip my bowler to him before striding back into Smythe's impromptu tailor shop.

"Everything's alright," I informed a huffing, puffing, pacing Smythe. "I talked some sense into him."

"So he's coming back to put on his costume?"

"Oh, I think it'd be best if he outfitted himself today."

And before Smythe could get to gnashing his teeth again, I bit the bullet. Chomped down hard on a cannonball, really.

I swiped the red Stetson off the desk and plopped it atop my head. Unfortunately, it fit.

"Unlike my brother," I said, reaching for a pair of white trousers, "I ain't too big for my britches."

Smythe kept on fretting and fuming at first, but the more I got myself looking like a candy cane, the more he calmed down. I even managed to get the lay of the land from him at last.

The competition was to kick off at noon with a ceremony in the White City's much ballyhooed Court of Honor. All the contenders would be present, and the contest judge—William Pinkerton, eldest of Allan Pinkerton's heirs and head of the Pinkerton National Detective Agency's Chicago office—would preside.

"Pinkerton ain't gonna compete himself?" I managed to ask as I buckled on my chaps.

"No," Smythe said.

"But he'll have a man in the ring for him, right?"

"No."

"You mean you're havin' a World's Greatest Sleuth competition without a contestant from the world's biggest detective agency?"

"Yes."

"Hmm," I said, inviting elucidation.

Which Smythe did not provide.

So I tried again.

"Hmmmmmmm."

"It couldn't be helped!" Smythe cried. "Pinkerton wanted to keep his precious agency 'above the fray.' He was willing to act as judge, however, and he oversaw the creation of the contest rules."

"Oh ho! I've been wonderin' about that. What are the rules, exactly?"

"I don't know. Pinkerton wouldn't tell us. *Real* detectives don't get a rulebook to play by, he says."

"Sounds like Mr. Pinkerton don't think the rest of us *are* real detectives."

Smythe said nothing.

I'd used up my daily allotment of "Hmmmmms"—not to mention all our time—so I let the matter drop.

The first step toward the door was the hardest. I don't just mean that metaphorical-like, either. My boots, chaps, holster, and vest were new-leather stiff, and I couldn't so much walk as waddle. It chafed something fierce, too, and before I was even in the hallway I was already aching in the places a man least likes to ache.

"Who is that your brother's talking to?" Smythe asked.

I pivoted stiffly on one heel to square myself the way he was facing. Old Red was far off down the hall, in what looked to be a broad, open lobby. With him was the little round-faced gent I'd seen staring at us earlier.

I tried to shrug, but my vest was hard as armor and my shoulders wouldn't budge.

"I got no idea," I said.

I began wobble-walking toward Gustav, the leather of my costume squeaking so loud it sounded like I was crushing a mouse with every footfall. My brother and his new pal turned to watch me approach with pop-eyed stares that did not bode well for my impending debut before the public at large. As I drew up close, however, the squat stranger's expression changed, his disbelief displaced by a grin so wide it would've looked right at home on a jack-o'-lantern.

"Otto Amlingmeyer!" he blared with an enthusiasm usually reserved for cries of "Land ho!" or "Gold!" "I am a great admirer of yours, young man!"

"You don't say. I didn't know I had any, other than me."

The man laughed so hard I worried he might rupture something.

"Priceless! You and your brother—you're exactly like in your stories!" He looked me up and down and cocked an eyebrow. "Well, maybe not *exactly*."

"You've read my stories?" I marveled. Though Smythe had purchased several yarns from me, I'd only seen two in print—and one of them little more than five minutes before. I could hardly believe anyone else had ever laid eyes on the things. Yet the little fellow nodded with such vigor his top hat nearly flew off.

"Read them and loved them! The stories themselves, anyway. The magazines they appeared in, on the other hand . . ."

Smythe had followed behind me, and the little man glared at him, his delight giving way to disdain.

"Really, sir," he said. "You finally have some material of integrity and quality, and what do you do with it? I mean, egad—'Buckaroo Sleuths of Rustler's Ranch'? It's like something dreamed up by a six-year-old. I can't imagine that was the original title."

He glanced at me for confirmation.

He was right, of course: I'd titled the tale "Holmes on the Range." Not worthy of Shakespeare, maybe, but hopefully a notch above what a six-year-old could manage.

Still, I played it safe and just shrugged.

"And those covers!" the man went on, railing at Smythe again. "They make these fine young men look like something from under Barnum & Bailey's big top."

"Publishing, *sir,* is not the stuff of literary salons and poetry journals," Smythe harrumphed back. "Capturing the fancy of the reading public requires boldness and verve and . . ." He stopped himself and straightened up to his full height. "Who the devil *are* you, anyway?"

"We already know each other, actually." The stranger offered Smythe his hand. "Armstrong B. Curtis, Esquire."

Smythe actually gasped, then tried to turn it into an innocent cough.

The handshake was over fast.

"What brings you to Chicago, Mr. Curtis?" Smythe asked stiffly.

Curtis gave him a coy shrug. "Just wrapping up some unfinished business. Speaking of which, I really should be going. Big Red." He took his leave of me with a friendly nod, then turned toward my brother. "Old Red. May I say what a pleasure it was chatting with you. Best of luck."

"Thank you, sir. I enjoyed our little talk, too," Gustav said. "I hope we'll be seein' more of you."

Curtis's smile went so wide I could hardly believe one face could contain it. When he turned to go, I almost expected him to leave it hovering in the air behind him like Mr. Carroll's Cheshire cat.

Gustav and I both turned to Smythe, our quizzical stares saying in unison, "Well . . . ?"

"The man's a fanatic," Smythe told us, voice atremble. "I just hope he's not here to disrupt the contest somehow."

"Why would he do that?" I asked.

"Cuz of how he feels about Mr. Holmes," my brother said. "That's what you meant when you called him a fanatic, am I right?"

Smythe nodded. "He's turned Sherlock Holmes into a sort of god. In his eyes, every other magazine detective's a fraud. A false idol for him to tear down. And the little crank doesn't keep his opinions to himself."

"Sounds like someone else I know," I said.

Old Red scowled at me.

"What did Curtis want with you?" Smythe asked him.

"Just to talk. He asked if I was me, shook my hand, then started in about the Man. Really knew his stuff, too. Quoted Holmes, talked about the Method, compared my brother's stories to John Watson's. Every now and then he'd go all forgetful, though. Need me to remind him of this or that. Almost like he was testin' me."

Down at the end of the hallway, Curtis passed another Guardsman and pushed through more ornate glass doors. The blast of a brass band echoed in from somewhere just outside.

"I'm sure he *was* testing you," Smythe said. "He wrote the Nick Carter exposé."

"The Nick Carter what, now?" Gustav asked, his face puckering up as it would whenever Carter came up. To him, the man's always been "Blockhead Numero Uno"—undoubtedly the most famous magazine detective, aside from Holmes, but (according to my brother) the dimmest as well.

"The article about him," Smythe said. "In *Scribner's Magazine*. The one that caused all the uproar."

"We ain't heard about no uproar."

Smythe gaped at my brother, then at me. "You mean you really don't know? I can't believe you haven't read of it. I mean . . . why do you think I wanted you here today?"

I peeked down at my new duds. "You have a sick sense of humor?"

"Nick Carter doesn't exist!" Smythe said. "Curtis proved it!"

"Doesn't exist? So there ain't really no Nick Carter?"

"That's generally what 'doesn't exist' means," Gustav sniped. Somehow, he seemed utterly unsurprised to learn that Blockhead Numero Uno was, in truth, nada. "Curtis proved it how?" he asked Smythe.

"Oh, that doesn't matter now."

Smythe pulled out a pocket watch and checked the time. From the look of profound gloom that came over his face, you'd have thought it was the Hour of Judgment. And in a way, I guess it was.

"The important thing is you're going to walk outside with me and prove to all the world how real *you* are."

Smythe snapped his watch shut and started for the doors Curtis had just passed through. Gustav and I reluctantly followed.

"You ready to be famous?"

"I am ready," my brother said, "to smack you upside the head for gettin' us into this."

"Just grit your teeth and think of Miss Corvus and you'll be fine. We get through this, she'll have us on Colonel Crowe's payroll for sure."

"I'd rather just give you that smack."

It was nerves talking, I knew, so I didn't sass Old Red back. Even if we'd fallen into our usual bickering, though, it couldn't have lasted long: Once we walked out into the Court of Honor, neither of us had the breath left for anything but gasps.

Stretching out before us was a long lagoon, so large you might've called it a lake if it hadn't been dwarfed by the infinite blue of Lake Michigan beyond it. Huge statues jutted up out of the water—naked women, flute-playing children, men riding rearing fish-horses, an entire life-sized barge—while fountains shot foamy-white arcs high into the sky.

To the right of the lagoon was a long, stately, bepillared building as big as anything we'd yet seen. You had to pity it, though, grand as it was, for to the left was a structure so vast it could swallow the other whole and a half dozen like it. It stretched on so far you couldn't see the end of it. You couldn't even be sure there *was* an end to it.

There was much more I didn't have the presence of mind to note beyond hazy impressions: What are all those columns down there and how do the boats in that big pond move so fast with no one rowing and is that actually a statue of a *cow* over yonder? I couldn't pause to think any of it through, not with a uniformed band nearby hammering away at "The Liberty Bell March" for a throng hundreds strong—a good portion of it staring at *us*.

Old Red grabbed hold of my arm and muttered something I couldn't quite hear.

"What's that?"

"I said, 'Holy shit!'" my brother bellowed just as the band went pianissimo for a piccolo solo.

I can't say the *entire* crowd turned to stare at us. It sure felt like it, though.

"Look!" a man shouted, pointing at me. "It's Buffalo Bill Cody!"

"Naw, that ain't him!" someone hollered back.

"Yes, it is!"

"No, it isn't!" another man joined in. "That's Annie Oakley!"

At last, there was agreement.

Everyone laughed.

"Come come come!" Smythe prodded us, head slick with sweat. He waved at a gazebo bandstand about fifty yards away, and when I looked at it I saw a cluster of frock-coated dignitary-types up there looking back at *us*. "They're waiting!"

Gustav was still clutching on to my arm as we started for the bandstand, and I heard a woman nearby hiss-whisper, "Oh, my . . . the little one's *blind*."

"Must've stared too long at the big one's clothes," some wag replied, and there was more laughter.

Old Red let go of me and marched on with as much dignity as he could muster. I tried to follow suit, but mustering dignity's not easy when walking in chaps so starchy-stiff you can't bend at the knee, and I ended up lumbering along with all the easy grace of the town drunk on Saturday night.

When we reached the stairs up to the bandstand, a pair of Columbian Guards parted to let us pass. A big, bluff, bushy-mustached man met us at the top of the steps.

"So, Smythe," he said, looking me and my brother over like we were something even the most indiscriminating cat wouldn't have bothered dragging in, "your new champions made it."

"Yes, yes. Here they are, Mr. Pinkerton. Otto and Gustav—"

"Amlingmeyer" turned into a strangled wheeze halfway out of Smythe's mouth.

Mr. Pinkerton—Mr. William Pinkerton of the Pinkerton National Detective Agency—hadn't waited for Smythe to finish.

"Alright," he said, turning away, obviously addressing himself to someone else. "Let's get this over with."

Just beyond the man, till then hidden behind his bulk, was a toothy grin so big it seemed to just float there in the air. It was pointed our way . . . and standing behind it was Armstrong B. Curtis.

"Awwww, hell," Old Red said.

He wasn't even looking at Curtis, though. He was eyeing the folks clustered up at the back of the bandstand—our competition, I presumed. Among them was a dark-haired beauty cut from the same lovely cloth as Diana Corvus, and beside her was a little gent who looked for all the world like her employer, Col. C. Kermit Crowe. It took but a blink for me to realize why the resemblances were so striking.

It was them.

5

PALPITATIONS
Or, The Contest Kicks Off with Another Kick in the Pants

I think I'm palpitating . . . I think I'm palpitating," Smythe puffed, pressing both hands to his heaving chest as he gaped at Armstrong B. Curtis.

"You have *got* to be kiddin'," said I, widening my eyes to a size approximate to a pair of dinner plates as I gawped at Diana and Colonel Crowe.

This left it to my brother to provide calming comfort, which he did in his usual gentle, compassionate fashion.

"Get a move on, ya idjits," he snapped, grabbing both me and Smythe by the arm and jerking us away. "This is bad enough without you two just standin' around starin' like a couple heifers chewin' cud."

As Old Red dragged us toward the clump of ladies and gents huddled at the back of the gazebo, a slick-dressed, fiftyish fellow separated himself from the pack and sidled up to Smythe.

"It was a shock to me, too," he said, voice low. "Curtis. Up here. With Pinkerton. I don't know what they're up to, Urias, but I can tell you this much: We've been stabbed in the back."

36

Smythe was whimpering when the man slithered away again.

Though Curtis was too far away to have overheard the conversation, it was obvious he knew what it was about—and found it rather amusing. Smythe he flashed his cheek-cistending grin. Me and Gustav he offered an apologetic shrug. Then, at a whispered word from Pinkerton, he turned and stepped up to the podium at the front of the bandstand. The brass band by the edge of the lagoon wrapped up "The Thunderer," and the final, rushed *bah-bum-bum!* was still echoing out toward the lake as the little man addressed himself to the crowd.

Just about everything he said after "Good afternoon!" I missed, however, for I was deep in conversation with Diana. Not that either of us was actually saying anything. When I leaned out to stare in wonderment at the lady, though, I found her looking our way, and the following passed between us.

My slack jaw: *What are* you *doing here?*

Her sorrowful frown: *Competing against you, obviously.*

The way I raised my hands, the palms up: *Well, how could you let that happen?*

Her elegantly arched eyebrow, pointed first at me, then at my brother and his shaded cheaters: *I'd say you have some explaining to do as well.*

My blush as I remembered what I was wearing: *Shit.*

Then Colonel Crowe stepped in to join the conversation. There wasn't much of him—he was short enough to make even Curtis look like Goliath—yet he could prove a formidable obstacle when he set his mind to it.

His malicious glare: *What are you looking at, you EXPUR-GATED UNPRINTABLE?*

I busied myself looking elsewhere.

My gaze fell first upon my brother—who was giving me a dose

of "EXPURGATED UNPRINTABLE" himself. For once, I couldn't begrudge him his truculence. Here we were supposedly winning the colonel's favor, and instead we end up squared off against him. If the man didn't hate us already for costing him his job with the Southern Pacific, beating him out of $10,000 prize money would surely do the trick. Yet if we *didn't* win the contest, why should he bother hiring us?

We were damned if we did, damned if we didn't . . . and damned if I knew what to do about it.

So absorbed was I in all this I only barely noticed that Curtis was lulling the crowd to sleep with some sort of fable about Christopher Columbus.

"—which has been secreted somewhere within the confines of the White City," he was saying when I actually started paying attention. "Only I, the Puzzlemaster, know where it is. So it will be for the next four days. At noon precisely, our contestants will gather here to be given clues as to the egg's whereabouts. Every day they'll have the chance to find it, and every night I will hide it again. Whosoever has located the egg the most times by two o'clock Thursday will be our winner."

"Uhhh . . . did he just say 'egg'?" I asked Smythe.

He goggled his eyes at me. "Haven't you heard a word he said?"

I shrugged. "Yeah. 'Egg.'"

"I'm doomed," Smythe said. At least he was over his palpitations.

Curtis, meanwhile, was introducing that great American (according to him) William Pinkerton. There was a smattering of applause—and one "Boo!" I was actually surprised there weren't more, what with the Homestead Strike fiasco little more than a year old and the Anti-Pinkerton Act fresh-passed by Congress. The Pinks may be heroes to some, but they're villains to just as many others.

Pinkerton slowly scanned the crowd from left to right as he stepped up to the podium. I got the feeling that heckler wouldn't live long if Pinkerton spotted him.

"You know my name and what it stands for," he said. "Nearly half a century ago, my father invented the modern detective profession. Today, despite the best efforts of agitators and cranks, the Pinkerton National Detective Agency remains synonymous with integrity and efficiency. Crime and radicalism know no greater enemy, and democracy and capitalism no better friend, than the well-trained, *professional* private detective."

The man's lack of brevity was matched only by his lack of zeal. Of all those listening to his speech, he himself seemed the least interested in it.

"But there is another kind of detective," he went on. "One typified by the late Sherlock Holmes: the talented novice. His passing was a tragic loss for his followers—some of whom are standing behind me at this very moment. For the time has come to answer the question: Who is now the World's Greatest Amateur Sleuth?"

"*Amateur* Sleuth?" I said.

"Talented novice?" Old Red spat.

"Dooooooooomed," Smythe moaned.

Whatever enthusiasm the audience had once possessed had been smothered under Pinkerton's wet blanket, and I fancied I heard groans when he consulted a piece of paper fresh-pulled from his pocket. The speechmaking was over, though. It was time for introductions.

"Will it be King Brady"—Pinkerton squinted down at the paper and frowned—"monarch of the New York detectives?"

A young man who'd been standing near us stepped out to the center of the gazebo. He was a big buck blessed with features so pretty-perfect no woman could look upon them and not swoon, and he acknowledged the cheers that greeted him with a wave and a cocky grin. He was no Nick Carter, fame-wise, but Old Red and I knew his magazine well, and he certainly had ol' Nick beat out in one important respect: He existed.

"Will it be Boothby Greene," Pinkerton read out listlessly, "English heir to the genius of Sherlock Holmes?"

A tall, lean, sharp-featured fellow joined Brady. Though I'd never heard of him, he struck me as strangely familiar-looking, and as he nodded to the crowd I realized why. He was a dead ringer for Holmes himself (or at least the Holmes I'd come to know from the illustrations in *Harper's Weekly*).

"Will it be Eugene Valmont," Pinkerton went on, "French master of the sleuthing arts?"

A compact, square-faced fellow with graying red hair and a bulbous nose lined up with Brady and Greene.

"Will it be Little Red Amplyminor, the Holmes of the Plains?" Pinkerton droned after a distracted glance down at his notes.

Smythe grimaced and squeezed his eyes shut tight. "Father, why hast thou forsaken me?"

"The Holmes of the Plains" was more succinct.

"Feh," he grunted, and slowly, sheepishly, he slouched out to join the competition.

"Or," Pinkerton went on, "will it be railroad detective Colonel C. Kermit Crowe and his daughter, the beautiful and brilliant Miss Diana Crowe?"

The colonel and Diana lined up with the others.

"And there you have it," Pinkerton declared. "Fizzle blop de ginkle shmertz. Clopthrobble fuff oaka heng holla diffin."

Of course, that's not *exactly* what the man said. Yet that's sure what it sounded like to me after his earlier words—"daughter" and

"Miss Diana Crowe"—started to sink in. Once they did, it was only the stiff leather of my costume that kept me upright.

"Puzzlemaster," Pinkerton said, turning to Curtis. (In spite of the "Diana Crowe-Crowe-Crowe" still echoing in my ears, I could understand English again.) "You have the clues?"

Curtis held a little bundle of envelopes up over his head. "Here, sir!"

"Then you may proceed."

This Curtis did, stepping up to each contestant in turn—the Crowes (the *Crowes*!?!), King Brady, Boothby Greene, Eugene Valmont—to hand over an envelope.

As he gave the last one to Gustav, he peeped over at me.

"Your brother might need help with this part. On account of the trouble he's having with his eyes."

I was still in such shock I felt like my own eyes were spinning like pinwheels, yet I managed to stumble up next to Old Red and mumble out my thanks. Curtis might have been a fanatic, by Smythe's measure, but at least he was a kindly one: He'd read my stories, so he knew my brother was illiterate—and how it would shame him to have that fact brought up in front of the other sleuths.

Curtis threw me a wink, then returned to Pinkerton's side.

"Gentlemen!" he called out. "And lady," he said more softly, with a nod Diana's way. "Deduce!"

6

THE CONTEST (ROUND ONE)

Or, We Go on a Wild Goose Chase and End Up Laying an Egg

The band struck up a song. The mob hurrahed. The contestants tore into their envelopes.

I gaped at Diana Crowe and drooled on myself.

Or so I imagine. There was no mirror there in which to see myself—and I thank the good Lord for it.

I suppose I should be grateful, too, that Diana didn't see me in such a state: She was too busy reading her fresh-opened clue with her father (*father!?!*) to throw more meaningful glances my way. Which meant my slack-jawed, pop-eyed "Huh?" went unanswered.

When Gustav and I had first met the lady, she'd called herself Diana Caveo—this because she was a spy for the S.P. Railroad Police. The second time our paths crossed, she was Diana Corvus, though this name she also abandoned whenever convenient, bald-faced lying being one of her specialties while on the job. Off it, too, I had to figure, for never in all our time together had she even hinted that Colonel Crowe was more to her than a particularly nettlesome employer.

"I said *mmm-MMM*!" I heard my brother growl. When I looked his way, I realized he must've been clearing his throat at me for quite some time, for upon his face was a scowl and in his hand—unread, of course—was his clue.

"Oh. Right. Let's see now."

Inside the envelope Curtis had handed him was a small card, perhaps four inches by six. Upon it were these words, pounded into the heavy paper in the slightly smudgy gray-black lettering of a typewriter:

```
A bleeding edge along the east
A famous dodge for northbound beast
Southwest is where you grip the pan
Go back, go back!
And you'll advance
```

"Most intereSTING," someone said, and I found the Frenchman, Valmont, peeping down at the note. "Your massage is not the same as mine."

"What's yours say?" Old Red asked.

Valmont smiled and tucked his card away in his coat. "Oh, I would tell you, but—*quel dommage*—it is *en français*."

He offered us a little bow, turned, and headed for the steps off the stage.

He wasn't alone, either. Greene, the faux Holmes (who says I don't know any French?), was striding away as well. The famous King Brady was still staring down at his card, beetle-browed, but when he noticed the others hurrying off he barked out a laugh and said, "Clever . . . but not clever enough to stump *me*! Miss Larson?"

A slender blond woman separated herself from the dignitaries at the back of the bandstand, and the two of them set off together.

Colonel Crowe marched off next with his arm around his daughter's (*daughter's!?!*). He took care to attach himself to her left-hand side, thus keeping his puny self between her and us as they walked past.

"Diana *Crowe*," I groaned once they'd started down the stairs. "I can't believe it."

"Maybe you shouldn't," Gustav said.

"What's that supposed to mean?"

"That apple fell pretty damned far from the tree, you ask me. Like a mile away."

"You mean cuz she's twice as tall as him? But why would they be lyin'?"

"I don't know. All I *do* know is we're the last 'sleuths' still standin' here." My brother flicked the card in my hand. "And that still don't make a lick of sense."

"Let's break it down a line at a time, then," I suggested. "'A bleeding edge along the east.' Could be it's something on the eastern edge of the fairgrounds. Maybe a hospital or a slaughterhouse."

"The Exposition's got its own slaughterhouse?"

"Well, no. Not that I know of. It's got just about everything else in the world, though."

"But 'go back,' it said. We just showed up today. How can we go back to anything? We ain't been nowhere."

As we spoke, I could hear the murmurings and mutterings of the crowd growing louder. Folks were getting restless, and I couldn't blame them. If the two of us were any indication, puzzle-solving was every bit as exciting a sport as a staring contest or competition napping.

Old Red swiped a hand at the clue card, exasperated. "Alright, forget the bleeding part. What was next?"

"'A famous dodge for northbound beast.'"

"A famous *dodge*?"

I nodded. "It's an odd choice of words, alright. The only famous dodge I know of is Dodge City."

"Yeah, and that's . . . hel-lo!" Gustav jerked his head at Armstrong B. Curtis. "Our Puzzlemaster there's read your yarns. Which means he knows where we hail from."

"Peabody?" I said. Then, just barely resisting the urge to smack my forehead (an urge my brother no doubt shared): "Kansas!"

Suddenly, it all made sense.

The bleeding edge to the east: the "Bleeding Kansas" border war with Missouri.

The famous dodge for northbound beast: Dodge City, the West's best-known cattle town.

The pan grip to the southwest: the Oklahoma panhandle.

And the "go back, go back": I had no idea.

"He wants us to go back . . . to Kansas?"

"Don't seem like such a bad idea," Old Red muttered, eyeing the crowd.

"Hold on a tick. I just remembered—"

"Are you just gonna stand there all day?" someone shouted out.

"Yeah!" another voice chimed in. *"Do something!"*

Gustav spun around, face flushed. He was indeed about to do something. He was about to tell our public to shut the hell up.

I caught his arm just in time.

"Allow me," I said, and I cleared my throat, stepped around my brother, and addressed the audience. "We need a map of the White City—pronto!"

I would've said "immediately," but "pronto" seemed to suit my costume better. Funny thing, too: It worked.

"Here!"

"I've got one!"

"Take mine!"

45

"Come on," I said to Old Red, and I tried to stride manfully from the bandstand.

I say tried because the attempt was unsuccessful: It's impossible to "stride" down stairs with one's legs strapped to red leather splints, and a waddle is anything but manly. Still, I made it to the bottom of the steps without breaking my neck, and this I counted as a victory.

The crowd had thinned a bit since the ceremony began. Some folks had hustled off after Valmont and the Crowes and the rest; others had just drifted away upon realizing, perhaps, that the contest wouldn't involve us solving an actual on-the-spot murder. Yet there were still more than enough spectators to swarm me, and I quickly had my pick of maps. I accepted a dog-eared guidebook from a beaming young lady, receiving in reply to my tip of the hat a blush the memory of which I cherish to this day.

"Every state in the Union's put up a big display here at the Fair," I said as Gustav slid up beside me. "All we gotta do is find . . . a-ha!" I lifted a hand up over my head, the index finger jabbing at the clouds. "To the Kansas Building!"

There were huzzahs and applause, and a gray-haired gent clapped Gustav on the back.

"Good luck, Little Fred," he said.

More encouragement rained down upon us: "Go get 'em, boys!" and "You can do it!" and "America's counting on you!"

Never have I seen my brother look more miserable—and keep in mind, I've seen him beaten, shot, blown up, and lynched.

"Yeah, yeah. To the Kansas Building," he mumbled, shooing me forward with both hands. "Please."

And we set off . . . very, very slowly. My outfit was rubbing me raw from the waist down, and every step felt like I was wading into a pool of razor blades. At the pace we were setting—about equal to a three-legged mule in full pack—we'd make it to the Kansas Building just in time for Christmas.

"Can't you go no faster?" Old Red snapped at me.

"Not without sawin' my legs off. Too bad Smythe didn't give us a pair of horses to go with the . . . well, lookee there!"

"Lookee where?"

"*There.*"

Up ahead, just around the corner as we left the Court of Honor, a dozen boater-wearing lads were lounging about in wheeled chairs. FEAST YOUR EYES, SPARE YOUR FEET, a sign above them said. SEVENTY-FIVE CENTS AN HOUR.

One quick negotiation later, we were speeding away. We'd promised our young attendants an extra two bits apiece if they could get us to the Kansas Building within five minutes, and God bless them, they meant to collect. They were so eager, they didn't even notice that neither my brother nor I had a watch.

I assume we got stares aplenty as we zoomed north through the fairgrounds: It's not every day you see what looks like a blind man and a cowboy carved out of candle wax getting pushed around in wheelchairs. I didn't even notice any gawping, though, for I was too busy doing it myself.

The gravel paths we followed took us along the lagoon, which stretched on and on and on to our immediate right. To our left was the long, angel-adorned facade of the Transportation Building, its bright red paint a shocking smear of crimson through the heart of the White City. Then it was back to *blanco* for the Choral Building, the Horticulture Building, the Women's Building—a Building, it seemed, for everything under the sun but Ham and Eggs and the Piece of Lint Stuck to the Bottom of Your Sock.

"Almost . . . there," my attendant rasped (oh, how his face had fallen when he'd been assigned to ferry husky me instead of my runty brother). "We've . . . reached . . . the . . ."

"Save your breath for pushin', friend," I said. "I see."

We were passing another majestic dome-topped building—the men who planned that fair sure loved their domes—and this one had the word ILLINOIS over the doorway. Around the corner was a grand Spanish mission (CALIFORNIA it read across the front) and a dark, high-roofed manor house (WISCONSIN) and an ornate, twin-towered palace (INDIANA, of all things).

KANSAS couldn't be far off now.

State pride forbids me from discussing at length my reaction when it first came into view. Suffice it to say this: The Michigan Building it was not. Or the Washington Building or the Minnesota Building or the Nebraska Building or . . .

Anyway, the exterior—so boxy, so boring, so punily domed—didn't matter. It was what we'd (hopefully) find inside that counted.

We left our huffing, puffing beasts of burden outside and went bounding up the steps toward the building. (I was able to bound now, having finally had the good sense to unstrap my chaps.)

"I was a mite preoccupied when Mr. Curtis was explainin' the contest," I said to Old Red. "What exactly are we lookin' for again?"

"An egg."

"I heard that part. But what kinda—?"

"I was a mite preoccupied myself, dammit."

"Oh. Wonderful."

I didn't have to ask what had distracted my brother. It would be the same thing that had distracted *me*. Which left us both in the same boat now: the leaky kind with no paddle one usually finds adrift up Shit Creek. Fortunately, there was someone on hand to toss us a lifeline.

When we hustled into the Kansas Building, we found a dozen men and women waiting just inside. They were clustered before a photographer's tripod, staring expectantly at the entrance.

"Gustav and Otto Amlingmeyer?" asked a muttonchopped man wearing a ceremonial sash. From the tone of his voice, it was clear he was hoping to hear a "No."

"That's us," I said.

The man winced, cleared his throat, and held out his hand.

"As president of the Kansas World's Fair Board of Managers, it is my great honor to—"

"That for us?" Gustav asked. He nodded at an envelope in the man's other hand. It was identical to the one Curtis had given us back at the bandstand.

"Yes, it is."

"Thanks."

Old Red snatched the envelope away, spun on his heel, and made a beeline for the doors.

"But . . . but . . ."

"Sorry, folks—we're in a bit of a hurry," I said. "Need a picture for the folks back home before we go?"

I threw one arm around Mr. President, the other around the wide-eyed matron beside him.

"Fire away," I told the photographer.

He pushed the camera button, there was a blinding flash, and then I was gone in a literal puff of smoke.

I caught up to my brother outside. He'd already ripped the envelope open and pulled out yet another small, stiff card. I took it and read out the following:

Large shrinks to small
With the right point of view

49

```
Just as small turns to large
With a lens to look through.
So for giants so tiny
You can't see them by eye
Go to the biggest of biggerers
And look to the sky.
```

"Tiny giants?" Old Red fumed. "The biggest of biggerers? This is bullshit!"

"No, it's not," said Basil, the young fellow who'd been pushing me around. "It's obvious."

"Yeah," said Al, Gustav's wheelchair man.

They were resting in their chairs at the bottom of the steps, and as we came down to join them they looked at each other and spoke in unison.

"The Yerkes telescope."

"The what?" Old Red asked.

"The world's biggest telescope," said Basil.

"Right in the middle of Columbia Avenue," said Al.

"Over in the Liberal Arts Building," said Basil.

"We can have you there in five minutes," said Al.

"For two more dollars," said Basil.

"Apiece," said Al.

"Why, you little—" said I.

Basil jerked his chin at a man in a dark overcoat scurrying down the path toward the North Dakota Building. "Hey, you're lucky we're still here at all. That guy just offered us two bucks to go with *him*."

The man peered back over his shoulder just long enough to give us a glimpse of bushy black beard.

"He tried to hire both of you?" Old Red asked. "What for?"

Al shrugged. "He didn't say. He just wanted us to leave before you—"

"But you didn't so thank you so let's go!" I said, sprinting for Basil's wheelchair.

The young men sprang to their feet, but Basil was shaking his head as he did so.

"We flipped a coin," he told me. "You're with Al now."

"Well," I said to Al as I plopped myself in his chair, "I assume that means you *won*."

"Yeah, right," Al groaned, and off we went.

Basil and Al took us west past more grandiose state buildings and the imposing colonnades of the Fine Arts Museum before swinging south through a whole new stretch of wonders I won't catalog here except to impart my general impressions.

"Whoa! What in the—? Oh, my. Is that really a—? Golly. Egad!" And so on.

Basil and Al were as good as their word, reaching the massive Manufactures and Liberal Arts Building in mere minutes. Yet it took minutes more just to get to the right entrance.

"Telescope . . . south . . . end," poor Al gasped as we rolled along the loooooooooooooooooooong eastern edge of the building.

To the southwest, near a canal-spanning footbridge back to the Court of Honor, I could see the very bandstand from which we'd started. We'd traveled in a huge loop through the White City, ending up not a hundred paces from where we'd begun.

The gazebo was deserted now, the crowd and the band and Pinkerton and Smythe and all the rest of them nowhere in sight.

"This . . . is . . . it," Basil said, staggering to a stop.

Al just let my chair go and bent over panting as I coasted the last few feet to the doors.

"Thanks, boys! We'd have been lost without you!"

"We . . . noticed," Al said.

I hopped from my chair and stuffed my hand in my pocket.

My stiff, scratchy, *empty* pocket.

"Oh, no."

Basil and Al shot each other the same weary-eyed glower.

"Let us guess," said Basil.

"You left your money in your other pants," said Al.

"Well, I did!"

"Here's all we got for now," Old Red said, and he smacked what looked like three nickels, a penny, and some crumbs into Basil's hand. "We're good for the rest, though, don't you fret."

"Yeah!" I called over my shoulder, following my brother as he pushed through the doors. "We'll come back and pay you soon as we're done winnin' in here!"

Unfortunately, the Liberal Arts and Manufactures Building isn't just notable for its size. Its acoustics are pretty awe-inspiring, too. Or, in this case, nausea-inducing.

My last words—"soon as we're done winnin' in here!"—echoed out through the vast cavern of glass and steel, turning hundreds of heads our way just as the band nearby launched into the French national anthem.

Ahead of us, looming up over the crowd, was an immense spyglass atop a tower three stories tall. A spiral staircase wound its way up to it, six figures spaced out along the steps.

King Brady at the bottom.

Diana and Colonel Crowe halfway up.

Armstrong B. Curtis and William Pinkerton up a little higher.

And at the top, one hand clasped in Pinkerton's, the other cradling a gleaming golden egg the size of a brick, was the Frenchman, Eugene Valmont.

7

MISS LARSON

Or, A Newshound Appears on Our Trail, and She Seems to Smell Blood

I longed to creep into a dark corner and quietly disappear, but there was no such corner to creep to. The Manufactures and Liberal Arts Building was (and remains) the largest man-made structure in the world, and the interior was vast and open, as if God had reached down from His cloud to plop a giant birdcage over an entire town. True, I could've darted into the art gallery to our left or the display of German clockworks to our right or any of a dozen other showrooms within quick dodging distance. Hell, I could've simply whirled around and bolted out the door. Gustav and I were still getting stares aplenty, though, and turning tail would only multiply our humiliation a hundredfold. So I stood my ground and applauded for Eugene Valmont, and Old Red did the same.

"Don't worry, Brother," I said through a glued-on grin. "We'll have other chances to come out ahead. There's three more days of this, remember?"

"Three more days of *this*? And that's supposed to make me feel better?"

"Ummm . . . yeah?"

The band wrapped up "La Marseillaise," and the crowd started to scatter in every direction.

"Round two begins tomorrow at noon in the Court of Honor!" Armstrong B. Curtis bellowed. "Don't miss it!"

"Come on," my brother muttered. "Let's get outta here before—"

"Hey, Deadwood Dick!" a man called out. "Better luck tomorrow!"

"Yeah!" someone else threw in. "See if you can't find that egg instead of just getting it all over your face!"

There was a smattering of laughs as we fled for the doors.

"Otto! Mr. Amlingmeyer! Wait!"

I looked back to find a big, black-clad blob clumping after us. Urias Smythe.

We stopped just long enough for him to catch up. "Gimme six bucks," I said, hoping to head off another "I'm dooooooooomed." "We got us some expenses."

"*You've* got expenses? Do you realize what all this is costing me? How much I'm paying for the honor of rack and ruin? I can't afford to—"

"Please, Mr. Smythe," I sighed. "Just think of it as an advance until I'm wearin' my own britches again."

Smythe produced his billfold and pulled out six ones with such obvious pain you'd have thought he was peeling away strips of his own skin.

"Thanks," I said. "And just so's you know, this is money well spent. You wouldn't want people sayin' your champions was deadbeats, would you?"

I stepped outside looking for Basil and Al and found them talking to the willowy, fair-haired woman King Brady had squired away from the bandstand—Miss Larson, he'd called her.

"Deadbeats," Al was telling her.

"And none too bright," Basil added.

"They wouldn't have made it as far as they did without us," Al said.

"And what's the story with the big one's clothes?" Basil asked.

"It looks like someone shellacked him," Al said.

Miss Larson was encouraging them with nods and mmm-hmms while she wrote down their every word.

I walked up waving the bills in my hands like little flags. "Uh-hhh, fellers?"

"Oh," said Basil.

"Oh," said Al.

They both looked ashamed. Which didn't stop them from taking the money.

"Well," said one.

"We'd better get back to work," said the other.

And they grabbed their wheeled chairs and went whizzing away.

"As you can see," I said to Miss Larson, "deadbeats we are not."

I couldn't help noticing she didn't write that down.

Though she still looked pretty, up close I noticed she wasn't simply slender but almost gaunt. She seemed to be but a few years older than me—somewhere in the vicinity of twenty-five, I'd have guessed—yet she looked somehow withered, desiccated, like all the juice had been baked right out of her.

"Otto Amlingmeyer," I said with a tip of the Stetson. "Pleased to make your acquaintance."

"You haven't made it yet," the lady replied dryly. She put pencil to notepad and leaned to look past me. "Any thoughts on today's outcome, Mr. Smythe?"

Smythe stepped up to join us, Old Red lagging a little behind, moving slow and wary. Women of a certain age—approximately fifteen to fifty—tend to spook my brother, and he looked like he wanted to give this one the kind of distance you'd usually reserve for something with a rattle at the end of its tail.

"I couldn't be more pleased with the turnout," Smythe said. "We had more than eight hundred spectators on hand, by my count."

"Five hundred twenty-nine by *my* count," Miss Larson said, "but that's not what I was asking about. I'm wondering how it felt to see your 'sleuths' come in last."

She hung those quotes around "sleuths" with just the slightest pucker of her thin lips. Other than that, her face remained utterly blank, her voice flat.

"That . . . well . . . I . . . uhhhh . . ." Smythe wiped a hankie across his sweat-beaded brow, then tried again. "It's . . . uhhh . . . well . . . I . . ."

"What Mr. Smythe's trying to say," I cut in, "is that you seem to have overlooked something, miss. My brother and I did *not* come in last. Boothby Greene, I believe, has yet to put in an appearance."

Miss Larson conceded my point with a little tilt of the head.

"So," she said to Smythe, "how did it feel seeing your 'sleuths' come in *second* to last?" She swung her dead-eyed gaze back my way. "Better?"

"Much."

"Actually, miss, I got questions for *you*," Old Red said. He'd been half-hiding behind Smythe, but now he stepped out and managed to drag his gaze up from his own toes. "Like, for one, are you from *McClure's Magazine?*"

The lady nodded. "I'm Lucille Larson, *McClure's* special correspondent. However did you guess?"

Gustav looked irked by the suggestion that he'd stoop to guessing when a thing might be deduced.

"You're obviously a reporter," he said, "and it only seemed natural *McClure's* would want someone here to write up their contest for 'em. Which leads me to my next question: How'd *you* feel findin' out Mr. Curtis was runnin' things? It don't seem like him makin' up the rules was in the plan anyone agreed to, and as I understand it he's been known to write for another magazine."

"How did I feel?" The lady shrugged in a listless way that suggested she rarely felt much of anything. "Curious, mostly. I am a journalist. That's my nature. For instance, I keep wondering: Did something happen to your eyes or are those spectacles just an affectation?"

Old Red's fingers—slightly atremble, I noticed—brushed over the rims of his shaded cheaters.

"Yeah, something happened. But I get by."

"What a relief." Miss Larson turned back to Smythe, pencil hovering over paper again. "So you didn't have to replace a boy detective with a blind one, then?"

Smythe twitched as if his plush bottom had been pricked with a pin. "Yes, well, I, ummmm . . . ah!"

Something off to the north, in the shadow of the vast building behind us, slapped a smile of relief onto the man's blubbery face.

"So you've joined us at last!" he crowed.

The rest of us turned to find Sherlock Holmes strolling up to join us. More or less. (The latter, Armstrong B. Curtis probably would've said, if he could but prove it.)

It was the Englishman, Boothby Greene.

"I get the uneasy feeling," he said, "that you're *not* waiting here to congratulate me on my imminent victory."

"I'm afraid not," Smythe chuckled. "You'll have to do better

57

tomorrow if you want to make good on your publisher's investment."

"As much as I appreciate Mr. Blackheath-Murray's patronage,
it's not him I'm worried about. It's what will happen to me back in
England if I let a Frenchman win. I hope you're not about to tell me
that it was M. Valmont who—?"

Smythe nodded, grinning.

"Ah, well," Greene sighed. "I can but hope tomorrow's challenge proves a better showcase for my humble talents. Riddles and
trivia don't often come into play in real detective work. Observa-
tion and ratiocination—those are the province of a true sleuth."

"Hear, hear!" I cheered. "Couldn't have said it better myself."

"I don't doubt it," Miss Larson said.

I looked over at my brother, wondering why he didn't weigh in:
He was passing up the chance to both pontificate on detecting *and*
rag on my big mouth, which seemed mighty unlike him.

Old Red hadn't even been listening, though. He was staring at
Diana Crowe.

She and her father (and I'll pause here for a final *father!?!*) had
just left the Liberal Arts Building and were headed for the footbridge
to the Court of Honor. If they'd noticed us, they hadn't let on.

A hand planted itself on my back and began pushing me the
same direction as the Crowes.

"Well, I'm sure you have some questions for Mr. Greene here,"
Smythe said to Miss Larson. He put his other hand on my brother's
back, but Gustav's glare had him snatching it away so fast you'd
have thought he'd touched a hot griddle. "We need to be toddling
along. There's that . . . man we need to see about that . . . thing.
Remember?"

"Yeah, right," I dutifully replied. "Can't keep the man with the
thing waitin'."

"I understand entirely," Miss Larson said. From the way her pinched face seemed, for just a moment, on the verge of a smirk, I believed she did.

"Oh," Greene said as we started walking away, "I don't think any of you were on hand for the formal invitation this morning. Blackheath-Murray is hosting a dinner to celebrate the commencement of the contest. At Rector's Restaurant, I believe it's called. Seven o'clock. All the other contestants and sponsors will be there."

He stole a glance back at the bridge. Diana and the colonel were now halfway across.

"Including your friends the Crowes," Greene said with just the slightest arch of an eyebrow. Apparently, the man didn't just look like Holmes: He could see like him, too. "I hope you'll join us."

Smythe never stopped moving toward the bridge. "Well, it's been such a busy day . . ."

"I'm looking forward to observing a dinner party with so many notable detectives," Miss Larson said. "If the Amlingmeyers weren't to come, it would be such a *conspicuous* omission, don't you think?"

"As if we'd pass up an invitation to Rector's!" Smythe said, still back-stepping away. "Until tonight, then!"

He finally whirled around and scurried off. I scurried along beside him while Old Red fell behind, unwilling to commit himself to more than a trudge.

"You wasn't worried we'd embarrass you, were you?" I asked Smythe.

He let that slide by without reply.

"Blast it all," he muttered instead. "I'll have to get Cohn back again."

"Who's Cohn?"

"Your tailor."

"He ain't *my* tailor," Gustav said.

"Oh, so you'll be wearing your own tuxedo, then?" Smythe threw over his shoulder. "Because you're not getting into Rector's without one."

"Well, then it's high time we were tuxed," I answered for Old Red. "Right, Brother?"

"Feh."

"Feh?" Smythe turned to me for a translation. "What does that mean, anyway?"

"It means 'Anything you say, boss,'" I replied.

"It means '*Feh*,'" Gustav said.

He was still staring ahead, at the Crowes. They were on the other side of the canal now. The colonel had his arm wrapped around his daughter's again, and he didn't seem to be escorting her so much as chaining her to his side.

"Looks like Pa Crowe's keepin' a tight rein on his daughter," I said. "Don't expect we'll get many chances to socialize. Be a shame to pass one up when we had it."

Behind me, Old Red grumbled something I couldn't quite catch.

"What was that?" I asked.

"I said," my brother growled back, "anything you say, boss."

8

PRÉLUDES

Or, Our First Brush with Haute Cuisine Ends with Several Low Blows

Take your average badger on a bad day, poke him in the eye, step on his toes, and wrap him in swaddling clothes, tight. Then put chipped ice down his back. I guarantee you, he'll look happier than my brother in a tuxedo.

Yet though Old Red snapped and snarled as much as that badger might while our tailor Mr. Cohn got him gussied up, he stood still for it. Maybe it was the fact that Cohn—a hunchbacked old fellow ever muttering around a mouthful of pins—had to spend so much time poking needles into his "inseam" to get the fit just right. Or maybe he just wasn't awake enough to kick up a fuss: Two straight days of the collywobbles on the train had left him weary and worn, and he'd spent the afternoon catching up on his sleep in the dingy hotel that was serving as contest HQ.

Once he was betuxed, Gustav just stood in the corner of our little room as stiff as his own starched collar while Cohn moved on to me. When Cohn was done, Smythe begrudgingly paid him, begrudgingly ushered us out of the hotel, begrudgingly hailed a hansom, and—once he'd begrudgingly packed himself into the cab with us—seemed to begrudge us every breath of air we stole from his lungs.

"You don't seem very enthused for a feller on his way to a free dinner," I said as we clip-clopped north.

We were jammed into that cab like three peas in a two-pea pod, and Smythe had to do some writhing just to look at me.

"Why should I be enthused? You heard the questions that wretched Larson woman was asking this afternoon. It's sure to be more of the same tonight. And if Armstrong Curtis is there as well?"

Smythe shivered.

"Have some faith, friend," I said. "Me'n'my brother might make a better impression than you think. And ain't it in the lady's interest to make us look good? Wouldn't reflect well on the contest if we was just a couple yokels, and it's her bosses sponsorin' the thing."

"*Co*-sponsoring," Smythe corrected. "Everyone but Eugene Valmont had to pay their way into the competition. Three thousand dollars each—and now the damned Frenchman's winning!"

"Oh, that's just for today. Tomorrow I betcha we'll—"

"Why didn't Valmont ante up?" Old Red cut in.

Up to then, he'd just been watching the city streets slide past with a sour glower upon his face. Now he turned away from the elevated trains and overloaded drays and clogged sidewalks and gray buildings and leaned forward to look past me at Smythe.

"We wanted contestants from abroad. Professionals. Policemen," Smythe explained. "To legitimize the competition. We couldn't very well ask them to come all this way *and* give us money they probably don't have."

"Was it the same with Pinkerton?" Gustav asked. "You needed him to 'legitimilize' things?"

Smythe nodded glumly. "We thought it would shore up our credibility. Detectives don't get much more real than the Pinkertons. And it's not like they couldn't use our help, what with all the anti-Pinkerton rabble-rousing in the yellow press these days. That's why it was such a shock to see Armstrong Curtis in charge of the contest. You'd almost think Pinkerton wanted to turn the whole thing into—"

"A trap," my brother said.

"I was going to say 'circus,' but . . . oh, God. You're right. It *does* feel like a trap, doesn't it? If Pinkerton wanted to crush us for good, he couldn't have asked for a better opportunity!"

"Oh, come now," I chided. "Why would William Pinkerton want to—?"

I didn't even get to finish. Smythe buried his face in his hands and started sobbing.

"I'm dooooooooooomed!"

"Hmm" was all Old Red had to say to that. His work done, he turned back to the window and said no more for the rest of the ride. Which left it to me to hand our patron a hankie and pat him on the back and generally behave like a human being until he could pull himself together.

Smythe had only just snuffed his last sniffle when we came to a stop before Rector's Restaurant. Even from outside, it was obvious this was a far cry from the gristle-and-beans lunch counters my brother and I were used to. A long red carpet stretched out from doors held open by greatcoated valets, and candlelight shimmered softly in the lattice-glass windows. Inside, I could see, all the ladies were in evening gowns and all the men in tuxedos or black tails . . . even the busboys.

Gustav followed me and Smythe in with slow, hesitant steps, as if we were leading him into a snake pit rather than the city's swankiest eatery. Yet though he was still wearing his tinted spectacles—he never took the things off, no matter how dim the light—I knew it wasn't just poor eyesight that was slowing him. I couldn't help but think the same thing he was: that it must be obvious how little we belonged there. Any second, I reckoned, some freshly stuffed pluto-crat would wave us over to clear his dishes.

After a few words with the maître d' (and it soothed me some-what that I knew what a maître d' was), we were led through the restaurant and up a set of stairs to a private room on the second floor. Here we found the dinner party already under way.

Or the dinner, at any rate. "Party" would suggest gaiety and laughter, and the gathering we walked in on was about as festive as a Baptist wake.

Everyone was gathered around a long table set with a dizzying array of plates, bowls, goblets, glasses, and so much elaborate silver-ware I wouldn't have been surprised had George Hearst clawed his way from the grave to stake a claim to it. One didn't just see all these beautiful settings, either—one *heard* them, for every clink of metal or glass against china seemed to crack like thunder in the awkward silence hanging over most of the room.

Of all those present (and I saw nearly everyone who'd been up on the bandstand that afternoon), only King Brady was talking. The handsome young "monarch of the New York detectives" had my preferred seat—the one next to Diana Crowe—and he was blathering away at the lady about the time he fought off a gang of bank robbers with his feet tied together, a blindfold over his eyes, and an orphan tucked under each arm. Or something like that. I was gratified to see the look of dubious boredom on Diana's lovely face—and even more gratified when she spotted me and Gustav and smiled. It was a small smile, though, and one she tucked away fast with a glance at her father.

"Ahhhh, so glad you could join us," said our host—Boothby Greene's publisher, Blackheath-Murray. At least I assumed it was Blackheath-Murray. I'd noticed the fleshy, middle-aged, mustache-sporting gent standing next to Greene in the gazebo that afternoon, and he was at the head of the table now. Beside him was an empty seat, and the only contestant I didn't see in the room was Greene himself. "I hope you'll forgive us for beginning the *préludes* without you."

"Of course, of course," Smythe mumbled as he claimed the free spot next to the man.

That left three chairs for Old Red and me to choose from, and it was obvious why Smythe hadn't wanted any of them for himself. They were at the opposite end of the table, clustered around William Pinkerton and Armstrong B. Curtis.

Once we had ourselves seated—Gustav next to Curtis, me between my brother and a sullen Colonel Crowe—there was a quick round of introductions. Most everyone we'd already encountered in one way or another, including the French sleuth Valmont and lady journalist Lucille Larson. So that left only one person I didn't already know to put a name to: the flashy-dressed swell who'd whispered to Smythe about being "stabbed in the back" by Pinkerton that afternoon. He, it turned out, was one Frank Tousey, publisher of *New York Detective Library*, King Brady's magazine. His neck had to be stuck out as far as Smythe's, money-wise, and though he was doing no blubbering about it you could see the strain. The fellow was throwing down champagne like he was trying to douse a fire in his belly.

"So where's Mr. Greene?" I asked once all the unenthused how-dos were out of the way.

"Delayed, I'm afraid," Blackheath-Murray said. "He'll be along shortly, though."

A silver bucket sat on a stand near the table, and Curtis lurched to his feet and snatched a bottle from it.

"Still," he said, and just from that one word I could tell he'd been matching Tousey chug for chug, "there's no use waiting any longer for our first toast."

He sloshed fizzy gold into the tall, narrow glasses before me and Gustav, and after refilling his own with the last foamy drops, he plopped the bottle back into the bucket upside down.

"To the World's Greatest Sleuth!" he said, raising his champagne high.

The rest of us reached for our glasses—Old Red almost upending his in the process. Between the restaurant's dim light and his own dark spectacles, it was a wonder he could even see the thing in the first place, let alone get a hand around it.

"The World's Greatest Sleuth," everyone repeated, and me and Gustav finally got our first taste of champagne. To my considerable disappointment, it was basically ginger ale without the bite.

Curtis waited till everyone was midslurp to finish his toast.

"May he rest in peace!"

He flashed a demented grin, then drained his glass.

A waiter appeared out of nowhere to replace the bottle our Puzzlemaster had emptied, while another swooped in to place plates before Old Red and Smythe and me. On each was a single puff of flaky pastry sandwiching something brown and gooey that oozed out over the sides.

This, apparently, was the *préludes*.

"*Cassolette d'escargots au beurre persille,*" Valmont said, and he kissed the tips of his fingers.

"Oh. Uh. Lovely. One of my favorites."

I speared the thing with my fork and popped it into my mouth.

It wasn't bad, though perhaps a tad slimier than the steak and pota-toes I would have preferred.

Old Red just let his be. In fact, he seemed reluctant to so much as touch the cutlery lest he be accused of trying to pocket it.

"Tell me, Brady," Curtis said as he refilled his glass again. "That robbery ring you were describing to Miss Crowe a moment ago. The one you broke up single-handed. I've been following all your recent cases quite closely, but that one isn't familiar to me."

"That's because it hasn't appeared in the magazine yet. It'll be in next month's issue. The title's 'The Adventure of the Silver Dwarf.' "

Brady spoke with such breezy ease I had to conclude this par-ticular King had no clothes when it came to detecting: He hadn't even noticed that Curtis was baiting him.

His publisher didn't miss it, though. Tousey was giving Curtis the kind of look you see on a cat just before it spits at you.

"Well, it's an incredible story," Curtis said. "Truly in . . . credible. So many narrow escapes! So much derring-do!" He put on a rueful expression and shook his head. "I'm afraid that sort of thing won't help you much this week, though."

"That's too bad," Brady replied with a cocky shrug. "Because it's not all puzzles and ciphers out in the real world. Nine times out of ten, it's pure muscle that wins the day."

"That sounds more like your philosophy, Mr. Pinkerton," Lu-cille Larson said. Her tone was languid, detached, even as her gaze bored into the man like an auger. "When it comes to strikebreak-ing, at least."

Pinkerton looked pained.

"Force has its place," he said, "but I believe what I said in my speech this afternoon. The most important components of true de-tective work are diligence and professionalism, plain and simple."

"Ohhhhh, much *too* plain! Much *too* sim-PELL!" Valmont protested. On his blocky face was an eyeball-bulging expression that conveyed either surprise or an overexcess of coffee consumption. "You are not descri-BING a sleuth. You are descri-BING a banKARE. A druggist. A shoe sellsman."

"Precisely," Pinkerton said. "At the end of the day, there's little that separates the successful detective from the successful businessman."

"Lee-tell? Lee-tell? Ohhhhhh, there is so much that sep-a-rates them. It is infinite what sep-a-rates them! Yet it is all contain-ED here." The Frenchman tapped the side of his head. "Imagination. Vision. To see not just the pee-says on the chessboard but the invisible pattern of their porpoise."

Valmont snatched up a salt shaker and zigzagged it through the air.

"Why does the rook go wee-wee-wee?"

He slammed the salt down in front of a startled Blackheath-Murray, then grabbed a roll and whipped it this way and that, sending crumbs flying.

"Why does the knight go zeeeee-blow, zeeeee-blow?"

The roll was flattened in front of Miss Larson's plate. Then it was a stray fork's turn to fly.

"To what end does the queen go vish-vash!"

Valmont plopped the fork into Blackheath-Murray's ice water, then moved a pop-eyed stare slowly around the table.

"The sleuth will look about himself and ask, 'Why are these pawns and kings doing what they do? Are the pawns really pawns and the kings really kings? Indeed, can one even say what game they truly play?' To dis-en-tingle all this . . . it is the greatest game of all!"

"Piffle!" Colonel Crowe scoffed. "Detective work isn't some

diversion for our amusement. It's life and death, and all that matters is getting the job done and done right. Only amateurs and fools take it lightly."

He might have been rebuffing Valmont, yet by the time he finished he was glaring at me and Gustav.

Other than the toast to Holmes, my brother hadn't made a sound since we'd sat down. Now, though, he wheezed out something whispery and incomprehensible.

He coughed and tugged at his collar and tried again.

"I couldn't agree with you more, sir," he said. "I may still be an amateur, as you figure it, but I take detectivin' as serious as anyone at this table. I been makin' a study on it for some time now—and been through one calamity after another for my trouble. This much I've learned, though: You can't boil sleuthin' down to a simple set of rules and homilies and expect that to get you to the truth or justice or whatever you wanna call it."

"I'm surprised to hear that from you, Old Red," Curtis said. "Don't tell me you've lost your faith in Mr. Holmes."

"Not in the Man, exactly. But I've come to have my doubts about followin' in his footsteps. I ain't so sure anymore another feller could do what he done. Outside of a magazine, anyhow."

Curtis aimed one of his big sickle-blade grins at King Brady and Frank Tousey. "On that much, at least, we're entirely in agreement."

"I, on the other hand, beg to differ," someone said from across the table, and when I glanced that way I was surprised to see it was one of the waiters.

He was an olive-skinned fellow with a thick black beard—a Greek or Turk by the look of him—and after sliding a mixture of greens, cheese, and what seemed like sagebrush in front of Pinkerton, he shocked us all by sliding *himself* into the empty seat to the man's right.

"I'm sorry to hear your faith has been shaken, Mr. Amling-meyer," he said. "Let me assure you, however: Sherlock Holmes's spirit remains very much alive. His intellect. His love of a challenge."

The waiter scratched at his beard high up near his left ear. A little strip of skin and hair seemed to come loose, and the man pinched at the dangling flap and peeled it away.

"His flair for theatrics . . ."

In a moment, the waiter's whole beard was gone, and with a few swipes of a napkin most of his swarthy darkness had smeared away as well.

What remained was Boothby Greene.

There were gasps and stunned laughs, and Curtis even applauded.

"You been servin' us the whole time?" asked Old Red, looking so awestruck you'd have thought Holmes himself had just materialized before us like Jesus appearing to the apostles.

Greene gave him a nod. "Soup to nuts—or *escargot* to *salade de chèvre chaud,* at any rate. I do hope you'll all forgive my childishness. I have a weakness for the dramatic, and I put on such a poor showing this afternoon I couldn't resist a little prank to even the score." He offered Curtis a small bow. "Unofficially, of course."

Curtis bowed back. "Too bad I won't be awarding bonuses for clever charades, Mr. Greene. You wouldn't be the only one to pick up a few extra points."

"What's *that* supposed to mean?" Frank Tousey said.

He'd never stopped glowering down the table at Curtis, and even Greene's little floor show hadn't wiped the frown from his face. The man was a wick soaked in alcohol, and now it took but the slightest spark to light him up.

"You'll find out," Curtis said.

Tousey swung himself toward Pinkerton before finally exploding.

"What's this all about? We came to you because we wanted this thing to have some kind of integrity, and what do you do? Hand us over to the very loon who'd like nothing better than to show us all up as frauds!"

"If you want to convince people your 'sleuths' are real," Pinkerton grated out, "who better to test them than the man who proved Nick Carter doesn't—?"

"Oh, please!" Tousey howled. "A stupid schoolboy scavenger hunt *for a golden egg*? That was no test. It was horseshit, pardon my French."

"Sir! There are ladies present!" Colonel Crowe protested.

"Can I quote you on that?" Miss Larson asked Tousey.

"Actually, *en français* it would be *merde de cheval*," Valmont said.

Tousey ignored them all.

"If your little friend there doesn't stop his insane insinuations—*now*—I've half a mind to sue you for . . . where do you think you're going?"

Pinkerton was pushing back his chair and tossing his napkin onto his plate.

"I told you this would happen," he said to Curtis.

"Yeah." Curtis nodded eagerly. "Perfect, isn't it?"

Pinkerton glowered at him a moment, then stood. "My apologies, Mr. Blackheath-Murray. This was no way to repay your hospitality." He looked down at Curtis like the man was something unpleasant stuck to the heel of his shoe. "We're leaving."

"Just when it's getting fun?"

"*We're leaving.*"

"Alright, fine," Curtis sighed. "I've got an egg to lay anyway."

Instead of standing, though, he turned to the rest of the guests. "Before I go, let me leave you with a few choice morsels to chew on along with your snails and cheese."

"Snails?" I said. I don't think anyone heard me.

Curtis was turning his attention to Eugene Valmont.

"You could ask the *monsieur* there about what the French newspapers call '*L'Affaire des cinq cent diamants.*' Or ask Colonel Crowe why he and his"—Curtis cocked an eyebrow and coughed—"'daughter' are suddenly at liberty to open their own detective agency. Or ask young Master Brady about his birthday or Mr. Greene how it is he doesn't seem to have one."

My brother tensed up beside me, no doubt sure his not-so-secret shame was to be aired out next: that he was putting on sleuthing airs when he couldn't even read. Yet Curtis spared him, his gaze sweeping over us like the Angel of Death on its way to the pharaoh's house.

"The plain truth is," he went on, "there are more mountebanks at this table than master detectives . . . and proving it is going to be child's play."

Curtis finally stood then—a bit unsteadily—and his grin returned. It didn't seem so much like a smile this time, though. It was more like a growling dog showing off his fangs.

"Speaking of which, I'd urge you all to turn in early. Today was just a warm-up. Tomorrow the real sleuthing begins . . . for you *and* me."

"Please. Allow me," I said to Smythe as Curtis and Pinkerton headed for the stairs.

I cleared my throat.

"Dooooooooooooomed."

9

THE CONTEST
(ROUND TWO)

Or, Curtis Flies the Coop, and We Encounter a Bad Egg

To say that the dinner party ended awkwardly might imply that it was ever anything *but* awkward. Which it was not. Unless you want to count mortifying, horrifying, and deeply painful. Which it was. So merely "awkward" was an improvement, I suppose.

Before Pinkerton and Curtis even made it down the stairs, Tousey drained his latest glass of champagne and proclaimed that he was leaving as well.

"Come on," he snapped at Brady as he rose to go.

King proved surprisingly pliant, for royalty, instantly hopping up to hustle after his publisher.

A moment later, Colonel Crowe announced that he'd lost his appetite, and he stood and hovered by his chair as a signal for Diana to lose hers, too. Gustav and I swapped puzzled frowns as she followed the colonel out. The Diana we'd known was daring and headstrong—certainly no slave to convention or decorum or even, on occasion, scruples. Yet now she was so thoroughly under Colonel Crowe's little thumb her spirit seemed to have been squashed flat. Maybe, I had to think, it was more than the lady's name we'd had wrong all along.

Next to go was Eugene Valmont, who announced that his "diges-CHON" had become "unseateld."

"Well?" Old Red said to Smythe as the Frenchman made his escape.

He got the answer he was obviously expecting.

"Yes, yes . . . let's go," Smythe muttered. "I've never felt more hugger-mugger in all my life."

That left only Lucille Larson to help Blackheath-Murray and Boothby Greene with their feast. I hoped they were all hungry.

"Well," I said as Gustav, Smythe, and I wedged ourselves into another cab, "if that's how the high and mighty dine, I'm glad I'm riffraff."

Smythe mumbled a reply that may or may not have been "I'm not."

Old Red tried to draw the man out with questions about Tousey and Pinkerton and the little innuendos Curtis had been tossing around. Yet all my brother got for his efforts were moans along the lines of "What does it matter now?" and "I don't know anything anymore!" At last, as our cab skirted the long Midway Plaisance that jutted west out of the White City like a knife in the back, Smythe could take no more.

"Driver! Stop!" he cried. "I'm getting out!"

He threw himself from the hansom before it even came to a full halt.

"You alright, Mr. Smythe?" I asked.

"I need air! A walk! To clear my head! Oh, my poor nerves!"

He scurried off toward the electric glow and chattering crowds and strange, gay music of the Midway.

I looked over at my brother. "Should we go after him?"

Gustav was eyeing the lights spinning slowly in the dark night-time sky. The Midway's famous Ferris wheel was still turning, despite the late hour, and hovering high above us one could see hundreds of faces peering out the windows of its huge, illuminated cars. It would be hard to imagine a mechanized contrivance better designed to turn my brother's stomach, and he gaped at it with something akin to horror upon his face.

"Smythe'll be alright," he said. "Though I don't see how goin' anywhere near *that* could soothe a man's nerves."

"Oh, I don't know. It might be real relaxin', swoopin' up into the clouds with the birds and the angels. In fact, I ain't leavin' Chicago till I've given it a whirl myself . . . and talked you into comin' with me."

"Feh," Old Red said.

I nodded. "Yeah. Feh."

Soon afterward, we were back at the Columbian Hotel, the ramshackle rattrap where all the contestants were staying. In the neighborhood around it were enough rooming houses to lodge every man, woman, and child on the planet, with beds left over should the population of another decide to take in the fair as well. On our one block alone was the White City Inn, the World's Fair Hotel, Keene's Exposition Lodge, and half a dozen others. In Chicago that year, making a mint in the hostelry business seemed as easy as painting a sign and hanging it over your front door.

Which was exactly what the owner of the Columbian seemed to have done. It was no more than a dreary office building hastily made over into an even drearier fleabag. The carpeting was poorly fitted and threadbare, the wallpaper peeling to reveal crack-veined plaster, the lighting so stingy and cave-like I almost expected to see bats hanging from the low ceiling, the "lobby" no more than a random scattering of mangy settees seemingly salvaged from the back of a junkman's wagon, etc., etc. Strangest of all was the front desk, which was, unlike any other front desk I've ever encountered, literally a desk parked in the front of the lobby.

And parked behind it when we came in: a wide-eyed, high-haired, middle-aged woman beaming so much sunshine you could tan your skin by her. This was Mrs. Jasinska, the Columbian's owner and, she claimed, general manager. I say "claimed" because nothing much seemed to get managed around the place, either generally or specifically.

"Why, if it isn't Mr. and Mr. Amnee[mutter]!" she cried upon spying us. (Like half the folks who aren't Amlingmeyers themselves, she could never get the hang of our name.) "Welcome back! Did you bump into your admirer?"

"Our admirer?" I turned to my brother. "See how this is workin' out? Now we got two!"

"What admirer?" Old Red asked Mrs. Jasinska.

"The bearded gentleman. You couldn't have missed him. He left not twenty seconds ago."

We had indeed passed a man on our way into the hotel, but he'd just hustled by us with the collar of his dark coat turned up.

"He wanted to know if you were staying here with the other detectives," Mrs. Jasinska said. "He was hoping to meet you."

"Well, he missed his chance. Breezed right by us."

"Probably didn't recognize us in these getups," Gustav growled with a bitter glance down at his tux. "Speakin' of which, I can't wait to be free of mine."

He was already whipping off his white bow tie as he tromped off toward the stairs. I bade Mrs. Jasinska good night in the more traditional fashion—by actually saying it—then followed.

Despite the drab dilapidation of the place, my brother and I had been afforded one unaccustomed luxury: separate rooms. So after a lengthy discourse on recent events (Me: "Well, that was a hell of a day"; Old Red, closing door: "Yup"), we parted ways for the night. I spent the next couple hours stretched out on a mattress as downy-soft as a pile of bricks while I pored over my Exposition guidebook. It was interesting, though hardly surprising, to find that the Columbian Hotel rated but one word in the chapter on local lodgings: "Avoid."

The guide was far more effusive—too much so, actually—on the myriad marvels of the White City. I was trying to pick out the highlights of the fair, anything that stood out for its distinctiveness or scale, like the Yerkes telescope. The problem: There were so many such things, a highlight anywhere else would barely rate as a lowlight here. Within a two-mile radius, you could find the Liberty Bell, the crown jewels of Germany, a solid silver sculpture of Justice, the world's largest dynamo, the world's largest searchlight, the world's largest lump of coal, the world's largest conveyor belt, the world's largest screw power testing machine (for those interested in screw power testing machines), and the world's largest "gray canary" diamond, whatever that meant.

Dizzying as it all was, I kept on studying, fancying it'd prepare me for whatever puzzles the next day might bring.

Ha!

The next morning, when it came time to costume myself for round two of the contest, I found that the only one of Mr. Cohn's creations I could bring myself to wear—and that just barely—was the oversized red Stetson. It looked mighty strange on a man in a black suit and brogans, I grant you, but I felt I had to make some concession to Mr. Smythe, if only to head off more weeping. Gustav topped himself with his new hat as well, and even went so far as to dress himself in the closest he had to "Sunday best," though I suspected this had less to do with Urias Smythe than with Diana Crowe.

When we returned to the Court of Honor just before noon, we found a much smaller audience than we'd drawn the day before. Riddle-cracking was most definitely a bust as a spectator sport. Yet that only compounded our humiliation, for the catcalls could surely be heard by one and all. "What happened to your red-and-white outfit, Tex? Saint Nick need it back?" was probably the *least* insulting—which is why it stands now as the only one I care to recall.

Up on the bandstand, we found the whole gang from Rector's, with one exception: Armstrong B. Curtis was nowhere in sight. I expected Pinkerton to wait for his Puzzlemaster to appear, but just a few minutes after our arrival—minutes we passed, alas, getting both guff from Smythe for not wearing our costumes and the cold shoulder from the Crowes—he trudged up to the podium alone. After a perfunctory welcome to the crowd and some halfhearted blather about the contest, he gave the sleuths their starting clues with all the enthusiasm of a fellow handing bullets to his own firing squad.

"Detectives . . . deduce," he said glumly when he was done.

We tore open our envelopes and pulled out the cards inside.

"Sweet Jesus," I sighed after scanning the first few lines.

"That bad?" Old Red asked.

I answered him by reading our "clue" out loud.

```
O, Nephilim; O, Atlas;
Be not haughty in thy pride.
O, Gog, Magog, and Behemoth;
We can cut you down to size!
The tiny stone
By shepherd thrown
Now weighs a ton
And flies for miles.
```

"Is that even English?" my brother asked.

"Well, it ain't French."

Eugene Valmont was already headed for the steps, a smile on his face and Lucille Larson on his arm. King Brady won a round of applause just for following after them, and Boothby Greene was soon on his way as well. A moment later, the Crowes swept past us, too. Once more, we'd be last out of the gate.

"Read it again," Gustav said to me. "Slow."

I obliged him.

"What the hell is a 'nephew-phlegm'?" he asked when I was through.

"I got no earthly idea. Same with them gogs. A behemoth, though—that's a huge, monster kind of a thing. And Atlas is a giant feller outta old legends. Supposedly carried the world on his shoulders."

"I know the feeling," Old Red muttered. "At least there's one part even I can figure out: the bit with the shepherd throwin' things. That's gotta be David goin' after Goliath. Which gives us another giant. So the stone that flies for miles . . ." He grimaced like a man about to burp up a meal he didn't like the taste of in the first place. "They got the world's biggest slingshot 'round here?"

"Not that I . . . hot damn! The Krupp Gun!"

"The *what* gun?"

"The world's biggest cannon, Brother! I read about it last night. Built by the Germans. Shoots a shell as big as a shed, and it *flies . . . for . . . miles.*"

"Well, where is the thing?"

I pulled out my guidebook, consulted the map, then stepped out toward the front of the gazebo.

"That way!" I proclaimed, pointing to the northeast.

A few folks cheered.

William Pinkerton rolled his eyes.

"If you would remain here till all our contestants have left," he said to the audience as I marched down the steps, Old Red on my heels. The brass band from the day before was once again lined up nearby, and Pinkerton swept an outstretched arm their way. "Major Bacon and His Hoosier One Hundred will treat us to a selection of favorite marches while we await today's champion."

"Champion*s*!" I hollered back. "These two geese are about to lay themselves a golden egg!"

"You are enjoyin' this entirely too much," my brother grumbled.

Without my red leather armor to slow us down this time, we were able to clear out of the Court of Honor at a good gallop. Along the Grand Basin with its fountains and gondolas and sun-dappled lagoon, around the Agriculture Building, across a bridge over a narrow canal, and there we were: the Krupp Gun Works Pavilion, a big girder-and-glass block plopped at the edge of Lake Michigan. Once we were inside, it was easy enough to find the Krupp Gun. There were dozens of cannons on display, but only one had a barrel half the length of a Chicago block. Waiting in its shadow was a stout gentleman with a walrus mustache and what could have been a walrus's gut and jowls.

"Allow me to velcome you to ze Krupp Gun Vorks Pavilion," he slowly intoned in a German accent as thick as *Hasenpfeffer*. "On behalf of Herr Krupp and all ze di-rrrec-tors of ze Krupp Gun—"

"Yeah, yeah." Old Red jerked a thumb my way. "Just give him the clue, would you?"

"*Vas?* Your pardon me, please. *Mein* English iz . . . *nicht so gut.*"

"The next clue! Hand it over!" Gustav barked, and he launched into our dear old *Vater*'s favorite phrase when snapping the reins on a stubborn mule: "*Befördern dein fette Arsch!*"

Us kids never knew exactly what it meant, but it always seemed to work on the mules. It worked on that German gent, too. Though his bushy eyebrows flew up high in surprise, he reached into his coat pocket and produced a small envelope.

"Here," he said as he handed it to me. "Now you vill get *your* fat asses out of my pawilion!"

I could have pointed out that my brother's ass is really rather bony, but I didn't get the feeling Herr Mustache would care to be corrected.

"Jawohl," I said instead, and we got our keisters—fat and otherwise—out of there. By the time we were scooting outside, I'd read our new clue through once and was starting in on it again.

```
They set themselves a mighty hurdle--
Enough to make one's courage curdle.
A task too vast for weaker ilk,
To them it was as mother's milk.
Success was theirs; they were not bowed . . .
Although, of course, they were quite cowed!
```

"Another damned riddle!" Old Red raged. "We was supposed to do us some *real* sleuthin' today!"

"Don't complain, cuz I already got this riddle licked. All we gotta do is run across that there bridge and duck into the Agriculture Building. I know exactly where that egg's gonna be."

You'd have thought Gustav would look pleased, but just the opposite. He scowled and growled out a "Feh."

"What's there to 'feh' about?"

"Oh, I may as well hole up in the hotel and leave all the detectin' to you. I ain't been no use in this thing yet."

"Now, now. Don't go and get . . . oh. Excuse me."

81

A tall, thin, heavily bearded man in a black derby and a long, loose overcoat had appeared in our path as we approached the footbridge. We tried to scoot around him to the right, but he stepped to the side to block us. When we moved to the left, he scooched over to check us again. There was something strangely familiar about him, and he glowered at us hatefully as he slid this way and that to stay in our way.

"Do we know you?" I asked.

"No, but you should! Everyone should!" he spat back, his words inflected with an accent I couldn't place. Then he reached out and snatched Gustav's cheaters right off his face.

A second later, the spectacles were on the ground, the dark lenses pulverized beneath the stranger's heel.

"Ha!"

The man stared at Old Red expectantly.

"Now why would you go and do a thing like that?" my brother said, meeting his gaze without a blink. It was a cloudless, sunny day, yet Gustav didn't so much as squint.

The bearded man looked profoundly disappointed.

I assume *I* looked profoundly surprised.

"You alright?" I asked Old Red.

"Yup."

"You ain't blinded by the light?"

"Nope."

"Well, how about that? Looks like you cured him, mister. Guess we owe you our thanks." I lunged forward and grabbed the stranger by the collar of his oversized coat. "And you'll have 'em soon as you explain what the hell you're up to."

"If you insist . . ."

The man suddenly spun away, flailing, and to my dismay I found myself holding nothing but coat.

"Ha *ha*! Try that on for size, you big hick!" He continued skipping backward, toward the Krupp pavilion. "Come on! Come and get me, clodhopper! You're not going to let me get away that easy, are you?"

I took a step toward him.

Old Red grabbed me by the arm.

"Clock's tickin'," he said.

"Right." I started to wad up the stranger's coat to throw at him, then changed my mind and slipped it on instead. "We'll call it an even trade: one overcoat for one pair of spectacles."

"Cowards!" the man hollered as we retreated across the bridge. "Come back here and fight!"

"I see you again, you'll get your wish!" I called back.

"Oh, you'll see me again, alright . . . when I want you to!"

And he cut loose with what my fellow dime novel scribes would probably call "maniacal laughter."

"What in God's name was that all about?" I said to Old Red.

"One puzzle at a time." We burst through the doors into the Agriculture Building. "Now . . . what are we lookin' for, anyhow?"

"Come on, and I'll show you!"

Arrayed before us was what could've been four state fairs under one roof. Within easy spitting distance were displays for farm implements, pesticides, wheats and grains, cigarettes, agricultural colleges, even ostriches. But not what I was looking for.

I dashed up to a jug-eared fellow standing before a wall of olive-tinted jars.

"The big cheese! Where is it?"

"The cheese! The cheese! Everybody wants to see the cheese today!" The man swept out an arm toward something green and slimy off to his right. "What about our map?"

I turned and beheld a huge, beautifully detailed rendering of the United States of America—made entirely from pickles.

"Yeah, hey, whooee, that's really something. The cheese, please?"

"Oh, alright. Right at the tower of chocolate, left at the statue of Columbus made from gum paste."

"Thanks."

I turned and darted off again, Old Red at my side.

"'Curdle,' 'milk,' 'cowed,'" my brother panted as we ran. "The riddle's about cheese, I see that. But what's 'the *big* cheese'?"

"You really need me to explain it?"

Gustav gazed at the dark pillar jutting up toward the rafters about fifty feet ahead. Melt it down and you'd have a pool of chocolate to rival the Great Lake outside.

"No," my brother said. "I suppose not."

After that, we just ran.

Half a minute later, we had the big cheese in sight. Or the vast iron vat that held it, anyway. It was on a wheeled platform not unlike a flatbed train car, and a set of stairs wound around it to the top.

THE MAMMOTH CHEESE FROM CANADA, it said on the side of the tank. WEIGHT 22,000 POUNDS.

Even if we hadn't seen the Mammoth Cheese—which would've been quite a feat, given that it was just a shade smaller than the moon—it would have been obvious we were in the right place. Clogging our nostrils was the overwhelming smell of cheddar, while clogging the hall before us was our audience from the Court of Honor.

William Pinkerton was waiting beside the cheese vat, Urias Smythe, Frank Tousey, and Blackheath-Murray clustered up beside him. Nearby, a pair of Columbian Guards stood stationed at the bottom of the stairs to the top of the tank, and upon a nod from Pinkerton they each took a step away.

"One side! Gangway! Sleuths comin' through!" I called out.

Unfortunately, Old Red and I weren't the only sleuths on the move: As a path cleared through the crowd, I could see King Brady at the far end of it, making for the cheese same as me.

"Oh, no you don't!"

We barreled toward each other like a couple trains on the same track, colliding at the foot of the stairs. After that, we collided again and again and again—on purpose—as we fought to be first to the top of the steps. Halfway up, we both went down on our faces.

"Excuse me," a woman said, and it wasn't until she was walking along my back that I realized hers was the voice I'd been so longing to hear the past day.

Diana Crowe was about to beat us all.

"Feh," my brother spat as he pounded up after her (and *over* me).

After that, I was done playing doormat, and I hopped to my feet just in time to hear the lady speak again.

"I'm sorry, Old Red. I'm afraid you're too late to . . . oh!"

A heartbeat later, I was at the top of the stairs with King Brady jostling up behind me.

"Is that what I think it is?" Diana was saying to Gustav. She nodded at a circle cut into the vat to allow for viewing of the cheese.

My brother stretched out on his belly and hung himself half in, half out of the tank.

"Yes, miss. It is," he said wearily. "So long as you think it's a dead feller facedown in cheddar. Hard to tell from up here, but it seems to me he's wearin' a tuxedo, too."

"Armstrong Curtis?" I said.

"I reckon so." My brother wriggled up out of the hole. In one hand he was holding a gleaming-gold orb. "Looks like he's given us at least one puzzle today he didn't aim to."

10

A MAMMOTH MYSTERY

Or, Gustav Eggs Diana On While King Brady Turns Chicken

"Curtis? Dead? In there?"

Behind me, King Brady burst out laughing.

"You're joking!"

His laughter stopped as suddenly as it had begun.

"Aren't you?"

Diana and Gustav ignored him.

"What's going on up there?" someone shouted.

"Yeah! Who won?"

More such cries echoed up from the audience packed in around the Mammoth Cheese.

"Pinkerton'll be up here any second lookin' for the winner," Old Red said. "And you know what he'll do when he finds out about our friend here."

Diana nodded. "We don't count as real detectives. He'll get rid of us as soon as he can."

"That's right. So if either of us is gonna do any clue-huntin', this is our chance . . . provided there's a distraction."

He held the golden egg out toward Diana.

She took it.

"I can't give you more than a couple of minutes," she said. "Make the most of it."

Gustav popped his head and shoulders back down into the tub. "I plan to."

Diana rose to go, and Brady and I stepped aside to let her pass.

"I'm glad you're talkin' to us again, miss," I said as she walked by.

The lady lingered to look at me, and though she didn't smile, I could tell a part of her wanted to.

"I am as well," she said. "I'm just sorry it took something like this to give me the opportunity."

When our audience caught sight of her at the top of the steps with the egg in her hand, a cheer went up, and Major Bacon and His Hoosier One Hundred launched into "American Patrol." The ruckus drew Diana's gaze away, and I could see that unsmiled smile wilt inside her.

Colonel Crowe was at the bottom of the staircase. Watching us.

"Don't worry, Otto," Diana said. "Now that we've started again, I'm going to see to it we don't stop."

She did smile, then—a big, blinding grin she slapped on for the benefit of her admirers. She was waving to them as she headed down the stairs.

Brady started to follow her with slow, stumbling steps.

"Whoa," I said, swinging in to block him. "Why don't you stay up here with us?"

Brady peered past me, down into the crowd, his eyes wide. There was a dusty splotch on the front of his coat and a smashed carnation in his buttonhole—the work of my own shoe in the midst of our tussle—yet he seemed too dazed to hold any grudges.

"But someone's got to tell . . . someone," he muttered.

"About the body? Oh, there's no rush. Mr. Curtis ain't goin' nowhere. And while the lady buys us a little time, we can do some investigatin'. Why don't you show me how the monarch of the New York detectives would go about it?"

"Yes, of course . . ."

Brady moved away from the stairs, but he only made it a few steps before his knees went wobbly and he had to stumble back and grab for the railing.

"Steady there, friend," I said, moving in to catch him should he swoon. "You alright?"

Brady nodded, though his face had gone as green as George Washington's on the one-dollar bill.

"It's the cheese vapors," he wheezed. "They're making me sick."

"Sure. It is pretty ripe up here, ain't it? Tell you what—why don't you just breathe easy and strike a heroic pose. My brother can handle the detectin'."

Brady nodded again and puffed out his chest as best he could. The band had stopped playing by now, and I could hear Pinkerton making some kind of pronouncement about the Crowes.

I walked over to Old Red's upturned keister and proceeded to have a conversation with it.

"So what happened to the man?"

"Looks like he got himself smothered."

"In cheese?"

"It ain't tapioca down here."

My brother had left his Stetson near the lip of the viewhole, and I considered placing it atop his rump and observing that his appearance had actually improved.

"Well, how'd he manage that?" I said instead.

"If I knew, I wouldn't be hangin' down here like a bat in a damned . . . hel-lo."

"You spot something?"

"I *smell* something."

"Other than cheddar?"

"Very other."

One of Gustav's hands snaked up to pull a small box from his coat pocket, and a moment later the inside of the vat lit up with the flash and flicker of a fresh-struck match. My brother's dangling body blocked my view, though, and I saw nothing of Armstrong B. Curtis save a little glimmer off his patent leather shoes.

"Careful with that lucifer, Brother. You'll melt all the evidence," I said. "Say . . . don't the flare off that thing hurt your eyes?"

"Now ain't the time for that."

Major Bacon chose that moment to fire up his Hoosiers again, and along with the blast of "The Washington Post," I heard the telltale mumble-buzz of a crowd dispersing. I moved back to the edge of the tank and peeped over the railing.

Down below, Diana was leaning in close to William Pinkerton, speaking into his ear.

"Five," I said.

Pinkerton snapped up straight and spun around to gawp up at me.

"Four."

He turned and waved over the nearest Columbian Guard.

"Three."

He sent the Guardsman flying away with a few whispered words, then hustled toward the staircase.

"Two."

He charged up the steps with more Guardsmen in tow.

"One."

"What do you think you're doing?" Pinkerton thundered.

"I," Gustav said, "am accumulatin' data."

He didn't bother coming out of the viewhole, so Pinkerton bothered for him.

"Get him out of there," he growled at the Guardsmen, and they proceeded to grab Old Red by the legs and lift him up like they were pulling a rabbit out of a hat.

When my brother's top half appeared, both his face and his match were smoldering.

"I ain't finished."

"Yes, you are," Pinkerton said. "Put him over there."

"Don't drop him on his head, boys," I said. "Our mama did the same thing when he was a baby, and—"

"This is *not* funny," Gustav snapped as the guards lowered him down and let him go.

"Yes, it—"

"A man's been murdered."

I shut up.

Pinkerton crouched down and squinted into the tank. "You didn't disturb anything, did you?"

"Oh, not much." Old Red snatched up his hat and jammed it atop his head. "I just borrowed the monogrammed hankie the killer left behind and used it to wipe up the message Curtis wrote in his own blood. *Of course I didn't disturb nothing!* But I did notice a thing or two. Or three or four."

"Get them out of here," Pinkerton said, jerking his head at the steps.

The Guardsmen gave Gustav a push toward the staircase.

"Don't you even wanna hear what I got to say?"

Pinkerton kept staring down into the vat. "Leave this to the professionals."

"You mean you and your tin soldiers here?" I said. "The ones who didn't even notice the body till the *amateurs* told 'em about it?"

That got *me* a shove from one of the Guardsmen.

"And see to it they don't come back up," Pinkerton said.

Brady got swept up with me and my brother as we were brushed away.

"Oh," Pinkerton said when we reached the top of the stairs. "If any of you breathes a word of this to the newspapers, you're out of the contest. And if you use the word 'murder,' I'll see to it you're in jail. Do you understand?"

"Yes, of course, Mr. Pinkerton," Brady said, voice cracking. "You can count on my discretion."

I just nodded.

Old Red said nothing until we were headed down the steps.

"Monarch of the New York ass-kissers is more like it," he grumbled.

If Brady heard him, he didn't let on. He just affixed a phony grin to his handsome face, doled out a few hurried handshakes to the well-wishers waiting at the bottom of the staircase, then darted away the first chance he got. He seemed to be making a beeline for a burly, bearded fellow watching us from beside a replica of the Liberty Bell made entirely from oats, but Frank Tousey intercepted him and steered him away. What any of them did next, I couldn't say, for our legions of adoring fans were falling upon us.

"Better luck next time," a plump, gray-haired matron said even as she went up on her tiptoes to strain for another glimpse of Brady.

"We're pulling for you," added her mousy, mustachioed husband. "Other than King and the Crowes, you're our favorites."

And with that, they drifted off in search of the map of pickles.

Just about everyone still lingering about was shoving in to congratulate Diana and the colonel. The exceptions being Old Red, who'd turned to gaze with bitter longing up the steps to the top of the cheese, and the Columbian Guards who'd pointedly positioned themselves in his path.

"Well, I do hope you got a rope on some decent clues," I said.

"Cuz we sure ain't gettin' another crack at the scene of the crime."

Gustav pushed back his Stetson and sighed. "I don't know *what* I got a rope on. But at least for once we'll have us some expert help untanglin' all the knots."

"That's right."

I looked over at the Crowes again. Just beyond the cluster of back-slappers around them I could see Boothby Greene talking to his publisher, Blackheath-Murray, and though Eugene Valmont had yet to put in an appearance, the Frenchman was bound to come scurrying along any second.

"If Curtis was murdered, the killer won't stand a chance with the World's Greatest Sleuths on the job," I said.

"I reckon not." Old Red squared his hat again, pulling the brim low, as if readying himself for a gust of wind he felt stirring around him. "Unless, of course, he is one of them."

11

LE PARFUM DE LA MORT

Or, My Brother Gets a Whiff of BS, and Our Fellow Sleuths Sling Some Around

Within ten minutes, we had them gathered: four of the greatest detectives the world had ever seen.

Well, the four greatest detectives we could find, anyway. (King Brady had disappeared.) The four greatest who were willing to speak to us. (Pinkerton was still atop Mt. Cheddar with the Columbian Guards.) And the greatness of three of these detectives we had to take on credit. (We'd seen Diana's firsthand in the past. Boothby Greene and Eugene Valmont and Colonel Crowe, though . . . ?)

So, to be a tad more accurate, within ten minutes we had them gathered: a great detective and three men who called themselves detectives but who, for all we knew, couldn't detect their way to flames if their pants were on fire. Still, it was a start.

All it had taken was a few quick whispers with the Crowes, a jerk of the head to Greene, and a Lucille Larson-ectomy for Valmont. (The Frenchman had come hustling up with the lady reporter attached to his side just as we were leaving the Agriculture Building. "There's a body in the Mammoth Cheese," Diana said.

"Pinkerton won't let anyone up to look at it." "Oh, really?" Miss Larson said, and she shot off for the cheese like she'd been fired from the Krupp Gun. Valmont we steered outside with us.)

Now here we all were, bunched up around a bench beside the shimmering waters of the Grand Basin. It had been a long, long time since I'd seen my brother crack a smile, and though he certainly wasn't about to pop off with one now, there was a grim satisfaction upon his face that counted, for him, almost as a grin. At long last, he wasn't just dreaming of being a sleuth. Here he was amongst people he might call peers, extraordinary individuals who shared his passion for detecting. And they weren't competing against each other now. They were gathered together for a common purpose . . . and they were looking at *him*.

He took in a deep breath and clapped his hands together.

"So," he said, "let's begin with—"

"Who put you in charge?" Colonel Crowe snapped.

"I just figured since—"

"Where are your speck-tickles?" Valmont asked.

"That's neither here nor—"

"It's a clear, sunny day," Greene said, "yet you don't seem bothered by the light."

"Like I said, that's not—"

"And your bruh-THERE's coat," Valmont said with a nod my way. "He was not wearing it when the contest began."

"Listen, could we just stick to—?"

"It barely fits across his chest," Greene observed. "As if it weren't his coat at all."

"Well, it's not, but that's a different—"

"I still want to know why we should be listening to you," Crowe said.

"Because he's the only one of us who's had a good look at the body," Diana told him. "What's more, he's the smartest man here."

Greene and Valmont looked surprised by the lady's endorsement. Her father simply looked exasperated.

"Now, Gustav," Diana said, "why don't you tell us what you saw?"

"Thank you, miss," my brother mumbled, and it took a moment more for the blush her words slapped across his face to fade away. "Mr. Curtis was still in his evenin' clothes, stretched out straight, facedown, arms at his sides. He was back a ways from that egg thing, which was smack-dab in the center of the cheese, right under the viewhole. So it might've been possible—if you wasn't payin' much mind to what you were doin'—to glance down and not notice the man at all. I reckon that's how he could fester there all day till we came along: They had the cheese blocked off for the contest, and all Pinkerton or whoever saw was that the egg was in place."

"Did you see anything indicating how Curtis might have died?" Greene asked.

"Oh, that was clear as day. He was mushed into the cheese pretty good. Mouth and nose totally covered. Ain't no way the man could breathe. Somebody suffocated him."

"Why 'Somebody suffocated him?' Why not simply 'He suffocated'?"

"Cuz cheese ain't quicksand, Mr. Greene. A feller ain't gonna smother in it without havin' him some help."

"I must disagree," Valmont said. "In one of my own cases in Frawnce, a diaboli-KELL master chef killed his wife by drugging her din-NAIR and arranging for her to collapse upon and asphyxilate in a carefully placed blancmange. He would have escaped ju-STESS if I

95

had not noticed the telltale odor of bitter almonds in the *coq au vin*. Rather than face the guillotine, he later killed himself with a poisoned beignet slipped to him by his love-AIR in a basket of . . . but I digress."

"You sure as hell do," Old Red said under his breath.

"I propose a similar scenario for M. Curtis—minus a crime," Valmont went on obliviously. "Our Puzzlema-STAIR came here last night to lay his egg. He was, as we all saw, quite detoxicated. So, when he climbed or fell down into the cheese recepti-KELL . . ." The Frenchman waved his hands before his face and fluttered his eyelids, wobbling from side to side. "He was overcome by che-DARE fumes, fainted, and—*voilà*—suffocated in cheese."

There was a long silence while we chewed this theory over. It left a bad taste in my mouth, though I couldn't say why. Fortunately, someone else could.

"Allow me to remind you, monsieur," Diana said. "We aren't talking about the Mammoth Camembert or the Mammoth Brie. Mr. Curtis died atop the Mammoth *Cheddar*. And you of all people should see why that makes a difference."

"Ah! *Touché*!" Valmont offered the lady a little bow. "You are not just a detec-TEEV, you are a true *connoisseur*."

"At the risk of sounding like neither," I said, "what's so special about cheddar?"

"It is zeamy ard," Valmont explained . . . if that particular grouping of sounds could be said to explain anything.

"Semihard," Diana explained with a good bit more success. "A nonsoft cheese."

"Well, there you go!" Old Red crowed. "Curtis's face is buried in the stuff! How could that happen on its own?"

For backing, he turned to the closest thing we had on hand to

Sherlock Holmes: Boothby Greene. Yet the Englishman shook his head.

"I hate to point out the fly in the ointment, as it were, but the answer to your question is 'Very easily.' We would consider butter hard when it's first taken from the icebox. Given time at room temperature, however, even so light a thing as a sprig of parsley might sink into it. Lying there as poor Curtis is—and has been for half a day, presumably—we might very well see the same effect. After all, it's *semi*hard cheese we have here, not parmigiana or pecorino."

"Not what or what?" I asked.

Valmont looked at me sadly. "They are more chee-ZES, *mon ami*. You do not have them in the West?"

"Friend," I said, "where I come from, there's two kinds of cheese and two kinds only: the kind that comes from a cow and the kind that comes from a goat."

Valmont's pity turned to horror.

"Jehoshaphat!" Colonel Crowe cried out. "This is getting us nowhere!"

Diana threw a glance at Gustav, her big brown eyes widening ever so slightly. She'd handed him a chance to show off—perhaps win her father over—and so far all he'd done was open up a debate about the relative hardness and softness of exotic cheeses. He'd have to do a lot better if he was going to prove himself the smartest man there.

"The colonel's right," he said. "Let's set the cheese talk aside, for now. There's something else that needs figurin'. Something mighty peculiar I noticed about the body."

"Yes?" Diana asked eagerly.

"When I swung in close to Curtis's head," my brother said, "I smelled dung."

Diana winced, while her father rolled his eyes.

"I hate to be undelicate," Valmont said, "but when a man dies, certain inavoidable processes are to be expec-TED. The result I like to call '*le parfum de la mort*.' The sickly-sweet smell of death."

"Hell's bells, I know what a stiff smells like," my brother fumed. "Ain't nothin' 'sickly sweet' to it, if it's fresh. Anyway, I'm talkin' about Curtis's head, not his trousers. I'm tellin' you, I got a whiff of dung. *Cow* dung."

"Could it have been a hair oil or pomade of some kind?" Greene asked.

"You ever heard of a pomade that smells like cow shit?" Old Red snapped back. He was growing so vexed, even his hero's stand-in wasn't spared a splash of acid.

"If you please, sir!" The colonel jerked his head at Diana. "Watch your language around the lady!"

Gustav swiped a hand at the man. "Aww, she's heard a lot worse outta me."

Diana's shoulders slumped, as if she wanted to pull herself down into her dress like a turtle retreating into its shell.

"Perhaps what you smelled was the cheese going rotten," Greene mused. "The odor of it is quite overpowering. I can only imagine what it would be like up close. In fact, I'm surprised you could detect any scent at all other than—"

"Mr. Greene," Old Red said, "I've been around cattle all my life, and I've spent many a looooonnnnng stretch ridin' behind herds thousands strong. So I've come across more cow pies than there are stars in the sky. Bury my head in cheese or stick garlic up my nose, it won't matter. You put a whiff of plop from a hay-fed Hereford anywhere near me, I'll know it. And that's exactly what I got a whiff of."

"Oh, well, when you put it like that, it makes perfect sense,"

Colonel Crowe sneered. "After all, what other deduction could we expect from the Holmes of the Range?" He swung his snarl on Diana. "Curtis was murdered by a cow!"

Dozens of tourists had ambled past since we'd started our little impromptu caucus. The ones nearby now stopped to stare.

"You are a card, Colonel." I guffawed for their benefit. "Now let me tell you the one about the chicken and the traveling salesman!"

The tourists went on their way again.

"All I know is what I smelled," Gustav said, quiet but firm. "And I smelled manure."

"Of course you did," Colonel Crowe growled. "Because you're full of it."

My brother let loose a gruff, aggravated sigh and once again turned to Greene for support. And once again, he didn't get it.

"I'm afraid I'm also unconvinced," Greene said, and he went on to roll out one of the (in my opinion) crumbiest of Sherlock Holmes's crumbs of wisdom, intoning it with somber, sonorous solemnity like he was reading scripture from the pulpit. "Let us not forget: 'When you have eliminated the impossible, whatever remains, however improbable, must be the truth.' It's safe to say that a killer cow is impossible while death by one's leavings would be highly improbable, at the very least. M. Valmont's theory, on the other hand, doesn't even strike me as unlikely. An intoxicated man met an untimely and undignified end. It's plain to see which way Occam's Razor would cut. That leaves us with an explanation that is, perhaps, disappointingly prosaic, for those in our line. Yet we shouldn't let a predilection for labyrinthine convolution blind us to the obvious conclusion."

I doubt my brother understood half of what the man said, but the gist he got, and he gave it a shake of the head and a quiet "Feh."

"Our English friend puts it very well," Valmont said. "If you were ho-PING, M. Amlingmeyer, that we would lunch an inquery of our own, I must disappoint you. I am a policeman myself. I will not interfere in an official investigation. Besides . . ." He drew up his shoulders in a rueful shrug. "I do not think there is anything to investigate."

"Fine," Gustav spat. "I guess some of us came here to play games, and some came ready for real detective work." He turned to Greene and threw his own Holmes quote at him. " 'It is a capital mistake to theorize before one has data.' I say it's too early to write this off as an accident. Especially when what little data we do have is so damned strange."

"I fear the data might not be the problem so much as its source," Diana said.

Old Red frowned at her. Or not at her so much as the truth she spoke.

No one was taking his clues seriously because he alone could vouch for them. And no one was taking *him* seriously because he was . . . him.

"We'll have to see what we can do about that," he said.

The "we" there wasn't lost on Colonel Crowe.

"Yes. You and *your brother* do that," he said, taking Diana by the arm and tugging her away. "There are still obscure clues to hunt for. Fanciful deductions to make. Heifers to round up for question-ing. We'll leave you to it while we prepare for tomorrow's contest."

"Our Puzzlemaster's dead," my brother said as the colonel and his daughter walked off. "How can you be so sure there's even gonna *be* a competition tomorrow?"

Colonel Crowe never looked back. Diana did, though—just long enough to throw us a look that seemed to promise . . . well, something. It wasn't much to cling to, but I grabbed it with both hands.

Greene and Valmont soon peeled themselves away as well, the two of them heading off together toward the long, column-studded Peristyle that separated the east end of the Grand Basin from Lake Michigan beyond. Greene, at least, had the decency to offer apologies before leaving. He knew he was letting my brother down.

"So much for our posse," I said as the Crowes receded to pinpricks in one direction, Greene and Valmont in the other.

"Yeah, well . . . us bein' on our own ain't nothing new."

"Nope. I do believe I'm tirin' of it, though."

Gustav turned to look at me. It was the first time I'd been able to look him full in the eyes in quite a while, and it was almost a shock to see the soft sky blue of them again. For some reason, I'd remembered them as steely gray.

"Me, too," Old Red said.

I was about to ask him about those eyes of his—why he'd kept them hidden behind smoked glass so long after he had to. Somehow, it didn't seem like the time or place for that, though, and instead I just said, "What next?"

Before my brother could answer, a heavy tromping sound turned us both back toward the Agriculture Building. A gaggle of Columbian Guards was trotting inside lugging what looked like stretchers—a lot of them.

"That," Gustav said. And off he went.

12

WALLS

Or, Pinkerton Tries to Avoid a Big Stink, and Gustav and I Go Hunting for One

Only two of the Guardsmen were carrying a stretcher, it turned out. The rest were toting dressing screens, which they proceeded to set up in a circle around the top of the Mammoth Cheese from Canada.

"They don't want an audience when they fish out the body," Old Red muttered.

"Why didn't you tell me you'd seen it?" someone said, and a thin, wraith-like figure popped out from behind a display of Professor Pertwee's Health Miracle Nut Butter.

My brother and I jumped halfway to the ceiling with a simultaneous, near-harmonious "Yahhh!"

"Miss Larson," I said after we'd taken a moment to catch our breath and climb back into our skin, "what are you doin' lurkin' around here?"

"The same thing as you: keeping an eye on the cheese," the lady reporter replied. "Now what about the body?"

"Why would you think we got a look at it?" Gustav asked.

"I talked to some of the spectators who were still milling around. They said you two were on top of the Mammoth Cheese before the Columbian Guards sealed it off. Diana Crowe and King Brady, too. Funny none of you told me that."

"Well, you didn't give us a chance, did you?" I said. "You went runnin' off like a bloodhound on the scent the second you heard someone was dead. What were we to do?"

Miss Larson gave me a long, hard look that made it clear she knew I was full of crap but felt it beneath her to come right out and say it.

"It's Curtis, isn't it?" she said.

She brought up her notepad and pencil and held them at the ready.

"Why does it chill me to the bone every time you do that?" I asked.

"What makes you think Mr. Curtis is dead?" asked Gustav.

"Really," Miss Larson said, "must you two answer my every question with more questions?"

I blinked her at innocently. "Oh . . . are we doin' that?"

She gave me a longer, harder look that said it was beneath her to knee me in the *huevos,* too, but she was tempted to do it anyway.

"What have we here?" Old Red said, and he nodded toward yet another Guardsman hustling past. With him was a grim-faced fellow in a dark business suit. The guards at the bottom of the steps didn't just swing aside to let the gent up. They hopped out of his way like a couple toreadors dodging a charging bull.

"Well, well," Miss Larson said as the man went clomping up the stairs. "Talk about the big cheese."

Gustav and I looked at each other.

He frowned. I shrugged.

"The big cheese?" I asked Miss Larson.

"Oh, no. You still haven't answered any of *my* questions. It's time for a little *quid pro quo*." The lady narrowed her eyes. "That means tit for tat. A deal. An answer for an answer."

Old Red rubbed at his mustache a moment before giving her a nod.

I brought up my right hand, spit in the palm, then held the hand out toward Miss Larson.

"Put 'er there, pardner," I drawled.

Miss Larson stared at me with such disgust you'd have thought I was offering her a handful of moldy lard.

"We know what *quid pro quo* means," I told her. (And it was even half true, for *I* knew.)

Point made, I reached for a hankie to clean off my hand—only realizing then I didn't have one on me. I ended up wiping my palm on the inside of my coat pocket as surreptitiously as I could.

"I've had bad luck with tits for tat before," Gustav said. "So if you don't mind, I'll do my askin' first." He jerked his head at the Mammoth Cheese. "What makes you so sure that's Curtis?"

Miss Larson accepted my brother's terms without a blink.

"He was missing this morning, for one thing. For another, the egg was found up there—I hear the Crowes were today's winners—and that means he was up there, too, at some point. And the way Curtis was acting last night, it would hardly come as a surprise to learn he fell victim to some kind of accident."

"You mean accident or"—Old Red gave the lady an exaggerated wink—"'accident'?"

Miss Larson just stared at him, her lips pressed tight.

"Alright. Yeah. It was Curtis," my brother said. "He was lyin' inside the tub, facedown, almost like he drowned. Now . . . my turn again. Who was that feller who just went up the cheese?"

"Daniel Burnham, the Exposition's director of works. And I'll give you a little more for free. You can bet he and Pinkerton are going to do everything in their power to keep Curtis's death under wraps, at least until the fair's over. The Exposition Company's got less than a week to grab as much cash as it can before going out in a blaze of glory. The directors, the vendors, the mayor—none of them will want to see these last days tainted. Now. Me again."

Miss Larson started to turn back toward the Mammoth Cheddar, then changed her mind and squinted at Old Red's face, instead.

"Why do you care?"

"Excuse me?" my brother said.

"Why come back here? Why ask questions? *Why care?*"

"A man's died under mysterious circumstances," I said. "We're sleuths. What else we gonna do?"

"I don't see any of the other sleuths here."

I shrugged. "They don't find what happened so mysterious."

"That still doesn't answer my question." Miss Larson turned back to my brother. "Why do you care?"

"I liked the man," Gustav said.

Miss Larson nodded. "Ahh, I see. Because you worshipped at the same altar. Still, you barely knew him, correct? It's not like Armstrong B. Curtis was your friend."

"No . . . but I reckon we might have us a common enemy."

"What does that mean? You're worried the killer's going to come after you next? Why should he do that?"

"We don't know why Curtis was killed, so we don't know what the killer was after—or if he's got it yet."

"But by openly pursuing an investigation, wouldn't you be provoking the killer, assuming there is one? Or is that part of your plan?"

"Hey. Yeah." I turned on my brother. "What she said."

Old Red shook his head. "Time for my next question. What do you know about Curtis, Miss Larson?"

The lady took in a deep breath. "He's from California. He's an attorney. He's made an obsessive study of the cases of Sherlock Holmes. He's made an obsessive study of the *rivals* of Sherlock Holmes. He's written an exposé of Nick Carter for *Scribner's,* and he might be planning another article along the same lines. He also might be crazy. And all of this should have been in the past tense, because he's dead. That's everything I know. Was there ever anything *really* wrong with your eyes?"

The way Miss Larson went sliding right into her next question caught my brother off guard. He seemed to remember at last that this was a young woman we'd been conversing with so intently, and he coughed and slouched and looked away.

Whether he could recompose himself enough to go on trading "tits for tat" proved a moot question, however, for at that moment Daniel Burnham came stomping down the steps from the cheese again—with William Pinkerton and half a dozen Columbian Guards right behind him.

Gustav and I spun around and pretended to inspect the nearest jars of Professor Pertwee's nut butter. This was no doubt a pointless enterprise, as with our Stetsons and contrasting, big-little frames, my brother and I would be just as recognizable from the back as the front. Fortunately, someone thoughtfully provided a distraction.

"Mr. Burnham! Mr. Pinkerton!" Miss Larson darted away from us. "A moment of your time, please!"

I can't say for certain how Mr. Burnham or Mr. Pinkerton reacted, for I went right on studying the label on Professor Pertwee's jar. (Note to Professor Pertwee: I'd get rid of the giant smiling peanut man, if I were you. It's danged creepy.) When I finally dared a peek around, Burnham, Pinkerton, and Miss Larson were all gone.

The two Columbian Guards who'd been stationed at the bottom of the Mammoth Cheese had apparently gone with them. In their place was a new Guardsman, one of the bunch that had brought the dressing screens up not long before.

Old Red eyed him warily.

"Think you can talk us past that feller?"

"No harm in tryin'," I said. "Unless he pulls his sword on us."

Gustav gave me a push toward the cheese. "Go on, then."

I went. My brother came, too.

The guard was a ramrod-spined fellow who appeared to be striving with all his soul to live up to the overdone ornamentation of his uniform. The piping, the epaulets, the braids, the badge, the plume-tipped cap, the gold-plated scabbard for his sword—you'd have thought he was Admiral Nelson instead of a two-dollar-a-day copper, and he wore a haughty, stern expression as puffed-up as his duds.

A smile and a "Howdy!" were out of the question.

"Afternoon, Officer," I said with the brusque, businesslike tone of a Colonel Crowe. "Mr. Amlingmeyer and I are assisting with the investigation, and we just need a moment to—"

Old Red and I skidded to a halt side by side. I'd hoped we could bluff our way up through pure momentum, but the Guardsman was purer inertia. If we hadn't stopped, we'd have flattened ourselves against his chest like a couple snow balls splatting on the side of a barn.

"No one goes up," he said. "Orders."

"I understand. Orders are orders. But I'm tellin' you, 'no one' means *them*." I jerked a thumb at the tourists strolling through the exhibition hall behind us. "Not the two of us. We're o-fficial."

"My orders were *no one*," the guard said. "Especially not a couple redheaded clowns wearing cowboy hats."

"Oh. Well, what if we were to take the hats off?"

The Guardsman did not surprise me by smiling.

"Beat it," he said.

"Come on," Gustav grumbled, spinning around and stomping away.

"Speakin' of orders, I've got one for you," I told the guard before following. "Only there are children present, so I can't say mine aloud."

A moment later, I was falling into step beside my brother.

"Shit—that's all we got to work with now," he said. "One little here-and-gone whiff of cowpat."

"Nothing new about that. We've had shit for clues plenty of times."

My brother, like the Guardsman, did not laugh, did not smile. I was probably lucky he didn't stop to kick me.

"Look," I said, "if you really smelled manure—"

"*I did.*"

"—which, of course, you did, then it's easy to figure what we should do next."

"Oh, yeah?"

"Yeah. We just go where the manure is."

"And where would that be? The Bullshit Building?"

"No need to get snuffy, Brother. I'm bein' serious. I've done some studyin' on the Fair, and I've got me a notion. A deduction, you might even call it."

"I can guess what *I'd* call it."

"Well, let's put it to the test, then."

I steered us toward the nearest exit. When we popped outside, we were facing the imposing, ominously droning Machinery Building not far away. A narrow, enclosed walkway snaked off from it, tendril-like, toward an identical wing from the Agriculture Building, and the two joined up to form something not unlike a high-walled stockade.

"Now, why do you think they'd feel the need to have them two buildings a-touchin' like that?" I asked Gustav.

"Why don't you just tell me?"

I started for the spot where the Agriculture Building and the Machinery Building came together. "Oh, come on. You've played coy with your deducifyin' so many times, you can't begrudge me one little moment of my own."

"Yes, I can," Old Red growled. But he followed me all the same.

When we were about fifty yards from the covered hallway linking the two buildings, my brother raised his head slightly and sniffed.

When we were forty yards off, he didn't have to bother, for the smell was swirling all around us.

When we were thirty yards off, you could hear what we were about to see.

The last twenty-something yards I can't report on, for they flew by too fast.

Gustav had broken into a dash, and I kept up. I wasn't going to miss the look on his face when he came out on the other side of that passageway.

In one door and out the other, and there it was: wide-eyed wonderment.

I pulled out my guidebook, flipped through the pages till I found what I wanted, and started reading.

" 'The Live Stock Pavilion is an oval amphitheater of diameters 280 and 440 feet, under the roof of which will be exhibited and judged the blooded stock of every description competing for the prize awards. Back of the pavilion are the tremendous live stock sheds, seventy-five in number, covering a space of forty acres. The collection of cattle contained here will be the most stupendous ever contemplated for—'"

"Christ," Old Red said, taking in the tall, white, pennant-pocked pavilion. "Even the damn barns 'round here are beautiful." He turned and gazed back at the high, long walls of the Machinery and Agriculture buildings. "Well, I'll be. It's a barrier. To keep the animal stink out of the White City."

"Works pretty good, too," I said. "I mean, to hide the smell of cattle from a man who knows it like you do."

That reminded Gustav why we were there, and he started off around the Stock Pavilion, not stopping until he could see the pens just beyond. In some of the closest ones were heavy-jowled red-and-white cows.

I stopped beside my brother and spread my arms wide. "Herefords, just like you said. And I already see enough meadow muffins to fill the Grand Canyon. Now all we gotta do is figure out how one of 'em got on Curtis's head."

Old Red's expression brightened. There was no actual smile, of course, those having been banished from his face long ago. But maybe, just maybe, you could call the little curl of the lip tucked under his mustache a smirk.

"Oh, I've got me a notion about that. A deduction, you might even call it."

"Let me guess," I sighed. "You ain't gonna tell me what it is."

"Revenge is sweet," Gustav said.

He started for the stockyards.

13

THE TRAIL

Or, The Killer's Tracks Take Us out of the Mire and into the Frying Pan

Revenge may be sweet, but the same can't be said of what you'll find carpeting a cattle pen. So I couldn't share my brother's enthusiasm as he crept along the edge of the stockyards giving the eye to each and every cow pie he could find. And he found plenty.

"You got us to the right haystack, alright," he said, crouching down to inspect a particularly intriguing mound of brown on the other side of the fence. "I just hope we can find the right needle."

"I wish it *was* a needle we were lookin' for. At least then I wouldn't have to worry about smellin' up my new—"

"Hel-lo!"

Old Red clambered over the fence and dropped down beside a prodigious heap near a corner of the pen. One edge had been mashed down and smeared across the ground.

"That our needle?"

"Most likely." Gustav knelt beside the patty, cocking his head to peer at it first from one side, then the other. "Unless someone's been breedin' cows to wear brogans." He pointed to a lumpy smudge on one of the fence rails nearby. "And climb outta their pens in 'em."

"So that settles it. Curtis paid a call on the cattle before headin' over to the Mammoth Cheese."

Old Red scowled at me, his eyes flashing such naked disdain I suddenly missed his shaded cheaters.

"Why would you assume this here footprint belongs to Armstrong Curtis?"

"Uhhh . . . because he's the one who smelled like shit?"

"Yeah. *His head*."

"You sayin' he did a handstand in there?"

"Just think about it," Gustav said. "Might make for a nice change of pace."

Up to then, the Herefords in the pen had been keeping their distance. But now a big, curious Bossie started ambling toward the fence with a thunderous "Moo!" She was a lot of cow, fifteen hundred pounds if she was an ounce—and my scrawny brother was squatting down directly in her path.

"Better move 'fore you're flat as that patty!" I called out.

Old Red didn't budge.

"Throw me your coat!" he barked.

"What?"

"I said—aww, hell!"

The heifer was almost on Gustav now, and he had to hop to his feet and leap aside to keep from being trampled.

The cow put a hoof down in our evidence, smooshing what little of it wasn't already smooshed.

"Dammit, Otto!" my brother raged.

"Hey, don't blame me. If you really wanted to save that thing, you should've used your new hat instead of goin' for my coat. Anyway, I'm not the one who did the steppin'."

The heifer lowed as if in apology and pushed at Old Red with her huge, wet muzzle.

"You I don't blame," Gustav said, giving her a pat. "Cows are *supposed* to be stupid."

He turned and scrambled over the fence, and then he was off, zigzagging away up the path that separated the cattle pens from the Stock Pavilion. His eyes were pointed straight down.

I didn't have to ask what he was looking for. When a man's walking around bent-over, nose-to-the-ground like a chicken pecking at grubs—and when that man happens to be my brother—you can bet he's hunting up a trail.

"Did you gentlemen lose something?" a kindly old man asked as we crossed his path, and once upon a time, I knew, I would've shot back "Only our minds" or some such. Now, though, I just tipped my hat and told him not to worry himself on our account.

This was what we did. This was what our lives looked like, thanks to Sherlock Holmes. I hadn't just come to accept it, I realized. I liked it that way.

Eventually, Gustav lurched and veered his way around the pavilion to the back of the Agriculture Building. After nosing around the first entrance we came to—and nearly ramming hat-first into a dozen tourists—he took to inspecting the windows lining the back wall. While by no means crude or ugly, they were simple pane-and-windowsill affairs, nowhere near as ornate as their awesomely large, arching brethren along the other three sides of the building. Old Red sped past half a dozen before skidding to a stop with a cheery (for him) "Well, well, well!"

On the sill was a conspicuous brown smudge.

With but a little fiddling, my brother got the window to crack open on pivoting hinges.

"You'd think with the World's Greatest Everything around here, they'd have 'em some decent locks," he said.

"I guess they weren't worried about someone makin' off with the Mammoth Cheese or the gum-paste Columbus or the Brooklyn Bridge made out of ham or what have you."

"Well, they should've taken more care. This thing didn't slow me down ten seconds, and everything I know about lock-pickin' I learned from Nick goddamn Carter."

Before I could ask what we were to do next, Old Red was doing it: He hoisted himself up and slithered through the window. I took a moment to make sure none of the passersby thereabouts were watching us and, finding that only two dozen or so were, took another moment to convince myself I didn't care. Then I followed my brother.

Being a fellow of some size, a certain amount of squirming and kicking and gut-sucking was required to get me inside, but eventually I teeter-tottered forward and spilled out onto the floor.

"And who's that?" I heard a woman ask.

"My brother," Gustav replied.

"I might've known," the woman said.

I rolled to my feet and found Old Red in one of the display stalls lining the walkways of the Agriculture Building. Looming up to one side of him was a cask the size of a railroad water tank with WORLD'S LARGEST FLOUR BARREL stenciled on the side. On his other side stood a plump old Negro woman with smiling eyes and apple cheeks and a yellow handkerchief wrapped round her head. There was a wall of red boxes just beyond her, each adorned with the woman's beaming face under the words AUNT JEMIMA READY-MIX FOR PANCAKES.

"Sorry to barge in on you like this, Miss Jemima," I said.

The woman chuckled. "It's Miss Green, thank you. Or Miss Nancy, if you prefer. The only place you'll find 'Aunt Jemima' is on those boxes. And no need to apologize. I was just sitting here waiting for my next performance."

"Oh?"

Miss Nancy nodded at a large stove nearby. The top was all griddle, by far the biggest I'd ever seen.

"Every quarter hour I whip up a stack of pancakes as tall as you. Wait around and you can have first pick of the next batch."

I suddenly realized that lunchtime had long come and gone with no actual lunch to it.

"Them Ready-Mix flapjacks any good?" I asked.

Miss Nancy peeped slyly to the left and right before whispering her answer.

"Not as good as mine."

"We ain't here to swap recipes," Gustav growled, and he got to stalking around eyeballing the floor.

"I think your skinny brother could use a nice big plate of pancakes," Miss Nancy said to me. "Might improve his disposition."

"Ma'am, if it were as easy as that to put him in a good mood, I'd buy every box of Aunt Jemima you got."

Miss Nancy laughed. Once again—as if I need to tell you—Old Red did not.

"You notice any strange stains here today?" he asked. "Anything smelly?"

"As a matter of fact, I did," Miss Nancy said. "There were five or six smears along the floor when I came in this morning. Looked like you-know-what, though for the life of me I can't see how it got here . . . and I'd really rather not know. I had one of the custodians mop it up first thing."

Gustav stopped his pacing. "So it's all gone now."

"Of course it is. I'm not going to stand here cooking all day with *that* under my feet."

"But you'd be willing to swear you saw it? If someone else asked you? The police, say?"

"I suppose." Miss Nancy glanced at the window we'd slid in through as if she expected the guards from the sanitarium to come climbing in after us. "Is it *important* that I saw doodie on the floor?"

"It's a matter of life and death!" Old Red declared, and off he went, staring at the floor again.

"My brother works for the sanitation department," I explained. "He takes these things very seriously." I tipped my hat and started after Gustav. "Thank you, ma'am. You've been a great help."

"I'll have to take your word for that," Miss Nancy said. "Come back in ten minutes if you want those pancakes!"

I caught up with Old Red just in time to keep him from walking into a pyramid of jarred capers.

"That's it," he said. "No more trail. Even if it hadn't been mopped up, I couldn't pick it out again—not with all the folks stompin' new stains over it all day."

"So what now?"

Gustav pried his eyes from the floorboards. "We don't need no footprints to know where the killer went once he was done here."

It took but a moment's thought to see what he meant.

"The Columbian," I said.

My brother nodded.

Whoever the murderer might be, it was obvious where he'd spent the night: our very own hotel.

14

STOLEC

Or, Though the Dung Trail Ends, We're Handed a New Load of Bull

We returned to our hotel. And I could simply leave it at that. "We returned to our hotel." Five little words. Yet that utterly fails to capture the drama of the ordeal. In fact, I could devote an entire chapter to our long, arduous journey, so fraught was it with peril and death-defying derring-do.

On Stony Island Avenue, it was a trolley that almost got us. On Sixty-fourth Street, it was a dray hauling garbage. And on Madison Avenue, we were almost flattened by an omnibus *and* a locomotive *and* a policeman infuriated by both Old Red's wide-eyed stumbling through traffic and his less-than-respectful reply when advised to "get [his] hick ass out of the damned street." Time and time again, I had to steer my city-hating brother out of harm's way (though it was considerably easier now that he didn't have his smoked spectacles half-blinding him). So it was every single time we ventured from the White City to our hotel and vice versa, but to keep this book from stretching out to the intolerable lengths favored by Mr.

STEVE HOCKENSMITH

Tolstoy and his highfalutin ilk, I'll just circle back to those five little words.

We returned to our hotel.

Mrs. Jasinska, the proprietress, was at her usual post behind the desk near the entrance, and she greeted us with the merry "Welcome back!" that was her custom.

"Ma'am," Gustav began gravely, "there's something I need to—"

"What do you think about poor Mr. Curtis?" the lady prattled on without a hint of anxiety or sorrow to cloud her sunny disposition. "So untimely. So tragic. So deliciously mysterious!"

"You know about that already?"

Mrs. Jasinska gave my brother a cheerful nod. "That lovely Miss Crowe told me all about it."

"She did?" It took Old Red a moment to stow away his surprise. "Well . . . it must have been a terrible shock to you, losing a guest like that."

Mrs. Jasinska nodded again—and, without realizing it, confirmed my brother's guess. Before that, we hadn't known whether Curtis was staying at the Columbian or not.

"Oh, yes. It truly is upsetting." Mrs. Jasinska leaned over her desk and dropped her voice, though there was no one else in sight. "You don't think he was *murdered*, do you?"

Gustav bent down and took to whispering as well. "Frankly, ma'am, I have my suspicions, which is why my brother and I have been doin' some pokin' around. And you know who could be the greatest help to us with that?"

"Who?" Mrs. Jasinska asked breathlessly.

"You. Cuz you're the only one who could get us a look at—"

The lady was shaking her head before my brother even finished.

"Miss Crowe asked that, too, and I had to give the same answer. I can't let you into Mr. Curtis's room. There was a Canadian gentleman who hung himself in two-twenty the first week of the Fair, and the police were ever so irritated with me just because I let some of the other guests in to have a peek. Dear me—the language those officers used! No, I'm afraid that's out of the question. But I'm sure I can be of service in other ways. Miss Crowe certainly seemed to think so. She asked me oh so many questions. You know, at first I wasn't sure how I felt about a young lady taking part in your little tournament, but she's won me over completely. Such a pretty, clever little thing, don't you think?"

Old Red cleared his throat and looked down to make sure his toes were still attached.

Yes. He did think.

"Would you mind tellin' us what you told her?" he said.

"Well, as I explained to Miss Crowe, I'm honor-bound to protect my guests' privacy. But . . ."

Mrs. Jasinska glanced over her shoulder. A stooped figure had begun shuffling over the sun-bleached lobby carpet. It was Jerzy, the Columbian's withered, weary-looking bell coot. (It had been many a year since you could have called him a bell *boy*.) He'd emerged from some shadowy corner, where I suspect his employer kept him propped up like a disused broom, and was now trudging toward us with all the speed and spritely vigor of a sleepwalking tortoise. At his current speed, he wouldn't reach the front desk until around June of 1902.

We were, for all intents and purposes, alone.

"Alright, you talked me into it," Mrs. Jasinska said. "Actually, it's rather exciting helping you sleuths with a real case. Do you think that wonderful Mr. Brady will want to question me, too?"

"Feh," Gustav growled. "I don't know any *wonderful* Mr. Brady. The only Brady I've seen hereabouts is about as wonderful as a dose of—"

I clapped my brother on the back with a forced laugh. "Always joshin' the competition, this one! 'Old Funnybone,' they call him. But all japes aside, ma'am, what is it Miss Crowe wanted to know?"

"Well, mostly she was curious about everyone's comings and goings last night. I told her the first coming *and* going were both Mr. Curtis: I saw him stagger up to his room in a shocking state around eight thirty, then stagger out again almost immediately."

"Was—?"

"William Pinkerton with him?" Mrs. Jasinska cut in before Old Red could get out another word. "No. He was alone."

"And when he went out, did it look like he was—?"

"Carrying something? Miss Crowe asked that as well. And the answer is yes, he was. He had a large brown valise with him. There must have been something quite heavy in it: He walked out at a tilt. Not that he was all that straight when he came in."

"The egg," I said to my brother.

He nodded, then turned back to Mrs. Jasinska. "What happened after Curtis left?"

"Why, you yourselves came in, actually. With Mr. Smythe. That was no more than five minutes after Mr. Curtis went out. I didn't see you two the rest of the evening, of course, but Mr. Smythe went out again a little before nine."

Gustav opened his mouth, but Diana apparently beat him to the next question yet again: This time, Mrs. Jasinska was answering before he could say a thing.

"To buy cigars, he claimed. I told him we have a variety of smooth-smoking coronas and robustos at far better prices than he'd find at any tobacconist's. Right here in my desk. But he didn't even want to look at them." Mrs. Jasinska opened her eyes wide and tilted her head to the side. "Suspicious, hmm?"

"Maybe the man's particular about his brands," I said. If the lady's coronas and robustos were as high-quality as her hotel, they'd be about as smooth-smoking as a rolled-up doormat.

"So when did Smythe—?"

"Return? Around ten thirty." Mrs. Jasinska waggled her eyebrows at Old Red. "Quite a ramble just to pick up some cigars."

My brother mused on that a moment, then bucked the thought off with a shake of the head. "Howzabout everyone else? When'd they get back?"

"By eleven thirty, when I lock the front door and retire, all our guests had returned but Mr. Curtis."

"Who was the last of us in?"

"That would be Mr. Brady."

"And how'd he look?"

"Oh," Mrs. Jasinska sighed, "magnificent."

"I mean," Gustav grated out, "did he seem distressed? Nervous? Was he mussed up? *Were his shoes dirty?*"

Mrs. Jasinska chortled. "I wasn't looking at his *shoes,* Old Funnybone."

My brother looked like he'd finally reached the tipping point where mere irritation spills over into the urge to kill.

"I was asleep not long after that . . . and such dreams I had!" Mrs. Jasinska went on, unaware how precariously her life hung in the balance. "And yes, before you ask, there was one more incident that night. As you know, I have a room just off the lobby, so as to be available if any of my guests need assistance. And sometime very late—I have no idea when—I was awakened by a thump in the rear."

"A thump in the rear?" Old Red repeated warily.

The lady nodded. "A muffled crash at the back of the hotel. It sounded like it was outside, in the alley. It might have been nothing—a cat knocking over a garbage can—and I went right back to sleep afterward. But I thought I should mention it. After that, it was a typically calm, quiet Columbian Hotel night. In the morning, however, who should come stomping in but Mr. William Pinkerton himself? Mr. Curtis had missed an appointment with him for breakfast, it seemed, and he was not happy to have been kept waiting. We went up to Mr. Curtis's room together and, after we'd knocked and waited for a respectable period, I let Mr. Pinkerton in."

"You let him go into Curtis's room, but not us?" I shook my head and did my best to look cut to the quick. "Really, Mrs. Jasinska . . ."

"I'm sorry, but I didn't know Mr. Curtis was dead at the time, did I? I assumed he was simply indisposed. Plus, it was William Pinkerton asking. How could I refuse? He's not just a magazine sleuth. He's practically a real policeman."

"He's pigheaded enough to be one, that's for sure," Gustav grumbled. "Anyhow, so in he goes, and then what?"

"He didn't stay long. I think he was as surprised as I to find the bed empty. He just walked around the room once, picked up a bundle of papers Mr. Curtis had left atop his dresser, then left."

"You let him take something out of a guest's room?" I asked.

"He said he needed it." Mrs. Jasinska shrugged. "And it was William Pinkerton."

"I think I'd like to try bein' William Pinkerton one of these days," I said.

"And after that?" Old Red said to Mrs. Jasinska.

"Nothing—until Miss Crowe returned from the fairgrounds with the bad news."

Gustav nodded slowly and rubbed his mustache, brow beetled. Mrs. Jasinska and I watched him a moment, waiting for more questions that didn't come.

"Miss Crowe stopped there, too," the lady said to me.

"Oh, I ain't done just yet," Old Red said. "I got three questions I know Miss Crowe wouldn't have thrown at you, cuz they all have to do with that 'admirer' who came in lookin' for us last night. The bearded feller."

"Yes? What about him?"

"Well, number one, you said he wanted to know if we was stayin' here with the other folks from the contest . . . which makes me wonder how he knew they was here in the first place. He say anything that'd explain that?"

"No, now that you mention it, he didn't."

"Alright. Number two, did he have an accent?"

"Yes, I believe he did. Not one I recognized, though."

"Fair enough. And number three." Gustav turned toward me. "Is that his coat my brother's wearin'?"

"His coat?" Mrs. Jasinska peered at the long, dark overcoat I'd claimed for myself that afternoon. "I don't know. It could be."

"So that feller who jumped us today . . . ?" I began.

"Was trailin' us last night," Old Red said. "Yesterday afternoon, too, I reckon."

"That's right. The bearded man who tried to hire away our wheelchairs. That must've been him."

"Yup."

"Curiouser and curiouser. Kinda muddies the waters, don't it? I mean, if the bearded man's hooked into this . . ."

My brother let that one just float out there, which was probably for the best. Mrs. Jasinska surely wouldn't have been pleased if either of us finished that particular thought.

Maybe the killer's not another guest at the Columbian like we figured.

"Is it my turn yet?"

Gustav and I turned toward the source of the phlegmy, heavily accented voice.

Jerzy had completed his voyage across the lobby at last.

"You talk so long, I know what you talk *about*," he said. "And I know you will want to talk about it with me just like the young lady did."

"Miss Crowe already spoke to you?" I said.

The old man nodded.

"I won't waste your time with questions, then," Gustav said. "Just tell me what you told her."

Jerzy slowly hoisted his bony shoulders up into a shrug. "About the night, I tell her nothing because I notice nothing. The ears, any-more? Not so good. And at any rate, this one"—he jerked his head at Mrs. Jasinska—"she gives me a closet for my cot, and in there I may as well be in my coffin, for all I can hear. You'd think with half the hotel empty, I would not have to sleep with mops and buckets, but no. That's not how we do things here at the Waldorf."

"Oh, Jerzy."

Mrs. Jasinska reached out to give the man a playful swat. Or maybe not so playful.

"So I hear not a thing," he went on. "In the morning, though? I see." Jerzy opened his rheumy eyes wide, milking the moment for all its melodrama. *"Stolec."*

"Stolec?" I said.

"The young lady asked about stains," Mrs. Jasinska explained with an uncomfortable squirm. *"Brown* stains. Perhaps with a certain odor."

"Oh!" I said. *"Stolec!"*

Jerzy nodded. "I cleaned it up, of course. You would not think I would bother, with what I am paid. I could have left it to the maids. But what can I say? I am devoted to my work."

"Where?" Old Red asked.

"Come. I will show you."

Considering the speed (or lack of same) with which the bellhop moved, we could have asked Mrs. Jasinska a lot more questions— gotten in a couple games of chess, even—before bothering to follow him toward the stairs. Yet we wished the lady a good afternoon and toddled along with Jerzy all the same.

"The 'stow-leck' was on the second floor?" my brother asked him.

Jerzy grunted.

"Where everyone from the contest's stayin'?"

Jerzy shrugged.

"Was it in front of a particular door?"

Jerzy grunted and shrugged.

"Just be patient," I said to my brother. "You'll get your answers soon enough."

"That I will. All of 'em, maybe. Cuz if those stains lead us to a specific room—"

"Then the feller we're huntin' *is* a guest here . . . and we'll know which one."

"That's about the size of it."

"So," Jerzy wheezed when we finally reached the second floor, "about the stains . . ."

He paused to catch his breath.

"Yeah?" my brother prodded him.

"There are no stains."

Old Red narrowed his eyes. "Cuz you wiped 'em up."

Jerzy shook his head. "Because there never were any stains. I just needed to get you away from that one."

The old man nodded back down the stairs, presumably at his employer.

Gustav groaned, shoulders slumping. "No stains . . ."

"But I can offer you something else," Jerzy said. "The girl wanted to know which room the dead man was staying in. You do, as well?"

Old Red snapped straight again. "That's right."

Jerzy raised a palsied claw of a hand, the wrinkle-etched palm pointing up.

"Pay the man," my brother sighed.

I reached into my pocket, pulled out a couple quarters, and started to hand them over.

Jerzy shook his head. "Don't even."

So I covered his palm with a greenback instead.

"The girl gave me five," Jerzy said.

"Then the girl is a spendthrift."

Jerzy just kept his hand out, saying no more.

"Oh, for God's sake, give him what he wants," Gustav snapped. "I swear, you are the worst briber I ever saw."

"I'll give *you* ten bucks to shut up."

"Feh."

"Two-twelve," Jerzy said once he'd pocketed his fee. And with that he shambled off toward the stairs again, perhaps headed to his closet for a celebratory nap.

"Hey," Old Red called after him. "One more thing—on the house this time, if you please. Who does your shoe shinin'?"

"For the guests?" Jerzy said. "We send the shoes out to a boot-black. At Kenwood and Sixty-first. Pyle, his name is."

"You still sniffin' after that cow flop?" I asked as the old-timer scuffle-stepped away.

"I ain't forgettin' about it, anyway. Right now, though, we got other business to attend to."

"Business in two-twelve?"

Old Red nodded. "I got me a hunch."

"Care to share it?"

"Nope."

"You know what? I think you're just bullshittin' when you do that. 'I got me a hunch,' you say, and then anything we find out later, you can claim you was thinkin' all along."

"Now you're catchin' on," my brother said in a tone you could almost call jocular. Something seemed to be putting him in an uncommonly good mood all of a sudden. "Come on."

A moment later, we were at the end of the hall, before room 212. I expected Gustav to fish out the little length of wire he's taken to toting around ever since learning (courtesy of the nonexistent Nick Carter) how to pick locks. So imagine my surprise when he just knocked on the door instead.

"Uhhhh, Brother," I said. "In case you forgot, Mr. Curtis ain't around to answer."

"I ain't forgot."

And then I heard the footsteps, and the door swung open.

"Finally," Diana Crowe said. "What took you so long?"

15

WILD CARDS

Or, Diana Reveals (Almost) All, and a New Clue Points to an Old Acquaintance

Diana rushed us inside and closed the door, and I was relieved to see the colonel hadn't been waiting with her.

I then envisioned what the man would do if he caught us alone in a hotel room with his daughter, and my relief turned to alarm.

"Where's your father?" I asked.

"He's not in the next room loading his shotgun, if that's what you're worried about," Diana said. "He's still at the fairgrounds. I told him I needed to lie down and collect myself after this afternoon's excitement."

I cocked an eyebrow at that, and when I glanced at Gustav I found him with an identical look of skepticism on his face. Diana wasn't the swooning type.

"He believed that, did he?" my brother asked.

"Probably not. He's determined to see as much of the White City as he can in preparation for tomorrow's competition, though, and he knew I'd be bad company if I didn't want to be there."

"Ain't he worried the contest's gonna be canceled?" I said.

"Certainly. Yet he wants to be ready, all the same. He's a military man. He plans for all contingencies."

"I see," I said.

Gustav cut loose with a "Hmmm."

The silence that then descended was so uncomfortable, if it were a shirt it would have been made from sandpaper and baling wire. Here we were at last with the woman who, from a certain point of view, had brought us to Chicago in the first place. Yet I found myself unable to even look into her beautiful brown eyes.

So I took in the room instead. There was so little to take, though—a scratch-gouged floor, a dresser, a bed little bigger than a bassinet, a window affording a breathtaking view of dingy brick across a trash-strewn alley. Soon I found myself simply looking off at nothing.

"So," Diana said.

"So," I said.

"He's your father," said Old Red.

"Not quite," the lady replied.

My brother squinted at her. "Not quite?"

"Oh, God," I groaned before I could stop myself. "You ain't married to him, are you?"

Diana looked at me as though I'd just asked her to change my diaper. *"What?"*

"Well, I mean, I'd noticed . . . both of us had . . . it's hard not to notice, really . . . that you and your dad . . . the colonel, I mean . . . that you two ain't exactly peas in a pod, looks-wise."

"Colonel Crowe adopted me when I was a child," Diana said, speaking slowly, as one would when addressing the village idiot. (And I cannot deny that, in our little village of three, I was the one for the job.) "He and my father served together in . . ." She shook her head and looked away. "It's a long story, and there's no reason to go into it now."

"Why didn't you tell it to us before?" Gustav asked.

Diana let out a long breath as one will when asked an obvious question one's pondered often—without ever coming up with a decent answer.

"When I first met you, I was a spotter for the railroad under orders not to reveal my true identity. After that . . . well, it becomes harder to explain. I was just being cautious, I suppose. Wary. Out of habit, perhaps. I've been hiding behind other names for a long time now, and I find I've grown to like it. I started working for the colonel nearly ten years ago, and in all that time, not half a dozen people with the Southern Pacific even knew who I really was. The colonel liked it that way. As you might recall, he was always convinced the railroad was riddled with spies. A certain . . . predisposition for distrust has always been one of his eccentricities."

"That's putting it kindly," I said.

When Diana went on talking, she was looking at Old Red alone.

"I saw such potential in you, such promise, and I just wanted to be certain of it before I put all my cards on the table. Plus, I knew it would be awkward when you finally learned everything." She threw me a look again, and I was relieved to see it included a wry smile. "I was well aware you might not have the highest opinion of the colonel yourselves. Believe me, though, I never would've wanted the truth to come out the way it did. We had no idea you two were going to be here, at first. When my father—" Diana's eyes flared, shooting me a warning I'd be wise to heed. "And, yes, Otto—I do think of him as my father. When he bought our way into the contest, he was told Mr. Smythe's representative would be someone called 'Dan Slick, the Dude Dick.'"

"Dan Slick, the Dude Dick?" My brother snorted. "That's worse than 'the Holmes of the Range.'"

I was gracious enough to let that slap pass without reply.

"Funny we ain't never heard of him," I said. "We've sampled every dime novel dick out there."

"You ever hear what happened to Mr. Slick?" Gustav asked the lady.

"No. We arrived Sunday afternoon, and by then the switch had already been made. Dan Slick was out, you were in. The colonel was actually quite enthused when he heard the news."

"Cuz now he'd have the chance to show us up for the country bumpkins we really are," Old Red said.

"Exactly. The colonel was with the Southern Pacific Railroad Police fourteen years. Then he hired you two, and he was sacked within half a week. You can't blame him for being bitter."

"I don't," Gustav said, "but I get the feelin' . . . well . . ." He drifted over to the window and pretended to inspect something down in the alley below. "The way he keeps herdin' you away from us makes me think there's more to it than that. Something other than him just holdin' a grudge."

Suddenly, Diana looked like she wanted her own window to stare out. Or escape through.

"You're right. There is something else," she said. "You know I've been trying to talk the colonel into hiring you for his new detective agency. Unfortunately, I was a bit too persistent. He's gotten it into his head that I have an emotional reason for wanting the two of you to join us."

"Emotional?" I said.

"Personal."

I think I got it then. Some part of me just wanted to hear the lady say it.

I furrowed my brow and cocked my head.

"Intimate," Diana said.

"Oh. Oh! You mean he thinks you've . . . you're . . . you

might . . . ? With one of us?" I had to gulp and loosen my collar before carrying on. "Whatever gave him that idea?"

"You did. You came right out and told him as much."

"When did I . . . ?"

I cut myself off before I could say something stupid. Alas, this is not something one's able to do *ex post facto*.

"My book."

Diana nodded. "Your book."

No wonder the colonel didn't trust us, given what I'd written about the lady. I may as well have sent a note to a pitchfork-toting farmer: *Will be behind the woodshed tonight defiling your daughter. Aim for the head.*

"I owe you an apology, miss," I said. "I always figured they'd cut that stuff out along with all the naughty words and blood and whatnot. And I never dreamed the colonel would read any of it."

"He's read it," Diana said. "As have I."

"What are you two talkin' about?" Gustav asked, finally stepping away from his window.

I started looking for one of my own.

One advantage to reading a book out for an audience—assuming you know that audience as well as, say, a brother—is the opportunity to skip the bits that'll get the chilliest reception. Or even spark a fight. So when reading my yarns to Old Red, certain passages I had a tendency to skim over with a droned "Etc. and so on and so forth." Which was fine with my brother, as he was only interested in the deducifying anyway and frowned mightily on flowery descriptions and allegedly humorous asides and other such folderol. But now the folderol had caught up to us.

"*On the Wrong Track,*" I said. "There are some parts in it that get a little . . . well, I guess I was pretty honest about how much we both enjoy workin' with Miss Crowe. How very, *very* much."

Gustav's face went the dark red of rose petals.

I was just glad *The Black Dove* hadn't seen print yet. That one would turn him purple.

"Etc. and so on and so forth, huh?" Old Red said to me.

"It was in the 'so on.'" I sighed. "How come this never happened to Doc Watson?"

"Doc Watson ain't a goddamn idjit."

"You might just be onto something there."

"Feh—enough of this," my brother spat. "You and me can pick it up again later. For now, it's neither here nor there. It's just good to know where we stand with Colonel Crowe—which is in the shitter, thanks to you."

"He apologizes for his foul language," I said to Diana.

"I'll handle my own apologies, dammit."

"He apologizes for that, too."

"No, I don't."

"*Gustav. Otto,*" Diana said, and she didn't go on till it was clear our traps were shut and were going to stay so. "There is no need for apologies. I grew up around soldiers. If I let a little swearing unsettle me, I would never have survived to adulthood. And, in any case, Gustav is right. So far as the colonel's concerned, you two are in the shitter. There is a way out, though. Colonel Crowe might be irascible, opinionated, distrustful, and not especially inclined toward forgiveness, but if there's one thing he respects, it's results." She looked at my brother. "I've told him again and again how brilliant I think you are."

I didn't *think* I grimaced, but I must have from the way Diana turned toward me and smiled reassuringly.

"And how brave and resourceful you are, Otto. But words haven't been enough. You've got to show the colonel what you can do. Prove you're the great detectives I say you are."

"And the manure clue didn't do it," Old Red said.

Diana shook her head. "The manure clue most definitely did not do it."

"It is a good clue, though."

"Most instructive."

"We found us some Herefords nearby, by the way. In the Stock Pavilion. And there were dung stains on a windowsill over to the Agriculture Building. Inside, too, we was told, though they'd been mopped up by the time we got to 'em."

"Well, then. That settles it."

"Couldn't be more obvious."

Gustav and Diana kept their eyes locked on each other as they talked, as was their way when bandying about clues. It was always like that when the two of them put their heads together: The rest of the world was blotted out entirely. Including me.

This time, though, I was determined not to be a blottee.

"Yup," I chimed in. "It's positively elementary."

From the looks on their faces as they turned toward me, you'd have thought it was the dresser that had piped up.

"Curtis leaves the restaurant," I said, "comes back here, and collects his clues for the next day's contest. Then he heads back to the White City and starts spreadin' 'em around. Somewhere in there, the killer gets to ridin' drag on him—and Curtis almost spots him. He finds a place to hide just in time, though: a cattle pen, where he mucks up his shoes. It's plenty dark by then, so when he sets off after Curtis again, he don't realize he's leavin' a trail. When Curtis goes into the Agriculture Building, the killer slips in through a window, for some reason. And when he finds Curtis up atop the Mammoth Cheese—passed out, maybe, like folks've been guessin'—he takes the opportunity to smother him. With his foot on the back of the man's head, you understand, so as to shove his face down deep into the cheese. In the process, he grinds that plop off the bottom of his shoe into Curtis's hair. Then he leaves, thinkin' everyone'll just chalk it up to some kinda bee-zar accident. Only he don't reckon on *us*."

Diana gave me a round of applause and a "Bravo!" Yet though my brother's always needling me about my detecting, he didn't seem particularly pleased to see me Holmesifying at his and the lady's speed now.

"Not bad," he muttered.

"So the manner in which Curtis was killed isn't really in question," Diana said, "and I daresay the motive isn't, either. At that dinner last night, Curtis flaunted his willingness and ability to publicly humiliate any of us. Brady, Greene, Valmont—he hinted at secrets he's uncovered about them all. And Tousey and Blackheath-Murray and Smythe all stand to lose thousands if their heroes' reputations are besmirched. So that gives us six suspects. A nice round number easily divided between the three of us."

"I'm afraid it ain't as tidy as that," Old Red said. "We got us a wild card." He looked to me while jerking his head at the lady. "Tell her about him."

I knew straight off who "him" was: the Bearded Man. I told Diana how he'd tried to steal our wheeled chairs, then come sniffing around the hotel and later yet waylaid us and smashed Gustav's glasses.

"Obviously, someone's trying to sabotage your chances in the contest," Diana said when I was done. "He meant to strand you at the Kansas Building yesterday, and today he tried to deprive Gustav of his shaded spectacles thinking it would slow him down or perhaps even blind him." She turned a quizzical look on my brother. "I've been meaning to ask about those glasses myself, by the way. Did you ever really need them?"

"We'll swap long stories, one of these days," Old Red said.

"Right now, I think it's about time we gave that coat a good goin' over."

I shrugged off the overcoat, a little embarrassed to realize I'd been carrying fresh evidence around on my back without even thinking of it.

"Got a tag here in the lining," I said. "'Manookian Bros. Fine Tailoring, Cleveland.'"

"Anything in the pockets?" Diana asked.

"Nope. That I would've noticed a . . . well, hel-lo, to coin a phrase."

There was an inside pocket I hadn't noted up to then, and when I slipped my fingers into it I felt a piece of thin paper.

I drew out a folded note and snapped it open. I started reading it aloud, was interrupted by my own "I'll be damned," then had to start over. This is what I read:

> Enclosed you will find the money order I promised your
> father. Please have him take you to the train station
> immediately. He knows where to find me here.
>
> Do not delay, my little friend! Many challenges lie ahead,
> but so, too, does glory!
>
> Your pal,
> Urias Smythe

The stunned silence that fell over us proved fortuitous. Without it, we might have missed the sound of footsteps echoing down the hallway.

Then the sound of a woman saying, "Right this way, Sergeant. Room two-twelve."

Then the sound of jingling keys.

16

THE MOTHER LODE
Or, New Clues Fall into Our Lap (After Our Laps Fall upon Them)

The room had no closet for us to jump in. The bed was too low to the ground for us to slide under. The dresser drawers were, as one might imagine, too small for us to dive into.

All of which left us only two options, so far as I could see: We could throw the overcoat over our heads and hope we'd be taken for a coat rack or we could simply make ourselves comfortable and wait to get caught.

My brother had a bit more imagination. So much so, in fact, for a moment I thought he'd forgotten we can't fly.

He threw open the window, turned to me, and whispered one word: "Out."

"But we're on the second—"

"What exactly are you looking for?" I heard Mrs. Jasinska ask out in the hall.

"In my line of work," replied a man with a soft Irish brogue, "one often doesn't know till one finds it."

"Ah. Well. Here we are, Sergeant."

That last I barely caught, for I was already slipping over the sill and letting gravity do the rest.

There was a heap of junk down in the alley below: metal garbage cans and boxes of discarded bric-a-brac and a stained mattress that, presumably, was too odiferous and lice-infested for even such as the Columbian Hotel. It was this last I aimed for.

I hit it, too. Or half of me did, anyway. My other half hit one of the trash cans, upending its contents all over myself as I oofed flat onto my back. I barely had time to notice the malodorous rubbish spilling over my belly and chest, though, for it soon had company in the form of my brother.

"Christ!" I wheezed.

"Up!" snapped Old Red.

I managed to stagger to my feet and clasp hold of his hands just in time to catch the plummeting form of Diana Crowe.

The three of us ended up in a heap back on the litter-strewn pavement.

"We're looking for clues," Diana said as she writhed her way over and off me.

(Knowing, as I do now, that she and her father might actually read this book, I will make no comment here on said writhing or any effect it might have had on me.)

A moment later, the three of us were pawing through garbage on our hands and knees.

"Found anything yet?" Gustav asked loudly.

"No," I blared back. "Golly, I'm starting to think this isn't a good use of our time."

A soft, lilting "Excuse me" floated down from on high, and we all looked up to find a pleasant-looking fellow sporting a neatly trimmed mustache and a bowler hat staring down at us from Curtis's open window.

The three of us stood up.

"Yes?" Diana said.

"May I ask what you're doing?"

"There've been some odd goin's-on round here," Old Red replied. "We've taken it upon ourselves to look into it."

"By going through the trash?"

"We got our reasons. We disturbin' you? Keepin' you from a nap or something?"

The man smiled and let a moment pass before answering. I got the feeling he was trying to decide whether to call us liars or play along.

"Oh, this isn't my room." He tipped his hat. "I'm Detective Sergeant Moses Ryan of the Chicago Police Department. You wouldn't be the Amlingmeyer brothers, would you? And Miss Diana Crowe?"

"That's right," Diana said. "It's a pleasure to meet you, Sergeant. Are you here investigating the death of Mr. Curtis?"

"Indeed I am, and it's most fortunate I've bumped into you like this. We've been trying to get word to everyone who's here for the contest: Mr. Pinkerton would like all of you to gather in the lobby in twenty minutes. He has an announcement to make. After he's done, I'll be conducting private interviews with each of you. If you think you could make yourselves available . . . ?"

"Of course," Diana said.

"Anything to be of service," I threw in.

Gustav just glowered.

"Splendid. Thank you so much," Sergeant Ryan said, and once again he smiled and tipped his hat. "Well . . . carry on."

He ducked back into the room and closed the window.

"For a lawman, he's awful polite," I said. "I almost expected him to invite us up for a slice of pie."

"Yeah," my brother muttered. "I don't like it."

"If the man was a bastard, you'd be happy?"

"Not happy. But happier."

Diana crouched down next to the overturned litter bin. "I think I've found something here."

"No need for more playactin'," I said. "The sergeant ain't watchin' no more."

"I'm not pretending." The lady reached into the can and pulled out a plum-colored wedge studded with big, thick teeth. "Correct me if I'm wrong, but this looks an awful lot like—"

"The jawbone of an ass," Gustav finished for her. "Painted purple."

I stuck a finger in my right ear and gave it a good cleaning. "Did I just hear you say that's the jawbone of an ass painted purple?"

My brother jerked his chin at the dark, L-shaped bone in the lady's hands. "What's it look like to you?"

I gave the thing a good long stare.

"The jawbone of an ass painted purple," I at last concluded.

"Well, there you go."

Old Red squatted beside Diana, peered into the garbage can a moment, then pulled from it a pair of clunky wooden shoes in which had been stuffed two huge potatoes.

"Time to call in the National Geographic Society," I said. "I think we just found the back door to Wonderland."

My brother just stood and tipped the can over, spilling its contents onto the ground. In amongst the to-be-expected newspapers and apple cores and cigar butts and such we found the following:

> • a stuffed squirrel clothed in a miniature tuxedo;

> • a copy of the book *Phrenology and Its Application to Education, Insanity, and Prison Discipline*, in which had been wedged a single turkey feather;

- a fruitcake with what appeared to be bits of gravel baked into it in place of the customary candied cherries and slivers of orange peel;

- a shattered bust of Queen Victoria (Diana recognized the subject from the combination of crown and jowls);

- and a small box containing a torn ferry ticket, several snail shells (shriveled-up dead snail included), a clove of garlic, and a yellow-brown lump my brother identified as rancid butter.

Once we'd sorted through it all—and managed to get our popping eyes back in our skulls—Old Red stepped back a ways and looked first at the trash can, then up at Curtis's window, then back at the can, then back at the window.

"You're thinkin' of Mrs. Jasinska's thump in the rear," I said.

"Yup."

"Excuse me?" Diana said.

"The noise Mrs. Jasinska heard last night," Gustav explained. "The crash in the alley."

Diana followed my brother's line of sight, nodding. "Yes. Of course. It would've been a straight drop into the garbage can from Curtis's room. So that settles it. The killer *has* been in the hotel. He was up there last night."

"Yup. Chucking all this out the window."

"A brilliant deduction," I said. "Only what is 'all this'?"

"Damned if I know." Old Red looked over at the lady, then whipped his gaze away again just as fast. "I mean *darned* if I know."

For a second there, Diana seemed to be stifling a smile.

"Unfortunately, we can't be sure this is everything that was thrown out," she said. "In a big city like this, you'll have vagrants picking through the garbage every night. Anything valuable or edible would've been scavenged by dawn."

"So for all we know, half our clues are gone," Gustav said glumly.

"You really think we need more?" I asked him. "This here's the mother lode. It's just too bad not a one of them makes any kind of sense."

"Everything makes sense," Diana said. "You simply have to find the right way of looking at it."

She turned to my brother for confirmation. He gave her a rueful shrug instead.

"I used to think that," he said. "I still might, on a good day. But I can't say this one's been especially—"

At that moment, the back door to the hotel opened, and the not-so-good day got even worse.

Sergeant Ryan stepped out into the alley, a big uniformed bull right behind him.

"Hello, there," the sergeant said. "You looked like you were having so much fun back here, we just had to join you."

"What grand timing," I said. "We were just about to run and fetch you, weren't we?"

Diana nodded. Old Red didn't bother.

Ryan cocked his head, eyes a-twinkle. "How fortunate it is we should come along and save you the trip. Now . . . what's that you've got there, hmm?"

I peeped over at Gustav for the go-ahead, and he gave it to me with a single downward jerk of the head. So I told the sergeant of Mrs. Jasinska's thump in the night and the curious curios we'd discovered under Curtis's window—omitting the fact that we'd discovered them by falling on them.

As I spoke, Ryan nodded in a pleasant, friendly, interested sort of way, though I got the feeling he'd be nodding just the same if I were telling him I was the king of the pixies. When I was done, he turned toward the pebble cake and the tuxedoed squirrel and the rest of it.

"So you found all this, you say?"

"Yes. He did just say," Gustav growled.

"Hmm. Very cluey, these clues of yours."

"What's that supposed to mean?" Diana asked. She didn't growl like my brother, but she sure wasn't purring, either.

"Well," Ryan said, "this is exactly the kind of thing one would read about in a detective story, isn't it? You know—'The Case of the Purple Jawbone' or 'The Turkey Feather Mystery' or the like. That you should be the ones to stumble upon such singular evidence strikes me as . . . ironic."

"You ain't suggesting we put these things here, are you?" Old Red asked.

"Oh, no. Why would you do something like that?" Ryan rolled his eyes heavenward and tapped a finger against his chin, as if struck by a sudden thought. "Aside from the publicity, of course. You are here to make names for yourselves as detectives."

"If you're gonna call me a liar, I wish you'd just speak it plain," I said.

"A writer of dime novels? Pass along anything but the unvarnished truth? Perish the thought! Believe me, I'm ever so grateful you brought all this to my attention, and you can rest assured I'll give it all the attention it deserves. Now, if you'd let me get to it."

Ryan stepped to the side and swept his arm out toward the door he'd come through a few minutes before.

We were being invited to leave—without our evidence—and the way the copper behind Ryan glared at us, it was clear the invitation was going to become an order right quick.

Gustav just glared at the two men a moment.

"Come on," he finally sighed, and he started for the door.

"You gonna let it go that easy?" I said as Diana and I started after him.

"They got the badges . . . dammit."

As we passed Sergeant Ryan, he gave us a genial tip of the hat.

When we stepped inside, we found ourselves in a long, dark corridor leading to the lobby of the Columbian Hotel. The big cop closed the door firmly behind us.

"It's too bad we didn't get more time with them clues," Old Red said, "but it ain't like we got nothing to do."

"Oh, yeah?"

"Yeah. We know exactly where Curtis's killer's gonna be in ten minutes. Heck, he might even be there already."

"There," Diana said, pointing ahead to the lobby. "Waiting to hear what Pinkerton has to say."

My brother nodded. "What say we join him?"

17

THE PROFESSIONALS

Or, Old Red Tries to Pin Down Some Suspects and Gets Needled Instead

When we got to the end of the hall, I leaned out for a cautious peep around the lobby. Only two of our colleague/competitor/suspects were already there: Eugene Valmont and Boothby Greene. They were sitting next to each other about fifty feet away, seemingly deep in conversation.

When I reported what I'd seen, Diana said it was time for us to part company again.

"I understand," I replied with a sullenness I found both embarrassing and impossible to squelch. "You can't have it gettin' back to the colonel we been workin' together."

"Yes, there's that," Diana said. "I was also thinking it would be to our advantage if *the killer* didn't know it."

"Oh. Yeah. Good point."

"What's more, a lady can't take a tumble in the trash and get away with it. I need to freshen up."

"When will we see you again?" I asked. "I mean, not just see you. Be with you. To talk to, I mean. About the—"

"Can you shake the colonel and meet us again tonight?" my brother butted in.

Diana nodded. "The Japanese Ho-o-den. Nine twenty."

"We'll be there," Old Red said firmly. He waited till the lady was gone to ask, "What the hell's a Ho-Ho Den?"

"Some kinda church, I think. In the White City. The guide-book says it's a 'temple,' Japanese style. It's out on that island in the middle of the big lagoon."

"Good. Sounds like the perfect place to meet on the sly."

"I just wish it didn't have to be on the sly."

"And who do we have to thank for that?"

"Well." I cleared my throat and held out an arm toward the lobby. "Shall we?"

"In a tick. There's something I wanna talk over with you first . . ."

A moment later, we were sidling up to the settee Valmont and Greene were sharing.

"Afternoon, gents," I said. "Waitin' for the big powwow?"

Both men stared at me blankly.

"The big pa-WOW?" Valmont said.

My brother eased himself into a shabby old armchair the color of a tombstone. "The meetin' Pinkerton called," he explained.

There was another divan next to the one the Frenchman and the Englishman were sharing, but I could see why Gustav hadn't settled his American rump upon it: It looked like it had, until all too recently, resided in the nearest dump, and there was no telling what smells—or occupants—might still be lingering in the vicinity.

I chose to stand.

"Yes," Greene said. "We were just speculating as to what Mr. Pinkerton will say."

"Afraid he's gonna call off the contest?" my brother asked.

"It might seem disrespectfell to M. Curtis, but . . . yes," Valmont replied. "We have come a long way to be here, M. Greene and I. To lose this opportunity because of an ill-timed axy-dawn would be most misfortunable."

"And then there's Mr. Curtis himself to think of," Greene added. "He saw his involvement in the competition as a tribute to his fallen hero. I rather think he'd want us to carry on."

"Tribute's a nice way to put it," I said. "The way Curtis was talkin' last night, it seemed more like a vendetta . . . against *us*."

"That's right," Old Red said. "He was throwin' around all sorts of hints about the dirt he had on folks. With you, Mr. Greene, it was something about not havin' a birthday. And you, Miz-yer Val-MONT . . . well, I couldn't repeat it even if I could remember it, but it was some kinda 'la affair' in the French papers."

Valmont folded then unfolded his arms, crossed then uncrossed his legs, turned his body this way then that.

His scowl didn't waver.

"Hmph," he said.

Greene, on the other hand, was all cool amusement. "Come, come, Valmont . . . we were going to be asked about it sooner or later. The only surprise to me is that Mr. Amlingmeyer beat Miss Larson to it."

"Not to mention the po-lease," Old Red said.

"It remains to be seen which tack the official inquiry is going to take," Greene replied mildly.

Valmont clasped then unclasped his hands.

"Hmph," he said again.

"Fine. I'll go first," Greene said. "I assume Mr. Curtis conducted research on all of us before coming to Chicago. The better to unearth our weaknesses. When it came to Boothby Greene, however, he would find none—because he would find nothing at all.

Boothby Greene has no birthday because Boothby Greene does not exist."

"I ain't lookin' at him?" I asked.

"You're looking at a man calling himself Boothby Greene, yes—but the name is a fiction."

Valmont stopped his fidgeting and hmphing and stared at Greene in naked fascination.

"So who are you?" he asked.

"A private inquiry agent of, I like to think, some skill—though that's not why Blackheath-Murray has high hopes for me." He gave both hands a *voilà* flourish just beneath his long, lean, oh-so-Sherlocky face. "I do fit a certain mold. And a highly profitable one, at that."

"And your real name is . . . ?" my brother asked.

The Englishman's prim smile turned wry.

"Shlomo Lindenbaum."

From Valmont: "Oh."

From Gustav: "Ah."

From me: "Whoa!"

Far be it for a fellow named Otto Albert Amlingmeyer to pass judgment on the mellifluousness of another's name, but it was a safe bet *The Adventures of Shlomo Lindenbaum* wouldn't exactly fly off the magazine racks.

We all gave this revelation a moment to sink in, then one by one we turned—Old Red and Shlomo and I—to Eugene Valmont.

"So it is my turn?" The Frenchman heaved a heavy sigh. "'*L'Affaire des cinq cent diamants.*' That is what M. Curtis was speaking of. 'The Affair of the Five Hundred Diamonds.' A great scawn-dell in Frawnce. The details are unimportant—and, for me, unpleasant to relate. But the *point essentiel* is that the case was bun-GELD and, as a result, I did not simply retire from the Sûreté. I resign-NED in disgrass."

"Disgrass?" Old Red said.

"Disgrace," I whispered.

"Right. Sorry."

Valmont shrugged. "*C'est la vie*. I am here to start again. Begin a new life, and begin it well. As is Monsieur . . . ?"

He turned to the man sitting next to him.

"Let's just stick with Greene, shall we?" Shlomo said.

"Of course. As is M. Greene. And you, too, M. Amlingmeyer. It is in all our interests that the competi-shawn continue. M. Curtis's death is a tragedy, but it need not be an ob-sta-clay."

"Ob-sta-clay?" Old Red said.

"Damned if I know," I whispered.

"Obstacle?" Greene guessed.

"*Exactemente.*"

My brother let loose with a hmph of his own.

"An inconvenience, you mean," he said.

Valmont took on a look of doleful dejection. "You make me sound so cold, monsieur."

"If the shoe fits," Gustav said, and his eyes met mine as he brought up a finger and lightly scratched the tip of his prodigious nose.

He was giving me a signal. One I wasn't much looking forward to, either. But Old Red had insisted, so I reluctantly reached into my vest pocket and pulled out my watch.

"Where is everybody, anyway? Must be almost . . . oops."

It was a hunter-case watch without a chain, so when I let the springing of the lid pop it out of my fumbling fingers, the little "accident" didn't look *completely* bogus. Only ninety-five percent. Ninety-nine tops.

The watch hit the carpet and, to my considerable surprise, bounced to a stop between Valmont and Greene's feet. The surprise being that the thing had actually ended up where my brother wanted it.

"I'll get it," Gustav said, and he slid from his seat and went down on his hands and knees.

Which was probably what gave it away, seeing as all he really had to do was ask Valmont or Greene to bend down and pick the watch up. There was no need to go to all fours.

Or linger on them so long.

Or suck in a quick, poorly concealed sniff.

"Monsieur," Valmont said, "are you smelling my feet?"

"No," my brother said. "Just picked me up the sniffles since comin' to . . ."

He glanced up and found Valmont and Greene staring down at him, the Frenchman cocking an eyebrow and puckering his lips, the Englishman looking like he was biting his to keep from laughing.

"Awwww, hell."

Old Red pushed himself to his feet and tossed me the watch.

"Told you," I said.

My brother shot me a "Shut up" glare and dropped back into his seat.

"Yes," he said to Valmont. "I was checkin' your shoes. You've both had 'em polished since yesterday, ain't you?"

"Merde," Valmont muttered, and if you don't know French, suffice it to say he was either identifying what my brother was looking for or commenting upon his technique.

"Your persistence does you credit, Mr. Amlingmeyer," Greene offered more charitably, "but I would point out that this hotel is several blocks from the fairgrounds. At least twice today, we've all had to cross busy city streets—and avoid what the carriage horses leave in them so plentifully. It would hardly have been conclusive should you have found what you were looking for."

Gustav tapped the side of his nose. "Remember what this can

do, sir. What I'm lookin' for came from a cow . . . and I'll know if I smell it a third time."

He threw a meaningful look at the stairs to the guest rooms.

"A *third* time? You mean you've come across it here in—?" Greene stopped himself and chuckled. "I see. Nicely played."

"Ah! Now this is more impressive than your flounderings on the floor," Valmont said. "More psychologi-KELL. I approve, monsieur! You suggest that you have uncove-AIRED a new clue in the presence of two suspects so you can then watch for any sign of pan-eek or perhaps await a telling countermove." He turned to Greene while waving a lazy hand at Old Red. "It is instructive to observe the process of detection from the oth-AIR side, *n'est-ce pas?*"

"I'm so glad to hear you think so," Gustav shot back, face flushing. "Then you won't mind tellin' me where you went after our dinner last night."

"Yes, by all means, let my education continue," Valmont said. "I retur-NED to the White City to prepare for the next day's competi-shawn."

"Prepare how?"

"I familiari-ZED myself with various notable exhibits, and, when the buildings began to close for the night at nine, I walked the grounds."

"Which exhibits did you take in?"

"Oh, a display of Remington typewriters, the gunboat *Niagara,* the Tiffany Diamond, a complete collection of the world's bacteria. I could continue the catalog for fifteen minutes, but *pourquoi?*"

"And in all that time familiarizin', you never laid eyes on Mr. Curtis or anyone else from the contest?"

"No. I saw no one I recogni-ZED, and I assume no one saw me."

"Hmmmm. Alright."

Gustav turned to Greene.

"Allow me to apologize in advance, Mr. Amlingmeyer," the Englishman said. "I'm afraid my narrative isn't any more reveal-ing—or self-incriminating—than our esteemed colleague's. After everyone else left the restaurant, Blackheath-Murray and I headed to the White City so that I might do more 'familiarizing' myself. We toured the Fisheries Building, stepped outside for the nightly fireworks, then retired for the night when the fairgrounds closed at eleven. Mrs. Jasinska can confirm that last. For the rest, I'm sorry to say, there is no corroboration I can offer. We didn't see anyone we knew all night."

"What about Miss Larson? She was still with you and Blackheath-Murray when me and my brother walked out."

"I'm afraid we didn't have the heart for entertaining after our little debacle of a dinner, and the lady departed not long after you did."

"Hmm." Old Red looked at Valmont. "You say the buildings over to the Exposition close at nine?"

"Oui."

"And the grounds close at eleven?" my brother asked Greene.

"That's correct."

Gustav threw both men a grimace. "So y'all just wandered around in the dark for two hours before comin' back to the hotel?"

"It was hardly dark," Valmont said. "The electrical lighting of the White City is quite magnificent."

"We'd all had a chance to see how the contest would play itself out, Mr. Amlingmeyer," Greene added. "Through puzzles requir-ing a familiarity with the Fair. Our wanderings might seem strange to you, but frankly I find it harder to believe that any of us would have stayed in his room."

"Bravo, M. Greene. An excellent point." Valmont turned back to my brother with eyes narrowed to slits. "Is that what *you* claim?

That after such a dramatic din-AIR and with so much at stake the next day, you simply went to bed?"

"Well, I—"

"That sounds like a man trying to establish an alibi," Greene said.

"Oh, that's—"

"*Oui!* Yes! And then after M. Curtis was found dead, M. Amlingmeyer engaged in a *spectacle ostentatoire* . . . a . . . a . . ." Valmont spun his hands in the air until the English words came to him. "An ostentatious show meant to establish that he alone was interested in catching the kill-AIR."

"A transparent attempt to place himself above suspicion," Greene said.

"*Exactement!* In addition, what are we to make of this mysterious odor that only M. Amlingmeyer can detect?"

"Now, really—"

"He was putting us on a false scent," Greene said. "Literally."

Valmont nodded. "It is quite damning. Or would be—"

"If we actually thought Mr. Curtis had been murdered," Greene finished for him.

The two sleuths grinned at each other.

Old Red fumed.

Usually he was the clever one, the crafty one, the one tripping folks up with words. Yet with less than a minute of effort, Valmont and Greene had just deduced circles around him. Never had I seen the tables turned on my brother with such complete and obvious ease.

This, I realized, was what it would look like to go up against a killer who knew more about detectiving than we did—a professional as opposed to talented amateurs like ourselves. If mystery-solving's truly a game, as Valmont had said at dinner the night before, then there was one conclusion I couldn't escape.

We were out of our league.

18

THE TEMPEST

Or, Pinkerton's Get-together Just About Blows Apart

My brother didn't have much time to seethe over Valmont and Greene's little humiliation. King Brady came through the hotel's front doors and (after pausing by the front desk to let Mrs. Jasinska bat her eyes at him) joined us in the lobby. He still looked a tad addled and ashen, as he had atop the Mammoth Cheese, but he managed to smooth away the jitters by the time he slipped into a seat across from me and Gustav.

There was some small talk along the "Where's Pinkerton and what's he going to say?" line, but my brother didn't join in. He just stared at Brady, seeming to perk up every time the man crossed or uncrossed his legs. I noticed his nostrils flare a few times, too, so by the time he reached up and scratched the end of his nose—giving me the signal to drop my watch again—I was ready.

I shook my head.

Old Red scratched harder.

I shook harder.

Gustav clawed at his big beak with such vigor I'm surprised his mustache didn't fly off.

"Excuse me, Mr. Brady," I said. "Would you mind if my brother smelled your shoes?"

"What?"

Brady gaped first at me, then at Old Red.

Valmont rolled his eyes.

Greene shook his head, his mouth puckered tight.

"It won't take but a second," Gustav sighed, and without waiting for permission, he went down on his knees before Brady, lifted up the man's right foot, and pointed at a chunk of brown crud wedged against the heel of his shoe. "Thought so. You've been in a cow pen."

Brady jerked his foot away. "So what if I have?"

Valmont's eyes stopped rolling and started bulging.

"You have?" Greene said.

"Would you mind?" Brady snapped at Gustav, who was still kneeling at his feet.

My brother got up and plopped back in his own chair.

"You paid a call on some Herefords today," he said. "Mind tellin' us why?"

"Because that's where Curtis sent me. My second clue in the contest today was hidden in the Stock Pavilion."

Old Red nodded, a familiar, faraway look coming over him. Inside his head, enough gears were turning to do Tom Edison proud.

"That explains why Curtis was over by them pens last night," he muttered. "He was tuckin' away Brady's envelope for today."

"Which tells us how the you-know-who came to follow him there," I said.

Gustav nodded, gazing off at nothing.

"So why didn't the you-know-who you-know-what him right

then and there?" I asked. "I don't imagine there was a crowd around the livestock in the dead of night. It would've been the perfect place to do the deed. Wallop him upside the head and make it look like a cow kicked him. Spook the cattle and flatten him. Smother him in plop instead of cheese. There would've been a dozen ways to get it done. Why carry on to the Agriculture Building and do it there?"

I half-expected the standard reply, courtesy of Mr. Holmes: "It is a capital mistake to theorize before one has data." Yet Old Red just shook his head again.

He had data. He was *trying* to theorize. Those gears of his weren't running smooth, though—the facts were grinding against each other like clockwork knocked out of synch. It was a wonder smoke wasn't coming out of his ears.

A sudden commotion kicked up by the front door, and we all turned to find our missing colleagues coming into the hotel in a herd. Some conversation amongst them was already well under way—and some fracas close at hand.

A couple fracases, actually. William Pinkerton and Colonel Crowe and Urias Smythe were going 'round and 'round about something, while Blackheath-Murray traded snarls with Frank Tousey. Miss Larson, meanwhile, was off to the side, furiously taking notes.

Watching them approach took me back to my childhood in Kansas and the times I spotted twisters bearing down on the farm. Only this time there was no storm cellar to flee to.

"—only thinking of yourself—!"

"—put this insanity behind us—!"

"—taking advantage of a man's death—!"

"—make amends for your duplicity—!"

"—save ourselves from utter ruin—!"

The hullaballoo drew the last of our party into the lobby:

Diana and Detective Sergeant Ryan. They came strolling in together looking so perfectly pleased and at ease, I almost expected to see a picnic basket dangling from Ryan's crooked arm.

Without ever letting up his carping at Pinkerton, the colonel collected his adopted daughter and steered her to a divan as far from me and my brother as possible while still keeping himself within shouting range.

"Is anyone gonna bother tellin' us what the heck is goin' on?" Gustav asked.

I don't think anyone heard him but me.

"Alright," said Pinkerton, striding over to stand beside Ryan, "that's enough."

Something about the way he said it made it so. The lobby went quiet.

"We're going to talk this through quickly and professionally, with no more outbursts," Pinkerton said. "Understood?"

There were a few sullen nods, then Pinkerton went on, addressing himself first to Old Red and me, then Valmont and Greene.

"Armstrong Curtis's death is being investigated by the proper authorities . . . and *only* the proper authorities. It's too early to come to any conclusions—"

"But here one comes anyhow," my brother said under his breath.

"—but every indication points to a sad accident, and we will move on knowing that we now honor not just Sherlock Holmes, but his greatest admirer as well. The contest will continue." Pinkerton switched his attention to Tousey and the colonel, staring hard. "As planned."

"Pardon my askin'," Gustav said, "but how else *would* it continue?"

Pinkerton did not pardon his asking. In fact, it looked like Pinkerton wanted to squash him into a ball and take him bowling.

"It could continue," Tousey sneered, "as something other than a farce."

"The matter's been settled," Blackheath-Murray said. "Let it lie, sir."

Boothby Greene's publisher had struck me as a mild-mannered fellow up till then, gentlemanly and affable, but there was steel beneath his soft, genteel appearance—you could see it glittering in his eyes.

King Brady's publisher had plenty of steel himself, though. Or brass balls, anyway.

"I will *not* let it lie!" Tousey thundered. "Not when we've been handed the chance to fix this crazy thing before Pinkerton makes laughingstocks of us all!"

"Hear, hear!" King Brady threw in, swinging a fist into the air. I think he was expecting more folks to join in with him—more than the nobody he got, at least—and his cheeks took on a touch of pink as his hand dropped back to his side.

"What are you proposing?" Greene asked Tousey. "That we toss out all the clues Mr. Curtis prepared and create entirely new ones?"

"Exactly. Pinkerton was supposed to come up with the contest in the first place. Let him do it now."

"I got another question," Gustav said.

Everyone ignored him.

"I already said no," Pinkerton snapped at Tousey.

"But *why*?" Tousey shot back. "Curtis was trying to make us look like fools—he told us as much last night. We should let him get away with it even after he's *dead*? No!"

Pinkerton was a big, bluff man, and all he had to do was lean forward and it felt like his shadow was falling over the whole room.

"Now, look here, you—"

Old Red poked a finger up into the air. "I got another question."

"I think Tousey's making good sense," Colonel Crowe announced. "Those silly puzzles . . . they're embarrassing. Why not come up with something worthy of *real* detectives?"

"Hear, hear!" Brady cheered, pumping his fist again.

"I will grant," Blackheath-Murray said, addressing himself to Tousey, "that Mr. Curtis's approach wasn't perfect. Still, to toss out everything he prepared is to invite chaos."

"I agree," Greene said.

"Invite chaos?" Smythe whined. He had a love seat all to himself, and it looked like he was going to collapse back on it in a dead faint. "What do you call this?"

Then the chaos *really* kicked in.

Blackheath-Murray was fussing at Smythe.

Brady was fussing at Blackheath-Murray.

Greene was fussing at Brady.

Tousey was fussing at Pinkerton.

Pinkerton was fussing right back at Tousey.

Colonel Crowe was fussing at everybody.

Smythe was fussing at God. ("What did I do to deserve this?")

Valmont . . . well, I couldn't tell who he was fussing at, his accent grew so thick.

Diana took it all in with the look of someone who'd rather be somewhere else—the South Pole, a Bolivian prison, the middle of a volcano, *anywhere*.

Ryan, on the other hand, seemed to be enjoying the show, while Miss Larson was scribbling so fast it was a wonder her notebook didn't light up like kindling.

And my brother . . . what *was* he doing, anyway?

I watched in helpless horror as he calmly rose to his feet, climbed atop his chair, cleared his throat, and hollered at the top of his lungs.

"*Put . . . it . . . to . . . a . . . vote!*"

Then he stepped down, reseated himself, and folded his arms across his chest.

The shouting was over. Now everyone was *staring*.

Pinkerton found his voice again first. "This isn't a Grange meeting. I'm in charge, and I've made my decision."

"Well, it looks to me like you got a mutiny brewin'," Old Red replied. "If you wanna stamp it out, a vote's the way to go. Cuz if it swings your way, Tousey there ain't got a leg to stand on, and this argument is over."

Diana raised a hand. "I second the motion," she said. "You might be in charge, Mr. Pinkerton, but it's our money at stake, not to mention our reputations. We should have a say in how we proceed from here."

"I third the motion," I said.

"I fourth it," said Valmont.

Colonel Crowe swiveled around to glower at Diana, but she kept her eyes on William Pinkerton. Unlike my brother, he wasn't one of those people you can *see* thinking. For all the turning the wheels may have been doing in his head, his jowly face remained stock-still for a long, long time.

"Alright," he finally said. "All those who think we should discard Curtis's clues and start from scratch, raise your hand."

Tousey's and Brady's hands were up first, of course, followed by Smythe's and Crowe's. The colonel's glare finally got through to Diana, and she reluctantly voted with her father.

I started to put my hand up again as well, but Gustav gave me a quick shake of the head.

"But you hate riddles," I whispered.

"I surely do," my brother said. "Now get that hand down."

I did as he said.

"That's five, then," Pinkerton said. "Now, all those who think we should see this through with the contest as it stands?"

Blackheath-Murray and Greene had their hands up first, followed by Valmont and, finally, Old Red.

"Come on, come on," my brother prompted me.

"Boy, this is a Chicago election, alright." I raised an arm. "You gonna cast a vote for Mr. Holmes, too?"

"Five. A tie," Pinkerton said. "And as judge, I can—"

"One party ain't been heard from," Gustav said.

He turned toward Miss Larson.

"Me?" The lady finally gave her pencil a rest. "I'm just an impartial observer."

"You're here representin' *McClure's Magazine*," Old Red reminded her. "Your bosses have as much ridin' on this as anybody. You need to weigh in."

The lady eyed him a moment, and though her face remained the same expressionless mask of ice, I could somehow sense the shift inside her as she reappraised the peculiar little fellow with the grubby clothes and the rough ways.

"Alright," she said. "I side with you and Mr. Pinkerton. It would be a shame to let Mr. Curtis's hard work go to waste. Let us honor him by carrying on as he intended."

"That's six to five, then," Pinkerton said. "We will move forward with the contest as is. Those who wish to withdraw—and forfeit their stake—are free to do so. Otherwise, the matter is *closed*."

Momentous words, those were. Funny thing, though: Nobody was looking at Pinkerton as he spoke them. All eyes were on Old Red.

Half the folks there looked like they were trying to figure out what he was thinking.

The other half? It looked like they were trying to figure out how to get his face into a chunk of cheddar.

19

THE OFFICE

Or, I Smoke Out a Lie While Gustav Burns Our Bridges

W ell, now . . . if you've concluded your business, I hope I might have a word."

Slowly, all the stares and glares directed at Gustav swung toward Sergeant Ryan. He was a mousy-looking man—lean and tidy and generally nondescript—yet there was a sparkle in his eyes that suggested unflappable amusement. My brother took in all around him with a perpetual glower, as if bitterly disappointed to find himself stranded on such a sorry world as this one, but Ryan was just the opposite. Everything that put a frown on Old Red's face slipped a wry little smile onto his.

"For those of you who don't know," he said, "my name is Moses Ryan, and I'm a detective sergeant with the Chicago Police Department. I'm handling the inquiry into Mr. Curtis's unfortunate demise, and it would be a great service to me if I could speak with each of you separately. Mr. Pinkerton has arranged for the use of the hotel office just behind me, so that we might have some privacy.

If you could wait here while I call you in one at a time, I promise you we'll be finished by—"

"I'll go first." My brother hopped off his seat and stalked toward the office. "I got questions for you, too, and I'd rather ask 'em away from all the rowdydow out here."

"Thank you. That would be fine," Ryan said softly, unfazed, smile still in place. "Mr. Pinkerton, would you care to join us?"

"I'd love to," Pinkerton muttered, and he fairly sprinted toward the office door.

Away from us.

He was wise to make his escape. Within seconds, Frank Tousey was grousing at Eugene Valmont for voting to keep Curtis's clues, which drew Blackheath-Murray in to defend the Frenchman, which drew King Brady in to back up his publisher, which drew Boothby Greene in to back up *his* publisher, which drew the colonel in to tell *everybody* they were fools, which drew from Urias Smythe a pathetic appeal to heaven for deliverance from all the uproar, which did *not* seem to draw in God at all, as the bedlam carried on unabated.

The ladies kept out of it, and I tried to follow their lead. I did slip in one small bit of detecting, though, just to cover my rump should my brother want to know how I'd made myself useful while he'd been off interrogating Sergeant Ryan.

"Got a match?" I said, sliding in beside Smythe.

I slipped a hand into my coat and began fishing around as if for a pouch of tobacco.

"I'm sorry," Smythe mumbled, too benumbed by all the hubbub to even look at me. "I don't smoke."

I'd meant to bum a stogie off him under the pretext of forgetting my rolling papers. If he'd really been out buying cigars the night before, as he'd told Mrs. Jasinska, perhaps the brand would have offered some clue. This was far, far better, however. I'd been digging for potatoes and struck gold.

"Oh, that's alright," I said, drawing a small white-and-green-striped packet from my pocket. "Neither do I."

I tore the wrapping off the pack and slid out a brittle stick of chaw wax—a new brand they'd been handing out free at the Fair. "Juicy Fruit," they called it (though, as I popped it in my mouth, I quickly discovered that it was neither juicy nor tasted of any fruit I've ever sampled, unless cardboard grows on trees).

Smythe eyed me, bewildered. Then he sucked in his breath as if he hoped to suck his words back in, too.

"I mean . . . I always keep some cigars on hand for . . . uhhh . . . you know. But I left them in my room."

"Sure. I understand. That's why I wanted a match, actually." I grinned around the sticky, tasteless lump in my mouth. "For the you know."

"Heh heh . . . yes . . . heh heh . . . ," Smythe said. And before I could ask him about the mysterious friend he'd summoned to Chicago—the glasses-smashing Bearded Man—he turned away and lobbed a random "Nonsense!" into the still-raging debate. This brought upon him a torrent of abuse from both the colonel and Blackheath-Murray, which Smythe seemed to prefer to any further conversation with me.

Soon after, the office door swung open and my brother tromped out throwing the words "And the same goes for you!" over his shoulder. Obviously, he'd been dealing with the local authorities with his usual deference and charm—which meant it was only a matter of time before we were both thrown in the pokey.

I hopped up and scampered after him as he stomped across the lobby toward the hotel's front doors.

"What happened in—?"

"Amlingmeyer the Younger," a gentle voice trilled behind me. "You're next."

I looked back to find Sergeant Ryan watching us. He pivoted and swept his arms to one side, gesturing for me to come into the office with him.

"If you please."

Now how can you say no to a policeman who actually says "please"?

"Where you gonna be when I'm done?" I asked Old Red under my breath.

"The alley," he whispered back quick. Then he swept past Mrs. Jasinska's desk, pushed through the doors, and was gone.

A moment later, I was stepping into the hotel office. It was a small, poorly lit affair cluttered with overflowing file cabinets and a battered rolltop desk. A telephone jutted from one wall, and there were brooms and buckets shoved in a corner.

William Pinkerton had claimed one of the room's two chairs. Ryan offered the other to me.

"Sorry about Gustav," I said as I sat. "He can be a tad . . . well . . . *that*."

"There's no need for apologies," the sergeant said. "Your brother's a man of deep passions, that's plain—and in the service of justice, no vice."

He leaned against the desk and smiled his serene little smile. If he felt a deep passion for justice, he was doing a good job keeping it deep—so deep I couldn't see it, at least.

"What got him so riled, if you don't mind my askin'?"

"Ohhhhh, I don't mind at all," Ryan replied. "Now could you tell me your whereabouts last night between eight thirty and midnight?"

It took me a few seconds to realize the sergeant didn't mind my asking because he had no intention of answering.

"My whereabouts was here. At the hotel. After that dinner 'party' I'm sure you've heard about, Gustav and I came back and called it a night."

"But the White City would be open for hours still. You didn't want to take another turn around the grounds? Prepare for the next day's competition?"

"I did prepare, Sergeant. I read up on the Exposition for a good long while before turnin' down the lights."

"What of your brother, though? As I understand it, studying from guidebooks wouldn't be his bailiwick—unless, I suppose, they had pictures."

I looked from Ryan, all innocent-eyed and affable, to Pinkerton, sitting there cold and hard as a marble bust of his father. If they'd badgered Old Red about his lack of learning, it wasn't a shock he'd stomped out shouting. The surprise was he hadn't kicked the door to splinters in the process.

"Look," I said, "Gustav was tired. Train travel don't agree with him, and he ain't fond of cities, neither. So he needed sleep, and he got it. Just ask Mrs. J up at the front desk. We didn't go out again all night."

"Oh, I did ask. And you're right: The lady didn't see you leave." Ryan shrugged. "I don't know what that proves, though. You and your brother have already demonstrated your familiarity with the back alley—as well as, I suspect, a certain persuasiveness when it comes to locked doors. Hmm?"

If that "Hmm?" was a cue for my confession, it didn't work. I said nothing.

"Otto . . . ," Ryan said soothingly. "I may call you 'Otto,' mayn't I?"

"Anything to keep things friendly, *Mo*."

No irritation showed itself on Ryan's face. Old Red once told me I could pick a fight with a marshmallow without even trying, but perhaps I'd finally met my match.

"Thank you, Otto," Ryan said. "I like to keep things friendly, too. And with someone like yourself, that's very easy indeed. Your brother, on the other hand . . ." He shook his head sadly. "A hot-tempered man, wouldn't you say?"

Of course I would say and have said, and at great length, too. Somehow, though, now didn't seem the time to say it again.

"Oh, he's just on edge, like everyone else around here now. In fact, you keep all them folks penned up in the lobby much longer, you're gonna have another murder on your hands."

"What makes you so sure we've got one now?" Pinkerton asked.

At that I had to laugh. "Come on, now. My brother can and I'm sure *did* explain it to you a lot better than I could. Ain't no reason to have me run through it again."

"Humor us, Otto," Ryan said. "Please."

"Alright, fine." I brought up a hand and counted it off point by point. "Dung in hair. Dung on window. Someone in his room. Everyone hated him. Smotherin' in cheese."

"What about smothering in cheese?" Ryan asked.

"What about it? It's completely preposterous, that's what."

"He was drunk," Pinkerton said. "You saw that yourself."

"Yeah, but . . . *smotherin' in cheese*?"

"Otto," Ryan said, "I've been a policeman for sixteen years. I've seen a man choked to death on a mouse. I've seen a woman who was accidentally strangled by her own hair. Smothering in cheese? I wager I'll see something stranger by the weekend."

"But it was cheddar," I protested. "That stuff's too hard for anyone to smother in accidental."

Pinkerton snorted. "Your brother said the same thing."

Somehow, this did not seem to stand my point in good stead.

"They flip the Mammoth Cheese once a month, Otto," Ryan said. "Otherwise, all the moisture collects in the bottom, and it loses its shape and turns to goo with a layer of crust on top."

"Let me guess," I said. "They flipped it yesterday."

"Two days ago, actually, but the result's the same. I'm told the top remains soft—almost gelatinous—for at least a week. Anyway, Otto, we don't *know* Mr. Curtis smothered to death. He might have had a heart attack just as he climbed in to hide that 'egg' of his. He could have died of a stroke as he crawled around in the tank."

"Sure. He *might* have been struck by lightning," I said. "He *could* have been clubbed to death by a leprechaun."

Ryan shrugged. "That's for the coroner to determine."

"Well, what about the dung, then? No heart attack or stroke would explain that."

"Strange that only your brother noticed it," Pinkerton said, sounding like he didn't mean "strange" so much as "suspicious."

"Oh, I don't know. I've met folks who wouldn't notice bullshit if it was served up to 'em à la mode."

In case there was any doubt that I'd met two such men very, very recently, I favored Pinkerton and Ryan with a big grin.

"I think you'll find, Otto, that you're dealing with more discriminating palates than you might imagine," the sergeant replied mildly. "Take your brother's glasses, for instance. That has a certain . . . bouquet about it. Yesterday, I'm told, he practically needed a white cane. Yet today, he was suddenly healed as if by the hand of Christ himself. Now, what are we to make of that?"

By the time Ryan finished, my smug smile was but a memory, and a feeble "You'd have to ask my brother" was the only answer I could offer.

"We did," Ryan said. "He told us—rather over-forcefully—that the question was immaterial. So it's to you I must turn for an explanation."

I shrugged miserably. "I ain't got one."

Ryan and Pinkerton looked at each other. After a long, silent moment, Pinkerton jerked his head toward the door.

"Thank you for your time, Otto," Ryan said. "You've been a big help."

"Have I?" I almost sighed. Perhaps from the sergeant's perspective I had been. Yet I knew I hadn't helped myself and Gustav any.

When I shuffled out of the office, I found Tousey, Brady, Smythe, and Colonel Crowe all clamoring to get in.

"Let me get this over with," the colonel said, trying to squeeze past me.

Tousey blocked him. "King and I go next!"

"Please, I beg you," Smythe said to Pinkerton. "Don't make me wait out here any longer. My nerves can't take it!"

"One side, pantywaist!" Crowe barked. "I'm coming through!"

"Oh, no you don't!" Tousey snarled.

"Oh, yes I do!"

Never had I seen such enthusiasm for the third degree. It was like finding a line of folks fighting to get into a dentist's chair.

A minute later, I rejoined my brother in the alley behind the hotel. He was pawing through more trash cans, and as I walked up a tattered, muck-splattered umbrella seemed to capture his attention.

"Come up with anything?" I asked.

Old Red tried to open the umbrella. It snagged halfway up and the handle broke off and something gray and gloppy—rotted cabbage, perhaps—oozed out from inside its folds.

"Yup." He threw everything back in the nearest trash can. "A whole lot of junk and a whole lot of rats. No more clues, though. How'd it go with Pinkerton and Ryan?"

"I think I *almost* got 'em convinced Curtis was murdered. The only problem is if I did, we'd be the prime suspects. That how it played out for you?"

"Come on." Gustav stood and started up the alley, bound for Hope Avenue. "We'll talk it out as we walk."

"Walk where?"

"The corner of Kenwood and Sixty-first . . . wherever the hell that is," Old Red said. "I reckon it's time you and me got our shoes shined."

20

UNCOMMON FEAT

Or, We Try Our Hand at Shadowing Suspects,
but the Shoe Ends Up on the Other Foot

Under normal circumstances, taking Gustav Amlingmeyer to get a shoeshine would make about as much sense as taking a pack mule for a pedicure. Spit was the only polish ever to touch my brother's boots, and even this was applied no more than once or twice per annum. Most times, every speck of trail dust to cling to the creased brown leather was worn with pride as a belle wears her bows or a soldier his medals.

But Old Red had a reason to shed some of his hard-earned grime now: We were on our way to see Pyle, the bootblack who shined shoes for the Columbian's guests, according to Jerzy the bell codger. My brother still had dung on the brain (as opposed to the dung *for* brains he frequently accused me of). If anyone had come back to the hotel the previous night with especially feculent feet, this Pyle might be our last chance to find out about it.

As we weaved our way through the chattering tourist clans clogging the sidewalks, Gustav grilled me on my talk with Pinkerton and Ryan. So as to have *something* encouraging to report, I threw in that I'd caught Smythe in a lie about needing cigars. Whatever had taken him out of the hotel the night before, it wasn't a hankering for a hand-rolled robusto.

"Add that to the note in the bearded feller's coat, and your Mr. Smythe starts lookin' like a man with things to hide," Old Red said.

"Wouldn't that just be the way? I finally find someone willin' to pay for my stories, and he turns out to be the next Lizzie Borden. So how'd *your* parley with Ryan and Pinkerton go?"

My brother shrugged. "Not much to tell. Pinkerton was the same way with me as you. Surly. Suspicious. Like he thought we had something to do with Curtis's dyin' like he did. Which don't make no sense at all considerin'—"

"He doesn't think Curtis was murdered."

"Or so he keeps sayin'. And Ryan I don't understand, either. He's cool, clearheaded, pleasant."

"Not like a lawman at all."

"Nope. At least the ones we've met. It's frustratin'. I couldn't get a lick of data out of him, yet much as I wanted to, I couldn't get properly mad at him, either."

"Could've fooled me, the way you was shoutin'."

"Oh, that don't mean I don't like the man."

"I'll try to remember that the next time you call me a goddamn idjit."

"Probably won't be long."

"No doubt."

"I just wish Ryan would *listen*. He seems too smart to be so dense."

"Well, I can tell you one thing that didn't do us any favors. Them specs you was wearin' when we come to town. Ryan wanted to know why—"

"Yeah, yeah. He asked me about that, too," Gustav muttered, and he let a big clump of sightseers come between us. After that, he was too busy zigzagging around sidewalk vendors and telephone poles to pick up the conversation again, and I got the message, plain as from Western Union: The subject was dropped.

Within a few minutes, we were at the corner of Kenwood and Sixty-first, and there we found a shoeshine stand worthy of the White City itself. While most bootblacks I'd seen plied their trade with nothing more than a box of polish and brushes or, at most, a couple chairs and footrests in a railroad depot, here was a long row of raised seats under a crisp white awning bearing the words WORLD'S GREATEST SHOESHINE—15¢.

"Fifteen whole cents just for a shine?" Old Red said.

"Well, it is the world's greatest. And the price sure ain't hurt business none."

Indeed, half a dozen men had ventured their dimes and nickels for the honor. Kneeling before each was a neatly dressed boy rubbing and buffing with such enthusiasm he could've put a blinding gleam on a pile of bricks.

A somber Negro of perhaps forty years of age paced slowly up and down the line, watching over the work with an air of austere gravity. When he noticed us staring his way, he smiled and tried to lead us to two empty seats.

"Oh, we ain't here for shines, sir," I said. "Are you Mr. Pyle?"

That was enough to wipe the smile clean off the man's face.

"What do you want?" he asked.

"We're detectives, sir," I said. "The private consulting kind. And we're conductin' an inquiry of a confidential manner that involves—"

"Shoes," my brother cut in. "The ones from the Columbian Hotel last night. That's what we wanna ask about."

"Did some go missing?"

"No, sir," I said. "It's nothing like that."

"Then this doesn't have anything to do with me."

And with that, the man moved off to prod one of the shoeshine boys with his toe.

"Andrew. Those shoes need paste polish, not wax."

"Yessir, Mr. Pyle!"

"Look," Old Red said, "we're only askin' for a few minutes of your time."

"Which I don't have," Pyle snapped back without turning to face us again. "I'm running a business here. I can't afford to stand around shooting the breeze."

"Why, of all the mulish—"

I silenced my brother with a hand on his shoulder.

"Mr. Pyle," I said, "it's not against the rules for a man to talk while he's gettin' his shoes shined, is it?"

"No."

"Well, then . . ."

I reached a hand around into the man's line of sight. In it was a five-dollar bill.

"Two for the World's Greatest Shoeshine. Keep the change."

The greenback disappeared.

"Right this way, gentlemen!"

Pyle ushered us to the nearest empty seats.

"I've been workin' on my bribin' technique," I said to Gustav.

He replied with a scowl that clearly said, *Five dollars?*

There's just no pleasing some people.

"Randall! Marcus!" Pyle barked, and a pair of young boys came scampering over, shoeshine boxes in hand. The older of the two—he was all of nine or ten—crouched down at my feet and got to work lickety-split. The other squatted down before my brother . . . and went bug-eyed at the sight of his dirt-caked boots.

"Is there a problem, Marcus?" Pyle asked sternly.

"No, sir!" Marcus replied, and he stretched a rag across Gustav's right boot and started buffing in vain. He would've been better served by a chisel.

"So, Mr. Pyle," I said, "you shine guests' shoes for the Columbian Hotel."

"*I* don't." Pyle nodded at Randall and Marcus. "My sons do."

"Ahhhh. I see. And how's that work, exactly?"

"We pick up the shoes after the stand closes at midnight. The boys shine them when we get home. Then we drop the shoes back off before we open the stand again at seven."

"My. You fellers ever sleep?" I asked the boys.

Randall glanced back at his father.

Pyle nodded.

"Not much this year," Randall said to me.

"There'll be time for sleep when the Fair's over. That's what Dad always tells us." Marcus rubbed with futile ardor at a deep stain just above Old Red's right heel. "What *did* you do to these boots? They look like they've been breaded and deep-fried."

"Marcus," Pyle said.

"Sorry."

Marcus redoubled his efforts to set a shine on the filthy, faded cowhide, but my brother waved him off.

"I know them things are grubby and I like 'em that way so let's stop dilly-dallyin', huh? You boys run across any shoes from the Columbian last night that struck you as particularly smelly?"

Marcus and Randall burst out laughing.

"Boys!" Pyle snapped. Then he gave Gustav a look that made it plain he, for one, was not amused. "You're looking for a pair of smelly shoes?"

"Not foot-smelly," I explained. "Dung-smelly."

Pyle waited for more explanation.

I shrugged. "Detectivin'."

"Alright," Pyle said. "Answer the man's question."

"They're all *kinda* smelly," Marcus said.

"Most of 'em have horsesh- . . . I mean, manure on 'em," Randall added.

"Well, did you notice any stains that wasn't normal, then?" Old Red asked. "Like blood, maybe? Or pomade? Or hair?"

Pyle glared at us. "Blood or pomade or hair?"

"Detectivin'," I said with another shrug.

The boys looked at each other.

"No," Marcus said. "There was nothing like that."

"The weirdest thing we saw all night was *clean* shoes," Randall said.

"Yeah!" Marcus laughed. "They didn't even have any Juicy Fruit on 'em!"

"Judas Priest." Randall rolled his eyes. "We had one old man come in here with *seven pieces* stuck to his soles."

"He could barely walk."

"And we could barely get it all off."

"We hate that stuff."

"But it's been good for business, so Dad loves it!"

"We get our five dollars' worth yet?" I asked my brother.

"You say there was a pair of shoes that was especially *clean*?" he said to the boys.

Randall nodded. "There wasn't a thing on 'em. No gum. No dirt. No dung."

"A careful stepper, huh?" I said.

"It wasn't careful stepping," Marcus said. "The shoes were washed off before they were put out for a shine."

Gustav practically sprang from his seat like a Jack from his Box. "How do you know that?"

"Shoe leather stiffens up when it gets wet," Randall explained.

"And the old polish was all smeared and spotty. Like someone had been working at it with a towel."

"Would you recognize them shoes if you saw 'em again?"

Randall and Marcus looked at each other again before shaking their heads.

"We shine a *lot* of shoes," said Randall.

"Well, could you describe 'em, at least?" Old Red asked.

"I think they were brown," said Marcus.

"Black," said Randall. "Ankle boots."

"Nuh-uh. Oxfords."

"No. Ankle boots."

"No! Oxfords!"

"Didja notice any kind of maker's mark on 'em, at least?" my brother managed to slip in.

"Naw," said Marcus.

"It would've been Italian, though," said Randall. "Like I said—we shine a *lot* of shoes. For a lot of foreign tourists. And those shoes were made in Italy, for sure." The boy frowned. "Or maybe France."

"I'd say England," Marcus said. "Or Germany."

"Well, that narrows it down," I said. "We're lookin' for either brown or black ankle boots or oxfords that were made in Italy or France or England or Germany. Maybe."

"That *does* narrow it down," Gustav sniped back.

Randall was rubbing his chin.

"They could have come from Spain," he muttered.

"Or Russia!" Marcus blurted out.

"Come on," I said to my brother. "Let's go before they pull out an atlas."

Before leaving, though, we made arrangements for Pyle to contact us should his sons come across the Italian/French/English/

German/Spanish/Russian ankle boots/oxfords again. Those "arrangements" being giving him our room numbers at the Columbian and yet another five-dollar bill.

In Chicago, we were learning, even the clues are expensive.

"A pair of cleaned something-or-others," I mused as we walked away. "That means what? The killer noticed the muck on his shoes once he was back at the Columbian?"

"Most likely."

"And if the shoes ain't American, we oughta be lookin' at Valmont and Greene and Blackheath-Murray?"

"Not necessarily. Lots of folks with money buy foreign-made shoes. It's just as likely to have been a swell from New York City."

"Like King Brady or Frank Tousey, you mean."

My brother shrugged. "Could be. Come to think of it, Smythe's not a bad dresser either, and his bearded friend had him an accent."

"Well, hell, it could've been Lucille Larson wearin' men's shoes."

I was joking, of course, but my brother nodded.

"Or it might just be that some other guest at the hotel wiped off his shoes before settin' 'em out last night," he said.

"In which case, it has nothing to do with us, and this has been a complete waste of time."

"That'd be the size of it."

We were both silent for a few strides.

"You know," I said, "I do so appreciate these little chats of ours. If not for them, I might get to feelin' downhearted about our prospects."

Old Red tapped the side of his head. "If you don't wanna know everything I'm jugglin' up here, then don't ask me to——"

He grabbed me by the arm and jerked me toward the nearest doorway.

"What the hell?"

"I just saw Smythe crossin' over to this side of the street," Gustav said. "He's headed this way, but I don't think he spotted us."

"Yeah? So? I wouldn't recommend jumpin' out to say 'Boo.' It'd probably kill him."

We'd dodged into a curio shop larded with commemorative baubles and knickknacks, and my brother took cover behind a rack of Exposition postcards.

"He might be goin' to meet up with that bearded feller," he said.

"Ahhh, I get you. If he is, we'll be right behind him."

I picked up a throw pillow, held it up even with my face, and pretended to admire the embroidery (WORLD'S COLUMBIAN EXPOSITION, it said over a needlework Ferris wheel) until Urias Smythe's big, round form scuttled by outside. Old Red and I gave him a moment to put distance between us, then slipped out after him.

Now, we've all seen folks with a guilty look about them, but what Smythe had was a guilty *walk*. It was slow paced yet long strided, as if he was in a hurry to get somewhere but was trying to hide it. He was ever glancing this way and that, too, and at one point he looked so far back over his shoulder I thought his head was going to take to spinning like a globe.

Gustav and I stopped and turned our backs to him, and my brother stretched out an arm as if noting some point of interest in the distance.

"If you *really* wanted us to be inconspicuous, we'd stop wearin' Stetsons," I said.

To this, he chose to make no reply.

"Well, I'll be damned," he whispered when we took off after Smythe again. "*We're* bein' followed."

"What?"

"A ways back there's a gent with a thick, dark beard. When we turned around, he turned around."

"It must be him, then. The Bearded Man."

"Naw, this one's burlier. Older, too."

Smythe looked over his shoulder again.

We pivoted toward a shop window.

About forty feet back, I noticed out of the corner of my eye, a big, bearded man spun to face the brick wall to his left. Perhaps he'd merely stopped to admire the poster plastered there, but I had my doubts: It was an advertisement for "Doc Healey's Feminine Regulator, the Elixir for Women."

"I see him," I said under my breath. "But how do you know he's trailin' us and not Smythe?"

"I *don't* know. What say we find out?"

We let Smythe move on up the sidewalk without us. He was crossing the street toward the Midway Plaisance, the mile-long strip of amusements considered too lowbrow to be part of the White City itself, when the Other Bearded Man started after him again.

"You get one arm, I'll get the other," Gustav whispered.

"Right."

Once our quarry passed us, we whirled around and caught up to him fast. Old Red hooked himself to the man's left arm. I did the same on the right.

"Hello, friend," Gustav said. "You mind chattin' with us a moment?"

I had only a couple seconds to register my impressions: the mass of muscles under the man's heavy coat, the bushy gray eyebrows beneath the low brim of his slouch hat, the crow's-feet around his dark eyes, the thick black beard that was entirely *too* thick and *too* black. Then he spoke in a raspy-rough voice—"Yes"—and after that there was one and only one thing my senses could make out.

A bone-jarring blow to the side of the head.

Oh, and then darkness.

21

THE JOSS HOUSE

Or, We Lose Our Chance for Answers by a (Clump of) Hair

For a moment, everything around me went black, as if all God's creation had been snuffed out like a candle. A few blinks and the world returned, however, and I found myself (somewhat to my surprise) still on my feet, my brother staggering stunned beside me.

After a couple more blinks, I managed to work out what had happened: The Other Bearded Man had stopped walking, jerked his meaty arms from our grips, and clobbered us with the hardest objects at hand—each other's heads.

He'd clapped our skulls together, and it was only our hats that had prevented him from leaving considerable dents. While we stumbled around the sidewalk blind with pain, he'd hustled away.

A cluster of curious tourists had stopped to gawp at us like we were another display at the Fair—the World's Biggest Fools, perhaps—and Old Red snarled at them as he punched the crown of his hat back into shape with a furious jab.

"Y'all wanna watch a show, go find Buffalo Bill! He's got a tent around here somewheres!"

Folks stopped staring and started doing their best to ignore us.

"Come on," my brother said to me, and he jerked his chin at something up ahead. "That slippery bastard ain't got away yet."

I followed his gaze.

Up a stretch of sidewalk and across a busy street was the Midway Plaisance. A hulking figure crowned with a black slouch hat was mixed in with the crowd walking through the gate.

Gustav took off after the Other Bearded Man. I took off after Gustav.

When we reached the cross street, my brother didn't just run out into it without slowing. He ran out into it without bothering to look to either side to see what might flatten him if he didn't stop. Perhaps this was the only way he could get himself to dash across the avenue at all, like a horse that can't get past a fire without a saddle blanket over its head.

Whatever the reason, it worked. Drivers yanked hard on reins, hansoms swerved, a streetcar operator hurled curses, yet Old Red just shot past like they weren't there, alighting on the opposite side of the street with neither a scratch nor a glance back. I stayed on his heels the whole time and, by some miracle, managed to survive the crossing as well.

"He knows we're after him," Gustav said as we jogged past the gates the Other Bearded Man had scuttled through not a quarter minute before. "Only question is which way he's gonna duck."

Indeed, our quarry hardly lacked for hiding places. Imagine all the nations and wonders of the earth shuffled like a deck of cards and dealt out again willy-nilly. That would be the Midway Plaisance.

Within easy sprinting distance was an Irish castle, an African village, a Moorish palace, an ostrich farm, an Old Country hamlet of the type our dearly departed *Mutter* and *Vater* grew up around, a series of ramps and chutes upon which screaming youngsters were whizzing around in what looked like bobsleds, and, towering over it all, the mighty Ferris wheel.

Not that my brother noticed any of it. He still had his gaze glued to that bearded fellow—right up to the moment the man ducked behind a pair of passing camels (and the tourists who'd apparently paid for the privilege of riding them) and disappeared.

"Dammit!" my brother spat.

He tore around the camels and spun in a quick circle.

"There!" he declared when he stopped his twirl, and he pointed at the nearest attraction. Two ornate towers loomed up over the entrance, each featuring curling roofs and five or six gaily painted widow walks festooned with hanging bells. CHINESE THEATRE & TEMPLE OF WORSHIP, a sign nearby said.

This was the place the guidebooks called the Joss House. Though we'd never laid eyes on it before, we knew it well, for we ourselves played a role in destroying some of the ancient treasures it once displayed. (Note to those planning on sending a train full-steam into a ravine: You might want to detach the baggage car first.)

If Gustav recognized the building for what it was, he didn't let on. He simply charged inside, ignoring the indignant Chinaman shouting "Hey! Twenty-five cents!" as he whipped past.

"Sorry about my friend there," I said. "He just gets a trifle over-excited by Chinese theater. If I may ask, did a big, bearded man come hurryin' in here right before us?"

"Yes." The Chinaman held out his hand. "And *he* didn't forget to pay."

"Right, right." I forked over four bits. "One more question. Is there any other way out of here? A back door or some such?"

"Not for customers, no."

"Ha! Did you hear that, Brother? We got him!"

Old Red was scurrying around the ornately decorated lobby, the centerpiece of which was a statue of what looked like an elongated dog with the skin of a lizard and the head of a goldfish.

"I heard," my brother said. "You stay here in case he tries to slip back out. I'll see if I can't corner him."

"That feller just walloped the two of us together, and you wanna go at him alone?"

"This time, I'll be ready."

There were three halls leading off from the lobby, and Gustav picked one and bolted off into it. The echoes of his footfalls faded quickly, and though I kept listening intently for shouts or the sounds of a scuffle, all I heard was distant music I can only liken to "Camptown Races" as played backward by two out-of-tune fiddles and a musical saw. (In the interest of fairness, I hereby encourage my no doubt multitudinous Chinese readers to track me down and give me their unvarnished opinion of "Camptown Races" played forward.)

After a couple minutes standing vigil, I looked over at the gent working the door.

"Say, as long as I'm not actually going in . . ."

The Chinaman was an older fellow outfitted in traditional silken robes and pillbox hat, yet he spoke with no hint of an accent, and his next words demonstrated his mastery of both the English language and American business practices.

"No refunds."

I went back to waiting. Yet though there was a steady flow of folks out of the building, I never saw the Other Bearded Man.

Eventually, Gustav shuffled out looking disgusted. In his hands was a big black bundle—a rolled-up coat, I saw once he got up close.

"I thought you were manhuntin', not clothes shoppin'," I said.

Old Red unrolled the coat. Wrapped up in it were a slouch hat, crushed flat, and a U-shaped patch of black hair with an oval hole dead center.

"That ain't what I think it is, is it?"

My brother nodded glumly. "I found these stuffed under a seat in the theater."

"Sweet Jesus . . . a fake beard. I thought them things only existed in Nick Carter stories."

"And King Brady stories," Gustav said. "And Boothby Greene stories, too, should anyone ever write any."

"Yeah, maybe. Only that feller wasn't Brady or Greene, if that's what you're thinkin'. He was older. Bigger."

"I know. And he could be anywhere, by now. I figure he walked out right past us not long after we got here."

"Well, at least we got another new coat out of it. Why is it these bearded SOBs feel such a need to build up our wardrobe? Speakin' of which . . ."

I reached for the coat, but Old Red just shook his head.

"I already checked. The tailor's tag's been removed. Same for the hat. The pockets are empty, too."

"Damn. This feller thinks of everything."

"Yup. Knows how to fight dirty, too. That little trick he pulled when we put the pinch on him? That surely wasn't the first time he's done that."

"So we're up against another professional, you're sayin'?"

Gustav looked out at the Midway, slowly moving his gaze over the dozens of sightseers strolling this way and that through the gloomy gray of oncoming evening. Any twenty or thirty of them could have been the man we were looking for.

"Oh, yeah. He's a professional, alright," Old Red said. "The question is . . . what kind?"

22

CONSPIRACY

Or, Three Birds of a Feather Flock Together and Find They Have a New Tail

Though we'd lost the (we now knew) Unbearded Man and had no way to find him again, we weren't finished yet. It was Urias Smythe we'd been following in the first place, and it sure looked like he was headed for the Midway Plaisance when we got side-tracked. So we decided to make a sweep for him.

The Midway was not an easy place to sweep, however. Night was coming on, for one thing, and even with electric lights flaring to life all around us, there was still more than enough shadow to hide a hundred men, let alone one. For another thing, a search there-abouts could prove an expensive prospect. The Midway was a purely for-profit, pay-as-you-go enterprise, and if we wanted to hunt through the Ottoman Hippodrome or the Hawaiian cyclorama or Hagenbeck's Animal Show or the Turkish, Javan, Laplander, or Dahomey villages, we'd have to shell out two bits a go just like ev-eryone else.

We made a circle around the base of the Ferris wheel in the center of the Midway (Old Red keeping his back to the massive

186

contraption the whole time) and ended up before the warren of shops and fake mosques known as "A Street in Cairo."

"It's no use," my brother said. "This ain't the prairie. Five strides any which way, and a man could disappear."

"That don't mean we gotta give up stridin' ourselves. And if we split up, we could cover twice as much ground."

Gustav stroked his mustache a moment, mulling it over. Then his expression soured and he turned toward the barker shouting at passersby from a Street in Cairo doorway.

"Step this way, gentlemen, step this way, and feast your eyes on Little Egypt and her famous—her infamous!—'belly dance.' Some call it the *danse du ventre,* some call it the Hoochie-Coochie, but I guarantee, my friends, I gehr-own-TEE, that you will call it unforgettable! Just twenty-five cents, one quarter of a dollar, will buy you sights and sounds so exotic, so hypnotic, you will swear you've been transported *à la* magic carpet to a sheik's harem in far-off Araby!"

Old Red swiveled his glower back my way.

"You almost had me," he said.

I shrugged. "Hey, who's to say Smythe *ain't* in there?"

"Me." He threw another glance back at the barker. "Lord . . . he talks almost as much as you."

"Well, you know the best way to shut me up, and I'd say it was about that time, if we're givin' up on Smythe."

"I ain't hungry."

"You would be if you knew what was good for you. We ain't slowed down long enough to eat in what . . . eight, nine hours? Think of your brain, if not your stomach, Brother. It's gotta have something to work on."

"Well . . ."

"Good!"

I started tugging Gustav toward the German village nearby—and, more importantly, the huge German beer garden I'd read was inside.

"Some schnitzel and potato salad, and you'll be a new man," I said. "And we'll finally get us a chance to talk without bein' on the run, so you can tell me why you . . . what?"

Old Red had stopped dead in his tracks.

"On second thought," he said, "I think you were right about us splittin' up. Huntin' for Smythe or studyin' up for tomorrow's contest, either or, we can do a lot more apart than together."

"Oh, come on, now . . ."

I took a step toward him.

He took a step back.

"Don't forget," he said. "We're meetin' Diana at the Ho-Jo Pen at twenty past nine. I'll see you there."

Then he turned and hurried off toward the eastern end of the Midway.

"It's 'Ho-o-den,' you stubborn fool!" I shouted after him. "How you gonna find it when you can't even say it?"

Gustav just waved a hand over his head without looking back. He wouldn't come out and admit it, of course, but I knew what he was running from. Whatever the story was behind those spectacles of his, he wasn't ready to tell it yet.

I just stood there for a minute, thinking, before I was sure.

Yes, *I* was still ready to eat.

I carried on to the German village.

After some schnitzel and kartoffelsalat that wasn't a patch on my mother's, I headed into the White City. Though I stayed on the lookout for Smythe and the Bearded Man and the Unbearded Man and Gustav, too, my heart wasn't really in it. Here I was, at liberty at last at the World's Columbian Exposition. It was time to do me some sightseeing.

For simplicity's sake, I confined myself to the Manufactures and Liberal Arts Building. As it housed by far the biggest assemblage of displays at the fair, I reasoned, odds were the competition would take us there again before the week was out. Unfortunately, though I hoped to get the lay of the land, it proved unlayable for anyone without the exploring skills of Columbus himself. Inside the gigantic building were exhibits touting the wares of nearly every nation on earth, and there wasn't a field of enterprise known to man that didn't get its own sizable section. A family could spend a week just perusing the wing devoted to stoves, and the collection of gas lamps and fixtures took up enough acreage to accommodate a small farm.

With so much to see, my eyes and mind wearied fast, one display blurring into the next, and eventually only the most vivid experiences made any impression at all.

A man playing a beautiful melody on Beethoven's grand piano.

An up-down ride on an Otis-Hale "elevator."

The world's largest "gray canary" diamond sparkling as it spun on a rotating pedestal of pure gold.

I was standing mesmerized by this last when I felt a tap on the shoulder, and a Tiffany & Co. clerk informed me that the building was closing for the night. Nearby, a brawny fellow—no clerk, he—was frowning at me as he tugged on the heavy sliding doors that would turn the Tiffany Pavilion into its own little fortress for the night. His suit coat bulged slightly at the right breast in a way I recognized right off: Like me, the man had a fondness for shoulder holsters.

I tipped my hat and got on my way.

It was nine o'clock, almost time to rendezvous with Gustav and Diana, yet outside there was no lack of light. Electricity blazed everywhere and on everything, and if you'd taken the time to count them up, I do believe the Westinghouse bulbs would have outnumbered the stars above. Great searchlights upon the rooftops were throwing beams of color all around the fairgrounds as well, bright circles of emerald, azure, and scarlet sweeping over the buildings and water and people.

The Wooded Island, home to the Ho-o-den, was lit up, too, though it was rows of round red paper lanterns that did the job. They gave the island's garden-lined paths a soft pink glow, like the light of a dawn that never quite came.

"Beautiful," I said as I sat down next to Old Red, who was waiting on a bench facing the squat, boxy Japanese temples.

"Spooky," he said.

"Hello," said Diana.

We both hopped to our feet.

The lady was smiling as she walked up, and I wanted to tell her the Exposition wasn't a patch on her when it came to radiance—dark hair, dark eyes, dark dress, yet still she seemed to shine. Somehow, I managed to hold myself to an "Evening, miss" and a tip of the hat.

"Where's the colonel?" Gustav asked, throwing glances this way and that as though he expected the man to leap from some black patch brandishing a tomahawk.

"He's concentrating on the northern end of the White City tonight," Diana said. "He got it in his head that we could familiarize ourselves with the fairgrounds twice as quickly if we split up."

"What an interestin' idea," I said. "The colonel got it in his head or someone put it there?"

The lady's smile turned sly. "Oh, it was the colonel's idea . . . I just helped him have it."

"Crowe lets you run around unchaperoned at night?" my brother grumbled. "When there's a murderer on the prowl?"

"I work for the colonel, remember? The White City's probably the *nicest* place he's ever let me run around unchaperoned. Anyway, he still doesn't believe there has been a murder."

"Did you tell him what we found this afternoon?" I asked. "The stains in the Agriculture Building and all that peculiar whatnot dumped out Curtis's window?"

"I did . . . though, of course, I had to improvise a bit in the telling. If he knew we'd been working together, he wouldn't let me out of his sight a second the rest of the week."

Gustav snorted. "And he still ain't convinced something shady's goin' on? That mule-headed little—"

"You can hardly blame him when William Pinkerton and the police are treating Curtis's death as an accident," Diana cut in. "Speaking of which, were you able to pry anything useful out of Mr. Pinkerton and Sergeant Ryan this afternoon?"

I shook my head. "All we got from them was guff."

"It was the same for me, I'm afraid," Diana said. "They were impervious to persuasion. Fortunately, Guardsman Karr was in a far more loquacious mood."

"Guardsman Karr?" I said.

"Loquacious?" said Old Red.

"Talkative," I said. Then, again: "Guardsman Karr?"

But it was my brother who answered.

"Let me guess. He's one of the Columbian Guards who was lockin' up the Agriculture Building tonight."

Diana told him he'd guessed right—and that she wanted to know how—with a cocked eyebrow.

"You wanted to meet here at nine twenty," he explained. "Not nine, not nine thirty, not even nine fifteen. Well, this ain't five minutes' walk from the Agriculture Building, and that closes at nine. So it stood to reason you was givin' yourself a quarter of an hour to—"

"Oh, stop showin' off," I snapped. "Miss Crowe wanted to catch one of the guards at closin' time. You don't gotta flower it up with deductions." I turned back to the lady, and suddenly my voice was dripping honey. "And this Guardsman Karr had something to say, did he?"

He did, and Diana proceeded to spool it out for us.

Every night, it was Karr who locked the Agriculture Building's westernmost doors—those nearest the Stock Pavilion. And exactly twenty-four hours earlier, a gentleman had come stumbling up to him waving an OFFICIAL badge. The man declared himself to be Armstrong B. Curtis, Esquire, and he said he had "confidential business" to conduct inside. Alone. Every Columbian Guard knew of the contest, of course, and they all had orders to cooperate with Mr. Pinkerton's associate Mr. Curtis no matter how eccentric his requests might seem. So Karr reluctantly let Curtis in (the reluctance stemming largely from the wobble and weave of the man's step). After waiting twenty minutes for him to come out again, Karr had gone in to hunt him down and drag him out. Curtis was nowhere in sight, though, and after a brief search, Karr gave up looking. One of his fellow Guardsmen had let Curtis out through another exit, he figured. Or the man had simply staggered out the way he'd come in while Karr was hunting for him. Of course, it never occurred to him to check the Mammoth Cheese of Canada for a new occupant. He just locked up and called it a night.

"Goodness," I said when Diana was done. "Loquacious don't even do it justice. Sounds like Guardsman Karr did everything but act it out with puppets."

Diana shrugged. "It was the least he could do for the dead man's grieving widow."

I gaped at the lady a moment, then offered her a deep bow. "Allow me to say what a pleasure it is to be workin' with you again, Miss Crowe."

"Yeah, yeah—that all helps paint the picture," Old Red said. "Howzabout after Otto and me got called off to the office this afternoon? You able to finagle any new data outta Brady or Tousey or the others?"

"I'm afraid I didn't get the chance to ask questions. I was too busy answering them. Miss Larson took quite the interest in you after you left. Where you're from, what you're like, how you came to be here—she wanted to know everything."

"Well, what do you expect? She might seem like a cold fish"—I spread out my arms as if putting myself on display—"but who doesn't warm to good looks and charm sooner or later?"

"It was actually Gustav she was interested in. Exclusively."

"Really? I am both puzzled and appalled." I rubbed my chin as I mulled it over. "And maybe relieved."

"Enough tomfoolery," Old Red said. "It's our turn."

He didn't need to say any more than that. My brother handles the deducifying in our little partnership, while recapitulations, banter, and walloping people are usually left to me. If it was time to swap information, then I would be the swapper.

I described what we'd dug up the last few hours: Valmont's scandal back in France, Boothby Greene's real name, the conspicuously clean shoes from the Columbian, and, last but certainly not least, the genuine master of disguise who'd taken an inexplicable interest in Urias Smythe.

Diana listened intently, if without reaction, up till this final revelation. After hearing of the Unbearded Man, however, she frowned and furrowed her brow.

"We've been focusing all our energies on individuals from the contest group. If the killer has outside allies, though, that means we're up against some kind of conspiracy."

"Conspiracy?" Gustav said. "I don't know if I'd use as fancy a word as that."

"What other word applies?" Diana replied. "We've got two outside parties we can't account for: the Bearded Man and the Unbearded Man. And someone broke into Curtis's room and meddled with his things, which tells us his death wasn't simply the result of an argument gone wrong. There was a specific purpose behind it—a purpose we don't yet know."

"Well, if all that makes it a conspiracy, then I guess . . . you're . . ."

Old Red's words trailed off, and his gaze shifted ever so slightly to the right, so that he was squinting over Diana's shoulder at one of the island's dimly lit paths. I could see nothing there but round balls of reddish lantern light and the black, blobby shapes of shrubs and topiary, but from his sudden, rigid stillness, I knew my brother saw something more.

My fingers twitched out of habit, anxious to wrap around the grip of a gun I didn't have.

"You may as well come on out," Gustav said. "I reckon you've heard just about everything."

About thirty feet from us, a shadow broke in two. Half seemed to be a rosebush. The other half walked toward us. It was so small, at first I took it for a lost child.

Diana gasped as it drew up close.

"So now you know," Colonel Crowe said to her. "Your doting old godfather isn't half as gullible as you like to think."

"You followed me? Eavesdropped on us?"

"I'd say it was my right when I'm being lied to."

"Colonel," Old Red said, and from the muted tone of his voice

I knew he was working hard to tamp down his usual tetchiness, "if you were eavesdroppin', then you know we ain't makin' any of this up. Something's afoot here. Something strange and dangerous."

Colonel Crowe stepped up to Diana. It looked like he meant to take her by the arm and drag her away, but he stopped beside her instead.

"Yes," he said. "I grant you that. It seems I was hasty in my judgment this afternoon. Yet that still doesn't make any of this our business. Diana and I are here to win a contest, not do Sergeant Ryan's work for him."

"But if the contest and the *murder* are tied up together, it is your business, sir," Gustav replied. He paused a moment, giving the colonel a chance to dispute that "murder," but the little man said nothing. "And if the points start pilin' up the wrong way, who's to say Curtis is the only one who's gonna end up dead?"

"It's in your own interests to look into this with us," I threw in. I'm supposed to be the persuasive one of the two of us, so it was purely out of habit. It was also a big mistake.

The colonel's expression instantly soured. "I'm surprised you'd want any assistance from 'the kind of military mind that could make Custer look like a model of common sense and cool-headedness.'"

I went numb from head to toe.

Colonel Crowe was quoting one of my own books back to me.

"Oh, well, heh heh, that was just an unfortunate turn of phrase for comical—"

"My brother is a horse's ass, and for that I apologize," Old Red said. "That don't change the situation, though. We'd all be better off if we worked together."

Colonel Crowe just stewed for a moment (while I fumed over that "horse's ass" crack).

"I'll think about it," the colonel finally said, and at last he did wrap an arm around Diana and begin guiding her away.

"Good night, gentlemen," the lady said.

Before she turned her back to us fully, she favored us with a quick wink.

"That woman," Gustav said, shaking his head, once the Crowes were gone.

I shook my head, too. "Oh, yeah. That woman."

My brother threw me a dubious look. "Do you even know what I'm talkin' about?"

"Sure." I pointed at the path Diana had just departed on. "That woman."

Old Red sighed in a way that seemed to call me a horse's ass all over again.

"What?" I said.

"She knew the colonel would follow her. She wanted him to overhear that conversation. She set up the whole thing so he'd see there's no hanky-panky between us and we ain't crazy to say Curtis was murdered."

"Ohhhhhhhhhhhh."

I pushed back my hat and whistled and said the only thing that seemed to fit the moment.

"*That . . . woman.*"

23

PROMISES, PROMISES

Or, We Fail to Hold a Suspect's Feet to the Fire,

and Gustav and I Go Toe-to-Toe

We returned to our hotel. And aside from one "Shit!" in the midst of a particularly close call with a hard-charging hansom, my brother said nothing.

"Hel-lo!" was the word (or words?) that finally broke his silence. We'd just stepped onto our floor at the Columbian to find two pairs of shoes set out for shining. One was beside a door about halfway down the hall, the other no more than six steps from us.

Gustav pounced on the nearest shoes, snatched one up, and stared down into it.

"We got us a maker's mark," he whispered.

When I was close enough to look inside for myself, I saw a circle of words stamped into the dark leather of the insole.

RUGGERO E ROMANO • MILAN

"Italian," I said, careful to keep my voice low. Most likely, the shoe's owner could be found lounging on a bed just beyond one very thin door.

My brother grunted, then flipped the shoe over to get a look at the sole. Stuck to it were four blobs of white goo, two on the heel, two closer to the toe. All had been smashed flat into wavy-edged discs about the size of a quarter.

"What the hell is that?" Old Red said softly.

I leaned in and gave the little globules a whiff.

"Juicy Fruit."

"Oh."

My brother gave the shoe a smell, too, not restricting himself to the flattened chewing wax. I was just wondering whose aroma he was sampling when Fate handed me the answer. And as is usual with Fate, I've found, it didn't go about it gently.

The door before us swung open, and there stood Frank Tousey gaping down at us.

"What in God's name are you doing?"

"Admirin' fine craftsmanship!" I enthused, bolting upright. "You might not believe it, but I'm something of a fashion plate, when finances allow, and I've been mighty impressed by your sartorial sense. You, sir, are pure gentleman from head to, quite literally, toe. So I couldn't resist the urge to learn where you'd acquired such stylish footwear."

As I spoke, Gustav straightened up beside me and folded his arms across his chest. Tousey looked back and forth between the two of us, the sneer on his face making it clear he regarded the Amlingmeyer brothers with the same esteem one would usually reserve for Juicy Fruit—or worse—stuck to the bottom of one's fine Italian shoes.

"You were right when you said I might not believe it," he said. "Because I don't."

"You always wear Eye-talian-made shoes?" my brother asked.

Tousey barked out a nasty laugh. "Don't tell me you're a fashion plate, too."

"Nope. Just curious."

"Well, the answer's yes." Tousey pointed at his feet, which were clad in nothing but black socks. "Except when I'm just trying to get to the damn water closet to take a damn piss. Now would you step aside, please?"

I got out of the man's way.

Old Red didn't.

"There's one more thing I'd like to ask, long as we're havin' us a chat. Last night, Mr. Curtis said something puzzlin' about your man Brady: that we should ask him about his birthday. You know what that was all about?"

"Yes," Tousey said. "It was about Armstrong Curtis being a complete madman. Now *get out of my way*."

Gustav finally moved aside, and Tousey stepped into the hall, picked up his shoes, and tossed them into his room. Then he closed his door—and pulled out a key and locked it, for good measure.

"You know," he said, "if you two had one brain between you, you'd forget about Curtis and concentrate on the contest. Because in case you hadn't noticed, nobody but you is in any hurry to stir up a stink the last week of the Columbian Exposition. If—*if*—that Sergeant Ryan decides Curtis had help smothering himself, you can bet the Exposition board, Mayor Harrison, and probably Grover goddamn Cleveland wouldn't want him saying so until after the Fair's . . . oh, forget it. I'm about to bust."

He hustled down the hall toward the WC. My brother just stood there watching him, silent and still.

"What're you lookin' at?" I asked.

"I'm hopin' he don't make it."

Tousey reached the end of the hall, pivoted stiffly, and fairly threw himself into the privy.

"Oh, well," Old Red said. "Let's get a look at them other shoes."

They were outside Smythe's door, they were high-sided black-and-white button-ups, and they were not, it turned out, Italian.

No, they were English, the products of (embossing on the sole told us) GUNDRY & SONS, SOHO SQUARE, LONDON.

"Damn," Gustav sighed. "Don't nobody make nothin' this side of the Atlantic anymore?"

I brought up a fist and let it hover a couple inches from the door.

"Shall we ask Smythe what he's got against American shoes? We could throw the Bearded Man in his face, too. About time we asked about that note."

Old Red thought it over a moment, then jerked his head at the other end of the hall, back toward our rooms. He didn't speak till we were both well away from Smythe's door.

"You saw how Tousey bluffed his way past us. Let's not waste our ammunition on Smythe till we got him dead to rights."

"Dead to rights doin' what?"

"Whatever it is he's doin'," Gustav said with a shrug. "In the meantime, might as well call it a night."

He stopped before his door. I did, too.

"I'll take first watch," I said as he pulled out his key.

Old Red froze. "What makes you think we're bunkin' together?"

"The fact that there's most likely a murderer a door or two down, and he no doubt knows we been sniffin' around after him."

"Our doors got locks."

"So did the one to Mr. Curtis's room. So did that window into the Agriculture Building. A lock ain't nothing to bet our lives on—and you'd admit that yourself, if you weren't so stubborn."

"I ain't bein'—"

"Yes, you are. You're bound and determined not to talk about them cheaters of yours. So much so, you were about to make a fool mistake just to avoid it. Well, if it'll keep you from slittin' our throats for us, I'm willin' to make a deal: no questions about your eyes tonight."

My brother squinted at me a moment before heaving a mighty sigh. "Promise?"

"You got my word."

"Fine." Old Red opened the door. "But if you break it, *I'll* kill you."

Soon after, he was stretched out on the bed, while I was on the floor with my guidebook and a useless Peacemaker. (Well, the shiny new Colt that came with Mr. Cohn's cowboy costume wasn't *entirely* useless. We had no bullets for it, true, but the ivory handle would make a fine club, if need be.)

"Night," I said.

"Night."

I let a minute pass. Then another. Then another.

Just when I heard my brother's breathing deepen, catch in his chest in that raspy way that would soon be snores, I spoke again.

"Funny thing about promises, though . . ."

"Christ. Here we go."

"A few months back, you promised there'd never be any lies between us again. Yet then you up and lied about your eyes."

"I never lied about that."

"Oh?"

"No. I just . . . let you make some assumptions."

"Like thinkin' you was still hurtin' when you really weren't?"

There was a long pause.

"Yeah. I coulda got rid of them glasses a week ago."

"Why didn't you?"

There was an even longer pause.

"Hey, I'm on watch here," I said. "If you're waitin' for me to fall asleep, it ain't gonna work. So you'd best just answer me: Why?"

Gustav mumbled something.

"What was that?"

"I said, I don't know!"

Of course, that's an old dodge, "I don't know." It usually means "I don't want to say." Yet I could tell my brother meant it. He was as baffled by himself as by any mystery he might set out to solve.

"Theorize, then," I said. "Guess."

To my surprise, Old Red tried.

"I reckon maybe . . . I liked havin' a reason to fail. An excuse. If this detectivin' thing don't work out, you know what we got to fall back on."

"Sure. Nothing."

"I was gonna say droverin', but yeah. Same thing. We ain't got no jobs, no family, no home. If I can't give us any of that again . . . I guess I didn't want it to be cuz I just wasn't good enough."

Good God, do my ears deceive me? I almost scoffed. *Old Red Amlingmeyer, the Holmes of the Range . . . humble?*

This wasn't the Holmes of the Range I was hearing, though. It wasn't even Old Red Amlingmeyer. It was just Gustav, my brother, stretching his neck out like a tortoise leaving its shell. And I'm glad it wasn't Big Red Amlingmeyer who answered him. It was his little brother Otto.

"Of course you're good enough," I said. "You're better than good enough. You're great! If you weren't, I wouldn't have dragged you to Chicago—and you wouldn't have Diana Crowe fightin' for you the way she is. Sure, she likes us, but that ain't what it's about. The lady's a professional, and she can see you could be, too. Maybe the best there is. And if you've lost sight of that, then you're as bad as Smythe and Pinkerton and Tousey and the colonel, cuz you're makin' the same mistake they are: judgin' yourself by your second-hand clothes instead of your first-rate mind."

"F-"

"Don't you 'feh' me! That's false modesty. That's them specs all over again, and they are gone. You ain't got no excuses, and you ain't gonna need any. Cuz whether it's by winnin' the contest or ropin' in a murderer or both, you're gonna prove to the world what Diana and I already know—and you never should've forgotten."

This, I believe, was altogether too much brotherly approbation for Gustav to take, and he felt the need to cut through it with a good Old Red–style snarl.

"I ain't been runnin' around today chasin' bullshit and beards to make myself look good! A man's dead, and we're rubbin' elbows with his killer. That's what matters. To think of turnin' that to our advantage somehow . . . I will give it a 'feh'! *Feh!*"

"Alright, alright. You can consider me chastised and the subject dropped."

"Good."

I busied myself with my guidebook, pleased to have squeezed not just an explanation from my brother but some honest-to-goodness soul-baring. I hadn't managed to drag an apology out with it, but one can't expect more than one miracle in a day.

Just when I'd started to think Gustav was asleep, I heard him speak.

"I'm sorry I wasn't square with you," he said softly. "It won't happen again, I swear."

I put my book down and crawled over to the side of the bed.

"I truly appreciate that," I said. "Still, let's see you cross your heart and hope to die, this time."

There was a muffled thud, and everything went black.

Old Red had hit me over the head with his pillow.

"Close enough," I said.

24

FAVORITES

Or, An Idol Gets Tarnished While Someone Surprising Takes a Shine to Gustav

When the time came to return to the Court of Honor for the next round of the contest, we found Major Bacon and His Hoosier One Hundred tooting out Sousafied favorites for a throng twice as large as the one that had packed in around the gazebo the day before. Gustav stopped at the edge of the crowd, pausing to work up his nerve before wading on into it.

"Wouldn't you know," he grumbled. "A man gets killed, and out come the buzzards."

We were attired as we had been the day before—him in rough work clothes, me in a suit, both of us topped with Stetsons—and enough folks recognized us to draw a steady stream of back-pats and go-get-'ems as we made our way toward the bandstand. Old Red endured the attention with obvious uneasiness, body rigid, face twitchy, eyes ever darting this way and that.

"Relax, Brother," I told him. "Folks are just showin' their support. I know it's not in you to smile, but could you at least look like you ain't about to bite 'em?"

"I'll try. But there are sure a lotta fellers with beards around here."

"Say . . . there are, aren't there?"

My eyes started doing some darting, too.

When we finally reached the gazebo, we found our path blocked by a small, milling herd of clamoring men. There were perhaps a dozen of them, all wearing cheap suits and boaters and identical looks of frenzied intensity. They were squeezed in around the stairs up to the platform, the only thing keeping them from rushing it, it seemed, being a single Columbian Guard standing on the first step.

"Was he drunk?" one of them shouted at us.

"Was he crazy?" another called out.

"Did you see the body?"

"Was he really trying to eat the cheese?"

"Did the ghost get him?"

"What's King Brady like?"

"Yes, kinda, yes, I doubt it, what in God's name are you talkin' about, you couldn't print it even if I told you, and who the heck *are* you, anyway?" I replied.

The men didn't really need to answer my question—especially not when they all bent over little pads of paper and got to scribbling like a pack of Lucille Larsons. To the left of them stood a man behind a camera-topped tripod, but apparently he didn't think us worth any flash powder.

"Was the 'I doubt it' to the ghost or eating the cheese?" one of the newsmen said.

"What have you got against King Brady, idol of millions?" another asked.

"Take your pick," I said. It seemed like a fine enough reply to either question.

My brother, meanwhile, had a question of his own. "What was that about a ghost?"

"The ghost of Sherlock Holmes!" said a stubble-faced fellow in a white seersucker suit so wrinkled it looked like an unmade bed. "It materialized in the Administration Building at the stroke of midnight—just after Curtis Armstrong was killed!"

The other reporters groaned in chorus.

"Aww, pshaw," said one.

"Where does he get this stuff?" said a second.

"It's Armstrong Curtis, Phil," said a third.

"That's the *Journal* for you," said a fourth.

"Just ignore him," said a fifth.

"That's what *we* do," said a sixth.

"Hey!" said a seventh. "Here comes King Brady!"

Then my brother and I were the ones being ignored, apart from cries of "Step aside!" and "Let the man through!"

Gustav and I dutifully hopped out of the way as Brady and Frank Tousey came striding along smiling.

"Was he drunk, King?"

"Was he crazy, King?"

"Did you see the body, King?"

"Was he really trying to eat the cheese, King?"

"Did the ghost get him, King?"

"What are you really like, King?"

"King! King! Look this way!"

"No pictures!" Tousey snapped, his smile gone in a flash, and he bolted forward to block the camera with his chest.

The photographer responded by calling Tousey several unprintable (though, in my mind, entirely accurate) names.

"I'm sorry," Tousey said, drifting back to Brady's side, "but if someone wants a picture of King, they'll have to pick up a copy of

New York Detective Library." He held his hands up toward Brady's so-perfect-it-hurt face. "You don't just give away something like this for free, do you?"

The newspapermen wasted all of half a breath on obligatory chuckles, then launched right back into their questions—the same ones shouted twice as loud.

Standing off to the side as we were, I could see Tousey put a hand to the small of Brady's back and give him a little pat. It was almost as though he was cranking the key on a windup toy, for Brady immediately opened his mouth and got to making noise.

"I know you're curious about Mr. Curtis's untimely passing, but I'm not the person to turn to for answers. My good friends at the Chicago Police Department have the matter well in hand, and when the wheels of justice are turning smoothly, there's no need for King Brady to intervene. Should those wheels bog down, however, the authorities know that King Brady, as always, stands ready to help."

"And Gustav Amlingmeyer stands ready to puke," Old Red grumbled. We slinked off unnoticed as King Brady went on extolling the virtues of King Brady's unparalleled King Bradyness.

When we reached the top of the stairs, we found Diana, Colonel Crowe, William Pinkerton, Lucille Larson, and Urias Smythe already there. I started steering us toward the Crowes, curious to know if the colonel had altered his thinking in the past half day, but Miss Larson peeled herself from Smythe's side to intercept us.

Smythe looked relieved. Gustav looked alarmed.

"Well, it's all settled," Miss Larson said, and she slid in beside my brother and took him by the arm. "For the rest of the afternoon, you're the exclusive property of *McClure's Magazine*."

"E-excuse me?" Old Red stammered.

"Each day of the contest, I've followed a different sleuth. After your little performance yesterday, Mr. Amlingmeyer, I decided you should be next."

"M-my little performance?"

My brother was blushing and staring at the floorboards and generally looking like he'd gnaw off his own arm to escape the lady. The day before, with a fresh murder on his mind, he'd seemed to forget that this was a prettyish woman. Now, though, with her bony frame pressed up close, his old gal-jitters were back bad as ever.

"Yesterday, during the gathering in the lobby, everyone else was bickering, dithering," Miss Larson said. "You were the only one to actually *do* something, and it was beautiful."

"Oh? What'd I do?" Old Red asked as if he didn't know the answer.

For me, it wasn't an act. "Yeah . . . what'd he do?"

Miss Larson shook her head and smirked.

"Still answering questions with questions," she said. To Gustav. She was paying me no more mind than you would a speck of dust floating by on the breeze. "You can stop being coy."

My brother was looking at anything and everything but the lady—the crowd, the Grand Basin, the ceiling, his shoes.

"Coy?" he said.

To my surprise, Miss Larson started to look annoyed. The surprise being that she hadn't started sooner.

"Everyone was arguing about how to continue the contest," she said. "By putting it to a vote, you forced each and every one of us— even me—to take a stand one way or another. Commit ourselves. Whether the contest would continue as is was secondary. In truth, you were fabricating a pretext for assessing possible motives."

"Miss, you sure use a lotta ten-cent words." Old Red finally met the lady's gaze. He was able to hold it, too. For two or three seconds, anyway. "But I expect you're right. I wanted to know where folks stood with Curtis gone. Cuz that'd tell me who most *wanted* him gone."

He took to picking at a loose thread on his sleeve.

"See?" Miss Larson said, finally speaking to me. "Beautiful."

"That's a word I never thought I'd hear applied to my brother," I said.

"Either you're the only one who believes Curtis was murdered or you're the only one who's willing to act on it openly," Miss Larson went on, speaking to Gustav again. She tightened her grip on his arm, pulling him tighter to her scrawny side. "Either way, that makes you the most interesting man here right now."

Old Red squirmed like a worm on the hook.

Then, just like that, he stopped. His spine straightened, so he wasn't cringing anymore, and he looked over at the lady with a gaze that stayed steady.

"Two days ago, the most interestin' gent around was King Brady, am I right?"

"I followed him the first day of the contest, yes. For reasons I'm sure are quite obvious. He's by far the most famous detective here."

"What'd you think of his sleuthin'?"

Miss Larson shrugged. "I didn't really see any. He just ran around a lot."

"Well, from what you could see, did it seem like the man lived up to his reputation?"

"Not for a second. I'd say the man's a conceited fraud."

"You mean like Nick Carter? Just a pipe dream?"

"Uhhhh, Brother," I said. "That'd be kinda hard to pull off, wouldn't it? You know. Seein' as the man's *right down them steps.*"

Miss Larson was shaking her head. "No, no," she said to Gustav. "Brady's a real detective, alright. You see stories about him in the legitimate press from time to time. News articles, I mean, not entertainments. He's a private investigator in New York City. That's fact. It's just that Tousey's built him up to be the American Sherlock Holmes when there's nothing remotely clever about him."

"Or brave," Old Red said, no doubt thinking of the way Brady went weak at the knee when we stumbled upon Curtis's body the day before.

A great "Hurrah!" went up from the crowd, and the band launched into Sousa's "The Gladiator."

King Brady was at last headed up the stairs to join us on the bandstand. He paused every couple steps to wave or doff his hat, the cheers growing louder and wilder with each repetition.

"Go get 'em, King!"

"We're behind you all the way, King!"

"Show us what you got, King!"

"Yeah," Gustav muttered. "Come and show us what you got."

No doubt about it, King Brady was the people's favorite.

In a very different way, it seemed, he'd become my brother's, too.

25

THE CONTEST
(ROUND THREE)

Or, My Brother's Suspicions Come to a Head, and I Get In over Mine

Before long, **Boothby Greene,** Blackheath-Murray, and Eugene Valmont followed King Brady and Frank Tousey up onto the bandstand. As soon as all us contestants were lined up, Pinkerton stepped to the podium and addressed the crowd.

If his introductory speech Monday had been halfhearted, he was down to quarterhearted now. He re-presented the competitors with all the zeal of a schoolboy giving a report on the benefits of eating spinach, then asked for a moment of silence "for those whom tragedy has kept from being with us today." The silence wasn't particularly silent, though, what with the splashings of the nearby fountains and occasional cries along the lines of "We love you, King!" After all of ten seconds, it was over, and a great cheer went up as Pinkerton produced the clues, held them aloft, and turned to hand them out.

The second our envelope was in my hand, I tore it open and read out the neatly typed message within.

Then I asked God what He had against us.

```
Foul swamp! In thy slow, oozing flow
Of murky and muddied water,
Black as the grave where no light goes,
No thing can grow; so we ask how
Leviathan can say "Meow"
And sire there such monstrous daughters
```

"Sweet Jesus. It don't even make enough sense to be a proper riddle."

"It don't matter," Old Red said.

"It don't?"

"Nope."

To the right of us, Valmont, Greene, and the Crowes were all still puzzling over their own clues, but—much to the delight of the masses—King Brady was on the move, marching with quick, certain purpose toward the stairs.

"We ain't goin' on no wild goose chase today," my brother whispered. "We're just chasin' *him*."

"You mean you wanna trail him? But what about the contest?"

"What about it?"

The low, growly tone of Gustav's voice told me there was no use arguing—which usually doesn't stop me from doing it anyway. This time we had an audience, though: Lucille Larson had been standing with Tousey and Smythe and Blackheath-Murray as Pinkerton ran through the preliminaries, but now she swooped in to lay claim to us again.

"So?" she said, nodding at the clue card in my hands. "Cracked it already?"

I looked at Old Red. "Oh, it's cracked, alright."

"Come on," my brother said, and he led us down the steps.

It was easy enough staying on Brady's trail. About fifty people seemed to have the same idea, clumping up around the man as he tried to stride away from the bandstand. He gathered up such a flock, in fact, Tousey took to the podium to urge people to let him pass.

"Our sleuths have work to do, folks! Don't worry—you'll see them again soon! Just wait here in the Court of Honor, and all will be revealed!"

Most of Brady's followers dropped away, yet a small gaggle scurried along after him as he turned up the path leading north between the Electricity Building and the Mines and Mining Building.

We took the turn, too.

"Where are we going?" Miss Larson asked.

"Won't know till we get there," Gustav said.

The lady followed his gaze to King Brady's back forty yards up.

"Is this part of your investigation or are you just cheating?"

"Miss," I said, "if we was cheatin', would *he* be the one we stick to?"

"So what is it you think you'll gain by following him?"

"I got me a hunch," Old Red said.

Several strides went by in silence.

"And your hunch is . . . ?" Miss Larson finally prompted.

"Oh, he never speaks 'em aloud," I told her. "If he does, the Hunch Fairy won't make 'em come true."

Miss Larson looked back and forth between me and my brother as if trying to decide which of us was, at that particular moment, the most irritating. I reckon she came to a conclusion, too, for she took her notepad and pencil from a drawstring bag and started writing even as we walked.

Up ahead, Brady was now hustling across a bridge toward the islands in the great lagoon just north of the Grand Basin. Despite his quick pace, he still had followers (other than us)—a small flock of schoolboys skipping along at his heels. As the caravan followed the path curving along the southwestern edge of the Wooded Island, Gustav slowed to keep us just around the bend from Brady, and for a moment we lost sight of him. That moment stretched into two when the path straightened out again.

Brady was nowhere in sight.

"Shi- . . ." I caught myself just in time. ". . . oot."

"Thank you," Miss Larson said.

"*There.*"

Old Red pointed at another bridge stretching west over the lagoon again. Brady was scurrying over it, the young pups still capering along behind.

"Where the heck's he goin', anyway?" I said.

Miss Larson made a sound that could've been called a chuckle, perhaps, had there been any genuine amusement to it.

"I think I can tell you. It was the first place he went Monday, too. Today he's just been a little more circuitous about it."

She nodded at a low black building on the other side of the bridge, between the Choral and Horticulture buildings.

"And what exactly is that?" Gustav asked.

"Oh, I'd hate to spoil the surprise."

The lady was right. We weren't halfway over the bridge ourselves when we saw Brady duck into the structure she'd pointed out. The kids didn't follow, drifting off instead looking profoundly disillusioned. I knew why when we got close enough to see the sign out front.

"Public Comfort Building," I read out.

"Huh?" Old Red said.

"The john," I explained.

"Oh." My brother squinted at the building. "It's nicer than most places we've called home."

Miss Larson dutifully jotted this down, much to my chagrin.

"So this is where Brady came first thing on Monday?" Gustav said.

Miss Larson nodded. "He was in there at least ten minutes." She shrugged. "Nerves, perhaps."

Old Red shuffled his feet and tugged at the brim of his hat. "Hmm. Yeah. Maybe. And when he came out?"

"He'd had a brainstorm. He led us straight to the New York Building, where he found his second clue. Then he came here *again*, and after that it was on to the Yerkes telescope. Valmont beat him to the egg by mere seconds."

Gustav jerked up straight, eyes agleam. "He solved both riddles while he was in there?"

"Yes."

"Some folks do their best thinkin' in there," I pointed out.

Old Red ignored me.

"And when he came out he almost won the contest?" he asked the lady.

"Yes."

"That tears it. I'm goin' in."

"You're *what*?" I said.

My brother started toward the door gentlemen were filing in and out through. "Y'all wait here."

"Good idea," Miss Larson said.

Gustav disappeared into the Public Comfort Building, leaving Miss Larson and me outside in a state of most extreme *dis*comfort. Somehow, I got the feeling loitering around public lavatories did not strike the lady as inspired Holmes-style sleuthing, and with her every little scribble in her notepad, I could feel our portrait in *McClure's* grow less flattering. When she was done writing ("Why did I think these fools knew what they were doing?" no doubt), she looked over at the clue card I still clutched in my hand.

"Doesn't it bother you to just give up on that?" she asked. "After today, you'll only get one more chance to score. You can't even win. The best you could hope for is *not* being the only team that doesn't score at all."

"I've been doin' my best not to think about that."

The lady kept staring at the card. "May I? Just out of curiosity."

"Sure. Don't expect it to mean anything, though. This one Curtis must've come up with by just throwin' things at his typewriter."

I gave her the card.

"Oh," she said upon glancing at it, and she handed it right back with an air of embittered boredom. "Is that all?"

"You mean you get it?"

"You mean you don't?"

I shrugged helplessly.

"Well, I suppose you would be at a disadvantage," Miss Larson said. "It is a little . . . literary."

I read the clue through again myself. "'Leviathan can say "Meow"' is *literary*?"

"It's a burlesque of a Poe poem. 'To the River.'"

I stared back at her blankly.

"'*To . . . the . . . River*,'" Miss Larson repeated. Then, growing ever more exasperated, "Leviathan was a *sea monster*."

"Well, that I actually knew alre-DAMN!"

Miss Larson cocked an eyebrow at me. Most of the tourists around just flat-out stared.

"I mean dang," I said, hopping from foot to foot like I had to visit the gents' myself. I could barely keep my legs from breaking into a sprint.

I knew where the next clue was. We still had a shot at winning after all . . . only my brother was doing Lord knows what in a fancy-ass privy.

Was he in danger? I didn't think so.

Did he really need me around? I couldn't see how.

Would he be pissed if I ran off without him? Of course.

Did I care? That was a tougher one. So I let my legs decide.

They started running.

"Tell my brother where I went!" I shouted over my shoulder.

"I'm not Western Union!" Miss Larson replied.

Then I was around the corner of the Horticulture Building, out of range of the daggers she was staring my way. I suppose it must sting a woman's pride some, being abandoned by not one but two men outside a WC.

I consulted my guidebook as I ran (and, in the process, nearly bowled over a group of sightseeing nuns like so many big black tenpins). Across another bridge, back onto the Wooded Island, past the Japanese Ho-o-den, across yet another bridge, and I'd be there.

The Fish and Fisheries Building.

It wasn't nearly so imposing as its dome- and statuary-studded brethren thereabouts, I saw as I dashed toward it. In fact, it looked like nothing so much as three overgrown bandstands connected by long colonnades, with some turrets thrown on here and there for show. Once I'd raced up the steps and darted through the nearest door, however, I beheld a sight that, at first, seemed not just imposing but outright impossible.

I was in a darkened hall bracketed on either side by long pools of light-dappled water. Which wouldn't have been so amazing, except that said pools had been mounted to the walls like living pictures, and one could walk up to them and see eye to eye with lazily swimming fish—something I wouldn't have thought possible without sticking one's head in a lake.

I'd read of aquarium tanks, of course, yet it still took my mind a moment to accept the reality of those before me. As I walked up the hallway, I couldn't help but feel like an Egyptian chasing Moses into the Red Sea . . . which would come crashing in on both sides any second.

"Uhhh, y'all got any catfish in this place?" I asked the first fellow I passed who looked at all official—a chubby little cherub of a man with a ribbon pinned to his lapel reading DOCENT.

"Have we got catfish?" he chuckled, shaking his head, and directed me to the building's eastern wing.

I understood his amusement a minute later, when I saw the following words posted beside a particularly popular water tank:

ICTALURUS FURCATUS
WORLD'S LARGEST CATFISH IN CAPTIVITY
CAUGHT IN THE MISSISSIPPI RIVER BY MR. HECTOR DeJEAN
MARCH 16, 1893

Lurking at the silty bottom of the tank was either Mr. DeJean's *Ictalurus furcatus* or a tree trunk with fins, whiskers, and gills. One fillet from the thing would get a family of four through a long winter.

I had no time to pause and ogle "Leviathan's monstrous daughter," though. It was the docent ogling *me* I was more interested in. He was standing to one side of the tank, a hand dipping into the pocket of his frock coat.

"You're one of the Amlingmeyers?" he said.

"That's right."

I stepped toward the man.

He drew out an envelope and started to give it to me.

A hand shot out and snatched the card away.

I said a word I can't repeat here.

A dark shape whirled around and hustled up the hallway.

The Bearded Man was back, and he was making off with my next clue.

This was Bearded Man #1, to be precise—Urias Smythe's pal, the one who'd done a dance on Gustav's glasses. He only got a couple seconds' head start before I shoved aside my astonishment and bolted after him. He peeked over his shoulder at me as I gained on him, and I caught a glimpse of dark skin and curly black hair and wide, panicky eyes.

"*Urgle!*" he cried. Or something like that. It was no word I'd ever heard, yet I got the distinct impression it was cousin to the curse I'd popped off with a moment before.

Fear spurred the man on faster, and that—combined with my collision with a burly tourist who'd blundered into my path on his way to admire the seahorses or some such—stretched out his lead again.

"Help! Stop! Thief!" I called out.

The Bearded Man had almost reached an exit, but before he could dart through it a pair of upstanding citizens moved to cut off his escape.

"*Urgle!*" he said again, and he veered to the right and threw him-self through a door marked NO ADMITTANCE.

Seconds later, I was ignoring the sign, too.

The door led to a room chockablock with cabinets and crates and, in one corner, a spiral staircase of black iron the Bearded Man was busy spinning up.

I reached the top not five steps behind him, finding myself at the end of a long, narrow metal walkway that curved in a broad circle, the end out of sight. Beneath it were huge pools of water: the build-ing's fish tanks as seen from above.

The Bearded Man was racing away from me again, his footfalls on the walkway's iron-mesh plates pounding up deafening echoes.

This was my second day chasing Bearded Men, though, and I guess I was getting better with practice. I was on this one fast, and I managed to snag him by the collar of his long (new) coat, then spin him around to face me.

"Alright, mister—the masquerade party's over!"

Then I did something I feel kind of bad about. Instead of just snatching the envelope back, I reached out and grabbed the man's beard. I guess our encounter with the Unbearded Man had given me ideas.

"A-ha!" I said, and I yanked down hard.

The beard itself did not come off, though a few curly hairs and bits of skin did.

The Bearded Man—the Really Truly Not-Fake Bearded Man, one could call him—screamed.

"Oh, God. I'm sorry," I said.

"*Urgle* you, cowboy!" the man bawled back, and he brought up the envelope he'd stolen from me and threw it as far as he could into the nearest tank.

"No!"

The pale yellow paper of the envelope darkened fast as it soaked up water. I could see it going limp, too. Starting to sink.

I had two choices: try to hold on to my catch or go after bigger fish.

I tried for a compromise, clipping the Bearded Man across his newly thinned chin whiskers before hurling myself into the tank below.

I plunged deep into the dark water, catching a murky glimpse of stunned faces staring at me through the glass before I started kicking my way back to the surface. As I swam, I felt something both rough and slimy brush against my left ankle, and it only then occurred to me to wonder whose tank I was taking a dip in.

They didn't have sharks on display, did they? Squids? South American piranha? Eels? *Alligators?*

I thrashed back toward the walkway with an *"Urgle!"* of my own. Just as I got my hands on iron and tried to hoist myself out, something big bumped up against my upper thigh.

Now, I'm rather partial to my thighs, and the image of one going in chunks down the gullet of some ravenous sea creature did, I'm afraid, no small damage to my dignity.

Meaning I started kicking and screaming.

A fierce pressure locked on to me, and I was dragged away.

And, more importantly, *up*. By the wrists.

I was being fished out by a pair of Columbian Guards. Unfortunately, they were alone on the walkway. My punch hadn't been enough to hold the Bearded Man. He was gone.

"Thanks, boys," I panted. "Guess I let myself get a little unnerved there for a second."

"You alright now?" one of the Guardsmen asked, moving his hand to my shoulder.

I nodded. "Just need a minute to catch my breath."

"Fine." The Guardsman's fingers tightened till it hurt. "When you're ready, we'll take you over to the Security Department. You're under arrest."

26

ARRESTED DEVELOPMENTS

Or, I Find a Familiar Face in the Pokey, and a Familiar Beard Reappears as Well

The witnesses who saw me chasing a thief didn't help. My being in an official Exposition-approved contest didn't help. My *begging* didn't help.

"Sorry, son," one of the Guardsmen said as I was marched, sopping wet, out of the Fisheries Building. "If Jesus H. Christ Himself jumped in with the fish, we'd have to arrest Him."

"Oh, well," I sighed. "Least I'm in good company."

That held true when I was locked up in the Columbian Guard's little holding cell as well, for my brother was there already.

"What're you doin' here?" I asked as I plopped down next to him on the cell's lone bunk.

He grimaced miserably. "You first."

I spun out the tale.

"You get back that clue card, at least?" Old Red asked when I was done.

I shook my head. "Damned thing turned to mush out there in the water. So . . . why are you in the hoosegow?"

222

My brother threw me a warning glare. "Don't laugh."

"Why would I laugh?"

"I'm serious. You laugh, we're gonna tussle."

I put on a lugubriously long face. "Do I look like I'm about to laugh?"

"Alright." Gustav sucked in a deep, weary, wary breath. "I was arrested for peekin' at folks in the privy."

"Oh, sweet Jesus." I put my head in my hands. "You should've warned me not to *cry*."

"Brady wasn't out in sight, but there were gents in all the stalls, so I had to . . . well, I had to crouch down and do me some lookin'. And wouldn't you know it, one of them Guardsmen chose that very moment to come in and water the flowers."

"What did you think you was gonna catch Brady up to?"

"I don't know. But I'll tell you what I *did* catch him at."

Given where Gustav had done the catching, I wasn't sure I *wanted* to know. Still, I looked up and gave him a "What?"

"Just sittin' there, drawers up . . . with the fellow we caught tailin' Smythe yesterday doin' the same the next stall over."

"The Unbearded Man was there?"

"Yup."

"Were they talkin'?"

"I wasn't there long enough to tell."

"Be quite a coincidence if they weren't."

"So it would."

"Well. Well well well."

I was still letting this sink in when Gustav spoke up again.

"Brother?"

"Yeah?"

"Would you mind movin'? You're gettin' the bunk all soppy."

And here I thought he was going to thank me for not laughing.

223

As I stood and shuffled toward the cell door, a man apparently dressed as Napoleon Bonaparte marched in to inspect us. His uniform was similar to that worn by the Columbian Guard, only it was even more flamboyant, with enough gold braid and piping to trim ninety-nine of Major Bacon's Hoosier One Hundred. From the look the man gave us, if we'd been soldiers under his command, a firing squad would've been summoned immediately. The gents who followed him in—William Pinkerton and Urias Smythe— looked no more pleased to see us.

The military man introduced himself as Col. Edmund Rice, commandant of the Columbian Guard, and he proceeded to lecture us at length on the error of our ways. We were disrupting the Exposition. We were embarrassing our nation before all the world. We were (or, to be more precise, *I was*) responsible for the death by blunt trauma of two innocent softmouth trout. We were lucky we weren't bound for a *real* jail. We were rubes and imbeciles and generally unfit to live.

And we were free to go.

"Don't let me lay eyes on either of you ever again," Rice barked as a Guardsman scuttled in to unlock the cell door. He left with stomps heavy enough to drive penny nails through solid steel.

"If we could have a moment," Pinkerton said to the Guardsman, and the man nodded and followed Rice out. "Alright, let's hear it. What's your excuse?"

"Don't you mean our *explanation*?" Old Red asked.

"That depends on what you have to say." Pinkerton turned his glare on me. "Well?"

So I rolled it all out: the Bearded Man, the Unbearded Man (leaving out that we'd first come across him tailing Smythe), Brady's suspicious behavior. When I was done, Pinkerton kept staring at me a moment, expressionless, before pronouncing judgment.

"You're out of the competition."

I've never heard the death rattle of a dying walrus, but I'm guessing the sound that came out of Smythe was pretty close.

"I'll try to get your money back," Pinkerton said to him.

Smythe instantly brightened. "Really?"

"I doubt Tousey and the others will agree to it, of course. But I'll try."

The walrus died another horrible death.

"You can't kick us out of the contest," I said. "We ain't broken no rules."

"This contest has rules?" Gustav snorted.

"Exactly!"

"You're right," Pinkerton said to me. "There's no rule against jumping into fish tanks or making a scene in a men's washroom. But the directors of the World's Columbian Exposition Company allowed this competition to proceed only upon *my* guarantee that it would not disrupt the Fair. Your behavior today violated that agreement and put the entire contest in jeopardy."

"Oh, the contest ain't in no jeopardy," Old Red said with a dismissive swipe of the hand. "You can't tell me a carcass in the Canadian cheese ain't enough to put an end to things, but a man fallin' into some water is. Naw, you ain't gonna give us the boot."

"I'm not?" Pinkerton said. He didn't sound convinced.

"Nope. Cuz if you went and did that, what switch would you have to lick us with should we go to the papers with all this? You saw them newsmen buzzin' around today. They ain't talkin' murder yet—maybe cuz they're tryin' to protect their fair city and their fair fair, just like you. But we can surely persuade one of them to see things as we do: that there was a murder in the White City . . . and right under William Pinkerton's nose, to boot."

"Are you trying to blackmail me?"

"Yup."

Given how Pinkerton was looking at us, I was tempted to close the cell door again. I would've felt safer.

"You know I could have you thrown in the Cook County Jail with one word," he said.

"Sure. And if you do, Mr. Smythe'll just go tell the newspapers where we are."

"Well, now!" Smythe cried, horrified to find himself dragged into this. "I don't know if . . . I mean, you shouldn't assume that . . . well, I suppose I might . . . oh!"

"If he did that, I'd have *him* thrown in jail," Pinkerton said.

Smythe gasped.

Old Red shook his head. "You're playin' a weak hand out too long, Mr. Pinkerton. Time to fold."

Pinkerton and my brother stood there looking each other in the eye so long I started to think I could just leave, maybe go get something to eat, then come back and find them still at it.

"Get out of here," Pinkerton finally said.

"You mean get out of here and don't stir up a stink in the papers and then come back tomorrow at noon for the next round of the contest?" I asked.

"*Yes.*"

"Will do, sir! Come on, come on, come on, let's go."

I herded my brother out of the cell and through the door. Smythe fled before us down the hall, scurrying like his britches were on fire and he was looking for a trough to sit in. We found him waiting for us on the building's front steps when we came outside.

"Oh, why couldn't you leave well enough alone?" he moaned.

"Don't you read them stories he sends you?" Gustav shot back with a jerk of the head my way. "I ain't the kind to let a thing like this go."

"Why not try it for once? Just to see how it feels? After all, Curtis was no friend of yours."

"He certainly wasn't any friend of *yours*."

"No, he wasn't, but . . . say! What's that supposed to mean?"

Gustav carried on down the steps. There weren't many: The Columbian Guard was headquartered in the Service Building, one of the least ostentatious structures in all the White City. Slap it in the middle of Kansas, and it would have served admirably as a county courthouse, but here it seemed puny and plain.

"We've lost enough time dilly-dallyin'," Old Red said. "There's another new trail for us to follow, and I want to pick it up while it's fresh. And if it leads to another privy or another fish tank, that don't matter to me. We'll keep on doin' what we gotta do, damn the consequences!"

I started after him, then stopped and turned back to Smythe. "Hey, who won today, anyway?"

"Boothby Greene," Smythe said glumly. He was watching Gustav march away like he was toting his very soul off to a bonfire.

"It's neck and neck, then. Valmont, the Crowes, and Greene all got one point each. So if we get to the egg first tomorrow, it's a four-way tie . . . and at least no one can say we *lost*."

Smythe didn't even look at me. "Oh. Joy."

I took off after my brother, catching up to him just as he rounded the southwest corner of the Service Building.

"So what's this new trail you're so anxious to pick up?" I asked.

"Ain't that obvious?"

Old Red whirled around the way we'd just come, then whipped off his Boss of the Plains and stole a wary look back at the front steps of the building. I took off my own hat—Stetsons not allowing for much stealth when peeking around corners—and leaned in for a peep myself.

Smythe was headed north, feet moving fast, fingers twitching.

"You know what's up thataway, don't you?" Gustav said.

"Oh, only the Horticulture Building, the Women's Building, the Palace of Fine Arts, and forty-something state buildings. But I assume you're talkin' about the Midway Plaisance."

"Yup. Right where we lost him yesterday."

"You think he's off to the same spot again?"

"Maybe yes, maybe no. I only know there ain't no man, bearded or unbearded, who's gonna keep me from seein' where that feller's headed this time."

He gave Smythe another moment to put more distance between us, then stepped out onto his trail.

27

WOES

Or, We Lift the Veil on Smythe's Secrets,
and He Brings Down the Curtain on Us

We kept well back as we followed Urias Smythe north. One glance over his shoulder, and my brother's little ruse would be in vain. I resisted the urge to needle Gustav again about the big sore thumbs we had atop our heads and the need to switch to more discreet bowlers or boaters, for it wasn't just our Stetsons that were conspicuous this time. I was without a doubt the only gentleman thereabouts whose suit was soaked through to the skin, and I had to walk at an awkward waddle lest my sodden, clinging underthings get to chafing me in spots still tender from the leather clown suit I'd been forced to wear two days before.

Gustav also wanted us back a ways so as to spot anyone new who took to doing what we were, but the Unbearded Man didn't end up tagging along that day . . . so far as we could tell. Fortunately, it was easy to keep an eye on Smythe from quite a distance thanks to his broad, hunched back and half-bald pate and bustling, ungainly pace.

Just as he reached the end of the long west-facing facade of the

Horticulture Building, with the Women's Building and all the state buildings still ahead to the north, Smythe cut left and hustled out of the White City. Which cinched it right there: He was indeed returning to the Midway Plaisance.

"What do you think keeps drawin' him back here?" I asked Old Red.

"I reckon it's where he comes when his feathers get ruffled. The first time he disappeared—when he went off to get cigars he don't smoke—was right after that crazy dinner party. Yesterday, he came here again after he got a grillin' from Pinkerton and Ryan. Now here he is fresh from seein' us behind bars."

"You think he comes to consult with somebody? The Bearded Man, maybe?"

"Could be. That letter we found certainly made out like they was up to something together."

"But the Bearded Man's been tryin' to wreck our chances in the contest. Why would Smythe want him to do that?"

"I don't know. Didn't you notice, though? When Pinkerton said he was bootin' us outta the competition?"

I nodded ruefully. "Yeah. Smythe was actually relieved—so long as he thought he could get his ante back."

"And if the contest had been canceled yesterday, after Curtis turned up dead, he would've. Everyone would've. After all, no contest, no winner. No winner, no prize."

"Are you suggestin' that we are so entirely uninspirin' as champions that Smythe would kill a man just to get out of backin' us?"

My brother shrugged. "Gotta ask yourself: 'Who is it who profits by it?'"

I smiled despite the sudden gust of wind off the lake that cut through my damp clothes like a Bowie knife through wet paper. The quote was a new addition to Old Red's inventory, coming as it did from the latest (and apparently last) Holmes story to appear in *Harper's Weekly,* "The Naval Treaty."

"Seems like forever since I heard you spout off like that," I said. "Good to hear you talkin' like the Man again."

"About time somebody around here did."

We were on the Midway now, a Javanese settlement to the right, an encampment of Samoans to the left. Smythe passed them by without slowing.

"Well, at least now we know the Bearded Man ain't from Samoa," I said. "But if Smythe's comin' here to meet him, don't that mean he spends his days in one of these here villages or castles or what-have-you? I mean, Smythe didn't have time to send word he wanted a parley. He'd have to just know the man would be here."

"Hmm," Gustav grunted.

Translated from Gustavese, this means "Good point."

The natatorium, the panorama of the Alps, the diorama of Pompeii, the Turkish and German villages—all quickly fell behind us as the Ferris wheel loomed ever larger.

"Looks like he's goin' for a spin on the wheel," I said. "I told you I'd get you on that thing before we left Chicago!"

My brother said nothing, though I thought I caught a little twitch of his lips. Maybe he was praying. If so, his prayers were answered, for once: Smythe turned right, into "A Street in Cairo."

"That there's the perfect place to meet someone on the sly," Old Red said. "All them alleyways and cafés and quiet corners and—"

Smythe veered off into the theater where the hoochie-coochie girls plied their trade.

"That is not a quiet corner," I said.

"Hrm," Gustav grunted.

Translated from Gustavese, this means "Shut up."

"You know," I went on, "if you'd have just let me look for him in there yesterday like I wanted to, we—"

"Shut up."

I shut up. When my brother goes to the trouble of saying it in English, I generally listen.

We paid our way into the theater, ignoring both the disapproving scowls of the passing ladies and the up-and-down sneer the ticket taker gave my still-soggy suit. The entrance hall led to a high-ceilinged lobby lined with elaborate scrollwork and murals depicting veiled women in diaphanous pantaloons dancing for hookah-sucking sheiks. In the center of the room was a plush round couch upon which sat two stout gentlemen speaking in low tones. Neither one was Urias Smythe.

The sound of shrill, high-pitched pipes squeaking out a repetitive yet strangely compelling melody drew us through the room like the song of a laryngitical siren. On the far side of the lobby was a set of double doors, and pushing through them we finally found ourselves in the theater proper.

Or the theater improper, I should perhaps say, for what was transpiring on the stage looked, at first, like a whorehouse hit by an earthquake. Gyrating wildly this way and that were girls in outfits so thin and skimpy all the material put together wouldn't make a nightgown for a midget. Their exposed bellies they sucked in and pushed out and swiveled and shimmied in time to raucous music played by fez-wearing men seated on pillows to one side of the stage.

Their audience—two hundred strong and male, every one—filled the room both with their bulk and the noxious smells of their cigars and sweat. Most were attempting to maintain some sense of decorum, looking upon the pulchritude wiggling and jiggling before them with studious expressions of mild, polite interest, as though they were missionaries forced to endure some heathen ritual they'd have sooner skipped if not for fear of offending the natives. The rest dispensed with such pretense, stamping their feet and clapping their hands and hooting with an unbridled delight the others no doubt envied.

"There," Old Red said, and he nodded at a familiar figure working his way toward the stage.

We sidled into a shadowy corner from which to watch Smythe make his rendezvous. He didn't seem to be searching for a particular face in the crowd, though: His gaze remained glued to the dancing girls.

"Funny," I said, squinting at the dark-haired, wide-hipped gal who seemed to be monopolizing Smythe's attention. "That don't *look* like the Bearded Man."

"Just wait. And watch."

Of course, I couldn't imagine a place I'd rather do some waiting and watching, though it proved a challenge to keep my eyes on Smythe. Every time I did manage to glance at the man, he looked more happy and relaxed than I'd ever seen him. If he was up to some kind of skullduggery, he sure was cheerful about it.

Much as I hated to bring our surveillance to an end, after thirty minutes or so even I couldn't deny we wouldn't be surveilling anything useful.

"You thinkin' what I'm thinkin'?" I finally said.

Usually, my brother hates to admit that he'd stoop so low as to share a thought with me (or that I had thoughts anyone could share), but there was no avoiding the obvious.

"Yeah," Old Red said, starting toward Smythe. "Might as well stop wastin' our time and come at the man straight."

Smythe didn't notice us as we approached. He wouldn't have noticed the approach of a herd of buffalo, in fact, so enraptured was he by the oscillations onstage. I think Gustav had to tap him on the shoulder four times before he finally turned around.

"Oh, my!" he said when he saw us. His eyes popped wide and his spine snapped straight and his wattles quivered and swayed.

"We need to talk," Old Red said. "Outside."

"But . . . but . . . but . . . of course."

A minute later, we were back on the Midway, all of us squinting and blinking even in the dimming light of the early evening sun. A passing matron shot us a haughty glare as we left the theater. Her husband gave us a wink.

"Now what's this all about?" Smythe asked. He tugged down on his vest and smoothed back the nonexistent hair atop his head in a vain effort to regain his poise.

"That was a clumsy lie you told Mrs. Jasinska Monday night," Gustav said. "About wantin' cigars you don't even smoke."

Smythe shot me a resentful look. "Yes, well. Force of habit, I suppose. It's what I tell my wife when I want to get out of the house and . . . you know . . . whenever I need a little privacy. She knows I don't smoke, of course, but she understands."

"And it was here you was comin' to for your 'privacy'?" Old Red asked. "That night and yesterday afternoon, too?"

"Yes. I find it calms me in times of anxiety."

I jerked a thumb at the theater. "That *calms* you?"

"It distracts me from my woes." Smythe put on his wounded puppy face. "I have so many."

"Well, I reckon we got another for you," Gustav said. "That bearded feller we told Pinkerton about? The one who was so anxious to see us lose? Well, we got a letter offa him when we tangled yesterday. And it was from you."

Smythe looked genuinely surprised. "From me?"

I did my best to recite from memory. "Enclosed you will find the money order I sent your father. Have him take you to the train station at once. He knows how to find me. Don't delay, my little friend! We face many challenges, but glory lies ahead. Your pal, Urias Smythe."

"Ohhhhhhhh, nnnnnnnnnoooooo . . ."

Smythe clapped his hands to his head and held them there as if trying to keep his skull from exploding.

"You wanna tell us why your friend's been tryin' to trip us up in the contest?" Old Red asked.

"He's no friend of mine. At least, not anymore. Not now that I know who he really is."

"And that would be . . . ?" I prompted.

"Billy Steele, Boy Detective."

My brother and I looked at each other. We knew Billy Steele well. He'd brought us to Chicago, in a way, for the magazine devoted to his adventures was so gloriously, stupendously awful I'd felt encouraged to approach the publisher with my own humble tales. *If they'll commit this BS to print*, I'd thought, *the folks at Smythe & Associates Publishing are gonna think I'm the next Mark Twain.*

"I hate to tell you this, Mr. Smythe," I said. "but your boy detective has a beard and doesn't seem to have been a boy since the Civil War."

"Yes, I know that *now*! But I didn't last week. He'd always represented his stories to me as true, just like you do."

"Hold on a tick," Gustav said. "I just remembered one of Miss Larson's cracks about us the first day of the contest. She said something about you replacin' a boy detective with a blind one. I never got a chance to ask about it in all the brouhaha, and now I guess I don't have to."

I saw where he was headed and finished for him. "We weren't your first choice for the competition. Billy Steele was."

"No, alas. Dan Slick, the Dude Dick was my first choice. Then I found out he doesn't exist."

"So you turned to Billy Steele," I said.

"No. I turned to Lady X, Society Sleuth."

"Let me guess," Gustav said. "Doesn't exist."

"Precisely. So I sent for the boy . . . only he turned out to be a forty-year-old Armenian named Emile Agajanian!"

"*Then* you called for me and my brother," I said.

"Yes. Much to my relief, you both actually existed . . . though to be honest, I was almost hoping your stories would prove as exaggerated as Agajanian's. I needed someone who'd go along with the costumes and props—who'd be the Holmes of the Range of my covers. And to discover that your brother isn't just as physically unimpressive as you've described him but every bit as disagreeable as well . . . ?"

Smythe sighed and shook his head sadly.

Old Red, to my surprise, did not remove said head from Smythe's shoulders.

"What I don't understand," he grumbled, "is why this Agajanian would come to Chicago if you thought he was a kid. Didn't he know it would be a problem, him bein' him?"

"No. He actually thought it shouldn't matter. When I told him he couldn't be in the contest, he flew into a rage. It was a frightful thing to see. It left me positively discombobulated for days!"

"So on top of bein' a fraud—" Gustav began.

"The Bearded Man's crazy," I said. "I guess that shouldn't come as a shock, given how he's been actin'."

"Just how deep does his crazy run, though, and in which direction?"

"I don't follow you."

My brother turned back to Smythe. "You think Agajanian's mad enough to try to mess with the contest, somehow?"

"Well, yes. Obviously, from the things he's done to you."

"I ain't talkin' about us. I'm talkin' about the contest."

Smythe's face turned the color of buttermilk. "You mean would he . . . ? Could he have . . . ? *Curtis?* That never even occurred to me. I don't know."

"You got any idea where he's stayin'?"

"No. Not anymore. He was going to check into the Columbian Hotel, of course, but after our quarrel, I don't know where he went."

"That's how he knew to look for us there," I said to Old Red. "Maybe how he knew where Curtis was stayin', too."

Gustav nodded vacantly, staring off at nothing. Then his gaze locked on Smythe again, eyes narrowed to slits.

"There's something else we ain't let you in on yet. That other feller my brother told Pinkerton about? The *Unbearded* Man? The one tied in with King Brady? When we first crossed paths with him, he was followin' *you.*"

Smythe's complexion went from buttermilk yellow to moldy cheese green. "Following *me*? You're sure?"

"Yup. He was but twenty steps behind you when you came walkin' thisaway yesterday. You got any idea why that might be?"

"No, really, I . . . wait just a minute."

I hoped this was the sort of "wait just a minute" that precedes a till-then-forgotten memory that cracks a mystery wide open. You know the kind: "Hang on . . . now that I think of it, I saw the butler walk out of Mrs. Moonbeam's room with a bloody axe just before she was found decapitated in bed. Do you think that might be significant, somehow?"

Sadly, it was not to be.

"That means *you* were following me, too," Smythe said. "Just like today. You didn't simply stumble upon me back there. You've been watching me. Spying on me!"

"Just lookin' out for you," I lied. "There've been some mighty shady goings-on, and naturally we were concerned about—"

"Flapdoodle!" Smythe barked. "You've been sneaking around behind my back prying into my private affairs. After all I've done for you! You wreck my nerves, you squander my money, you put me in dutch with William Pinkerton, and now what? You suspect me of murder? I've had it! We're done. We're through. I want nothing to do with you from now on!"

He whirled like a great flabby top and started stomping away. After he'd gone but a few steps, though, he stopped and faced us again.

"Unless you get to the egg first tomorrow. Then perhaps we'll talk."

He flashed us a fleeting, tight-lipped smile, then went on into the theater. He had troubles to forget, and he was the lucky man who knew just how to go about it.

Me, I didn't feel so lucky.

28

THE CHOPHOUSE

Or, A New "Friend" Treats Us to a Meal, but It Ends Up Going to the Dogs

Heartbreak never hits you where you want it to. The shoulder you want to cry on, the booze you want to guzzle, the sheets you want to pull up over your head—they're not around when you need them most, nor do they come running when you call. No, you've got to make the Trudge. I'm sure you're no stranger to it yourself, dear reader: that long, dejected slog to consolation when your mind has nothing to do but dwell on your failures and your heart has nothing to do but break a little more.

I've undertaken the Trudge several times in my life. Few were more discouraging than the one I took there in Chicago, though. After months trying to sell my stories and *years* scrambling not to starve, my first publisher, my one backer, my much prayed-for patron had just told me to go to hell—and now I had to walk eight blocks to my hotel in a suit that felt like someone had tried to wash it with me still in it.

I was not, in short, in high spirits.

"For a feller who's so tight-lipped, you sure managed to get a lot of foot up in your mouth back there," I said to my brother.

"I'm sorry things went that way," Gustav said. I was about to let loose a hosanna in the highest in thanks for this miracle—two actual apologies in as many days!—but then he added, "The question had to be asked, though."

"Not like that, it didn't. I know you can muster a light touch when you want to, but no. You just went and dropped the Unbearded Man on Smythe like an anvil off the roof. Couldn't you have finessed how we first run across him? Smoothed it out a little? You know. Lied?"

"Sure, I could've, but . . ." Old Red sighed and looked over and up into my eyes. "Alright. I should've."

I gave him a clap on the back of the brotherly/manly kind that says "Apology accepted—what's done is done."

"Aww, it probably don't matter, anyhow," I said. "I get the feelin' Smythe wasn't gonna be our bosom chum by the end of the week, no matter how things played out. And there's other publishers than him. Maybe I oughta run some of my stories under Blackheath-Murray's nose."

"Why not Frank Tousey?"

"Ha! First you admit you were wrong, then you crack a joke! You are in rare form today, Brother. I don't know what to expect from you next. A belly dance?"

Gustav did not, of course, bust out with some hoochie-coochie, nor did he look in the slightest amused, and I began to wonder if he'd been joking at all. I couldn't imagine Tousey desiring any dealings with us, though, excepting the dirty kind that would keep us from asking further questions about King Brady.

Imagine my surprise, then, when we walked into the Columbian Hotel only to have Tousey himself cheerfully halloo us from the lobby.

"Just the gentleman I was hoping to see," he said, bustling up to me. "There's something I'd like to discuss with you. Your brother as well, of course. Would you care to do it over dinner? On me?"

"I don't know, Mr. Tousey," I said. "Arsenic doesn't agree with me."

It wasn't much of a quip, I admit, yet the way Tousey roared you'd have thought I was Oscar Wilde.

"I don't blame you for being suspicious after the way I spoke to you yesterday," he said once he caught his breath. "Please. Let me make amends for my rudeness."

"That's mighty nice of you, sir," Old Red said. "It'd be ungracious of us not to give you the chance."

"I hoped you'd see it that way!"

"Do y'all mind if I at least run up and put on something dry first?" I said. "Feels like I been walkin' around with tadpoles in my pockets."

Tousey laughed again. It was a little unnerving, actually, having someone guffaw at my every funny. I was more used to silence or, at most, "Feh."

"Tell you what," Gustav said, "is the place you got in mind close by, Mr. Tousey?"

"Sure. It's just over on Sheridan. The American. It's a chophouse."

"Fine. Why don't you run up and get changed, Otto? We'll head over to the American and put in an order for you. By the time you get there, you'll probably have a steak waitin'."

"Sounds good to me."

Before bounding up the stairs to our room, I was treated to the bewildering sight of Old Red and Tousey chatting amiably as they strolled away. It was like seeing two rattlesnakes sit down to take tea together. I couldn't imagine it'd be long before the fangs came into play.

I washed up and threw on a new suit quick as I could, then scurried over to the American no more than a quarter hour behind the others. When I joined them at a table in the middle of the restaurant, they were still gabbing at each other in a pleasant, relaxed way I found remarkable. My brother had taken my earlier admonishment about finesse and smooth talking to heart, it seemed, for going fifteen whole minutes without grievously insulting someone ran contrary to his very nature.

"Mr. Tousey was just tellin' me how this here contest got started," Gustav said as I sat down. "It's quite a story."

From the way he said it, I knew it was a story he'd be passing along soon, too—with some deductions mixed in with the telling.

"We were talking about you as well, Otto," Tousey said.

"Oh? Comparing notes on your admiration and envy, I trust."

"Something like that," Tousey chuckled.

"Mr. Tousey's been readin' your tales," Old Red said. "He's a big admirer. Maybe as big as Mr. Curtis was."

Tousey was reaching for a glass of red wine and, for just a second, he froze solid.

"I certainly liked what I saw." He took a quick sip that couldn't have done more than moisten his lips, then put the glass down again. "I did have a few thoughts, though."

I felt my upper arms and shoulders tingle and tighten, as if someone had ever-so-lightly swiped an icicle over the skin.

" 'Thoughts' as in criticisms?"

Tousey smiled. He was a dapper man, with gold cufflinks and rings on his pinkies and a diamond-studded stickpin through his silver satin cravat, and somehow the smile seemed like just one more little bauble he affixed to himself so as to make the right impression.

"As in suggestions, Otto," he said soothingly. "To make your stories more palatable to the masses. Sand some of the edges off."

"I didn't know my stories were edgy."

"They could just be a little smoother, that's all. Simpler. Pithier."

"Not so danged gabby," Gustav said.

I glared at him.

He seemed to enjoy it.

"Shorter would be good, yes," Tousey said, "and you've got some trimmings I think should be trimmed, to be frank. Those chapter headings of yours, for instance. Are they really necessary?"

"I don't know about necessary, but I like 'em."

Tousey shook his head. "They're old-fashioned and they slow the reader down. Cut them. And those prologues you always put at the beginning? The 'preludes,' I think you call them. What are those for?"

"That's just me trying to start things off with something exciting. To grab folks' attention."

"But then you have to circle back later to explain it. It's confusing. Anyway, who's going to remember by chapter nine what happened in the prologue? You don't *want* anyone to remember. You just want them to keep turning pages, pushing ahead, not looking back."

"Well, maybe, but—"

"I know what I'm talking about," Tousey cut in. "I put out dozens of dime novels every year. And when I look at you, do you know what I see? Raw clay just waiting to be molded by the right hands. A good publisher could turn you into the next John Watson. But with the wrong publisher, you're going to keep making the same mistakes, and that'll get you nowhere. Tell me, Otto—what's Urias paying you per word?"

"Per word? I don't rightly know. He gives me two hundred bucks for the long stuff, twenty for the short."

Tousey rolled his eyes. "As usual, Urias doesn't know what he's got. Otto, you shouldn't accept anything less than four hundred dollars for your next novel . . . and I want you to accept it from *me*."

I had to put my hands flat on the table to steady myself. When I was a kid, I once took a roll down a hill in an empty flour barrel, and when I stumbled out I hadn't felt half as dizzy and disoriented as I did now. Things had gone too fast in a direction I hadn't expected.

"I truly appreciate the offer, sir. In fact, you wouldn't believe how fortuitous your timing—"

"Of course, we'd hate to betray Mr. Smythe like that," my brother said. "Especially now, with everything that's been goin' on."

Tousey nodded. "I understand. It's only natural that you'd have some reservations. Take your time. Think about it."

He picked up his wine and took another sip—a longer, deeper one this time that left a little crimson crescent on his lips.

"Don't take *too* long, though," he said. "In fact, I think you should probably make up your minds before dessert."

That grounded me fast. I once again knew exactly where I stood. It wasn't a good place, but there's a comfort in the knowing.

"Long as we're all bein' so friendly," I said, "do you mind if we ask you a question or two?"

"That depends on how friendly the questions are."

Tousey chuckled again, as if this had been some joke. The coldness of his eyes, though, made it plain it wasn't.

"Well, we won't be askin' 'em out of spite," I said, and I turned to my brother and gave him a look that said, *Got your anvils ready?*

"We saw a man followin' Mr. Smythe yesterday," Old Red said. "Tall feller wearin' a fake beard. Today I saw him again—meetin' with your man Brady. Who is he?"

"A mysterious stranger with a fake beard?" Tousey scoffed. "You can't be serious."

"Oh, I can be," Gustav said. "I am. And it makes me wonder: Would you still be our friend if we keep tryin' to figure out who that man is?"

I could have sworn someone opened a door and let in a cold wind off the lake. The temperature around our table seemed to drop ten degrees.

"No," Tousey said.

"And you would be our friend if we stopped?"

"Yes."

"I just wanted us to be clear on that."

"Let's *be* clear, then," Tousey said.

Old Red shrugged. "We ain't friends."

Tousey didn't waste another second looking at him.

"Hutchings," he said, turning away and putting up a finger.

Tousey must have been a regular customer there, and a healthy tipper to boot, for the maître d' heard him on the first call and came scurrying over quick.

"Yes, Mr. Tousey?"

"Do you own a dog, Hutchings?"

"It just so happens, I do, sir," the man said without blinking an eye. I got the feeling Tousey could've asked "Do you have two heads and purple skin?" and he would've replied "No, sir, I don't believe I do" with equal aplomb.

"What's his name?"

"There are two of them, actually, Mr. Tousey. Copperfield and Nickleby."

"Ah. So much the better. I have a treat for Copperfield and Nickleby, Hutchings." He pointed across the table at me and Gustav without taking his eyes off the maître d'. "Please take these gentlemen's steaks home with you tonight and give them to your dogs."

"Very good, sir."

"Also, if the gentlemen are still sitting at this table in two minutes, summon a policeman."

"Absolutely, sir. I hope you're not being annoyed."

"I am, but it's no fault of yours. I apologize for the inconvenience."

"Think nothing of it, Mr. Tousey."

Hutchings bowed ever so slightly before hustling away. I found the smug satisfaction on his face puzzling until I realized the size of the gratuity he had to look forward to—not to mention the steaks.

"No need to get the law mixed up in this," Old Red said, pushing back his chair. "We'll go."

I got to my feet, too. "We got work to do, anyhow. Ain't that right, Brother?"

"It sure is."

Tousey went right on ignoring us, focusing himself instead on draining his wineglass and admiring the paintings of (ironically enough) cowboys and cattle drives that lined the wall.

We left.

Halfway back to the Columbian, Gustav started to steer us into another, lower-rail chophouse, but I wouldn't follow him inside.

"Thought you'd wanna talk it all through over some food," my brother said.

I just shook my head. It had taken me a couple months to lose my first publisher, and a couple minutes to lose my second.

For once, I wasn't hungry.

29

TROUT IN THE MILK

Or, We Angle for More Facts and End Up Hearing Something Fishy

s my brother and I carried on back to the Columbian, a funny thing happened. It was my second Trudge of the day, and I didn't feel up to filling the silence between us with gab—yet Old Red, of all people, did.

"Got some good data outta Tousey 'fore he tried to buy us off," he said. "Turns out the contest was his idea. Or so he tells it. Said he saw *McClure's* was gonna publish Doc Watson's last Holmes story and set out to find an 'angle' for makin' hay off that. Cooked up the competition, roped Smythe in, then the two of 'em took it to *McClure's* together. It was Smythe's notion to do it in Chicago and get Pinkerton involved. You know who recruited Curtis. The Crowes bought their way in after that notice ran in *McClure's* last month. But with just them and King Brady and Dan Slick, the Dude Dick, lined up, the *McClure's* crowd didn't think the contest was 'international' enough. So they signed up two sleuths from Europe on their own."

Gustav gave me a long, wide-eyed look that obviously prompted me to name names. I went ahead and did it before he could barrel straight into a streetlamp.

"Eugene Valmont and Boothby Greene."

My brother shook his head. "Eugene Valmont and Gareth Lestrade."

"Lestrade! As in Inspector Lestrade? Scotland Yard Lestrade? Holmes's . . . ?"

Neither "friend" nor "foil" seemed to suit the man perfectly, so after a little thought I had to go with the admittedly awkward "acquaintance Lestrade?"

Old Red, to my relief, finally looked where he was going just in time to avoid a head-on collision with a family of six. He weaved his way through them, ignoring their "Hey!"s and "Well, I never!"s as he answered me.

"The very one. Agreed to come over and compete—for the widows and orphans fund, of course—but had to bow out at the last minute. Some kinda fracas on the job, apparently. Got thrashed so good, he'll be laid up for weeks. By then, Blackheath-Murray had heard of the contest, though, so *McClure's* still got themselves an Englishman. That was as far as we got before Tousey launched into his eyewash about you."

"You don't need to remind me what happened after that."

"Yeah, well, still . . . ," my brother began, but whatever he'd been about to say got hacked away by a cough, and he started up again with a whole new thought. "Tousey played it pretty cool, but he's gotta be spooked to try something so obvious."

"I just wonder what he'll try next."

"You and me both, Brother."

Up ahead, I saw a sure sign my Trudge was almost over: Jerzy, the Columbian's cadaverous old bellhop, was standing beside a hansom as it was loaded with trunks. The cabdriver and what I assumed was a soon-to-be-former hotel guest were doing all the work while Jerzy waited to do his part: lightening the tourist's pockets of whatever spare coins they might contain.

Inside, we found Mrs. Jasinska beaming her usual sunshiny smile from behind her desk, and I planned to bask in it no more than the second or two it might take to sweep past her and head for the stairs. There was a pillow in our room with my name on it— either to sleep upon or smother myself with, I hadn't decided which.

Mrs. Jasinska waved us over to her desk, however, and when we stopped before it she leaned toward me, grinning.

"Aren't you the belle of the ball this evening? A certain personage gave me this."

She slid a folded slip of paper across the desktop. *MR. OTTO AMLINGMEYER* had been written on it in the fine, frilly hand of an educated lady. I picked up the note and opened it. The message inside was simple, if not exactly direct.

> *218*
> *D.*

I thanked Mrs. Jasinska, ignored the insinuating wink she gave me in reply, then told my brother what the note said as we made our way across the lobby.

"So we've been invited to pay a call on Miss Crowe," Gustav said.

"What makes you so sure it's a 'we' sorta invite? It's just my name she wrote down."

Old Red threw me a look hot enough to boil water. "Cuz it's just you that can read."

"True. Still, if she wants to see the both of us, I can always run back down the hall to fetch you."

"After you've showed up at her door alone?"

"I don't see the harm."

"And if the colonel should spot you? Or if he should be waitin' in that room with her, expectin' to speak with the both of us? Or if he should've told Miss Crowe to write the note thataway so he can make doubly certain you ain't got improper designs on his god-daughter?"

I chewed that over a moment.

"I see the harm," I said.

We went to room 218 together.

Diana answered at my knock. When she swung the door wide and invited us inside, I saw Colonel Crowe seated upon the bed, a map of the White City spread out beside him. A pair of men's hats—one a boater, the other a stovepipe—sat atop the dresser just beyond him, while a big steamer in the corner bore the initials "C.K.C."

For C. Kermit Crowe. This was the colonel's room, not Diana's.

I shuddered like someone had walked over my grave—and that someone was an elephant.

"We waited for you after the contest ended this afternoon," Colonel Crowe said once the door was closed. "You never showed up."

"We got sidetracked," my brother said, and he turned to me while jerking his head at the colonel.

I was being cranked up like one of Mr. Edison's phonograph machines over in the Electricity Building, and out again came all we'd seen, heard, and learned that day: Brady and the Unbearded Man as neighbors in the WC, me and the Bearded Man tussling over a clue, Pinkerton's short-lived threat to throw us out of the contest, the Bearded Man at last becoming the Named Man (a.k.a. Emile Agajanian, a.k.a. Billy Steele, Boy Detective), Smythe's win-or-else ultimatum, and Tousey's attempted bribe.

It took a while to get it all out, and for the first time the day didn't seem like a total loss: In spite of all our setbacks and blunders, we'd gathered up quite a pile of new facts, and now I could lay it before someone who'd (hopefully) appreciate it.

"Well, one thing's obvious," Colonel Crowe said when I was finally through. "Tousey and Brady are trying to cheat, somehow."

"At the very least," Gustav said.

"Meaning you think they killed Curtis?"

"Meanin' we still don't know what's really goin' on around here."

"Don't you find it curious," Diana said, "that even with the Unbearded Man as a confederate, Brady would remain one of the few contestants who hasn't yet won a point?"

Old Red and the colonel took a silent moment to (I assume) ponder this mystery. Me, I was pondering the fact that the rest of those "few contestants" the lady had mentioned were me and my brother.

"Well," she went on, "the colonel and I didn't have quite the day you did, but it wasn't wholly without developments. We were followed both during and after the contest, for instance. By a bearded man."

"Couldn't have been one of ours," I said. "The Unbearded Man was with Brady in the jakes, and that Agajanian feller must've been followin' *us* to snatch our clue the way he did."

"Only one way to look at it," my brother said. "There's another other bearded man."

I groaned and put a hand to my forehead. "Just when I thought we were gettin' somewhere . . ."

"Describe him," Gustav said to the Crowes

The colonel did the honors.

"Dark beard, not too thick. Average height, average build. It was hard to pick out particulars. He kept his distance, and he was wearing a long coat and a slouch hat, pulled down low."

"Of course," I said. "It's part of their uniform."

"After the contest," Colonel Crowe carried on, "when we noticed he was still shadowing us, we split up and tried to set a trap for him. I assume he spotted it. He simply disappeared."

Old Red grunted. "So he's a professional, too. Like the Unbearded Man. I wonder why he was followin' *you*?"

"For that matter, why was the Unbearded Man followin' Smythe?" I said. "Seems to me we ain't gonna nail a name to either gent till we know what they're after."

"I reckon you're right."

My brother spent the next few seconds absently stroking his mustache.

"Fortunately, it's not only new questions we have to share," Diana said. "We got an answer today as well. I'm sure you remember that Mrs. Jasinska saw Pinkerton take a bundle of papers out of Curtis's room yesterday. I can only assume the right moment never arose to ask him about it."

I nodded. "All our moments were about yellin' and threats."

"I'm happy to say that wasn't the case for us. Pinkerton's really not a bad sort, if you approach him the right way. I struck up a conversation with him this afternoon and managed to coax him into talking about Curtis. Those papers Mrs. Jasinska saw—"

"Were the clue cards for the contest," Gustav said. "All of 'em for the whole week, typed up neat and ready to go."

"That's right," the colonel said. "How did you know?"

My brother shrugged. "Had to be them. Otherwise, how could Pinkerton keep the contest goin' the way he has? Y'all get anything else out of him?"

"Yes and no," Diana said. "I asked about those queer objects we found in the alley. The squirrel and the fruitcake and the box of dead snails. Pinkerton just brushed it all off as meaningless.

According to him, you'll find all kinds of odd things when you dig around in a Chicago trash can."

Old Red snorted out a "Feh." "There's odd and then there's odd under a murdered man's window."

"Seems to me the oddest thing of all is a so-called sleuth who ain't curious about a stuffed squirrel in a tuxedo," I said.

"I disagree entirely," Colonel Crowe shot back. "The squirrel and the snails and the rest hurt your case more than they help. Such grotesqueries lend the whole affair the flavor of a schoolboy prank."

Gustav turned sharply toward the little man. He said nothing, though, and his eyes quickly lost their focus, so that he was no longer looking at the colonel so much as through him.

Colonel Crowe turned to me. "Is he having some sort of seizure?"

"You could call it that. It's just a thought that's seized him, though. Don't bother askin' him what it is, cuz he won't tell."

"I don't like servin' up ideas till they're fully baked," Old Red muttered, still staring at nothing. Then he blinked, shook his head, and was truly with us again. "Y'all round up any other data today?"

"I'm afraid that's it," Diana said.

Colonel Crowe hopped off the bed. Standing up added all of five inches to his height.

"I suggest we gather again tomorrow after the contest to compare notes . . . assuming you two don't end up in the clink again."

He walked to the door and reached for the knob.

"That sounds fine," I said. "But before we call it a night, don't you think we oughta come up with a plan for tomorrow? Figure some way we can get our hands on one of them bearded fellers, say? I mean . . . we are workin' together now, ain't we?"

Colonel Crowe opened the door.

253

"I wouldn't call it 'together,'" he said. "More like 'in tandem.' We'll see you tomorrow."

The four of us passed around good nights, and then Gustav and I were in the hall, the door closing firmly behind us.

"That's progress, at least," I said as we walked away.

"Is it? What was that remark about bein' 'in tandem' all about?"

"Means we're workin' toward the same thing at the same time, only not necessarily as a team."

"Well, horses runnin' against each other in a race are 'in tandem,' then," Gustav pointed out. "Far as the colonel's concerned, we're still the competition."

"I suppose. I don't think you can blame the man for it, though. Remember: He had to put up part of the prize money just to be here. All we can do is not win. The Crowes stand to *lose*."

"Hmm," Old Red said.

We'd paused outside the door to his room to finish our talk, and just as he fished the key from his pocket, two of our neighbors appeared at the top of the stairs nearby.

"Good evening, gentlemen," Boothby Greene said. "Calling it a day, are we?"

His publisher, Blackheath-Murray, was beside him, and both were dressed in black tail coats and trousers—not so gussied up as tuxes, but close. No doubt they'd been out celebrating Greene's victory in the contest that afternoon.

"Oh, I'll put in some more time readin' up on the fair," I said. "But yeah—we'll turn down the lights soon enough. A man needs his rest if he's gonna keep gettin' up and losin' every day."

"Now, now. Don't lose heart, Mr. Amlingmeyer," Greene chided me. "I didn't score my first point until the third day. Who's to say you won't score yours on the fourth?"

"We didn't see you at the closing ceremony, after Greene here found the egg," Blackheath-Murray said. "Did you make it to the Mines and Mining Building?"

From Tousey, I would've taken this as a jibe. The Englishman seemed truly curious, however, and I saw no hint of derision on his round, fleshy face.

"We didn't even know that's where things ended up today," I said. "We were a mite distracted."

"By your inquiries into Mr. Curtis's demise, I presume," Greene said.

"Something like that."

"Interestin' things we been findin' out," my brother said. "You might change your mind about Curtis dyin' accidental if you knew it all."

Greene shook his head. "I think it's most likely a case of a trout in the milk, if you'll pardon my saying so. And if it isn't, Sergeant Ryan's the man to handle it. It's not for me to stick this in." He tapped the side of his beak-like nose. "Someone might get hurt."

Blackheath-Murray and I chuckled dutifully, but Gustav merely narrowed his eyes and turned his head to the side, as if there were a sudden gleam off Greene that might blind him.

"Well. We shan't keep you from your rest any longer," Blackheath-Murray said. "Good night."

He and Greene turned to go.

"Oh, sirs—before you go?" Old Red said, and from the hesitant, raspy sound of his voice I could tell it was an effort to force himself to speak. "I've been thinkin' I need to change my style. Spruce up my wardrobe, not dress so rough. And I, umm . . . I been admirin' your shoes. I wonder if you'd be so good as to tell me where you got 'em?"

Greene and Blackheath-Murray exchanged a little bemused look. They knew what Gustav was up to. He knew they knew, too, and it was embarrassing the hell out of him.

"You're in luck, actually," Greene said. "It just so happens Blackheath-Murray and I share a fondness for American shoe-makers." He nodded down at the shiny black shoes on his feet. "Selby & Harte of Chicago."

"Mine as well," Blackheath-Murray said.

"Thank you, gentlemen," Old Red said. "I'll uhh . . . I'll have to pick up some of them Selby & Hartes for myself."

"A fine idea—you could follow in worse footsteps than mine," Greene said, and he and Blackheath-Murray headed off to their rooms as we finally went into ours.

"I am so thrilled to hear you're finally gonna stop dressin' like a saddle tramp," I said. "First thing tomorrow, we'll drop in on Mr. Cohn and have him whip you up a frock coat and kid gloves and spats and—"

"Alright, alright. So it wasn't the smoothest fib in the world."

My brother swept off his hat and plopped backward onto the bed.

"At least you got some good data out of it," I said. "Now we know American gentlemen only wear European shoes, and Europeans only wear American. Shall I run down to police headquarters and share the news with Sergeant Ryan?"

"Ha ha."

Gustav hadn't bothered taking off his boots and coat, and he wasn't about to, either. He simply put his Stetson over his face, sig-naling to me that his day was done and first watch was mine.

"Funny to hear Greene talkin' like Mr. Holmes," I said.

Old Red said nothing.

"Quite the odd turn of phrase, ain't it?"

Nothing again.

"'Circumstantial evidence can be very convincing, as when you find a trout in the milk,'" I recited. "'The Adventure of the Engineer's Thumb.'"

"'Is occasionally,' not 'can be,'" my brother said from under his hat. "And it's from 'Noble Bachelor.'"

I knew he wouldn't be able to resist.

"So," I said, "we gonna talk about tomorrow?"

"What about it?"

"Well, what are we gonna do? You got some kinda plan?"

More silence. Then: "I'm workin' on it."

"Asleep?"

"Better than awake and gabbin'."

"It's gonna be our last chance, you know. To catch the killer. To end up something other than laughingstocks in the contest. To put ourselves back on track for some kinda future other than—"

"*Snore,*" my brother said.

"Alright, fine. Be that way."

And he was.

This time, the silence lasted the rest of the night.

30

THE IMPOSSI-BELL

Or, A Shot in the Dark Hits the Bull's-eye, but Only One of Us Can See It

I t was all well and good that I was nighthawking first, for I doubt I could have nodded right off anyway. Thoughts of the next day plagued me. I could see my brother and me failing to catch Curtis's killer, failing to score a point in the contest, failing to swing Colonel Crowe around to respecting us. Failing, in short, at everything but failing, at which we would be a great success.

I tried to divert myself with further studies of the White City, propping myself against the wall with my guidebook in my lap. The sheer scope of the Exposition soon overwhelmed me, though. Every page was so packed with the Biggest This and the Greatest That and the Most Expensive the Other, I started wondering what mankind was trying to prove. We seemed like little more than children waving our broomstick horses at heaven shouting, "Look at us, Pa! Look what we made!"

One tidbit did make an impression, however. I finally found an explanation for the curious thingamajig we'd been hunting all week: "the Egg of Columbus." The copper egg, it turned out, had been borrowed from an exhibit created by Edison's famous rival Nikola Tesla. Through the means of modern scientific hoop-di-doo and alakazam, Mr. Tesla could make the egg whirl in circles. Having never seen a spinning metal egg, I had to take the guidebook's word for it that this was akin to an eighth wonder of the world.

If you're asking yourself why, then, this was "the Egg of Columbus" and not "the Egg of Tesla," you're not alone. I was wondering the same thing, and I found the guidebook's explanation so interesting I spoke aloud for the first time in an hour even though I had no idea if Gustav was awake or not.

"I ain't talkin' here," I said. "Just readin'."

From there I spooled out a tale that went more or less like this.

One day after returning from his voyages, Christopher Columbus was at some kind of wing-ding with a bunch of Spanish bigwigs. Before long one of these nabobs saunters up to him and says, "You know, Chris, what you did wasn't such a big deal. Why, if you hadn't bumped into America, some other son-of-a-gun would have." And instead of just telling this wisenheimer to kiss his Columbian behind, our hero picks up an egg (the Spanish gentry always keeping uncooked eggs on hand for unforeseen contingencies) and says, "I can make this thing stand up on end. Can you?"

After some scratching of their pointy heads, the hoity-toities pop off with the Spanish equivalent of "Bullshit!" So Columbus smiles, taps the egg on a table till the peak of the oval cracks a mite, then leaves it balanced there, standing on end.

Now, the moral of this story, it would seem to me, is not to engage in bar bets, because there's always some stupid gag that'll let a fellow get the better of you. But this was not the point that

259

Columbus or Tesla—or Armstrong B. Curtis, I assumed—had meant to put across.

Just what the point was, I couldn't quite say . . . though I did briefly try.

"So the feller who knows the best party tricks always comes out on top?"

Old Red said nothing, and I went back to reading silently to myself. A few hours later, he sat up and swung his feet off the bed, and he and I swapped places without a word. Sleep didn't come easily to me, but it came. It didn't go again till some hours later, when my brother ushered it out by leaning in over the bed and speaking.

"The point is, everything seems obvious in hindsight, and it's only a few folks who can see that the impossible is possible goin' ahead, not just lookin' back. The grand thing is to be able to reason *forward*—and then follow through on it."

"And good morning to you," I said through a yawn.

I sat up and found Gustav holding a powder blue card under my nose.

"What the heck is that?"

"You tell me. Someone slipped it under the door a minute ago."

I took the card. Written on it in a swoopy, swirling, curlicued hand were these words:

M. Gustav Amlingmeyer & M. Otto Amlingmeyer

The plaisure of your company is requested at Rector's
Restaurant this morning. Breakfast will be provided. So,
also, will answers. I know who killed Armstrong B.
Curtis. Coffee will be served at 9.

Your humble servant,
Eugene Valmont

"Free breakfast, huh?" I said. "Think we oughta go?"

This was, of course, a joke (though you wouldn't have known that from the stony silence that followed it). Not long after, we were stepping into the selfsame banquet room in Rector's in which Boothby Greene and Blackheath-Murray had hosted their disastrous dinner party three days before. Indeed, the Englishmen were back in place at the head of the table, and before them sat their former guests, all of them positioned just as they'd been Monday night. The only absences, excepting ourselves, were William Pinkerton and (for obvious reasons) Armstrong B. Curtis.

"So good of you to come, *mes amis!*" Valmont said as we came in, and he hopped up to usher us to our old chairs. As we followed him, we exchanged strained greetings with our fellow contestants. Diana, the colonel, King Brady, Greene—they were all stiff and distant, obviously on edge. Frank Tousey glowered at us. Urias Smythe avoided our eyes. Only Lucille Larson looked like she was enjoying herself, though she didn't bother with any pleasantries for our benefit. She just sipped cheerfully at her coffee and kept her gaze moving up and down the table, as if anxious to see who was going to pull a gun on M. Valmont first.

"The tableau is almost complete," Valmont said. "Now we need only wait for . . . a-ha! And here we are! With noninvited guests, I see. So much the beh-TAIR!"

William Pinkerton had appeared at the top of the stairs we'd just mounted, his invitation in his hand. With him were Sergeant Ryan and a uniformed policeman.

"What's this all about, Valmont?" Pinkerton said, giving the invite a wave.

"A nefarious plot. A mad scheme. An ingenious ruse. All this, it is about." Valmont stepped behind Pinkerton's empty chair and pulled it away from the table. "If you would be so good as to sit, I will explain."

Pinkerton obliged, though he didn't look like he saw anything good about doing so.

"And where would you put me and Officer Kurtz, then?" Ryan asked. "I assume you'd rather have us to the side lest we spoil your 'tableau.'"

"Just so," Valmont said. "There at the top of the stairs would be perfection. *Merci.*"

Ryan bowed slightly and smiled even slighter. Valmont wasn't just leaving him by the stairs. He and his fellow copper were now blocking the only way out.

The Frenchman returned Ryan's bow, then began pacing slowly around the table.

"I have asked you all to join me here," he said, "so that once more we may see all the pieces of the puz-ZELL laid out before us. Or, if you prefer, all the pawns and queens and kings in their proper place upon the board. In this way, we can best identify the roles they have played in the diaboli-KELL game of death in which we find ourselves."

"I hope you'll pardon my interruptin'," my brother said, "but the last time we talked about Curtis's death, you didn't see nothing diaboli-KELL about it."

Valmont nodded, looking chagrined, as he kept circling the table. "Yes. I have changed my mind upon this subject, and I have your bru-THERE to thank. Yesterday, Sergeant Ryan questioned me about certain men who may or may not have taken an unwhole-fulsome interest in the competi-shawn. Men with thick black beards. I knew nothing of this, and I pressed the sergeant for de-tails, but, like a good sleuth, he remained tit-lipped. However, this morning, I read in one of your Chicago newspeepers an account of a chase through the Fisheries Building—a chase involving Otto Amlingmeyer and a mysterious bearded man who disappeared soon after M. Amlingmeyer jumped into a tank of man-eating sharks. I am pleased to see, monsieur, that you escaped intact."

"Oh, God," Smythe groaned.

"Just for the record, I didn't go swimmin' with any sharks," I said. "Though I don't doubt that makes for wishful thinkin' for some."

"But there was a bearded man?" Valmont asked. "He did interfere with the contest?"

"Sure, but we know UMM."

That I said "UMM" and not "YOW!" was something of a miracle, considering how hard my brother brought his heel down on my toe. This was his gentle way of suggesting I not reveal what we'd learned of Emile Agajanian, Embittered Bearded Fully Grown-Up Detective. Smythe could be counted on to hold his tongue as well, for surely he wouldn't be anxious to admit how badly his Billy Steele debacle had come back to bite us.

"We know there's at least two other bearded fellers lurkin' about," I said, "but neither of them was in the Fisheries Building."

"This is ridiculous," Tousey growled. "Just what are you suggesting? That the competition's being sabotaged by a secret League of Bearded Men?"

"We've seen one of them ourselves," Colonel Crowe said. "He was following us yesterday during the contest."

"Poppycock. You're just letting your imagination run away with you."

"The man M. Amlingmeyer encountered yesterday was no fiction of imagination," Valmont said. He hadn't stopped pacing the whole time. "There were dozens of witnesses to the chase. So. We have at least one Bearded Man we know without doubt to be real. Or, I should perhaps say, we have at least one Man we know without doubt to be real. The beard, on the other hand . . . ?"

He stopped walking directly behind Diana, then whirled toward Boothby Greene and jabbed a finger at him.

"*You*, M. Greene, we know to possess both a false beard and the skill to wear it undetec-TED. For is it not true that you fooled us all with just such a subterfuge in this very room the night of M. Curtis's death?"

"How can I deny it?" Greene replied coolly. The pointing finger of suspicion seemed not to unsettle him in the slightest. "I would point out, however, that I could hardly have been wrestling with Mr. Amlingmeyer in the Fisheries Building when I was busy *winning the contest* in the Mining Building on the other side of the lagoon. I would also remind you, monsieur, that half the people at this table are skilled inquiry agents. I would think we've all had some experience wearing false beards." He looked at Diana and smiled. "With one exception, of course."

"You might be surprised," the lady said.

Valmont started circling again.

"You make a valid point, M. Greene. In fact, there is one of us at this tay-BELL who is often descri-BED as a 'master of dess-guise.' *You*, M. Brady!"

Once more, the Frenchman twirled around pointing a finger.

"Me?" Brady said. "Well, yes, alright, certainly. But why should I run around in a beard? Half the point of being here is being seen. We *want* people to see King Brady. To go home talking about it, tell their neighbors, pick up the magazine and say, 'That's the guy! He signed my guidebook!'" Brady waved a hand under his face and forced his lips into an unconvincing grin. "I mean, who'd want to hide this?"

"Indeed." Valmont went back to pacing. "But do we not all have parts of ourselves we choose to conceal? Masks we put on, for whatever reason?"

He stopped across the table from us, and I knew enough of his ways now to suspect it was Smythe he was going to bark at next.

"*You*, M. Amlingmeyer!" he said, and to my shock it was Gustav looking down the barrel of Valmont's pointed finger. "On the first day of the contest, you looked and acted like a man who can barely see. You had the slow, uncertain shuf-FELL, the bru-THERE who had to read for you and lead you. You even had the dark spectacles of a blind man. Yet then—*voilà!* On the second day, all is changed, without explication. I put it to you, monsieur, that you yourself were attempting a deception, only it was disrup-TED in some way by the death of M. Curtis!"

"Yup," my brother said.

Valmont blinked at him. "Yip?"

"*Yes*. I was tryin' to fool folks. I wanted them to see me as hobbled. I've been doin' it for quite a while now, actually, in a lot of different ways."

"And what is the porpoise of this pretext?"

Old Red shrugged. "It can come in right handy, bein' underestimated."

"Ahhh. *Naturellement.* It all begins to fall into place."

Valmont puts his hands behind his back and started wearing a groove in the carpet again.

I leaned in close to my brother. "You alright?"

I figured he'd be upset, finding himself forced to admit in public something he'd just barely been able to say in private just to me. The only emotion on his face, though, was slow-simmering exasperation, and it was pointed at Eugene Valmont.

"I'm startin' to think this whole thing's just a trip to the fishin' hole," he muttered.

"We must turn our attentions now to the one who is *not* with us," Valmont said. He spun on his heel so he was facing Pinkerton, but the scowl on the man's face seemed to convince him a poking finger would be a bad idea. "You, M. Pinkerton . . . so far as we know, you were the last of us to see M. Curtis alive."

"What of it?"

"How would you describe his mood?"

Pinkerton shrugged. "We all saw it. He was keyed up, a little drunk, reckless, I guess one could say obsessed."

"Ah! 'Obsessed'! *Mais oui!* There we have the crux of the ma-TEHR, for to explain all that has happened we need to delve into the deep, dark waters of the psychologi-KELL."

To my disappointment, he started walking around the table again. Watching him was starting to make my neck hurt almost as much as listening to him hurt my brain.

"Why was Armstrong B. Curtis here? This we know, because he told us. He intended to humiliate us. To show us up as frauds unworthy of the throne vaca-TED by his fallen hero. More than his hero. His idol. His god. And where has his god gone? Two and one half years ago, he simply"—Valmont fluttered his fingers and flapped his hands—"disappeared. Oh, we have all heard the rue-mares. The attempts on his life in London, the sudden flight to Switzerland, the last, mysterious sighting near the falls at Reichenbach. Yet we know almost nothing, and when M. Sherlock Holmes left this world, he did it as would a divini-tay. He left behind no body, no blood, no untidy mortal mess. He may as well have ascended into the clouds in the arms of awngels . . . to return one day with a blast of trumpets, the more fanati-KELL might even say."

I stole a peek at my brother, for he had a fanati-KELL streak himself: More than once, he'd told me he was skeptical about the whole Holmes-over-the-waterfall story. All he did now, though, was frown.

"What does any of this have to do with us?" Tousey asked.

"Everything! Because M. Curtis was about to lose that perfect ending to his god's goss-pell. Thanks to you, mademoiselle."

He was looking at Lucille Larson.

"Me?"

I would've thought the lady's gaunt, bony face hardly had the flesh to spare for a smile, yet I spied the hint of a smirk hoisting up one corner of her thin lips. I think she was pleased to find herself handed a plum role in the insane melodrama playing out before her.

"Your magazine, at any rate," Valmont said. "*McClure's*. Soon, it will publish Dr. John Watson's account of his friend's death at Reichenbach. That which has been shrouded in secrecy will be revealed for all the world to see. The myth of the god"—he brought up his hands, one high, one low, then smacked them together—"comes down to earth. For the acolyte, the disci-PELL, the *believer*, this prospect is both captivating and completely unaccepti-BELL." He pulled his hands apart again. "There is a spleet."

"A spleet?" I said.

"A spleet." Valmont tapped the side of his head. "In the mind. And this brings us to the final, the *greatest* deduc-shawn. Remember M. Curtis's last words to us before leaving this room. The first day of the contest was but 'a warm-up.' The real challenge was about to begin. Yet what did we get in the days to follow? I will tell you."

The Frenchman stopped and reached into his inside coat pocket. Out came one of the stiff clue cards we'd all come to know so well.

"*De la terre où les têtes couronnées une fois roulées, il sont venues à un grand jubilé,*" Valmont read out. "*Mais maintenant de lui goûte des larmes, et pourrait assaisonner mille bouillabaisses.*" He shook his head and put the card away again. "Translation: From the land where crowned heads once rolled, it came to great celebray-shawn; but now it tastes of tears and could season a thousand bow-ELS of soup."

"Your second clue yesterday," Diana said.

"*Exactement*. Leading to the fac-simile Statue of Libertay in the Mines and Mining Building." Valmont turned to the only sleuths there who didn't make it to the Mining Building the day before—me and Gustav. "Carved from salt, you see."

"Clever," I said.

Old Red, meanwhile, gave a little jerk in his chair, as if I'd repaid him for flattening my toes.

"Hel-lo," I heard him mutter.

Valmont didn't notice, though. He was already replying to me as he went back into orbit around the table.

"Cle-VAIR? No. I must disagree. How does this ri-DELL differ from what we were given on Monday, except that the doggerel is even more infantile and the French more execrable? Answer: It does not. Conclusion: This is not the real challenge M. Curtis was speaking of Monday night."

Valmont's voice rose steadily as he looped around us, and his pace picked up, too. In fact, if he kept it up, I figured it wouldn't be long before he was running screaming circles on the ceiling.

"I submit, ladies and gentlemen, that Armstrong B. Curtis could not abide the thought of his god being dragged back down to earth and supplanted in the firmament by one of us. So devoted was he to Sherlock Holmes that he chose to sacrifice himself upon the great sleuth's al-TEHR. It fits the facts, *mes amis*! Eliminate the impossi-BELL and whatever remains will be the truth, Holmes said. No no no! Not today! Today we must embrace the impossi-BELL, for—by design—that is where the truth lies! The man who killed M. Curtis *was* in this room Monday night, but he is *not* with us now, and that is because he . . . sat . . . *there*!"

When the Frenchman stopped and pointed this time, he was facing Armstrong B. Curtis's empty chair.

There were exclamations from all around the table—"Ridiculous!" from Colonel Crowe, "He's as crazy as Curtis" from Tousey, a simple "*What*?" from Pinkerton, etc. My brother didn't cut loose with his usual "Feh" or "Hel-lo," though. In fact, he barely seemed to be paying attention at all. His eyes were pointed at Valmont, but his gaze had turned inward.

"Consider the bizarre manner of his demise," Valmont went on, ignoring the ruckus he'd whipped up. "Consider his state of mind. Consider the outré clues unearthed by the brothers Amlingmeyer: cow dung in the dead man's hair, a rat dressed in a tuxedo, a box full of *escargot, et ainsi de suite*. Does it not begin to look less like a mur-DARE and more like a joke—with all of us as the butts?"

"Pardon me, monsieur," Miss Larson said. She seemed as astonished as everyone else, yet her surprise looked like more of the Christmas morning "Can you believe what Santa left me on the tree?" variety. "Did you just say a rat dressed in a tuxedo and a box full of snails?"

"*Oui*. Found in an alley behind the Columbian Hotel."

"It was a squirrel, actually," I said, "and how'd you come to hear of it?"

"The same way I learned of your League of Bearded Men."

Pinkerton twisted in his chair to throw a glare at Sergeant Ryan.

"This is all very interesting," Ryan said with his usual air of imperturbable cheer. "I think, though, that you just put your finger on the hole in your own theory."

Valmont nodded. "Indeed. The Bearded Men. They are not, however, a hole. They are the last piece of the puz-ZELL—the one that completes the picture. M. Pinkerton . . . if you would be so kind as to put it in place."

"I don't know what you're talking about," Pinkerton said.

"The truth about the disguise-ED men who have been adding such a delightful note of menace to this whole endeavor."

"Yes, I know that much. What I don't know is why you're asking *me* about them."

Valmont shook his head and clucked his tongue. "Come, come, monsieur. The time for charades is past. We know that you brought M. Curtis into the contest in order to embarrass your rye-VELLS. And we know that you, as head of the Pinkerton National Detective Awgency's Chicago office, have dozens of skilled operatives at your disposal."

The Frenchman lurched toward the table, his arm stretched straight out before him like a knight's lance, the index finger pointed at Pinkerton's heart.

"I put it to you that the Bearded Men are your agents, assigned to act as decoys and disruptions! That you have known from the beginning that M. Curtis killed himself as part of an elaborate hoax! That you intend to announce that you alone discov-AIRED Curtis's trickery after the contest is o-VAIR, thus ensuring our humiliation! Admit it, William Pinkerton! Admit it, and bring this ugly farce to an end!"

"I will admit nothing of the kind!" Pinkerton roared back. "Because it's complete hogwash! Those men, whoever they are—*if* they even are—are not Pinkertons! And as for Armstrong Curtis putting squirrels in suits and rubbing dung in his hair and smothering himself in cheddar, I can't even use the word that deserves with ladies present! If there's anyone here who needs to bring an ugly farce to an end, it's you! Now I suggest you stop pointing fingers, sit down, and *shut up.*"

Valmont nodded solemnly, turned, and walked to the empty chair between Blackheath-Murray and Miss Larson.

"I apologize to you all," he said once he had himself seated. "In the past, I have found that these lee-TELL confrontations can shock loose new facts, new connections . . . even confessions. But today?" He shrugged, then pulled out a pocket watch and checked the time. "*Très bon*. My timing, at least, cannot be faulted. The *pain au chocolat* should be arriving in but two minutes."

"Let me get this straight," I said. "You've been firin' blind the whole time? Shoutin' at us and makin' us squirm in the hopes someone would just fess up to the whole thing?"

Valmont dumped a lump of sugar in his coffee and began giving it a stir. "It has worked before."

"Did you even believe half of what you were saying?" Miss Larson asked.

"Oh, yes." Valmont took a sip of his coffee. "Half would be about right."

Pinkerton stood up and, without a word, walked away from the table. When he started down the stairs, Ryan and the uniformed cop went with him—though Ryan, at least, paused to offer a farewell in the form of a tipped bowler.

"Of all the presumptuous, arrogant, capricious wastes of time," Tousey grumbled, and he, too, stood up. "Let's go, King."

"I find I've lost my appetite as well," Boothby Greene said. A moment later, he and Blackheath-Murray were following Brady and Tousey out, and Smythe went slinking away at their heels.

"I think there's a French word for this," I said.

"*Déjà vu?*" Diana suggested.

"That's it. No one's gettin' me outta my seat before I eat this time, though."

My brother pushed back his chair and got to his feet.

"Come on," he said.

"But—"

"We got work to do."

Old Red turned toward Diana and Colonel Crowe, the long look he gave them saying, *All of us.* Then he headed toward the stairs alone.

"Well . . . thanks for the coffee," I sighed.

As I caught up to my brother, I was pleased to find Diana and the colonel doing the same.

"Valmont was right, and he don't even know it," Gustav said.

"Oh, please," Colonel Crowe scoffed. "You can't actually believe that preposterous story about Curtis killing himself."

"It ain't that the man was right about. It was all that talk shakin' something loose."

We'd reached the bottom of the steps now, and Old Red stopped and let us gather up together in a little circle before saying more.

"I think I know who murdered Mr. Curtis . . . and I definitely know how to smoke him out."

"Who?" I said.

"How?" said Diana.

Naturally, Gustav took things ladies-first.

"Simple," he said. "We let him have exactly what he wants."

31

THE CONTEST
(FINAL ROUND)

Or, The Last Riddle Turns Out to Be a Joke . . . and It's on Us

H ow do I look?"

I opened my mouth to answer.

"On second thought, forget I asked," my brother said. "I don't want to know."

I closed my mouth and (for the moment) kept it closed.

He was right. He didn't want to know. Nor did I want to know what *I* looked like, though I had a pretty good idea: I looked like a color-blind fool. A red-and-white-striped one, to be more specific.

I was once again in the leather cowboy getup I'd worn the first day of the contest, only this time I wouldn't be making a spectacle of myself alone. Old Red had agreed to let Mr. Cohn the tailor dude him up, too. For the final round of the competition, at least, Urias Smythe would have the matching set of court jesters he'd wanted.

So there Gustav was in white hat, white gun belt, white vest, red shirt, red trousers, red boots. Everything but the chaps. We'd both drawn the line there.

"Mr. Cohn, Mr. Smythe, if you don't mind," I said. "I'd like a moment alone with my brother."

"Of course," Smythe said. Despite Old Red's reversal, he'd remained so glum he lacked even the energy to pace, let alone palpitate. We were back in the same little office in the Administration Building we'd used as an impromptu tailor shop a few days before, and he'd watched Cohn fuss over my brother from his slump-shouldered perch atop the lone desk, a stack of empty boxes to one side, a typewriter to the other. He shuffled out of the room with all the pep of a man walking to the gallows.

Before going, Mr. Cohn leaned in to snap a loose thread off Gustav's trousers.

"The alterations . . . I don't know. I wish I had more time for the stitching." He straightened up and wagged a finger at Old Red. "Don't futz with that belt, or your britches might split."

"Don't worry yourself, sir," I said as I lead him out. "I will brook no futzin' from my brother."

Once I had the door closed behind the man, I turned back to Gustav. "Shall we?"

"Now's the time."

I walked over to my suit coat abandoned on the desk, reached into one of the pockets, and pulled out a smallish box. We'd done some shopping after leaving the restaurant that morning, us and the Crowes, and this had been our first purchase.

A box of .44 caliber cartridges.

We drew out our ivory-handled, silverplated Colts—up till now nothing more than particularly heavy decorations—and set about loading them. When they were ready, we looked at each other, nodded, then headed for the door.

I took hold of the knob . . . then paused to look my brother up and down.

"You know, it must be said—"

"No, it mustn't," Old Red cut in.

I forged on regardless.

"—you shouldn't have hid yourself away in them old puncher's duds so long. Clean you up, and you actually almost look like a goddamn hero."

My brother replied with what *he* felt must be said, as he feels it needs saying so very often: "Feh."

When we stepped out of the building, we found the crowd out front was the biggest yet: eight or nine hundred people, maybe even a thousand, all crammed in around the bandstand at the edge of the Grand Basin. The swarm was so large, in fact, there was no room along the water for Major Bacon and His Hoosier One Hundred, and the brass band was forced to take up residence near the steps of the Machinery Building fifty yards away. They were playing "The Gladiator" as we stepped outside.

"I wonder if . . . yup, there he is." I pointed to a tall figure halfway to the gazebo. "That's King Brady's song."

"Good timin', then," Gustav said as cheers went up all around the Court of Honor. "Maybe nobody'll notice *us*."

I glanced down at our eyeball-assaulting outfits. "Umm. Yeah."

My brother was nearly right, though. Brady might have been the only contestant other than us who had no chance of winning—the best he (or we) could hope for was a four-way tie with Greene, Valmont, and the Crowes—yet he was still the people's favorite, and their hurrahs were so deafening they must have echoed all the way up the lake to Milwaukee.

"You'd think he was ridin' into Jerusalem on an ass," I grumbled, but I don't think Old Red even heard me. He was too busy trying to take advantage of the distraction, and indeed as we hustled along in Brady's wake (with Smythe in ours), we only had to put up with two dozen wisecracks about our finery instead of the two hundred I'd expected. We also saw beards aplenty, of course, but none were attached to anybody who seemed to wish us any harm.

By the time we reached the bandstand, Brady and Frank Tousey were doing us yet another favor—entertaining the reporters camped out by the steps with bold predictions of imminent victory. We managed to slip by almost unseen.

There would've been no "almost" about it if Old Red hadn't leaned out over the railing when we were halfway up the stairs.

"Hey! You!" he called down to the reporters. "The feller in the white suit!"

A man clad in wrinkled seersucker turned to peer up at my brother. I recognized him as the newshound from the *Evening Journal*—the one who'd been shouting about "the ghost of Sherlock Holmes" the day before.

"That spook ever come back?" Gustav asked him.

"No," the man said sourly, obviously thinking my brother was guying him.

"Well, just keep your eyes open today, friend," Old Red said, and on he went to the top of the steps.

I'll say this for Boothby Greene and Blackheath-Murray and Eugene Valmont: They were all polite enough not to smirk or roll their eyes at our getups. (You'll notice that Lucille Larson and William Pinkerton are conspicuously missing from that sentence. The Crowes are as well, but I couldn't fault them for the looks on their faces. They'd been forewarned what we'd look like, yet the colonel still winced, while Diana stared despondently at Old Red like he was a kitten favoring a sore paw. Her heart obviously ached for his lost dignity—which had me wondering if she thought I had any to lose.)

A moment later, Brady and Tousey joined us, and it was time. Pinkerton said a few words from the podium, but I didn't hear a one of them. He could've fired off a cannon and I wouldn't have noticed, so lost in thought was I.

If I don't talk my way into an early grave, I might get seventy or eighty years to gallivant around this old world of ours. Yet despite all the thousands of hours I could still have ahead of me, this next one, I knew, was the most important, for every single minute to follow would bear its mark. We were being swept toward a fork in the river, my brother and me. To the one side was failure, to the other success, and the current was strong and our paddles small. We were going to have to row for all we were worth to make it downriver the right way, and what's more—and this scared me most of all—we were going to have to get lucky. And the one and only thing you can count on with luck is that it won't be there when you really need it.

"Contestants, deduce!" Pinkerton bellowed, and it was only then I realized he'd already handed out all the envelopes, and one of them was in my own hands.

I tore it open and read out the following words.

```
To find the treasure
Board a ship of the desert
Asail where the spinning wheel looms.
Enter ye there the pharaoh's tomb.
The prize you'll find hidden
In that black vault forbidden:
In Death's grip, yet free from harm,
Safe as the babe in mummy's arms.
```

"Hardly even counts as a riddle, it's so obvious," I said. "They may as well have just given us a map with a big *X* on it."

"Maybe that's the point," Old Red said. "Ain't the time to stand around jawin' about it, though. Lead on."

It was gratifying to be the first ones on the go, for once, and the assembled multitudes put up a satisfying roar of approval as we clopped down the stairs. We didn't get all the huzzahs to ourselves, though, for King Brady was right on our heels, and when we reached the bottom of the steps I glanced back and saw Diana and the colonel at the top.

"Clear a path for our sleuths!" Frank Tousey called out to the crowd. "And don't follow them, please! If you wait just a few minutes, I assure you, you'll have front-row seats for the thrilling climax of our competition!"

Miraculously, the sea of spectators parted, and we were able to cut east with no shoving needed. Our stiff new clothes slowed us, though, and before we even had the crowd fully behind us, Brady and the Crowes had swept ahead. By the time we rounded the Mines and Mining Building on our way out of the Court of Honor, Greene and Valmont had passed us as well. We were one minute into the final round of the contest, and already we were dead last again.

"God damn these crazy drawers," Gustav panted. "It's like tryin' to run with your legs in splints."

"You're the one who wanted us wearin' 'em."

"I was just givin' us an excuse to strap on our irons. If I'd known it was gonna be like this, I'd have . . . say."

Old Red was eyeing a gaggle of young men lollygagging nearby in their wheeled chairs. FEAST YOUR EYES, SPARE YOUR FEET, the sign hanging over them read. SEVENTY-FIVE CENTS AN HOUR.

"I'm way ahead of you, Brother," I said. "I didn't leave my money in my other suit this time, neither."

I wrestled a wad of crumpled greenbacks from my pocket.

"Cash on the barrelhead, boys!" I said as we hobbled up. "Ten bucks to whoever gets us where we're goin' fast!"

I would have added "Basil and Al need not apply," but our sharp-tongued young guides from the first day of the contest weren't there. Half a minute later, I knew why. As we went careening up the path between the Mines and Transportation buildings, I could see the two of them up ahead, jogging along behind their chairs—in which were sitting Greene and Valmont. Farther up, another pair of chair-pushers was steering the Crowes northward. In fact, the only contestant who didn't hire himself some wheels and extra legs was Brady: I spotted him dashing across the footbridge to the Wooded Island as we carried on north after the others.

Soon after, all our chariots were clumped up together beside the same gates. The wheelchairs weren't allowed out of the White City, it turned out, and our destinations lay just beyond, in the Midway Plaisance.

Valmont peeled off into Hagenbeck's Animal Show. Diana and the colonel darted into the Japanese Bazaar. Greene disappeared into the Moorish Palace. For us, it was back down the Street in Cairo, past the theater home of Urias Smythe's "soothing" dancers, past the shops and mosques and cafés and camels, to an imposing stone edifice bracketed by towering, rune-riddled obelisks.

This my guidebook had called "the Temple of Luxor," and inside we would supposedly find "the mummy of Ramses II, oppressor of the Israelites." We would also, hopefully, find our final clue in the contest—and our last chance to catch Curtis's killer, if Old Red's hunch was right. Before heading inside, however, we both paused to glance back up the narrow street we were leaving. We saw bearded men, but no one we recognized as a Bearded Man.

A mustachioed Mohammedan with pince-nez and red fez stood behind the ticket window, and when he saw us come up he smiled and waved us on.

"Mr. Pinkerton made all the arrangements this morning," he said. "I wish you luck."

"Thanks," I said. "I wish it, too."

From there, a narrow, gloomy passageway wound down to a series of low-ceilinged chambers packed with display cases and educational placards. The floor was sandy, the air musty and dusty, and nearly every inch of wall was covered with colorful "hiero-glyphs," which seemed to translate to something along the lines of "bird man eye squiggle woman cat sun squiggle snake dagger duck." Propped up in some of the corners were sarcophagi adorned with human faces and crossed hands, and a feeling of profound eeriness hung over everything—and that was before we even saw the bodies.

We found them in what was by far the biggest chamber in the place: a cavern-like space just beyond a pair of heavy wooden doors upon which hung a sign reading CLOSED FOR REPAIRS. (This last, we figured, was merely one of the "arrangements" Pinkerton had been seeing to.) In the middle of the room were half a dozen gilded coffins. Open.

Now, there's one thing about a corpse a man can usually rely on: It's dead and it's going to stay that way. Which might sound as obvious as obvious gets until you've laid eyes on one that seems to have half a mind to hop up and offer you a how-do, heartbeat be damned. As is the case, I quickly discovered, with those rag-wrapped bundles of bleached bone and beef jerky popularly known as "mum-mies." The first one I found myself face to shrivel-twisted face with looked to have all the heft left of your average piñata, sans candy. Yet staring into the black pits of its dead eyes, I could swear I saw a little flutter, a flicker, a glimmer of unholy life.

Of course, it was just a trick of the crypt's dim, shimmery light.

Yet even I, devout scoffer at hexes and hoodoo and spook-talk of all kinds, couldn't help but go goose-bumpy.

I glanced back at my brother, who was busy giving the once-over to a mummy of his own.

"Nothing tucked in here but one fay-row and a whole lotta old linens," I said, "but I'm tellin' ya, this is the place. Ain't nowhere else that clue could point to."

Old Red just said, "Nothing here, either," and moved on to the next carcass.

I was still giving my second stiff an uneasy eyeballing when Gustav let loose with a "Hel-lo!" I turned to find him pushing his face so close to one of the mummies it looked like he meant to whisper sweet nothings in its ear—which would've been hard, seeing as said ear had apparently fallen off some centuries before.

Slowly, gingerly, he snaked a hand into the casket. When he eased it out again, it was holding a small envelope of the sort we'd come to know so well. I hustled to Old Red's side as he tore it open. Inside, as always, was a small card. My brother handed it to me without even glancing at its contents.

The message was short and not especially sweet.

"'Ha ha,'" I said.

"I don't need no commentary," Gustav growled. "Just tell me what it says."

I flicked the hard-edged black type. "That *is* what it says. 'Ha ha.'"

Old Red squinted at the card, for all the good that'd do. I suppose he knows what an *H* and an *A* are, but put them together and they could spell "sauerkraut" for all he'd know.

"'Ha ha'?" he said. "What the hell's that supposed to mean?"

He got an answer right quick.

There was the crackling smash of shattering glass behind us, the whoosh of quick-fanning flame, and we whirled around to find a wide strip of the crypt—the section between us and the heavy chamber doors—ablaze.

Oh, and those doors? The only way out of the burial chamber? They were thudding shut.

Ha ha, indeed.

Only my brother and I weren't laughing.

32

THE CONTEST
(FINAL ROUND, PART TWO)

Or, The Last Riddle Is for the Birds,
Yet the Feather Goes in Someone Else's Cap

The fire wasn't huge . . . yet. A good leap might still get us across to the doors. The flames burned with an unnatural ferocity, though, putting off billows of black smoke and a heat so intense I felt like a pig on the spit from a dozen feet away. Whoever was out to get us, they hadn't just tossed in a lit match. This was turpentine or wood alcohol or gasoline at work.

I moved closer and tried kicking sand over the nearest finger of flame, but there wasn't much to kick. The sand on the floor turned out to be but an inch thick. Beneath it were plain, old-fashioned, *flammable* wood planks. We were better off leaving the sand where it was.

I reached up for my lapels, thinking to shrug off my suit coat and use it to beat at the blaze. Unfortunately, my fingers found not heavy, flame-smothering wool but the stiff, useless leather of my red vest. For not the first time (though perhaps the last), I cursed Urias Smythe and his idea of proper Wild West attire. I briefly considered snatching up one of the mummies and using it on the fire instead—they were so withered I couldn't imagine one would weigh any more than my coat. All that cloth wrapped around them would probably light up like a rag dipped in pitch, however, and I'd just end up holding the world's oldest torch.

I was out of ideas.

I turned to Gustav and found him with his back to the fire, examining first the high, steepled ceiling filling with smoke above us, then the far walls.

"See another way out?" I asked.

"Nope."

"A way to put out the fire?"

"Nope."

"Well, sweet Jesus, what do we do, then?"

"Only one thing left we can do." Old Red faced the doors again and put his hands around his mouth. "Help! Fire! Heeeeeeeeelllllllllllllllllllllp!"

It lacked the stamp of genius, perhaps, but just then wasn't the time to point it out. I simply joined in. And I must say, there are times genius is overrated anyway, for we could've lost many a precious second cooking up a brilliant scheme for escape when those cries for help might—and, in fact, *did*—produce a banging on the other side of the doors within seconds.

Why our would-be rescuers couldn't simply throw the doors open was clear a moment later. The doors finally started to part, but through the smoke I could see two dark lines cutting across the space between them at about waist height. Our would-be *barbecuer* had tied or chained the doors together.

At last, whatever was trussing them up gave way, and the doors flew open—and the two men who'd been putting their shoulders to them nearly stumbled forward into the flames. Fortunately for all concerned, they stopped just short of charbroiling themselves, and a moment later one was smacking at the blaze with his coat while the other dashed off to fetch buckets of sand. They were eventually

284

joined by the fez-topped fellow from the ticket booth (who exclaimed what I can only assume was the Arabian version of "Holy shit!" upon discovering his temple turned into a hickory smokehouse). Between the three of them and a dozen buckets of sand and a few final stomps from me and my brother, the second Great Chicago Fire was snuffed out before it could really begin.

With no more flames to worry about, I finally managed a longish look at our saviors. Of the two first on the scene, one was bearded, the other not, yet both seemed vaguely familiar. It was hard to see clearly through eyes still teared-up from all the smoke, though, and the third gent proved a distraction, what with his spluttered, near-hysterical questions of the "How did—? What could—? Did you—?" school.

"Perhaps you'd better go and fetch along an officer of the law," the bearded man said, and the sound of his soft, lilting brogue told me we had an officer of the law among us already. Gustav waited till the befezzed fellow had hurried away to address him by name.

"Good thing you were tailin' us today, Sergeant Ryan," he said, holding out his hand. "I assume that was you followin' the Crowes yesterday."

Ryan took my brother's hand and gave it a shake. "I've been keeping an eye on things, in my own quiet way."

I peered at the policeman's beard, which suddenly seemed so obvious in its falseness it wouldn't pass muster in a kindergarten pageant about the life of Lincoln.

"So the sergeant here's the Other Other Bearded Man?" I said to Old Red.

He nodded, then turned to the man beside Ryan—a tall, lanky fellow with sunken eyes and swarthy skin—and offered him his hand as well.

"We owe you our thanks, too, Mr. Agajanian. I'm sure glad you had a change of heart about us."

The man huffed out a bitter grunt, but he shook my brother's hand all the same.

"I am angry. I am not crazy," he said. "I could not stand by and see you die."

I squinted at the man's eyes and nose and found I knew them well. This unbearded man was the Bearded Man: Emile "Billy Steele" Agajanian.

"You shaved since yesterday," I said to him.

Agajanian slapped his hands to his lean, freshly smoothed cheeks. "Oh, such a deduction! I can see why Smythe prefers you two to the likes of me!" He dropped his hands and rolled his eyes. "Of course, I shaved. You pulled out half my chin whiskers yesterday! What's more, you had seen me up close twice. With my beard, I wouldn't get within thirty feet of you without being recognized. Without it, I almost got close enough to lock you in this room. Imagine my surprise when someone else did it first."

"Yeah. About that someone else . . . ," Gustav said.

"I don't think you'll like it," Ryan said.

"Oh?"

"He had a beard," Agajanian said. "Black. Very thick."

"A big man?" I asked. "Burly?"

Agajanian shook his head. "Not especially."

"That all you got?" Old Red said. "A thick black beard on a not so burly feller?"

"I think he was wearing a brown coat." Agajanian shrugged. "He was in and out very fast."

Ryan jerked his head at Agajanian. "And I was watching *him*."

I hung my head and groaned. "Oh, Lord, no."

"Yup. Looks like we got us Another Other Other Bearded

Man." Gustav dismissed this newest mystery with a wave of the hand. "We ain't got time to sit around paintin' pictures of him, though—and what's more, there ain't no need to. If we get to that egg quick, we'll find our answers. If we don't, we ain't gonna have nothin' but questions till kingdom come."

"What makes you say that?" Ryan asked.

My brother ignored him, turning instead to me. "We gotta get back to the Court of Honor. My guess is right, the egg's gotta be around there somewhere."

"What makes you say *that*?" I asked. "Mr. Another-Other-Other up and stole our clue."

"We don't need no clue to get within spittin' distance of the finish line. Every day so far, the egg's been tucked away in a building in direct line of sight of that bandstand we start from. They can't go any further off and expect an audience to tag along. Now, the egg hunt's taken us to the Agriculture Building, the Mines Building and the big long one with the name to match."

"The Manufactures and Liberal Arts Building," I said.

"Right. So that leaves what else in the Court of Honor?"

"The Administration Building—"

"Closed to the public," Ryan threw in.

"—and the Electricity and Machinery buildings."

Old Red nodded. "It's one of them last two then, if the pattern holds. Only choice now is to hightail it thataway, duck into them buildings, and hope we hear Major Bacon and his boys. If they're kickin' up their usual racket, that'll lead us in the right direction."

Agajanian shook his head with grim-faced admiration. "I owe you an apology. You *are* good."

"Save the pats on the back for later . . . if we get our man. Right now, we gotta skedaddle."

"Just a moment, Mr. Amlingmeyer," Ryan said. "A serious crime has been committed here. Innocent people could have been killed, and I'm not talking about you and your brother. What makes you think I'm going to let you go stir up more trouble?"

"You ain't gonna let us. We're just gonna do it. Come on, Brother."

Gustav stomped off toward the doorway—which was suddenly blocked by the Egyptian ticket taker and two blue-coated, potbellied Chicago bulls.

"Those two! They must have started it!" our fezzy friend cried. "They were trying to destroy my temple!"

"You there. Wild Bill," one of the coppers said to Old Red. "What's this all about?"

I turned to Sergeant Ryan again. "Alright, so we're back to askin'. But come on—you must've known all along we had us some skullduggery here, though you couldn't say so. Otherwise, why would you be runnin' around with someone else's hair stuck to your face? The Exposition's a big deal, with big-deal backers, I understand that. Your hands were tied. But that don't mean you gotta tie ours, too. Let us go, before it's too late."

The sergeant looked at me, saying nothing, the usual twinkle in his eyes as dead as the fire we'd just put out.

"Well?" the uniformed cop prompted. "Is anyone going to tell me what the hell's going on here?"

"I can do that, Officer . . . Haas, isn't it?" Ryan reached up to his ears and pulled a rubber band out from around each, and just like that his bushy beard popped free. "Detective Sergeant Ryan from Central Station. I happened to be here attending to a spot of police work when the trouble began. I'll explain everything. In the meantime"—he nodded at me and Gustav—"these two gentlemen are free to go."

"What about me?" Agajanian asked.

"You are not," Ryan said simply. Then he shooed me and my brother away. "Go on . . . and happy hunting."

"Thanks, Mo!" I called over my shoulder as we darted off.

"You won't regret it, Sergeant Ryan!" my brother added.

"I'm going to hold you to that, Mr. Amlingmeyer."

"But those men nearly burned the place down!" the Egyptian wailed as we scooted around him. "And just look what they did to my mummies! They're black as coal!"

"Oh, I assure you it wasn't their fault," Ryan replied. "As for your 'mummies,' you'll find there's more than enough gauze and papier-mâché in Chicago to make more."

The last thing I heard from the crypt was Agajanian shouting after us.

"I want my coat back!"

When we reached the gates to the White City again, we found but two wheeled chairs still waiting on the other side. Ours. Valmont, Greene, and the Crowes were all ahead of us somewhere.

"Did King Brady ever come thisaway?" Gustav asked our charioteers. "Good-lookin' young feller with dark hair? Natty dresser? In a hurry?"

"Sure, we saw him. Went out to the Midway not long after you, then came tearing back through a couple minutes ago."

Old Red gave himself all of two seconds to muse on that before throwing himself into his chair. "The Electricity Building! Go!"

I settled into my own seat, but before the poor soul tasked with pushing me could get to it, he handed me a small envelope.

"The lady said to give you this."

It was already torn open, and as we got to rolling southward, I slipped out the card inside and looked it over. It was another clue—the one the Crowes had just found tucked away along the Midway, no doubt. Diana had left it for me in case our own proved too tricky or we jumped to the wrong conclusion.

I looked over at my brother as his cart flew up the gravel path beside mine.

"We don't gotta rely on Major Bacon, after all! We got the Crowes' clue to crack!"

"Well, get to crackin', then!"

So I did.

The G___ C_____

```
Its cage does not itself entrap,
for it has no wind-borne wings to flap.
Neither is it gray or golden hued
(though its gleam a fortune does imbue).
It feathers a nest, but not its own;
just one in the hand could purchase a throne.
You'll find its like down man-made hole,
yet those who dig seek not for coal.
By now, assuredly, you know its name
. . . though why it's called that, no one can say!
```

I didn't just crack it, it practically came pre-cracked: Like our first clue of the day, this one was laughably easy. What wasn't so laughter-worthy, though, was the fact that we were headed to the wrong place.

"Forget the Electricity Building!" I shouted. "The Machinery Building, too! It's the Liberal Arts Building we want!"

"But—" Gustav began.

"I'm tellin' ya, the egg's in the Manufactures and Liberal Arts Building!"

There wasn't another "But." There wasn't an "Are you sure?" or a "Why?" Old Red just looked back at the young men panting behind us and said, "You heard him. Manufactures and Liberal Arts. Pronto!"

Not three minutes later, we were sprint-limping through the building as fast as our leather leggings would allow. We were behind most of the others, sure, but that didn't mean we were out of the running. As we passed collections of porcelain and pottery, medical supplies, musical instruments, photographs, stained glass, and on and on—not to mention what seemed like a million gawping sightseers—the sound of a great, murmuring multitude grew steadily louder. I was leading us the right way . . . and no one was cheering for a winner yet.

Then a deafening roar echoed through the massive hall like thunder, and a moment later Major Bacon's band added to the din. They were playing "The Gladiator," which told me exactly what to expect when we finally turned off the broad thoroughfare running up the middle of the building and got the Tiffany Pavilion in sight.

There was the crowd, parted up the middle by low-slung velvet ropes and a small army of Columbian Guards. Halfway up the red carpet that lead to the Tiffany exhibit of jewelry and pearls and precious stones were Diana and Colonel Crowe. Farther on a ways was Eugene Valmont.

Beyond them all, at the far end of the carpet, was King Brady.

He was coming down a stepladder set up beside the rotating column of gold atop which had rested, the last time I'd been there, the Tiffany Diamond, otherwise known as "the gray canary." The gem's pyramid-shaped glass case was empty now, and Brady had what I knew to be its latest, temporary occupant in his hands.

When he stepped off the ladder, he held the Egg of Columbus up for all to see, and the crowd hurrahed him again. Then he turned to the cluster of folks waiting for him at the base of the ladder—Frank Tousey, Lucille Larson, Urias Smythe, Blackheath-Murray, a small flock of newspapermen, and three overdressed swells I took to be representatives of Tiffany & Co. of New York.

With them was William Pinkerton. Brady gave him the egg.

And with that, the competition to find the World's Greatest Sleuth ended in a draw. The only thing it had established for certain was who *wasn't* the greatest: us.

Yet though the contest was over, our work wasn't. We carried on along the carpet, sweeping up the Crowes as we went. The four of us shared some hurried, whispered words before the colonel and Diana slipped under the velvet ropes and disappeared into the crush on the other side. Then my brother and I moved on to Eugene Valmont, each taking him by an arm without stopping.

"Well done, miz-yer," Old Red told him.

"Excusez-moi?" Valmont said, startled to find himself being hustled along between us.

"You're in a mighty exclusive club," I said. "The five greatest sleuths in the world!"

"What say we go congratulate your newest member?"

Gustav nodded ahead at Brady, who'd taken to throwing kisses to the crowd between bows.

"Oh. *Naturellement.* That would be the sportsmanlike thing to do, yes?"

"Yup," said Old Red.

"Exactemente," said moi.

Where the red carpet ended, the Tiffany Pavilion began, and strung out along its borders was more velvet rope. Strung out along *that* was a mixture of Columbian Guards and hard-eyed men in dark suits, all of them intent on keeping the rabble a safe distance from the treasure-packed cases on display. As we drew up close, two moved out to intercept us, but I kept my eyes locked on William Pinkerton.

"We have come to concede defeat," I announced. "May we humble commoners pay homage to the King?"

The guards looked back at Pinkerton, who gritted his teeth and nodded his head. We were allowed to pass through into the pavilion.

Brady didn't notice our approach: He was too busy gladhanding the stuffed shirts while Tousey blocked a photographer who'd set up his tripod nearby.

"Here you go. Someone else to kiss your ring," I said, and we deposited Valmont before Brady—then swept past to the stepladder he'd descended but a moment before.

Gustav started climbing. I turned and planted myself by the bottom step.

Tousey spun around and lurched toward us. "What do you think you're doing?"

"You ready, Brother?"

When I got no reply, I threw a quick glance back. Old Red had come around to the far side of the ladder before starting up, so as he stood there, feet three rungs from the top, he was facing our audience: a swollen sea of humanity overflowing into the exhibits and showrooms and galleries all around.

Gustav opened his mouth, but no sound came out.

There he was. A man who could hardly look a young lady in the eye gazing out at hundreds of them, not to mention their fathers and mothers and brothers and so on. A man who hated pretension and the putting on of airs making a spectacle of himself in a red-and-white leather suit. A man who didn't care for talking trying to address himself to more people than he'd ever spoken to in his entire life.

"Get down from there this instant," Tousey demanded, coming closer. Pinkerton was right behind him, and the guards were taking an interest, too.

I squared my feet and clenched my fists. "My brother's got something to say."

I just wished he'd hurry up and say it.

Then, at last, he did.

"Ladies and gentlemen, if you would give me your attention, please! These proceedings are not yet over! There are two important matters that still need to be seen to! One is fraud, and the other, I'm afraid, is murder!"

33

—

TWO BULLS IN THE CHINA SHOP

Or, My Brother Holds Court and Unmasks a Pretender to the Throne

There were four hundred and sixty-seven gasps, three hundred and twenty-eight *My God*s and *Good Lord*s, ninety-five nervous titters, thirteen screams, and four faintings. More or less.

There was also one "Don't just stand there—get him down!" courtesy of Frank Tousey. It was directed at the nearest guards, who turned, to a man, toward William Pinkerton. As did I.

"Gustav's laid the cards on the table," I said. "Best let him play 'em out, wouldn't you say?"

Just in case he didn't get the point, I let my eyes dart to the side, toward the reporters clumped up behind him.

Pinkerton had his choice of flaps: whatever Gustav meant to stir up or the two of us tussling with the guards in the middle of the Tiffany Pavilion, and the contest he'd overseen ending with a million or so dollars in property damage. Either way, the whole world would be watching.

"He can have his say," Pinkerton grated out.

"Thank you, sir," Old Red said, and then he looked out over

the crowd again and got to orating with a boom to his voice I never would've guessed he had in him. "Let's take the fraud first, shall we? A short while ago, everybody in this contest but one went tearin' straight to the same place: the Midway Plaisance. Our second clues of the day were hidden there. Everyone's. Includin' his." He pointed down at King Brady, who was gaping up at my brother with a strange mixture of hatred and helpless horror on his too-perfect face. "Yet he didn't hurry out to the Midway right away, as the rest of us did. Nope. We saw him headin' over to the Wooded Island first. Now, why would he do that?"

"This is ludicrous!" Brady protested. "I made a mistake, that's all. I went to the Japanese garden on the island when I should have gone to the Javanese settlement on the Midway. Fortunately, I realized where I'd gone wrong before it was too late."

Gustav shook his head. "I might be inclined to believe you if your 'mistake' wasn't so typical. You've been takin' these little detours all week. Why, the first day of the contest, Miss Larson there tells me, you ended up in a . . . a private spot when you should've been runnin' for your next clue. And then yesterday, I saw you head right back to the very same . . ." A touch of color came to my brother's cheeks as he debated the use of the words "privy" or "john" in his debut as a public speaker. ". . . uhh . . . location. Which was why you had to switch up and find a new place to go today."

"If you won't shut him up, I will," Tousey snarled at Pinkerton. Then he turned our way and started a step he never finished.

My hand was on the butt of my gun. My eyes were on him.

"Keep goin', Brother," I said.

Gustav cleared his throat and carried on with only the slightest quaver to his voice.

"It should strike us all a mite strange, friends. All week long, this feller's been shakin' hands, takin' bows, everything but kissin' babies. Yet when the time comes for the contest, he needs solitude all of a sudden. And anytime a camera's pointed his way, why, he turns his pretty face away while his publisher jumps in front of the lens. It only makes sense if you put it together with a comment the late, lamented Armstrong B. Curtis made Monday night. Mr. Curtis had done him a little snoopin' on us sleuths, you see, and he got to droppin' hints as to what skeletons we had hung up our in closets. 'Ask Mr. Brady about his birthday,' he said. Which makes me think Curtis had dug that birthday up somehow, and it didn't fit with what he found before him. Didn't fit the man. It did fit someone else here, though . . . and I think it's time he stepped forward and came clean."

There was a moment of silence that stretched on forever. It didn't seem possible so many people could stay so quiet so long. With my brother up on a stepladder smoothly sermonizing for a horde of hundreds, though, I suppose it was hardly the time to say what was impossible and what wasn't.

"The jig is up, as you yourself have been known to say, sir," Old Red said, gaze moving slowly over the crowd. "It'd go a long way toward clearin' all this up if you'd show yourself. Otherwise, what you been up to is gonna get wove in with Mr. Curtis's death, and I know you wouldn't wanna make that tangle any worse than it already is."

"This is ridiculous," Tousey said. I didn't need to remind him to shut up, though. Whatever he might've said next would've been drowned out by the sound of a thousand gasps.

A big, burly, bearded man was slipping under the velvet rope and stepping onto the red carpet about forty yards from us. Even from a distance, I recognized him straight off: It was the Un-bearded Man, another fake beard in place on his broad face. A couple Columbian Guards took hesitant steps toward him, but my brother waved them back.

"Let him come on up," he said. "He should've been with us all along."

A great wave of murmurings arose as the man came closer, growing louder with his every step. Gustav spoke again just when it seemed no single voice could be heard above the clamor.

"Do you wanna introduce yourself, or should I?"

The crowd quieted down.

The Unbearded Man stopped, feet planted wide, back straight. What with the fuzz over his face and his slouch hat pulled low and a black topcoat wrapped around his body, there was little to see of the real him. Just big hands, thick gray eyebrows, and a piercing stare. That was enough to give you the measure of the man, though. He'd been around a while and been through a thing or two and knew how to handle himself. And he wasn't happy to be where he was now.

"I'll do it," he said in a deep, gravelly-gruff voice. He turned his head to the side, speaking to the multitudes behind him without fully showing them his face. "I'm King Brady."

It was half a minute before the crowd quieted this time.

"I assume the masquerade was Mr. Tousey's idea," Old Red said as the din at last died down.

"Yes," Brady said. He was ignoring Tousey, who fumed at him while the other, younger "King Brady" practically cowered behind his back. "In my line of work, it pays to keep your real looks under wraps. My clients see me, of course. My contacts and the police in New York. But that's it. What they draw in the magazine . . . that has nothing to do with me, and that's how I like it. Tousey knew that. And he knew what he *wished* King Brady looked like. So he found a way for both of us to get what we want."

"He hired him a . . . a . . ."

"Proxy," I whispered.

"A proxy," Gustav said. "A Young King Brady to do all the posin' while the Old King Brady did the real deducifyin'. He picked up the clues, you tried to figure 'em out."

King Brady (the old, real one) nodded. "It was risky. If that actor there—and that's what he is, by the way—if he got his face in the papers, someone back in New York was bound to figure out the truth. With Armstrong Curtis stirring up doubt about all us magazine detectives, I couldn't afford for that to happen. Tousey assured me it wouldn't come to that, though. I didn't see any of this as cheating, by the way. It was still my wits pitted against all of yours. If anything, I put myself at a disadvantage, having to work through someone else."

"I reckon you did, Mr. Brady. And I appreciate that you did you a little detectivin' after Mr. Curtis died. Followin' Urias Smythe and whatnot. You turn anything up?"

Brady glanced over at Smythe, who was wearing a blush so deep he looked like an overgrown eggplant. "Nothing I'd care to mention here."

"Excuse me," Lucille Larson said, and she walked over to stare up at my brother from beside me at the foot of the ladder. "Is this where we finally get to the murder, Mr. Amlingmeyer?"

I glanced back, fearing I'd see Gustav lose his nerve at last. He'd been doing fine facing things safe from his roost, like a man peeking over the top of a rampart, but perhaps one overinquisitive young lady would finally throw him.

I needn't have wasted even the half second I spent fretting.

"Indeed it is, miss," he said with but a here-and-gone peek down at the lady. He was determined to keep the crowd with him, and he knew (because I'd told him as much) that meant making each and every person there feel like he was talking straight to them, up close and one to one. This he immediately got back to doing.

"As you probably know, we had us a tragedy the other night. The Mr. Curtis we've been speakin' of—the gentlemen who whipped up the puzzles for this contest—was found dead over to the Agriculture Building. I won't go into the particulars, so let's just say it could've been an accident, but there was reason to be suspicious, and our friend Mr. Pinkerton and the Chicago Police Department embarked upon an investigation of . . . admirable subtlety."

Our friend Mr. Pinkerton remained stone-faced. I could but hope he appreciated Old Red's uncharacteristic diplomacy, given that his "investigation" had been so subtle it could barely be said to exist at all.

"My brother and me were a little more blunt about it," Gustav went on. "Heck, we were two bulls in the china shop. We did get us some results, though. We learned that the killer—and yes, Mr. Curtis was murdered—might have been wearin' shoes made overseas. We learned he paid a call on Mr. Curtis's hotel room and threw some very odd objects into the trash, including a box of dead snails and some garlic and a ferry ticket."

The word "murder" had sent murmurs rippling through our audience, and with the snails and the garlic they grew louder.

Old Red put up his hands.

"Stay with me here, folks," he said loud and firm, and he swept the crowd with a stern look that would do any schoolmarm proud. It worked, too. Soon there was as much silence as one could expect from a thousand-ish people packed in together.

"Then this very day," my brother continued, "we learned that the killer has a way with a false beard, like just about everyone else around here, it seems, and that he's wearin' a brown coat. But none of that's nearly so instructive, as a certain English sleuth might say, as what happened right here not ten minutes ago."

Gustav looked around the hall again, and until he spoke there was such a hush a mouse fart would've seemed like the roar of a cannon.

"No one won. If the killer did away with Mr. Curtis out of anger or a thirst for revenge or what have you, why go to his room and mess with the man's things? And if he was hopin' to win the competition by gettin' an early peek at the clues, which were sittin' right there atop a dresser . . . well, why didn't he? Why would we have a four-way tie? What was the killer after? Miz-yer Valmont?"

The Frenchman was still standing a few yards off, where we'd abandoned him a while before, and his eyes popped wide at the sound of his name.

"Yes?"

"This morning at that little breakfast of yours, you said the clues you've been gettin' are in French—and it's been gettin' worse as the week went on."

"*Oui.* Yes. It is true."

"So the first day the French was pretty good?"

"Yes. *Très bon.*"

"And today?"

"Maddy-NING. I could barely make from it head or tay-ELS."

Gustav nodded sympathetically. "Yeah, I understand the feelin'. And you know what, folks? The French in Miz-yer Valmont's clues wasn't the only thing that got worse as the week went on. The clues themselves got dumber and dumber, even though Mr. Curtis warned us the night he died that things would be gettin' *trickier*. Well, it's obvious what happened—although I didn't see it till those snails pointed the way."

Old Red pointed over at the golden egg Pinkerton still held in his hands.

"Yesterday, that was hidden in the Mining Building near a copy of the Statue of Liberty carved outta salt. Now, I'll admit I ain't the most far-traveled or wide-read man, but I do know this: The Statue of Liberty is on an island you can only reach by boat, and it came from France—where, I learned earlier this week, snails in garlic and butter are actually considered food—and salt causes snails to shrivel up and die. So that box with the snail shells and the ferry ticket and the garlic? That was part of a puzzle Curtis thunk up that never got used. He didn't mean for us to be runnin' around after puns and bad poems all week. He was gonna scatter around real clues, set up little scenes or some such. We'll never really know, cuz the killer threw all that out and whipped up his own riddles based on what Curtis gave us the first day. Only his French wasn't as good as Curtis's, and it—and the riddles themselves—only got worse through the course of what must've been a very long night of writin'. So there we go. We've got half the 'Why?' figured. The killer wanted Curtis out of the way so he could muck with the contest. Yet that still doesn't give us the other half: 'To what end?'"

My brother took yet another long, silent look around. It wasn't that he was getting cocky with his dramatic pauses, though. I figured he was starting to wonder—as was I—how much longer we'd have to drag this out. If we were lucky, the last piece of the puzzle would be handed over wrapped in ribbons any second. On the other hand, if we weren't lucky—which is to say, if things went as per usual—we'd end up with more egg on our faces than a whole henhouse could produce in a month.

"Sherlock Holmes had him a rule for gettin' to the heart of dark deeds," Gustav said. "Accordin' to him, the question you need to ask yourself is this: 'Who is it who profits by it?' Now here, you could say, 'Nobody! No one won the contest.' But I'd say that's lookin' at it out the wrong window, cuz there's other directions to come at a profit. Those of you who've been followin' the contest from the beginning know the egg's been hidden in a different building off the Court of Honor each day. Yet today, for the first time, we came back to somewhere we'd already been before. This building—and not just that, but the part of this building that's home to the most valuable single thing in all the White City, so far as I know."

Gustav looked over at the tall, pyramid-topped pedestal upon which the Tiffany Diamond had once glimmered.

"A jewel's gonna be pretty safe up there. How's a thief even gonna get at it? Ain't just anybody who can pull up a ladder in the middle of the day. I assume this one here was set up at Mr. Pinkerton's request?"

By this point, all the Tiffany & Co. men nearby had broken into such a sweat they were practically gleaming like diamonds themselves.

"Yes!" one of them said. "Of course, we were happy to cooperate. When a man like William Pinkerton asks a favor—"

"What exactly are you suggesting?" Pinkerton growled.

"I ain't suggestin' nothing," Old Red said. "I'm just tryin' to show why things have played out the way they have." He focused on the Tiffany men again. "I assume the diamond was moved somewhere safe while the egg took its place?"

"Yes. We have our own vault here."

"And you got a guard on it, do you?"

The Tiffanys nearly jumped out of their spats.

"All the guards are up here to handle the crowd!" one of them said. He waved a floppy hand at the display cases and dark, oak-paneled cloisters that receded into blackness at the back of the pavilion. "But there's no way anyone could get past—"

"Where there's a will, there's a way," a man said from behind us, and Colonel Crowe and Diana marched out of the gloom no one could supposedly get to.

"Two ways, in this case," Diana said. "Ours and his."

Boothby Greene was walking between them—and their guns, which were surreptitiously pressed into his sides.

Gustav slumped and rubbed at his chin.

"Finally," he said under his breath. "I thought my damn jaw was gonna drop off."

"What's the meaning of this?" Blackheath-Murray demanded, puffing himself up with all the considerable indignation his big, bluff British frame could muster. "Unhand him at once!"

"I don't think that's such a good idea, sir," I said. "Seems Mr. Greene's gotten into the habit of killin' people, and I'd hate to give him another chance at it."

34

LINDENBAUM & CO.

Or, Old Red Sleuths Up the Jewels in His Deducifying Crown

There was another general uproar all through the great hall, but my brother didn't wait for it to die down this time. He'd been stalling with his speechifying, but there was no need to beat around any bushes now. It was high time to just chop the things down.

He didn't get off his perch on the ladder, though, and when he went on talking his voice still rang out loud and clear. He didn't ask our audience to quiet down and listen, either, yet this they did.

"You got anything to say for yourself, Mr. Greene or Mr. Lindenbaum or Mr. Whatever Your Real Name Is?"

"I'd prefer it if we stuck with Greene," the man replied with a small smile, "and I think what we have here is a simple misunderstanding. I was helping myself to a private tour of the Tiffany & Co. exhibit, yes, but I hardly think that justifies—"

Old Red was shaking his head. "Ain't no misunderstandin', I'm sorry to say. In fact, I understand things all too plain. I've got Mizyer Valmont to thank for that."

"You do?" the Frenchman said.

"Yessir. You gave the pot a right good stir this morning, and it scraped up more than you saw. It was the part about Mr. Greene and his little trick at the dinner Monday that cinched it. When you talked about it, I noticed you made you an assumption—the same one we all made that night: that when Greene whipped off that beard and said he'd been servin' up snails all along, he really had been. It was him who'd invited everyone to the restaurant, remember, so he knew none of us would be back at the hotel. Which gave him the perfect opportunity—by his own arrangement—to slip into Armstrong Curtis's room and get a look at the clues. He had to be sure Mr. Curtis hadn't handed them over to Pinkerton. Cuz if he hadn't, that meant there was only one person who knew what those clues were really supposed to be. And if he got rid of that person . . ."

Gustav threw a sidelong glance at Greene, inviting him to take over the story and spare him more blather.

"I don't know what you're talking about," Greene said. He still had on his little smile, though, and a strange one it was—like the smirk of a boy accused of stealing candy who's still got half a lemon drop in his mouth.

Old Red sighed. "I guess I'll just have to fill you in, then. Mr. Curtis told us all where he was headed Monday night—back to the fairgrounds—and you followed him and you killed him. Once that was out of the way, you had to get rid of his clues and whip up your own, because the whole point was to use this moment right here, the big finish of the contest, as a diversion. So them . . . props, I guess you'd call them, they had to go. The box of snails and the squirrel and what all. There was no way you could come up with such crazy clues for all us sleuths for today, and what's more Pinkerton couldn't carry on usin' the others without Mr. Curtis alive to explain what the heck they meant. So you had quite a night there in the contest's office in the Administration Building—where you knew you'd find the typewriter you needed to make your riddles look the same as Curtis's. I assume he had some extry cards in his room? Spare blanks you could borrow?"

Greene just kept on smiling.

Gustav went on talking.

"Well, anyway, by the time you were done, you must've been all played out, not on your toes. Cuz you let someone catch sight of you. Through a window or some such, I ain't heard the dee-tails. All I know is somebody thought they saw Sherlock Holmes lurkin' around that night, and you look enough like how they draw him to be the Man himself—or his ghost."

"This is ludicrous!" Blackheath-Murray protested.

My brother nodded. "You ain't the first person to say that to-day. Ludicrous don't mean untrue, though, and I got more to back it up, too. The killer got certain stains on his shoes, for instance, and after some sniffin' around I found out them shoes was foreign. Mr. Greene there knew I was checkin' up on that, and, as I'm sure you'll remember, he told me he always got his shoes from America. Selby & Harte of Chicago. That struck me as funny, at first. An Englishman comin' all the way to Chicago in Chicago-made shoes. Then I realized I had only his word for it that he had, and if he needed to get him some new shoes—cuz he knew I was huntin' his old pair, which came from Europe—what would he do? Why, get him some new, American shoes fast as he could."

"Oh, that's just rank—"

"Something else that don't sit right," Old Red plowed on over Blackheath-Murray. "The contestant who didn't make it here, Inspector Lestrade of Scotland Yard. He got jumped and beat so bad he had to bow out, I'm told. Well, that just has to make a feller wonder: Was that so's he couldn't recognize a certain somebody who'd be here? An English yegg with a talent for crackin' safes and a strikin' resemblance to Mr. Sherlock Holmes?"

"Ludicrous!" Blackheath-Murray snorted again.

"You have no proof," Greene said, still smirking.

"You want proof?" Old Red said. "Well, why don't *you* offer some. Prove to us you were huntin' for your second clue when you went to the Midway this afternoon. Show us the card that led you here."

Greene patted the pockets of his heavy coat. "Oh, my. I seem to have misplaced it."

"Don't bother pretendin'," Gustav said. "It'd be easy enough to send one of Mr. Pinkerton's boys over to the Midway to check, but we both know what they'd find: your clue still where Pinkerton left it for you. You didn't have time to grab it—cuz you had your hands full tryin' to roast me and my brother before gettin' back here. It was risky, comin' after us like that, but I guess you figured it was riskier lettin' us live. With what we'd dug up, we might've put the finger on you the second the big hullabaloo broke."

"The big 'hullabaloo'?" Greene said, cocking his head and batting his eyes.

"Come on now," Old Red replied. "I been tryin' to let you end this thing with a little dignity left, but oh well. Colonel Crowe? If you wouldn't mind?"

"Mind? We should've done this five minutes ago!"

The little man stuffed his gun away in a shoulder holster, then got to moving his hands over Greene's long coat. He pulled nothing from the pockets at first, but he did pucker his lips in a satisfied/irritated way all his own. He went on to unbutton the coat, which proved to be brown on the inside, with more big, flap-topped pockets.

"Reversible," the colonel reported. "There's the brown overcoat you were looking for."

There were mutters from the assembled tourists—what a story they'd have to tell when they got back to Topeka or wherever—and the noise of it grew ever louder as Col. Crowe started taking things from Greene's pockets and holding them up for all to see.

"False beard. Box of matches. Pepper-box revolver. Kit of tools . . . for safe-breaking, I'll warrant."

Yet the more he discovered, the more the colonel scowled, and when he was done with every pocket on Greene's person, from top-coat to suit coat to trousers, he grunted in disgust.

"It's not here."

"It is," Gustav said. "You're just gonna have to go at it a tad less gentleman-like." He looked back out over the crowd. "I would suggest that females, children, and the weak of nerve avert their eyes!"

"That won't be necessary," Greene said. "If I may?"

Old Red looked first at Diana, then the colonel, then nodded.

Greene turned his back to the crowd—with Diana pivoting with him, the barrel of her cute little derringer never leaving his side. She kept her gaze steady on his face as he fiddled around for a moment, and then the two of them turned again.

In Greene's hands was the Tiffany Diamond. He'd packed the jewel away with those of the family variety.

There was many a gasp, though all of them together couldn't match for sheer volume the sudden raspy intake of breath the three Tiffany men took in chorus. The one with the least wits scared out of him managed to scurry forward and—after carefully covering his fingers with a handkerchief—retrieve the diamond.

"Greene! How could you?" Blackheath-Murray said.

Greene gave him a nonchalant shrug. "Sorry, old man. I suppose I'm just a rotter."

"Oh, you ain't so bad," Gustav said. "There you are tryin' to cover for your chum, and that counts for something. But please.

Now that we got that big rock back and everything else out on the table, ain't none of us got to pretend anymore." He swung his gaze over to Blackheath-Murray. "From the beginning, I thought it was a tall order, one feller convincin' another to take a nap facedown in cheese. Makes a lot more sense if it's *two* men. And don't forget, you told me you wear them Selby & Harte shoes, too—which means you bought a new pair this week as well. And you can't tell me you put your money behind a would-be Holmes who just happened to be a criminal mastermind. Nope. You two are in it together. Grabbin' that diamond was what brought you both to Chicago in the first place."

As Old Red spoke, everyone near Blackheath-Murray—Smythe, Tousey, Brady, Pinkerton, the Tiffany gents—shrank back from the man like he was a leper asking for a hug. He stood stock-still, though, impaling my brother on a hateful stare.

"Bravo, Mr. Amlingmeyer," Greene said. "You're close. Yet you haven't grasped the full scope of our endeavor. From the beginning, this has been a two-birds-with-one-stone enterprise, and it's not necessarily over. For the moment, we need merely target a different bird."

I figured out what the man was getting at about half a second after Blackheath-Murray did—which is why the big Englishman got a jump on me going for a gun. His was a snub-nosed Webley Bulldog yanked cross-draw style from somewhere beneath his frock coat. As he brought it up, Greene snatched the wrist of Diana's right hand and jerked it—and her derringer—toward the ceiling.

Blackheath-Murray took aim at his "bird": Diana.

Now, I've never been much of one for quick draws, and if I'd stopped to think about it, I would've realized this was hardly the time to get in some practice, what with a thousand innocent bystanders in the vicinity. Stopping to think, however, would also get the lady quite dead. So I did what I suppose Gustav would say I do best and I *didn't* think. I just drew my Colt and fired.

There followed three sounds in such quick succession you could hardly tear them apart: the roar of my revolver, a *clank* as my shot hit Blackheath-Murray's Bulldog and ripped it from his grip, and the shattering of glass and porcelain as the bullet ricocheted away into the shadowy bowels of the Tiffany Pavilion.

Then there was silence. Then a great stomping of feet as Old King Brady and a platoon of Columbian Guards rushed in and threw themselves on Blackheath-Murray. Then a nasty little crack as Diana brought up her free hand and, with a deftness one had to admire, broke Boothby Greene's thin, hawk-like nose. Then finally, when it was clear the scuffling was over and the danger passed, the sound that really caught me by surprise: light rain falling on a tin roof.

It took me a moment to realize it was actually applause, and by then the little sprinkle had turned into a downpour. Hundreds upon hundreds of hands were clapping together, and there were whistles and hurrahs and yeehas, too.

I looked over at Gustav and found him blinking out at the crowd in wonderment as he came down off his ladder.

"Nice shootin', Brother," he mumbled, looking like a man both walking and talking in his sleep.

"I was aimin' at his head," I said.

That was when the dam burst and the mob surged forward, and before I knew it I was watching cheering, grinning men hoist Old Red up on their shoulders. I was next (though it took my bearers a little more work to get me off the ground), and in the distance, Major Bacon and his boys lit into "Home on the Range" as we were paraded around the hall.

We rode the churning current of the throng, my brother and I, sometimes close together, sometimes swept far apart. For years the two of us had been dragged this way and that by the wild tides of fate, yet never had it seemed so literal.

The third or fourth time we passed each other, at some point after every hand in the place had either shaken mine or slapped me on the back (or rump if that's all they could reach), I saw Gustav trying to shout something at me. All I could do was shake my head and shrug, though, for his words were swallowed up by the echoing blasts of the brass band and the chant our new admirers had taken up and would repeat again and again for what seemed like—and what I wished could have been—forever.

"World's Greatest Sleuth! World's Greatest Sleuth! World's Greatest Sleuth! World's Greatest Sleuth!"

35

HIGH TIME

Or, The Amlingmeyer Boys Finally Find Themselves on Top of the World

It was Friday, October 27, 1893, and my brother and I had just had our asses chewed by some of the most powerful men in Chicago, and life was beautiful.

"How'd it go?" Diana asked as Old Red and I came down the steps of the Service Building, HQ of the Columbian Guards.

"Better than expected," I said.

"I can tell that already," Lucille Larson said. "I don't see any handcuffs."

"Oh, they weren't gonna throw the World's Greatest Sleuth in jail."

I nudged my brother.

"Feh," he grumbled. "I do wish people would stop sayin' that."

"What would you prefer? 'One of the World's Six Greatest Sleuths' ain't got no ring to it—though I suppose it is more accurate now."

I couldn't help but break out in the big, self-satisfied grin I'd been wearing, off and on, all day. That morning, we'd been informed that the other (unjailed) contestants had voted to cede us Boothby Greene's share of the prize money. We were $2,500 richer.

And then, within minutes, $2,000 poorer once *we* ceded most of the money to Urias Smythe to help the poor man cover his expenses. Still, that put us five hundred bucks ahead, a small fortune (by our meager standards) that we immediately doubled thanks to Smythe's offer for my next book. This one would chronicle . . . well, everything you've just seen chronicled, dear reader, for you're lucky enough to hold it in your hands.

The day wasn't to be all happy songs and rainbows, though. We were summoned to the White City for a private interview with various personages of an important and seriously pissed-off type. But that was behind us now, and the sun was shining, and we had money in our pockets and clean clothes on our backs and two ladies waiting for us. There was only one thing to do: promenade and bask in life's bounty.

I offered Diana my arm, and she took it, leaving a blushing Gustav to either do the same for Miss Larson or look like an ill-mannered lout. He chose to be a gentleman—though it was touch-and-go for a moment.

Miss Larson entwined his arm in hers in a way that put me in mind of a snake wrapping itself around its next meal. Diana we'd invited along; Miss Larson had invited herself. She needed a "coda" for her article about the contest, she said, and I wasn't inclined to deny her, given that our newly burnished reputations were hers to smudge, if she so chose. Anyway, who doesn't love a good coda?

We started strolling north, along the western face of the Horticulture Building.

"What did they want from you?" Diana asked.

"Oh, just a pound of flesh or two. And more explanations," I said. "I had to run through the whole thing all over again."

Miss Larson turned a typically cool look on her escort. "You let your brother do the talking this time?"

"I'm all talked out."

"I think he sprained his lips yesterday," I said. "But no matter. As always, I stand ready to serve—so long as 'serve' means gab. Good thing my lips were ready for action, too, for there were some mighty big backsides that needed smoochin', pardon my *français*. Daniel Burnham, Colonel Rice . . . why, the mayor even sent some toady over to grouse at us about spoilin' Chicago's image with murder talk so close to the end of the Fair. The feller from Tiffany & Co. was nice, though."

"That must have been a relief," Diana said.

I nodded.

After bouncing off Blackheath-Murray's gun the day before, my shot had destroyed, of all things, a replica of a ruby-encrusted chamber pot Tiffany's had created for the actress Lillian Russell.

"They ain't gonna make us pay for the damage Little Sure Shot here did," Old Red said. "There might even be a reward for gettin' the Tiffany Diamond back."

"I'm hopin' for our own chamber pots," I said, holding up crossed fingers.

Diana smiled. Miss Larson and my brother did not.

"Anyway," I said, "that ain't the most interestin' tidbit we picked up. Once the poobahs had their say, we got to talk to Pinkerton and Sergeant Ryan just the four of us, and . . . may I, Brother?"

Gustav grimaced. "I don't know. It'd have to stay on the q.t. Just between us." He peeped shyly over at Miss Larson. "Not every son of a gun who picks up a *McClure's Magazine*. Agreed?"

"Do you see me holding my notebook?" the lady said.

I shook my head. "Miss, I must point out that you just answered a question with a question."

Either a brisk wind swept in off the lake or, as I had at times suspected, Miss Larson could cool the air around her ten degrees with nothing more than a look (specifically, the look she was giving me just then). Either way, I shivered.

"Fine," she said. "This is a statement: Whatever you tell me shall remain confidential."

"Thank you, miss," I said. "So. Greene's been doin' him more talkin'. His name's not Greene *or* Lindenbaum, by the way. It's Eddie Pegg, but let's not confuse things any more than they already are. Him and his pal Blackheath-Murray—not his real name—are part of some kinda crime ring over to London, he says. And according to him, Sherlock Holmes himself put their boss-man six feet under a while back, and they've been out to get him for it ever since."

"Isn't it a little late for that?" Miss Larson asked. "They may as well have sworn vengeance on George Washington or Genghis Khan."

But Diana saw where I was headed before I got there.

"He claims to believe what you do?" she said, turning to Old Red.

My brother nodded, looking rather pleased with himself.

"You've lost me," Miss Larson said.

"Greene says Holmes ain't dead," I explained. "That he's just gone to ground these past two years. Supposedly, Greene and his chum were sent here to smoke him out. Figured a man with Sherlock Holmes's self-regard couldn't resist the temptation to give our little tribute a look-see. They wanted the diamond, sure, but that was just another part of the lure. They were gonna get rich while gettin' revenge on a man the rest of the world thinks is dead."

Miss Larson gave me a long, appraising look, as if trying to figure out whether I was just telling another bad joke.

"That's—"

"Ludicrous?" I guessed.

"The word I was going to use is 'absurd.' What about the story *McClure's* is about to publish? 'The Final Problem'—John Watson's account of Holmes's death. Are you saying it's all a lie?"

"*I'm* not sayin' it. Greene is."

"Exactly. A cunning killer and thief. I would guess he's simply trying to keep his head out of a noose, somehow."

"What did Pinkerton and Sergeant Ryan think?" Diana asked.

I shrugged. "They thought enough of it to pass it on to us. I guess they figured it ain't likely, but if it's true, maybe the same folks that're after Holmes wouldn't be too pleased with us . . . though to my mind, you may as well worry you've made enemies of Little Bo Peep and Red Riding Hood, cuz they're about as real."

"And what do you think?" Miss Larson said to my brother.

"I think it is a capital mistake to theorize before one has data," he told her . . . and tucked up under his mustache was a crooked little pucker of a smile I hadn't seen in a long, long while.

[*Note to self: X out the preceding page before mailing this manuscript to Mr. Smythe. Or better still, tear it up. You know Holmes has gone to solve the Great Mystery in the Sky, but if Gustav wants to keep talk the man hasn't under wraps, best to humor him and avoid a lot of unnecessary aggravation.*]

"That ain't all we got outta Pinkerton," Old Red said by way of a conversation changer, and to ensure the palaver moved swiftly on from there, he added, "Right, Brother?"

"That's right. Turns out Mr. Pinkerton's not such a bad sort, after all. Not only did he admit he was wrong for tryin' to buffalo us these past few days, he actually up and offered us the very thing we've spent the last six months tryin' to get a rope on."

"He didn't!" Diana said.

"He did. Offered us jobs. Said the Denver office would probably be the place for us."

"You turned him down, of course."

"I told him we'd think about it."

"Oh, he's full of—" my brother began. He coughed and tried again. "Yes, we turned the man down."

"More than that," I said. "We told him he's got some formidable competition to look forward to, thanks to our new partnership: Amlingmeyer, Amlingmeyer & Crowe, Detectives."

"Don't you mean Amlingmeyer, Amlingmeyer, Crowe & Crowe?"

"Pardon me, Miss. Tell you what. Let's make it Crowe, Crowe, Amlingmeyer & Amlingmeyer." I looked over at my brother. "The first Amlingmeyer is me, by the way."

"The danged sign's gonna have to be ten foot by ten," Gustav said.

"Oh, we'll come up with something more pithy," I told him. "Howzabout the Holmes on the Range Detective Agency?"

"*No.*"

I was about to ask Old Red if "Holmes on the Range & Associates" suited him better when a man stepped into our path. A bearded man with, it turned out, a foreign accent.

"Gustav Amlingmeyer," he said.

He was a tall, slender gentleman with piercing gray eyes, yet as the four of us stopped before him what I found myself staring at was his thick though well-tended beard. It appeared real, but who could say in this day and age when every other man you meet is hiding himself behind a wall of fuzz?

Much as I'd hated our leather cowboy outfits, I'd have felt better right then if the holsters weren't stowed away in a drawer back in our hotel room.

"Yes?" Old Red said, and just from the hard, clipped sound of that one little word, I could tell he was thinking the same thing I was.

The man stepped toward him. "Might I congratulate you on your success yesterday?"

He held out a hand.

Gustav took it, and they shook.

"I missed the first days of the competition, but I'm so pleased I was here to witness its finish," the stranger said. "Well done, sir."

I tried to place his accent but couldn't quite do it. It sounded like Swedish by way of Edinburgh, or maybe Danish with a hint of Dublin.

"Thank you, mister," Old Red said. "It wasn't all me, though."

"Of course." The Swede-Scot/Dane-Dubliner/God-only-knew offered first Diana, then me, a little bow. "What is a detective without his stalwart assistants?"

Diana accepted the compliment with a gracious nod, but I thought I noticed a little hint of irritation in the hard line of her lips. She was a detective in her own right, and it must have rankled to be dismissed as an "assistant," stalwart or not.

"I gather you are an admirer of the late Mr. Sherlock Holmes?" the man said, turning back to my brother. "So much so that you call yourself—"

"I didn't slap that brand on me," Gustav snapped. Then he took in a deep breath and attempted an apologetic smile. "I'd never claim to be the Holmes of the Range. Far as I'm concerned, that's just something to shoot for, and I can only hope I'm gettin' closer to the mark with each try."

The stranger nodded. "Commendable sentiments. I have no doubt, from what I saw yesterday, that you will hit your target . . . and do Mr. Holmes great honor in the process."

He bowed again, then stepped around us and set off swiftly down the path. Old Red turned to watch him go with a puzzled, pensive frown.

"You should feel honored," Miss Larson said. "Do you know who that was?"

"Do you?"

"Yes, I do. I recognized him from a magazine illustration." She nodded at the tall, thin figure that was receding from us fast. "That was Johan Sigerson, the Norwegian explorer. The first European through the Nangpa La Pass."

"He's a long way from Tibet," Diana said.

"Well, sure. He just had to pop over to Chicago when he heard Old Red Amlingmeyer would be here." I clapped Gustav on the back. "You are movin' in illustrious circles now, Brother. Next thing you know, Grover Cleveland's gonna step up and ask for your autograph."

Old Red just kept watching Sigerson, brows knit, until Diana slipped between him and Miss Larson and steered him north again.

"Come along, Gustav. You have a promise to keep, remember?"

"Oh. Yeah," my brother said.

From the sound of his voice, you'd have thought he'd promised to dip himself in boiling oil. Come to think of it, from his perspective, the truth was probably about as pleasant. He was a man of his word, however, and after a little more strolling and twenty minutes in line, the four of us left the earth behind together.

Old Red kept to the center of the compartment at first, and he left all the talking to me and the ladies. When our car finally had its turn at the top, though, Diana took him by the arm again and said, "You really should see this."

"Yes'm," my brother said meekly, and he let the lady lead him to a free spot at one of the long windows. There must have been fifty or sixty people in that car with us, all of them oohing and ahhing over the view from the Ferris wheel's highest vantage, yet I didn't hear Gustav join in. Which was fine by me. I was just relieved he wasn't throwing up.

Beyond him and the beautiful woman on his arm, I could see blue sky and white clouds and just a sliver of the sun that had begun to sink toward the horizon from its highest height in the sky. Old Red was facing west, I realized then, and somewhere out there was the Kansas farm on which we were born and the cattle trails we'd somehow survived and the future I felt was just beginning even as this perfect day drew to a close.

Miss Larson cleared her throat.

"I'm sorry, miss," I said. "Guess I let myself get distracted."

She followed my line of sight—but didn't see what I was looking at.

"She's too old for you, you know," she told me.

She thought I'd been mooning over Diana. For some reason, I didn't feel like correcting her.

"Oh, I'll catch up. I'm gettin' older all the time."

"You know, that's what I like about you, Otto," Miss Larson replied. "You always make me laugh."

She wasn't even cracking a smile. I stifled both my sigh and, just barely, the urge to retreat to the window with Old Red and Diana.

This was the pinnacle of my brother's life in every way you might name. He'd come further and risen higher than either of us could have dreamed. In fact, it was hard to imagine things ever looking better for Gustav than they did right then, in that bright, hopeful moment with all the world stretched out before him, and Diana Crowe at his side.

So I stayed back. I wanted to give my brother every second I could to just glory in it until the wheel turned again, and the view changed.

ACKNOWLEDGMENTS

The author wishes to thank:

Rex Stout and Anthony Shaffer—for inspiration.

Crafty Keith Kahla, editor extraordinaire—for opening doors.

Elyse Cheney, agent par excellence—for blasting through barriers.

Jonathan Turner and Robin Holly, volunteer/draftee story consultants—for saving me from myself.

India Cooper and Bob Berkel, copy mavens—for saving me from myself some more.

Adam MacFarlane, Aldo Calcagno, Ashley Edward Miller, Bob Bartlett, Bob and Nancy Ortmann, Chris Jonard, Dan Amsden, David Kuskie, Don Collins, J. Steven York, James T. Allerton, Jen Forbus, Jenn Highfill, Jennifer Garlen, Jennifer McKenzie, Jeremy Lynch, Joan Gallo, Joee Bonee, Judy Bobalik, Julie Bestry, Lauren O'Brien, Lee Nelson, Linda Manning, Linda McMaken, Mark Baker, Matthew Szewczyk, Patti O'Brien, Rhoda DeCruz, Richard

Prosch, Ron and Sandi Hockensmith, Sarah Theubet, Shanna Derringer, Shawn D. Hilton, Stefan Nissen, Stella Mattioli, and the whole danged Posse—for buying this book. (You did buy it, didn't you?)

Les Klinger, Mike Whelan, Peter Blau, and all you fabulous Sherlockians out there—for welcoming me to the party.

D. J. Kenny (deceased), author of *Illustrated Guide to Cincinnati and the World's Columbian Exposition* (quoted in chapter twelve); Norman Bolotin and Christine Laing, authors of *The World's Columbian Exposition: The Chicago World's Fair of 1893*; Erik Larson, author of *The Devil in the White City*; and everyone behind the documentary *EXPO: Magic of the White City* and the Exposition Web site of the Paul V. Galvin Library Digital History Collection (http://columbus.gl.iit.edu/)—for doing all the hard stuff so I wouldn't have to.

Andy Martin, Hector DeJean, Kathleen Conn, and everyone else at St. Martin's Minotaur—for a great ride. Yeeeha!

Sophie Littlefield, Julie Goodson-Lawes, Ben Sevier, and Sarah Weinman—for listening to me worry and whine.

Mar, Kate, Mojo, and Izzy—for reminding me how much I *don't* have to worry and whine about.